AF226169

SHADOW BEAST SHIFTERS

DESERTED

JAYMIN EVE

Jaymin Eve
Deserted: Shadow Beast Shifters book 4
Copyright © Jaymin Eve 2021

For information: jaymineve@gmail.com
Cover designer: Tamara K
Editor: Jax Garren

This is dedicated to that one time when fucking your ex wasn't a bad idea.

The best way to stay up to date with the Shadow Beast Shifters world and all new releases, is to join my Facebook group here:
www.facebook.com/groups/jayminevenerdherd
We share lots of book releases, fun posts, sexy dudes, and generally it's a happy place to exist.

Desert Lands
Guardians
Shale
Fret
Holinfra

Delfora
Rohami
Yemin
Zealon
Orani
Wander

PROLOGUE

The Time Before

My scream was hoarse as I held my sister's body, tightening my grip as if pure will alone would keep her in this world with me.

But deep in my power... in my energy, I knew it was too late.

I'd been a warrior my entire life, and that training told me her injuries were beyond repair. At some point, there was too much damage, even for the long-lived and powerful.

Her vessel had fought until it had nothing left to give. Her power was returning to our collective, and it was time for me to release her from my hold and bless her journey to our sacred afterlife.

If only I could force my fingers to open.

"Mel," she coughed, her brown skin rapidly losing color as her lifeforce bled out into the desert lands. "You have all the power now. You can end this." Her words were whispered and broken, golden liquid on her lips as she spluttered out her final advice.

My brain immediately rejected the notion. "I can't," I rasped, angling my body so I was lying in the black sands with her—side by side, twin souls by choice rather than birth. "If I release the power, I'll no longer feel you with me." The very thought stole the air from my lungs, and I almost couldn't continue. My next words were choked. "What if I can't follow you and our treasora into the afterlife? The only way I can continue living this life and fighting all the battles is knowing that you're all waiting for me in the end."

The last member of my family was dying in my arms, and as much as I wanted to fulfill her final wish... I couldn't. The power, as she'd said, was all mine, and with that came a lot of responsibility. Using it all now to end this battle in the sacred Desert Lands would take everything I had, leaving me without a connection to my ancestors.

"I can't risk it," I whispered.

"Yo— you will find us," she replied fiercely. "We will find you. Death is the beginning of our next journey. War—" She spluttered again, and my heart stopped when her eyes rolled back for a beat before she found strength. "Warrior and heart," she whispered, "swift winds and sharp blades. Until our souls meet again."

That was our goodbye, and with that I felt her fade. My body trembled as I wrapped myself around her, holding her for the last time. My entire essence wept as I murmured the final sacred words that would guide her home. "Swift winds and sharp blades, my Lekakin. Beyond the meadows, your journey is done. Until our souls meet again."

My scream was no longer hoarse as I lifted my head and released the pain of this death. When my parents left this existence years ago, I'd thought I'd never experience such aching hurt again, but this was worse. There were only a few beings in this world who had ever touched me at a visceral level, and Leka was one of them.

Now I was alone.

Alone in a world that was bursting with pain and death and loss.

Her body faded before me as the energy she'd held settled into the well of power that filled our family coffers. Light and dark, destruction and creation, it warred within me until I allowed it to settle and flow. I controlled our power, and as Leka had said, I could use it to end this once and for all.

But that wasn't to be my fate today.

Today I was leaving this godforsaken world that had taken so much from me: the Desert Lands.

"Lale!"

I heard his shout, but I never turned back. Reece of the Rohami dynasty was an old friend of mine. My best friend. He was here with his brother, neck deep in this battle, on the shores of their sacred Delfora.

They fought to keep the power of this land from falling into the wrong hands, one dynasty pitted against another. The only reason Leka and I were here was to honor the longstanding friendship of our families. I owed Reece loyalty, but today I was done.

I'd lost enough. I'd sacrificed everything, and I had nothing left to give.

"Lale, are you okay?"

Rough hands landed on my shoulders, and as he spun me, the rich blue in his eyes captured mine. Those eyes had gotten me into a lot of trouble in my life, and even as I drew on my training and numbed myself to keep the pain from destroying me, I couldn't halt the memories of last night.

"We need your help," he said, pulling me closer.

My body shook, and I looked to my hands, covered in the blood of my enemies... and my sister.

"I'm done," I said my voice cold and flat.

Confusion tugged at his brow as he examined my features, and then that confusion morphed into anger, his eyes blazing as he narrowed them on me. His grip tightened, and I was again reminded how much bigger and stronger he was. In close combat like this, I would never best him. Thankfully, I had many other weapons at my disposal.

My power knocked him away, a sharp pointed attack that he hadn't expected. He landed on his feet, a powerful god of this world, able to control the sands and energy of the desert. By the time he was zipping back toward me, clearly pissed, I'd already taken off, sprinting toward the transport doorways that had been left for warriors to return to Rohami. Only from here could I open a pathway back to my world.

"Melalekin," Reece shouted from behind me, and even though I told myself not to look, I had to risk one glance back.

Our eyes met, and his held nothing but fury at my betrayal. I shook my head, pressing a hand to my mouth before I stepped through the transport.

I was done.

CHAPTER ONE

The air in the Library of Knowledge felt cooler than usual as I walked in from the Honor Meadows. Or maybe it was simply that the meadows were going through their warm transitional months, heading toward the wet season. My birth world was not like Earth, where the wet season consisted of literal rain for days or months. In the meadows, it was about the energy flow. The hotter it was, the less the free power disbursed, and when it cooled down, we all got a boost.

It had been a long time since I'd had to care about such things, thanks to being the last in a very powerful family of transcendents, but after the battle in the Shadow Realm, where I'd expended a decent chunk of my energy in an attempt to help my best friend Mera Callahan defeat the Danamain, I could use a boost.

A few cooler days to replenish my base would be welcomed right now.

I had no regrets about using my power; I'd been willing to throw as much as I could at the Danamain—to the point of death—to ensure my new family and the rest of the worlds survived. The fact that I'd been reborn, without the scars of the past dragging me down, was a bonus I hadn't seen coming.

Every day now was a new experience, especially with a best friend like Mera. She was turning all our lives upside down and bringing us together for some of her favorite Earth customs. I could feel her excitement this day thrumming through the bond we had. It was a fairly new bond—so new that we should barely even sense the other at this stage—but thanks to both of our unusual powerbases, we were forging new ground.

We'd even managed to mentally connect and talk in the realm, at the point of my death when a ton of power spanned between us. We hadn't been able to replicate that again, but I knew eventually we would. We had all the time in the world now.

As I hurried farther into the great library, my usual sense of awe filled me. This room contained all the knowledge of the worlds, and as a lover of knowledge, I'd never get enough of this place. It had been a solace to my soul for most of my very long life.

Probably why I felt almost the same sense of ownership over it that Mera did.

Speaking of, as I passed the shelves on Faerie, I came to what used to be a central reading area but was now a snow-field... Hence the new chill in the air.

"Angel! There you are!" Mera, the goddess in question, snapped as she appeared between some shelves about twenty feet away.

I hadn't seen her for a few days, and I took a second to note that there was a decidedly festive, and a little crazed, look about her. Her red hair was messier than usual, piled on top of her head with green tinsel threaded through the strands. She also wore a bright red Christmas dress stretched over her rounded stomach. Santa was on the front with the words *Ho Ho Ho... what the fuck did you just call me?* stitched underneath.

Glancing down at my simple, tan shift dress made from a light silk of Faerie—perfect for the meadow's hot season, it was clear that I'd underdressed for this occasion. Oh well, if I was a betting transcendent, I'd wager that Mera already had an outfit set out for me—a thought that was strengthened when Gaster, the goblin who ran this library, hurried past with a red hat perched jauntily on his head.

Trying not to chuckle, I moved forward to meet my friend, who was dashing toward me. It was a mystery to all of us how she managed to move so fast for someone in her very pregnant state, but one thing I'd learned was to never underestimate this particular being. She'd started life as a shifter before evolving into a goddess. A goddess who'd tamed one of the most formidable and scary "gods" in our worlds: *Shadow Beast.*

Truth be told, no one could ever truly tame him, but Mera had definitely softened some of his harder edges. The beast and I had always had a tenuous relationship, but thanks to Mera, we considered ourselves more friends than frenemies now. She was also the reason I used words such as "frenemy" and *all* the curse words, because why the hell not? Those of us long-lived either stayed with the times or we retreated from the worlds. At one point I'd chosen retreat, but now that I'd been reborn, I was embracing this new side of myself that did not carry the burdens of the ancients. The memories remained, but the pain was muted.

"Yo!" Mera was in my face now. "It's been days. I've missed

you. Also, are you here to help me set up for Christmas or what?"

I laughed, shaking my head—since her pregnancy, she'd been extra fiery. "Are you actually getting crankier? How long until the baby is due?"

Mera sighed, all but sagging against me, her frame far too fragile for someone who was technically indestructible. "Fucked if I know. Shadow keeps telling me it's best if we don't discuss how long and just enjoy the experience." She trailed off into a ton of curses and colorful phrases regarding the *Shadow Bastard,* finishing with, "Which is easy for him to say since he's not the one growing a beast spawn or experiencing these insane cravings. Or"—her face screwed up into angrier lines—"dealing with my ridiculous mate. You know that today is the first time in months he's left my side? He keeps growling at anyone who steps near me like the caveman beast he is, but today he had to head to the Shadow Realm because it just couldn't wait. And he left me with five fucking bodyguards. *Five!*"

The moment she said "five," I was hit with an urge to spin on the spot and return to the meadows. There wasn't much in the worlds that scared me, not after everything I'd seen and done, but one of Mera's five bodyguards was a male I'd rather not be in the same room as.

Reece of the Desert Lands.

I'd known him for what felt like forever, and once, very long ago, we'd been best friends. Now we were bitter enemies, and for some reason, recently, that bitterness had grown near out of control. After all of these centuries, I wasn't sure why he'd once again started acting like a royal dick, and I didn't have the energy or inclination to explore his newfound hatred for me. In truth, it was only a matter of time before we had no choice but to sort our shit out the old-fashioned way: battle.

My rebirth might have changed much of who I was, but my

fighting skills were as strong as ever. It would do him well to remember whom he was constantly challenging.

"Come on," Mera said, tugging my arm as she led me deeper into the great library, dodging shelves and other world's inhabitants, all of whom bowed respectfully to both of us. Mera barely noticed, though, her focus on the winter wonderland she was establishing.

"My Christmas event is in two days," she said in a rush. "Two freaking days. My baby's first Christmas. I'm just not ready."

"Your baby is not exactly born yet," I said tentatively because her moods were supremely unpredictable right now. "I don't think they'll mind if it's not quite the perfect Christmas."

She paused, and I braced myself for yelling. But instead, she sighed. "I'm being overbearing, aren't I? Shadow told me I was, but I just thought it was his usual asshole personality rising to the surface."

She rubbed a hand over her stomach, and despite the way she frequently and loudly complained about the trials of pregnancy, she already loved her child with a ferocity that should warn anyone meaning it harm to stay far away. She wasn't the only one, either. Shadow was downright scary these days, and when this baby was born, I had a sense that he might turn into the literal beast he was named after.

This child would be the most protected being in the Solaris System, and I'd be the first in line if any came at us with ill intent. For Mera, Shadow, and the baby—*my family*—I would fight the gods themselves... and even put up with a sand-weaving asshole.

An asshole who looked really good tonight, his huge warrior body clothed in a black shirt and pants. He wore his usual scowl as he watched us approach, but it didn't take away from his beauty. Reece's skin shone dark bronze in the low, twinkling lights strung around the snow-tipped Christmas tree. The blue of his eyes was searing, and what had once been my favorite color was now my least, no matter how pretty those dark lashes framing pools of cobalt were.

"Mera, you're not supposed to run off like that," he admonished, removing his glare from me to glare a touch less at her. "Sticking us with stringing up the lights was a terrible distraction, but lucky for you, I knew you didn't leave the library."

She poked out her tongue, hip-checking him gently. Their relationship was so easy and caring, and I had no idea how she'd achieved that with this dick. But that was Mera's way, her superpower. Taming angry souls.

It was a power I did not possess, but that was okay. I made up for my lack of people skills with exceptional blade skills, and I had no doubts about which were more important. Only one would protect my family when the time arose. And it would arise.

There was always something evil lurking in the wings.

"Angel, come on," Mera called, dragging me further into her winter wonderland.

She'd gone all out for the library's first Christmas. A huge fir tree dominated the space with its glistening, dark green, needlelike leaves liberally coated with snow on the higher branches. There was nothing below since we had a strict no-present policy for this event. This Christmas was about coming together as a family and celebrating the fact that we were all still alive, and oddly enough, I even felt some swirls of anticipation about experiencing this Earth holiday.

Around the time Mera started to hand out "ugly Christmas sweaters," as she dubbed them, Shadow's energy entered the library. He was back from the Shadow Realm, the world he was supposed to be ruling but instead was training and overseeing the new rulers. The realm had been corrupted for thousands of years, and while they were on the path to a brighter future, their issues could not be fixed overnight.

It would take decades to mend the scars, but the new Supreme Being was already bringing life and prosperity to her people. Shadow had chosen his successor well... or should I say Mera had, since it had been her wish to appoint one of the leaders from the Samsan Grove outlier island as the Supreme Being. And what Mera wanted, Shadow made happen.

Such was the power of a true mate bond and the obsessive nature of their relationship.

A second after I felt his energy, Mera's head snapped in the direction of her mate. When he appeared, her face lit up, and she was moving at her too-fast-for-pregnancy speed again. They came together in a way that was hard to watch—not because I wasn't happy for them but because their pure love was the same sort of love my parents had shared.

The Honor Meadows was famous for its warriors, but what many didn't know was that it was also built on true-love bonds. Soul bonds.

A bond I knew nothing of and, after this many years, doubted I ever would.

"You weren't long," Mera said to her mate when he was done kissing her senseless. She dragged him back toward the snow-covered tree. "Where're Inky and Midnight?"

"They're still in the realm, keeping an eye out for us and frolicking in the mists," Shadow said, somewhat distracted as he looked around. "I wasn't gone long, and somehow you found the time to completely redecorate the library."

Mera lifted an eyebrow at him. "You don't like it?"

Shadow's lips twitched. "It's perfect, Sunshine."

Her face lit up, and as she was leaning in to hug him, she paused. Tilting her head back, she started to sniff, then snarled.

"Hand it over," she snapped, and this time, Shadow actually laughed out loud.

To see that stoic bastard tip his head back and rumble his mirth was super unsettling. Sometimes I wondered if Mera was the fabled witch of the Solaris System.

"Shadow," Mera growled. "You do not want to fuck with a pregnant woman."

"You really don't," Len said from where he'd wedged his huge body into a small corner to hang more lights. He was dressed in his usual silver, duster jacket and all, and he was wearing a strand of red tinsel that Mera had clearly strung around his collar. His white hair was kept short and styled these days, the only length falling across his forehead, and his silvery eyes looked wilder than usual. "Can someone seriously tell us how much longer she'll be pregnant?"

Mera, who was too focused on her mate to bother with the fae, was all but wrestling Shadow in an attempt to search his pockets. The beast could have broken free, of course, but he was occupied with staring at her in a way that was dangerous to any of us standing nearby. Finally, she found what her nose had sniffed out, pulling a white paper bag from inside his jacket.

Her hands trembled as she hugged it to her chest. "You found one," she sniffed. "Aw, mate, I love you."

Shadow pulled her close as she opened the bag and removed a weird green... stick? "What the hell is that?" Reece asked in his usual tactless way.

"Deep fried pickle," Mera said, still sounding tearful. "I swear to fuck I've been desperately craving these, and no one in the dining hall has a clue what I'm talking about."

She took a bite and then moaned, and as flames sprang into Shadow's eyes, I knew my friend was about to disappear from the room. Sure enough, after Mera's second bite and moan,

Shadow's energy whipped through the space, and by the time I blinked again, he was gone, taking his Sunshine with him.

"The only surprise there," Alistair said, letting out a warm laugh before he ran a hand through his blue and green curls, "is that she didn't get pregnant the first day they met." His blue eyes, which were a few shades darker than his skin, softened as he stared after his friends. Alistair was one of the only ones so far to pull on a sweater, and he'd chosen a green one with a sequined tree and the words *Merry Treemas* on it.

"Those two stubborn souls had a lot of shit to sort out," Len said, shifting around to twirl more of the lights across the tree using fae energy. "But, damn, it makes me happy to see them like that. I think Shadow's turning us all soft."

Lucien, moving at vampire speed, punched Len on his shoulder, his green gaze piercing as he scowled. "Speak for yourself. Nothing soft about me." He dropped his gold sweater and ran a hand through his blond hair, sending the smooth strands into attractive tousles. He was wearing all black, as he often did, perpetuating the human's take on vampires as creatures of the night. His species did have some similarities, hence where the original myth came from, but they also had tons of differences as well.

"Simone," Len coughed out between laughter, not even remotely annoyed by the punch. "Softie."

Simone was Mera's shifter best friend, who was currently on Earth. Something had happened between Lucien and her, but none of us knew the details. Mera had asked, of course, but Simone had said that most of it she'd been compelled to keep secret—a gift only the most powerful of vamps could use—and that the rest wasn't worth mentioning.

Mera hadn't been too happy with the secrecy, but for now she was trying to "respect the stupid decisions people made" and had stopped asking.

"I've told you all before, Simone was under my protection, but that was it."

Lucien was the epitome of "he doth protest too much," but before Len could push him until war broke out, Reece moved out of the shadows. "I know we're here for this celebration," he said, looking like he wished he was anywhere else, "but I also need to talk to you about... well, I don't even really know, but I think something is going down in the Desert Lands."

What is it? Galleli asked as he lowered himself from where he'd been stringing lights and tinsel up high and tucked his gold wings behind him. Galleli, who'd also chosen not to wear his sweater, was a transcendent from the Honor Meadows. But unlike the rest of us, he never spoke out loud. I didn't know the exact reason why, but there was talk that his voice had, at one time, been a weapon that the weaker would succumb to.

Reece shook his head. "The deserts are uneasy; their sands of time drift through my energy. I'm being called into the depths of the Delfora."

"Have you spoken to the other dynasties?" Lucien asked turning more serious.

Reece nodded, stance strong and sure even if his words were not. "Yes, but none of them have noticed anything, which doesn't surprise me. I have the strongest connection to the sacred lands, and if trouble is starting there again, then I'd be the first to know."

"When is your next meeting of the dynasties?" Len queried, and I was grateful that many of the questions running through my mind were being asked without me having to say a word. Wouldn't want him to think I had any cares left for him.

"It's in six new-moons," he said shortly. "Which is also odd because we weren't due for at least another thousand or so moons. Someone has pushed up the timeline, and that in itself is suspicious."

The room fell silent, outside of another two or three goblins in Santa hats chatting as they hurried past.

"The Desert Lands is one of the oldest worlds," I finally had to say. "There are many powers there that cannot be disturbed, especially in the Delfora."

I knew that better than any; the powers under those sands had cost me my sister. Reece didn't look at me, but he also didn't sneer, which was an improvement.

"Yes, and with that in mind," he said stiffly, "I have a favor to ask. Will you all accompany me to this meeting? If my senses are correct, this could be a huge issue, and it's best if we deal with it straight away. We must ensure there's never another dynasty war." His eyes, blue embers of fury, met mine briefly. "The last one nearly destroyed us all."

"Of course, you don't even have to ask," Len said, slapping a hand on Reece's shoulder. "As Mera said, we're a pack now, and packmates stick together."

Reece let out a short laugh. "Yeah, she used that emotional blackmail to get us to hang up her damn Christmas lights, but I'll take it. I know Shadow won't want to bring her while she's pregnant, but with all of us there, she'll be safe. I'll speak to him tomorrow."

That had me standing a little taller.

Truth of the matter, I was curious about this meeting of the dynasties, especially if there was trouble afoot in their ancient and sacred Delfora. But curiosity wasn't enough to get me to voluntarily spend time with Reece in the world where I'd lost it all...

Unless Mera was going to be there. Where Mera went, so did I.

This time when my eyes met Reece's, there was a moment of understanding between us. I would go to the Desert Lands in six new-moons, back to the place where our friendship ended.

The place that held our past hurts and losses. The place my heart remained buried from more than just the loss of Leka.

Maybe, this time, I would exorcise the ghosts of the past, dig up the fragments of my heart, and finally let our feud go.

For good.

CHAPTER TWO

After a few hours, Mera returned with Shadow, and all of us listened as Reece discussed his plans. It took some convincing, but eventually Shadow conceded under the force of his mate's conviction that this plan couldn't go ahead without her.

"We should have Christmas today, though," Shadow added, "since we need to prepare for this journey and Reece has to head home to pave the way for us to be there."

Mera swallowed hard but didn't argue. "It's basically set up anyway," she said with a forced smile. "No reason not to go ahead."

I exchanged a look with Len, who let out a sigh and reached down to find his sweater. I followed suit, and one by one we all pulled them on, bringing a true smile to her face.

"Okay, this is perfect," she sighed.

Even Galleli, who generally didn't cover his chest, got into the spirit. His had holes in the back for his wings, since Mera thought of everything, and it reminded me of the convenience I now had in being able to retract and hide my wings when I wasn't using them. It had, at first, felt like a loss but was now an advantage.

"I'm so grateful for each and every one of you," Mera said, lifting her crystal glass, the water shining in the low lights. "Shadow, Angel, Galleli, Alistair, Reece, Len, Lucien, Gaster, Inky, and Midnight, who I wish were here for this…" That got to her for a beat, but she recovered and continued, naming all the goblins and many of the other regulars, and I barely managed not to laugh at the expressions on the other's faces: exasperation and love mingled so perfectly.

By the time we were done, Mera had us all sitting around a cozy fire—her specialty—with eggnog and hot cocoa. Even the beings here who didn't enjoy these sorts of beverages indulged her, and if I had to guess, every single one of us felt lighter and happier for the experience. I certainly did.

Christmas carols even started to play from somewhere, leaving us all with a little extra cheer.

Cheer I sensed we were going to need over the next journey.

WITH THE KNOWLEDGE that I'd have to return to the lands where I'd lost the last piece of my heart and soul, I took a few days to prepare myself by returning to the meadows and meditating in the most soothing sections of my territory.

Many of the layers in my world had been designed by members of my family, and I went to those to feel closest to them. My sister's was a desert, oddly similar to the Delfora where she'd breathed her last. Despite the pain I felt from the memories, I still stopped in there and sat in the warmth, feeling her essence deep in our power.

This was what I had been afraid of losing all those years

ago. Even when I'd fought the Danamain, I hadn't used all the power. I hadn't lost my family. In the end, as long as I could keep them with me, I would survive whatever was thrown my way.

After leaving my sister, I went to the layer that I felt the most peace in: my forests.

My rebirth had taken a lot of the pain from my soul, muting past griefs to the point that I felt lighter. Freed. But that didn't mean it would be easy to go back to the Desert Lands. It might actually be the hardest thing I ever did because I'd let everyone down that day. Reece, my family, my honor. Transcendents were warriors; we did not run from battle.

Reece had every right to be mad at me, but at some point, enough was enough.

I'd finally gained the maturity to know that I'd been punished enough. After centuries of fighting harder and longer than any other transcendent, forming no bonds, and beating myself up, I was done being Reece's punching bag. It was time to embrace the two sides of who I was now: a transcendent and a phoenix born of the Nexus.

The powers had merged perfectly, a meshing of two worlds, and I needed a blessing from the Tholi, our spiritual guide, to really cement the new sides of me. With that in mind, after a day of meditation, I found myself travelling out of my territory and into the skyland.

This was where our highest leaders, the strongest of each family clan, met to govern the imbalance in the worlds that we fought for. There were many worlds, many more than Shadow had bonded in his Solaris System. At one time, transcendents had balanced every single one, but today our numbers had dwindled so that we were only scattered among a dozen or so.

Our legacy was falling, but we would always fight. To the bitter end when the darkness claimed the light.

My wings were strong and sure as I flapped, lifting myself up into the false sky that hid the skyland. They were the same feathered appendages that I'd been born with, only now a fire lit up their amber lengths. I'd had a few mini breakdowns in the days after my change. So much of my identity... my worth, had been tied up in looking like my sister, and losing that had taken me by surprise. But now I was embracing it all.

My second chance.

As I ascended, the landscape around me grew paler, and the red in my wings became more pronounced until it looked as if they were on fire—as if the light within me was also out. Transcendents were born in a similar manner to humans; most of the worlds had evolved to share comparable reproductive means due to an original god. For us, though, it required more than just the usual processes. On top of genetic merging, there was also a sharing of light and energy. This inherited light remained inside of us, warming our essence and fueling our powers. With this rebirth, my light and dark sides could form one. A transcendent filled with the fires of the Nexus.

As my feet touch down on the silver cloud that was the entrance to the sacred land above, I hid my wings away, no longer needing them. The elders were no doubt aware of my changes, since very little got past them. They would have felt my power in the final battle, especially as many of the worlds' leaders had followed our journey. If we'd lost, there would've been little hope for anyone—we had been the last stand against Dannie.

As I padded along, I marveled at the illusion that surrounded me. It was as if I walked in the middle of a silver cloud. The first time I'd seen this skyland, I'd brushed my hands across its surface, hoping it felt as soft as it looked, only to find that there was nothing of substance there at all. Many of us had learned the hard way not to lean on the walls here, unless you wanted to plummet toward the meadow's surface.

It was quiet today in the skyland. During the council meetings, the elders, one from each of the most powerful families in the meadows, would be present. My father had been an elder, along with my sister, but when they'd both passed, I refused the role. I had no interest in governing this world, and the heavy guilt I carried over my sister's demise and the subsequent way I'd handled myself after, had convinced all of us that it was better if I stayed out of politics.

Even though the elders would not be here, our spiritual guide, the Tholi, never left. They were not a transcendent and had no race or gender. It was hard to describe their presence exactly, except as a swirling mist that contained all the power, knowledge, and energy that formed the heart of this world. The twelve elders existed alongside the Tholi, but the final power always rested within our *hearts*, which was exactly why the skyland moved constantly and was generally accessible only to those who were strong, trustworthy, and powerful enough to be elders. We had to protect our heart, because we all knew what happened when the heart was compromised.

As I neared the center of the skyland, the cloud curved out into a bubble, allowing me to move into it. A trickle of energy traced across my skin, and as always, it settled deep into my chest, hugging me like an old friend.

The Tholi's swirling silver mist was the same as I remembered, reminding me of the light versions of Inky and Midnight.

Welcome, Ancient One.

It always called me ancient one, even though I was young compared to its estimated age.

Kneeling, I lowered my head. "Apologies for arriving unannounced, but I have a mission I must leave for immediately and I believe that I should not go without your blessing."

As I lifted my head, the mist formed a very round ball, its warm presence drifting closer to wash over me. It took real effort to lower my barriers and allow it to search within me, feeling for the truth of what I'd said. But there was no point being here if I fought the blessing.

In truth, the presence was not invasive as it traced through my memories... my emotions... the tattered essence of brokenness that had tainted my soul once but was mostly gone now.

You have changed.

I nodded and stood. "Yes, I was reborn in the last battle. Death apparently did not want me this time."

You are important to the worlds still. Death knows that, as do I.

The word *important* rattled around my brain for a moment, and not because it surprised me—all transcendents were important—but because it had a different meaning now. I was important for more reasons than just keeping the balance and saving worlds.

I had a family again, and I liked to think that the reason death had passed me by, was to give me a chance to really live my life. Maybe they thought I deserved this second chance.

Maybe I even thought so too.

CHAPTER THREE

The Tholi didn't ask any more questions as I stood in its presence for what felt like hours, absorbing every ounce of the soothing and cleansing power that trickled across my skin.

I didn't feel physically stronger when I was done with my blessing, but I felt more at peace. And if I'd learned anything in my long life, it was that often, peace trumped power. Power could be stolen, earned and rewarded. It was everywhere for the taking.

But peace... was far harder to come by.

By the time I returned to the meadow land, I felt recharged and ready for what lay ahead.

It was time for me to head back to the Library of Knowledge.

First, though, knowing how difficult it could be to pull energy into an ancient and powerful world like the deserts, I decided to add a few extra layers of my family power into the well inside me—not as many as I'd taken to the Shadow Realm, but enough that I'd have reserves if needed.

The realm battle had cost me about a third of my power,

but I still held thousands of layers, leaving plenty to go around. Hopefully, there was nothing of great concern in the Delfora, for it was there that the ancient gods slept and none of us wanted them to awaken. Reece's connection to that land was in and of itself unusual, but not even he could stem the tides if the gods returned topside.

Once I'd taken a few layers of power, feeling them sink deep into myself, the light from my blessing mingling with the white force that was the energy I controlled. It had been a long time since I'd felt so strong, free, and weightless. A great start to what would be my new future.

As long as the ghosts that rested in the deserts left me be.

Once I was done taking power, I returned to the highest level of the meadows and opened a doorway to the library. The swirling portal now evoked feelings of home and love. *Mera's magic.* It was the sort of magic that I wished could be replicated across many species and worlds. Her mouth might be sassy, but her heart was pure and, most importantly, her soul was open and loving and kind, drawing all of us weary vessels into its warmth.

Stepping into the library, the scent of Shadow's magic engulfed me along with the parchment and ink. I'd been utilizing this space for what felt like lifetimes, and even with its current Christmas décor, every part of it was filled with familiarity and warmth.

The lights and tinsel now extended out into the shelves and around the doorways. Mera had been hard at work. Well, at least the goblin population—headed by their fearless leader Gaster—were hard at work bringing Mera's vision to life.

It did feel homey with peppermint and spruce scents joining the others, along with the fire that still burned in her makeshift fireplace. As I walked along, I ran my hands over the decorations, particularly loving the red and gold tinsel mixed with twinkling white lights.

Mera had taken a room already magical in nature and really dialed it up a few notches.

Using our connection, I followed her energy to where she was sprawled across a red chaise positioned near the tree. Our bond, still so newly formed, was somewhat muted between worlds, but here it thrummed in my chest like another line of power. There would come a time when we'd be able to find each other no matter where we were in the worlds, but for now, just feeling her presence was enough.

"Angel!" she shouted, her head lifting as she smiled at me and ate the last chocolate ball that had been in the bag resting on her chest. As she pushed herself awkwardly to her feet, I was surprised that Shadow wasn't hovering nearby in case Mera broke a nail. I was protective too, but these males thought that being pregnant made her a porcelain doll instead of the badass she was. My best friend was growing an entire god in there, and that was the greatest magic of all.

"Where's your entourage?" I asked, looking around like they might jump out of the shelves the moment I got too close.

"Would you believe that they were stuck to my ass all morning," Mera said with a cheery smile, "until I lost my ever-loving shit, and now they're lingering nearby pretending to work when I know they're silently 'protecting me' in their over-the-top ways."

There was a slapping sound behind us, and I heard Lucien snarl. "I told you so!"

Len snarled back. "You. Fucking. Idiot. Now she knows for sure we're here."

Mera rolled her eyes at me before shaking her head and raising her voice. "This is really getting old. Don't make me remind you who I am. I will literally fry your asses and give them to Midnight as a snack."

Shifting my stance, I examined the shelves closest to the Christmas tree and found the fae and vampire a few seconds later. I hadn't sensed them, so they were masking their energy. I could have sniffed them out if I'd dialed up my power, but I hadn't thought I needed to.

Before Mera could say anything else, Len and Lucien strolled out, dressed casually in their normal silver and black attire. The fae shot his brightest smile at Mera. "You know that Shadow will murder us if you're unsuper—"

"What Len meant to say," Lucien interrupted quickly, "is Shadow wants you protected while he's working out the finer details of this trip into the Desert Lands. We're here to keep you and baby Shadow safe."

Mera glared at them both, taking her time to really settle into the scowl before she finally let out an exaggerated sigh. "I know he means well, but that beast and I are about to have a very serious chat regarding boundaries. Mostly the fact that he needs some."

This time the snort escaped from me. "Really?" I said as she snapped her gaze my way. "You're just as attached to him. I'd wager that half your annoyance right now is that Shadow isn't here."

She wanted to argue with me; her face screwed up, red hair flying everywhere since it wasn't tied back. Only there was no way she could baldly lie to my face and not get called out on it. "You're supposed to be my best friend," she finally said, a smirk fighting to cross her lips. "I expect you to be on my side."

Now it was my turn to step forward and wrap my arms around her. Hugs were relatively new in my life, but Mera had changed all of us to the point that no one even blinked an eye at this sort of contact these days. Some of us might even be a touch addicted, not that we'd ever admit it.

Even with the belly between us, there was no space in our hug, and I wasn't even ashamed to admit that I closed my eyes and sucked up every ounce of the love she so freely gave. Mera was an anomaly in our world, and I'd always known Shadow was a smart bastard. He'd seen the gift in her from the moment he'd thrown her over his shoulder, and he's never looked back since.

"I'm always going to be your best friend," I said as we pulled apart. "We are family. Treasora. And no transcendent says that lightly."

They really don't.

Galleli's voice sounded in our heads as he drifted around the corner, his wings keeping him slightly aloft. Seeing him reminded me of my blessing, since he was an elder and had been to the skyland many times for council meetings. He was one of the oldest of our kind, with a powerfully bright energy. It was said that his voice was the most beautiful sound to ever grace the meadows. It was a voice that could make humans cry and supernaturals fall in love. His voice had helped to create much of the human lore of angels. On the flip side, it was also a weapon, and while I didn't know the story of why he'd stopped speaking out loud, I sensed that someone he should have protected had been hurt by his power.

Mera greeted him warmly, no longer put off by his way of communicating. She hugged him the same way she'd hugged me, all the while chatting normally. There was silence as Galleli spoke only to her before he tuned back to the rest of us.

Shadow sent me to tell you all that he heard from Reece and we're set to leave for the Desert Lands the day after tomorrow. The pair decided we need one or two more nights to fuel our energy and discuss strategy.

Mera nodded before reaching down to rub her hand across her belly. "There's no way I'm letting you all go without me, and Shadow knows that. Hence why he's acting like such a grumpy ass."

Lucien snorted out a laugh. "Just hearing a person talk about his grumpy ass like that and not get fried is such a novelty. I don't think the joy will ever wear off."

"It truly is a breath of fresh air," Len added, crossing his arms, drawing tight the front of his intricate silver coat.

"If Shadow sent you," Mera said, her brow creasing, "does that mean he won't be back for a while?"

He's still in the realm, Galleli confirmed. *Because we might be gone and out of communication range, he wanted to ensure Inky and Midnight were up to speed on what needs to be done to keep that world functioning.*

Mera's frown turned thoughtful. "Yes, that makes sense. There're no others we can trust, and we absolutely cannot let the Shadow Realm fall to ruin again. This is its last chance."

No one argued with her about that because the realm, which had been cut off from the rest of us for years, was finally free to participate in the global exchange of energy and alliances. Re-taking its place in the Solaris System was an important role to fill for many reasons.

"Shadow will wrap it all up," Lucien said with confidence. "He always does."

Mera nodded. "You're right. In the meantime, can anyone tell me what to expect in the deserts when we get there? This meeting of the dynasties sounds awfully political."

Despite my usual pang whenever the deserts were mentioned, a refresher was definitely in order. "It's going to be a bit of a story," I warned, indicating she should take her seat on the couch again.

I sat on her right, and Len dropped to her left. The other

two ended up in plump, red-and-green tartan armchairs across from us.

Somehow a padded stool appeared before Mera, drifting in from behind the tree, and as she let out a sigh and threw her feet up on it, I knew that even from the realm, Shadow was looking after his mate. Their true bond was a sight to behold.

When everyone was settled, I started, "The Desert Lands are one of the oldest worlds, even among the ancients. Old and very set in their ways. There are eight main dynasties, which act similarly to the royal families in the human world. The princeps, or leader, is an inherited position, and there's a hierarchy of power that ensures the strongest receive the best land and resources."

"Is it all dry and dusty? Sand dunes and oases?" Mera asked, her eyes bright because she loved knowledge as much as I did.

"Their world is a mix of sands," Lucien said with a low laugh. "Reece is from Rohami, with its red sands. He has control over them like no other in his world. The other dynasties are all from various shades of gold, brown, orange, and so on, except for the Delfora, a land of the darkest night."

As Reece's friend, Lucien would have explored the deserts many times, but in general, they were not open for any stranger to just wander through.

"So, this Delfora, it's a sacred land," Mera said. "What does that mean exactly?"

I waited a moment to see if anyone would answer, but when no one did, I spoke up. It was important that all of them understood what we were walking into here. "It's where the ancients sleep—the gods of the past, who were laid to rest to halt their path of destruction that would have destroyed the worlds. The Delfora has many securities in place to keep them from rising, and for that reason alone, no one steps on their sands."

"I thought Reece was a god," Mera said, her brow wrinkling. "Are you saying there're ancient-ier, powerful-ier gods than him?"

"A true wordsmith," Len said with a smirk. Just as the pregnant and hormonal goddess reached out a hand to smack him, he hurriedly added, "and no one really knows why Reece is more powerful than any other in the deserts. For some reason, he has a connection to the ancients, and with that, control over all the sands. Reece is the strongest of his dynasty. He'd be their leader if he wanted the role."

"Which he emphatically does not," Lucien drawled, shaking his head. "Ever since he lost his brother, Reece has chosen a nomadic life."

Mera let out a low breath, the sound sad. "He wears his losses like a shield, stopping others from getting close to him."

That day in the Delfora when I'd lost my sister was also the day his brother, Rhett, was injured in battle. A battle Reece thought I could have prevented.

It was no surprise that Reece still hated my guts, but even so, I remained loyal to him. Len had said that no one knew why Reece was considered a god, but that wasn't strictly true. Two of us knew.

It was a secret I'd take to my grave.

CHAPTER FOUR

By the time the guys were done filling Mera in on the politics of Reece's land, Shadow had returned, and we all followed him into the dining hall. Reece wasn't back yet, and I didn't bother to examine the lack of joy I felt at seeing his empty seat. Every part of me was just too aware of him now.

For centuries I'd been a robot, pushing all of my pain and loss down, pretending I didn't care, but the truth was I did care and always would.

As we entered the brightly lit room, I noted the way Shadow's gaze followed the exaggerated sway of Mera's hips. She wasn't waddling yet, but she was damn close. Fire filled his eyes, fire only for his mate, and I hid a smile as he hurried his stride to lift her into his lap before she could take her own seat.

The moment their bodies connected, his energy relaxed, and he leaned in to breathe deeply, clearly needing this moment after being separated from her in the realm.

"Don't mind us," Lucien said drily, sliding into one of the chairs opposite the loved-up couple. Len took the one next to him, Galleli another on that side as well, and I ended up beside the handsy couple in my regular spot. "We'll just be here," the vamp continued, "jealous bastards secretly loving *and* hating the fuck out of your happiness."

Mera's eyes were warm, sympathetic even, when she finally tore her attention from Shadow. "You know, you could still tell me what the hell happened with Simone, and maybe together we'll figure out how to rectify it."

Whatever teasing spark had been in the vampire's face faded into nothing, a blank slate of hidden thoughts. "There's nothing to talk about there," he said stiffly. "We might as well discuss the possibility of a relationship between a human and a pet dog. It's not going to happen, no matter how much it's searched for in your human porn sites."

Mera wrinkled her nose, shaking her head a few times like she was hoping to clear that imagery. "Firstly, what the fuck, Lucien? What sort of porn are you watching?" She shuddered. "And secondly, you'd better not be referring to Simone as the dog in that scenario, because you know I'll gut you. I love you, for sure, but she's my lifelong BFF. This girl throws down for her besties."

Shadow shifted in his chair, straightening to bring Mera and his body in line with Lucien, and I think that was the moment the vampire realized he was in trouble. Not that Mera needed a guard beast—she could handle herself, no issue—but facing the two of them together was not for the faint of heart.

Lucien held both hands up, the smallest of smiles playing around his lips. "I don't know whether to be terrified or turned on right now. I think it's both." Mera snarled, and the vampire-with-a-death-wish laughed. "Calm down, preggo. I would never refer to Simone as a pet dog. She's a gorgeous, strong, funny, and fiery shifter. She's just not the shifter for me. Now leave it alone."

With a frustrated look on her face, Mera let out a sigh and, for once, didn't push her luck. She just settled into her mate like he was a comfy couch, despite the fact that there was nothing soft on Shadow. The beast reached out and placed his hands on her belly, the size of them spanning nearly across the width. As he started to massage the swollen area, Mera's eyes fluttered closed, and this time her moan was not one of annoyance.

Leaning forward, I gently patted her cheek, and as her hazel eyes came into view again, I said, "Stop that, or Shadow will whisk you away. And we don't have time for that just yet. I need to know what the plan is for the Desert Lands."

She exaggeratedly pouted at me. "Awwww, you're no fun, Angel-face."

My chest tightened as warmth trickled through my center. Her nicknames meant more than I'd ever tell her. Mera had turned me into a sap, and after so many years of hardening my softer emotions, it was the oddest sensation to embrace them now.

"Reece has smoothed the way for us to be at the meeting of the dynasties," Shadow said, getting to business, and everyone shut up to listen. "This was one of my requirements if Mera was to be part of these proceedings. I don't want to fight the dynasties as well as whatever else waits for us there. Normally this sort of meeting would be for Desertlandians only, but Reece, being who he is, got special permission by citing that this was not one of the regular, sanctioned gatherings and therefore didn't fall under the same rules."

"So, we're leaving the day after tomorrow?" Mera asked, reiterating what Galleli had said earlier.

Shadow nodded. "That's the plan, but we can't do anything until Reece returns. Best to be prepared just in case." His hands had slowed as they stroked across her stomach.

Mera pushed herself up from where she'd been completely

slumped into him. "I need to visit Simone and Sam first. You know I check on them every few weeks. I can't disappear into the deserts for who knows how long and not let them know what's happening."

Len jumped to his feet gracefully, silver eyes alight. "Right! I almost forgot. I made you some new papers to communicate through. Wait right there."

He was gone just as Mera shot a rueful smile toward her baby belly. "Don't worry, I won't be rushing anywhere."

Shadow's hands drifted up from her stomach and over her chest to rest against the sides of her neck and face, holding her from behind. Mera's pupils dilated because, no doubt, this position reminded her of the many, *many* ways Shadow had brought her to screaming orgasms. We'd all heard it. We were all jealous of it. Their sexual chemistry and love of voyeurism had been harder to take since my rebirth because as the robot faded, the wants and needs of my body had begun to make themselves strongly heard.

An ember burned low in my center, and for the first time in... well, forever, I was ready to experience and experiment with my own sexuality.

My steamy thoughts were interrupted by Shadow. "If you need to move fast," he breathed into Mera's ear, "I will carry you. You and our baby."

The way he said "our baby" in his low grumbling brogue even had me wanting to fan myself.

"And I will take you to Earth to check up on your pack mates before we leave," he finished. "Sam especially since I know you worry the most about her."

Mera swallowed roughly, her voice understandably breathy. "Yeah, because despite her reassurances that she's fine and her pack is no longer hurting her, I sense that there's a lot she isn't telling me."

I'd gone with Mera a few times to check on Sam, and whenever we made it to her pack lands—the pack she had worked years to escape before all but running back to them—everything seemed perfect. At least on the surface. Sam had a nice house, the town was clean, and the shifters all looked strong and healthy. But there was an undercurrent in her pack. A feeling of darkness lingering below the light.

Mera had pressed Sam as hard as she could, assuring her that whatever it was, she could help, but her friend had insisted that for once she was dealing with the shit show of her life and everything was okay.

"Don't announce your arrival this time," I said. "Maybe we'll catch them unawares."

"I never announce it," Mera said, her eyes shiny as she thought of her friend. "But I do always visit Torma first. One of those bastards probably warns the other pack." Her expression hardened as she nodded. "Yes, you're right. This time I'll head to Sam's first, and with a little luck, their magical shine will have a few spots I can pick at."

"The packs have been working hard to clean themselves up," Lucien said, continuing with the dirty analogy as he leaned back and laced his fingers together over his front, "ever since Shadow decided to take an interest in them."

Shadow scoffed, eyes hooded. "You mean ever since Mera told me my 'children' were acting like a bunch of little shits and I needed to deal with them?"

Mera shrugged. "I said what I said. When you're a parent, you don't get to just throw them out into the world and let them be assholes. It's your job to teach them all the valuable life lessons."

Shadow's lips twitched, eyes amused. "I'm not their parent. If I were their parent, you and I would be in a rather precarious sort of situat—"

"Stop," Mera cut him off with a squeak. "Nope. No. No no no. I was reborn and no longer have any ties to shifter packs. We are a weird, messy combination of DNA that is in no way related, and this topic requires no further discussion."

Everyone laughed except for Galleli, but the smile on his face was as good as laughter for the stoic transcendent. Before we continued any further ribbing about the minute possibility of Mera being related to Shadow, since she was a born goddess from the same Nexus as Shadow's mother, Len reappeared, drawing our attention. "Got the parchment," he said as he dropped back into the chair he'd vacated a few minutes ago. "You'll be able to give a piece each to Sam and Simone."

He waved three pieces of parchment at her, and I noticed the invisible lines of power spanning between them all. This was Faerie magic stemming from crushed up gems infused into the paper itself. The connection between them would allow Mera and her friends to send messages between the worlds.

Mera all but dove across the table to hug the fae, only pulling back when her mate growled. "Thank you so much," she cried, her excitement spilling free. "This will give me such peace of mind. I'm still so sorry I lost the last one."

Len waved her off. "It's all good. They're easy enough to make."

More than a few at the table hid their expressions at that slight exaggeration of the truth. These parchments were rare and took an extraordinary amount of magic, skill, and control to create. For Mera though, we'd all remake the worlds, and that was a fact that would never change. In comparison, parchment was easy enough.

CHAPTER FIVE

The rest of the evening continued with those of us who ate ordering food. My new ability to enjoy food was a true gift in my life. Transcendents generally took their energy from the land, the world's power, and their own family line. We did not have the need—or digestive system—for food. But after my rebirth, I found I could indulge in both if I wanted, and I'd really developed a taste for eating.

Everything was just so delicious, sliding across my newly evolved tastebuds with ease. After years of just touching and smelling food items for enjoyment, I finally got to experience the most important sense: taste.

"I told you the pot pie was to die for," Mera crowed, all but beaming as she watched me shovel another forkful in.

"How do they get the pastry so flaky and buttery and perfect?" I moaned, chewing each delicious layer.

"It's magic," Mera told me seriously. "Swirling portals and the ability to walk between the worlds are great and all, but the food is the true magic."

She was in her own seat now, eyes closed as she took another bite. Shadow was beside her, sipping his drink and chatting with his friends, but all the while, his possessive gaze remained on his mate. I swear to creations, watching her eat was foreplay to that fucker.

Jealousy was another new experience I had to contend with, and while I'd never want to take Mera's happiness for my own—not in a million lifetimes—a small part of me craved to know what that sort of bond felt like.

Unconditional love.

It probably wasn't in the cards for me, and while I felt some reassurance that there was a peaceful future out there, even without a mate, I knew it would take time. Maybe what I really needed was someone to quench this fire burning in my body, and once that happened, I could return to focusing on what was truly important: peace.

Yes, that was a good plan. My mission—after the Desert Lands mission, of course—was to seek out a suitable sex partner and see what I'd been missing out on all these years. No longer would I deny my body, and in doing so, I felt reassured that peace would follow.

After all, there was no greater dream for a transcendent.

When dinner was done, the others left to rest and gather their weapons. They'd all be back soon though, along with Alistair, who was returning from Karn tomorrow.

"Will you come with us in the morning?" Mera asked me as she was dragged to her feet by Shadow.

"We won't have much time," Shadow reminded her. "Quick stops to Sam and then Simone. No lingering."

Mera didn't fight him. Reece rarely ever asked for help, so whatever was going on in the Desert Lands was a big deal and deserved all of our attention.

"If you want me there, I'm there," I told her.

Mera shot me her *what the fuck* expression. "You're my family. I want you wherever I am."

"Except in bed," Shadow grumbled, and then he scooped her into his arms, cradling her close to his body. "We'll see you in the morning, Melalekin."

A low chuckle escaped from me, and I had to shake my head as I watched his broad shoulders disappear so fast that it would appear he was running. Except the smug bastard was clearly in a casual stroll. Whatever Shadow did with his energy, the ways he manipulated it, could not be replicated by another. Except for maybe the one being I did not want to think about.

My eyes landed on Reece's empty seat again, and I forced myself to get up and walk away before I could dwell on his absence. Of course, that was a brilliant plan right until I stepped from the dining hall and all but smacked into him.

The pain of my past, here to torment me.

Heavy hands landed on my shoulders, and while I'd normally be swinging at this uninvited contact, I froze as a dry pine scent invaded my nose. That, along with that earthy, deserts-in-the-summer, was all Reece.

It was unclear if he'd known it was me barreling out of the dining hall, but with his senses it wouldn't take him more than a few seconds to figure it out. When the shoulder contact didn't cease, I found my eyes fluttering open as I tilted my head back to stare into his face. I was tall with a body built for battle, but when I was with this male, he made me feel petite.

I'd always loved and hated that about him.

"Reece?" I asked softly, my expression scrunching as I tried to figure out why he was still holding me. "Is everything okay?"

His face was unreadable, telling me nothing even as his grip remained firm. He pulled me closer, our bodies touching along their length, and I tried to ignore his hardness against me. I wasn't exactly soft, having honed my body into a weapon, but Reece was made of rock in comparison.

"Lale," he breathed, his irises swirling and tormented, and

fuck, my heart stopped. He hadn't called me that in... forever. It'd been forever.

I couldn't tear my gaze from him, those eyes that destroyed my control and invaded my dreams. They were my favorite part of the desert god, the blue a color unmatched in any of the universes with the darkest, thickest lashes framing them. And deep inside those depths, where most wouldn't see because you had to be very close, there was a galaxy of stars and magic. Magic that betrayed his connection to the Delfora.

Only a very select few—most dead now—knew that Reece had been conceived and birthed in the Delfora, a land filled with the energy of the ancients. It was an act that should have killed his parents and any child, but for some reason, it had been allowed. A completely forbidden act, now a secret lost in time.

It was the reason galaxies of power existed in his eyes, and it was also, no doubt, the reason he was being called back to their lands.

Since he didn't appear to want to release me any time soon, I went into defense mode. "What are you doing?" I snapped. If I stayed in his arms like this for one more second, I was going to do something truly fucking stupid.

My tone knocked Reece out of whatever had been brewing between us, and as he released me, blood rushed back into my limbs, my muscles pulsing hot and cold for a beat. Before I could say another word, he strode past me like nothing had happened, entering the dining hall.

From the moment he'd touched me, adrenaline had been rushing through my body, pumping everything into overdrive. Now that he was gone, this eased, and I fell against the nearest shelves, overstimulated and somehow also exhausted.

"No!" I chastised myself with a hard shake of my head. "Pull yourself together. Now."

It had been a while since I'd needed my own personal pep talk, but with everything that had changed in the past few months, Reece being back in my life was proving to be the catalyst that turned it all to shit.

We'd been so good at avoiding each other.

So damn good. No one even knew the true details of our tattered past. At least I'd never told anyone, outside of giving Mera some basic information. Knowing Reece, he wouldn't have divulged much either, but I had the sense that by the end of this little adventure in the Desert Lands, the truth would come out. After all, what happens in the sands doesn't always stay buried there.

CHAPTER SIX

That random meeting with Reece unsettled me to the point that I could not rest that night, and by the time Mera and Shadow appeared, both dressed in black jeans, plain white shirts, and black boots—looking couple goals and well-rested, the bastards—I was standing in the center of the library feeling like shit but ready to get to Earth. I'd even dressed in as close to human attire as I could find, with my own jeans, red checkered shirt, and sneakers. My hair was in a braid and my wings were tucked away, so I'd blend right in with the locals.

I really needed Earth to be done so that the Desert Lands could get done. Once this was all over, I would shove Reece back into the past where he belonged and get to working on my future. Speaking of...

"Did Reece find you last night?" I asked Shadow, my voice flat.

He paused at my tone, his flaming eyes narrowing as he took in my current expression. "He got a message to me that he'll bring us all across later tonight, if we're back from Earth in time."

Shadow spoke in his usual gruff demeanor while also staring into the deepest recesses of my psyche. "Don't," I warned him, and as we often did, our next communication was silent.

His glare said, *You and Reece need to sort this shit out before we get to his world. No one has time for it.*

I glared harder. *Listen up, asshole. This is not on me. I ignored him as expected, but Reece was the one who turned it into a war again. Talk to your friend.*

Before he could glare some new "words" at me, Mera, who'd clearly caught the silent exchange, cleared her throat. "What the hell happened?" she said. "What did Reece do?"

Mera knew some of our past, and she thought we both just needed to get over it and move forward. Decades of holding grudges was just too much for someone with so few years behind her to understand.

"Nothing," I said with a long exhale. "Nothing at all happened. It's just a tense situation."

In truth, nothing had happened. We'd exchanged about ten words and none of them with any significance. My pique had more to do with the way his damn eyes had stolen my soul.

Stolen and shredded it, especially when they'd turned icy.

Changing the subject felt like a very good idea right now. "Are we ready to get to Earth?"

"Yes!" Mera chirped, expression brightening. Her red hair, which was out in loose waves, bounced around her body as she wiggled. "I'm excited to give my girls this magic fae parchment. It will be nice to regularly exchange messages."

Shadow wrapped his muscled arm around her. "Yes, and with that in mind, we should get going. We need to be back here and on our way to the Desert Lands by this mid-moon."

Mera stilled and turned her head to look up with a furrowed brow. "Mid-moon?"

"Let's walk and talk," Shadow said, guiding her along the center path of the library. "The Desert Lands have a moonlike ball in the sky," he explained. "They call it the *yertin,* which roughly translates to sphere. The phases are new-moon in the morning when it's quite red and warm, then mid-moon at mid-day, half-moon in the evening when the red fades to a light orange-yellow, finished up with the dark-moon, which is a sliver of light in shades of blue and grey."

Mera hung on his every word, desperate for knowledge of the worlds. If she wasn't reading, loving her mate, or creating Christmas, she was questioning every being who stepped through the doorways, wanting to know of their lives.

"That's so exciting. I can't wait to see it," she said in a rush, "and the different colored sands. We really do need to get to Earth and get back here."

Despite her extra belly, she was the one to pick up the pace, moving us out of the library and into the white hall. Her smile remained in place as she chatted, until about halfway down the length she ground to a halt. She dropped her hands to her stomach, and Shadow and I were both at her side in a beat.

"Is everything okay?" I asked, my hand on my chest to feel for our bond.

Before I could explore it in detail, she let out a low sigh. "Every single time this baby kicks me, my heart swells. It's the weirdest sensation, but since I've moved past my fears of an alien invading my body, I can't imagine not feeling these daily flutters and kicks."

Her essence had already opened and connected to the life she'd created with Shadow.

"You are my own personal miracle," the beast whispered as he leaned down and pressed his lips to her stomach.

"They kicked again," Mera exclaimed. "Right when you

kissed me. I swear, this little one knows your power already, Shadow."

Shadow's rumble was a deep, broken sound. It hurt in my chest to hear it because I knew his life had been akin to my own—two souls who'd never thought they'd be whole. And yet here he was with everything he'd ever dreamed of. Despite our differences, I was happy for him.

"Come feel," Mera said, holding out a hand to me. I reached out without hesitation, wondering if this was the moment the baby would kick for me. No matter how many times I'd tried to catch their movements, whenever they felt my power, they stopped.

And today was no exception. Mera grasped my hand and placed it on the spot she'd felt the kicks, and the second my palm touched her shirt, not a movement could be felt.

We all stared down. "Baby doesn't like me much," I said, trying to keep my voice light, even though I felt slighted by a fetus.

Mera's warm palm pressed down on mine. "Not true. Baby is going to love Auntie Angel. Maybe your power is just a touch foreign to them at the moment."

It was a possibility, but since Mera and I shared a similar powerbase now, it seemed unlikely. Children of power were often unpredictable, and I guess I wouldn't find out what had this one rejecting me until they were born.

We were quiet as we walked again. Shadow controlled the hallway exit so that we arrived in Sam's pack, Clarity, which was located in the small town of Hrento in the Sierra Blanco Mountains of New Mexico. I'd been here a couple of times with Mera before, and since this time we'd shown up with no way for them to have been warned of our impending arrival, this was our best shot at finding their darkness.

As we entered the small town, it was quiet, and as always,

nothing screamed danger or unease here. Clarity Pack had built their base within a gorgeous, forested mountain range, giving the shifters a decent chunk of a few thousand acres to roam without worrying about running into any unsuspecting humans. Their township itself was smaller than Torma, where Mera had grown up, but since Torma pack was one of the largest in America, that made sense.

Clarity pack was filled with a lot of beta type wolves and only a few that could wear the mantle of alpha, which meant they weren't ever going to challenge Torma for top pack status, but in the overall pack hierarchy, they held their own.

As we moved further into the winding and narrow streets with wood cabin–style houses dotted in and amongst the trees, the few shifters who were lingering around scattered like scared mice, disappearing into their homes. This in and of itself was not odd since Mera and Shadow had already built quite the reputation among the packs, but usually someone was brave enough to approach and greet us.

We continued on, moving further into Hrento, a village which could be described as having a treehouse vibe. They had really worked in harmony with their landscape here, taking away as little from the natural habitat that they could. It was a nice place, and from what we'd observed, this pack appeared to be far less brutal and rigid with its members compared to Torma. Yet Sam had done everything she could to escape them.

And then she'd come back. All of it was confusing, and I didn't blame Mera for feeling the need to continually check in on her.

Mera's face was somber as she strode along, and I knew all of us were using whatever extra senses we had to probe at the undercurrents of this pack.

"It feels really calm today," I said, feeling barely a ripple in my energy.

"Too calm," Shadow said shortly.

Mera stopped walking, her face shadowed by the trees above as she closed her eyes and breathed deeply. "There's no one here," she finally said, opening her eyes again. "I mean, outside of those who vamoosed when we arrived, I can't feel any other energy."

Shadow was the one now to close his eyes and send out his power to probe through the shifters. They were his creation after all, and none could hide from him.

Letting them do their thing, I walked to the closest house, one with large pots of lavender gracing either side of the front door. Peeking inside, I noted the dark interior and a slightly stale scent wafting out from under the window.

Not only was no one home, but it appeared they hadn't been here for some time.

"The town is empty," Shadow said, and I turned to find them both on the front porch with me.

We'd all reached the same conclusion, and now we needed to find out why.

CHAPTER SEVEN

Mera's face was pale as she swallowed roughly. "This is bad."

"Let's find those few who remain," Shadow bit out, his annoyance spilling over in the clipped words. "They must know something. Maybe there's a pack mixer or meeting away from Hrento."

A normal male would have just gone door to door and knocked to find the ones who remained, but Shadow was never going to be "normal." He released his flames, the beast side of him poking its head out, and as that energy spilled into the mountains, ten shifters hurried out of their homes to stand before us.

Two of them—both females with very blond hair and tall, athletic builds—lifted their heads in an attempt to meet Shadow's eyes. But as soon as they did, his chest rumbled, and they dropped their gazes quick smart.

There was only one alpha here.

Okay, maybe two with Mera. "Where is the rest of your pack?" she snapped.

One of the males—who was almost on the ground, he held

himself so low—whimpered before choking out some words. "Away on pack business."

"What business?" Mera pressed, clearly frustrated at having to pry this information from them.

One of those two women who had initially hoped to challenge Shadow let out a huff. "There's a meeting of all packs in New Orleans this weekend. It's one of those yearly catch-up-on-business events, and this year our alpha didn't feel safe going without most of our members."

She eased her head up a touch. "We were chosen to stay behind to keep the town running and feed the livestock and such, but the others are all there. They'll be back next week."

Mera, who'd clearly had enough, let her flames fly as she reached down to touch the blond shifter's head. There was about a thirty-second pause as Mera searched through her memories.

"Okay, she's telling the truth," she finally said with a sigh. "And Sam appears to be safe in these memories. She looks unhappy but not harmed, so it appears that whatever is holding her here continues."

The blond shifter shook her head, dislodging Mera's hand. Shadow's chest rumbled—his protectiveness toward Mera had never been higher than since she'd fallen pregnant. And considering how high it'd been before...

"Do you have something you want to say to us?" he growled at the blond, and all of her fight died as she crumpled forward.

"Sam is none of your concern," she choked out. "She's doing her duty for the pack, just like the rest of us, and as long as she keeps her side of the bargain, we will all be okay."

She now had Mera's complete and total focus. "What bargain?" she snarled, taking another step closer. Shadow didn't like that. His expression darkened but he knew that these beings were no true threat to his mate, so he refrained from dragging her back.

"What fucking bargain?" Mera pushed harder. "We'll get it from you one way or another, so you might as well save yourself the torture."

I hid my smile. Mera was so unlike other powerful beings. In general it bothered her to use her power against others, especially those weaker, but if you hurt anyone she cared about, you'd better start praying to whatever god you worshipped because you were on your way to the afterlife.

"She stays to protect the pack." Another shifter spoke up—a lanky, dark-skinned man who had been silent until this point. "Our alpha promised that if she stayed and mated his son, who is not quite of age yet, that we would all be protected from any further pack punishments."

He lifted his head fully, and unlike the others, almost managed to meet Mera's eyes. "Sam owes us nothing, but she stays for us regardless."

"Why would the alpha want her for his son?" Mera's voice lowered as she shook her head. "It makes no sense since she's already a rejected mate."

"His older brother was the one who rejected her," the man said, face drawn. "The previous future alpha, who was killed by his father after Sam left."

"Why?" Mera pressed.

"The alpha found out that the reason she left was because his son rejected her. That was when his obsession started."

The blond female laughed without humor. "He wants the strong bond of a true-mated alpha. He's obsessed now with recreating it with his youngest son."

"And Sam is the one he's chosen," Mera said softly, sucking in a few deep breaths before turning to meet my gaze. I wasn't sure exactly what she was thinking, but it was clear that we had a lot to discuss once we were away from curious shifters.

"I need you to give this to her when she returns," Mera finally said to them, pulling free a piece of the parchment. "She can write on this paper, and I will get the message. The alpha cannot know about it, either." Her gaze turned darker. "I want you all to swear that you will not screw up this simple task. I know your energy now and can track you without breaking a sweat."

Technically, Shadow could, and judging by the smile playing around his lips, he enjoyed Mera secondhandedly using him as a threat.

"We promise," one of them squeaked. "We will guard this parchment with our lives and give it to Sam with your words as soon as she returns."

"Thank you," Mera said with a nod. "Appreciate the help."

Her face was blank, but those of us who knew her quite well could see the worry burning in her eyes. She didn't say a word until we'd walked toward the edge of the town and Shadow had called a doorway, but as soon as we were in the white hallway, she broke.

"What the actual fuck?" Her growl was loud. "Sam and I have near mirror-image pasts." Her breaths came in and out harshly. "She never told me her mate was also an alpha's son."

"Do you want to go to New Orleans?" Shadow asked, his concerned gaze locked on his clearly stressed-out mate.

Mera slowed her breathing in an attempt to calm herself. Almost worked too. "As much as I do, I could see in their memories that Sam is physically safe. She's also had more than a few opportunities to allow us to help and has refused. Showing up there is not going to change that. Not to mention I'm probably the last person she wants to see."

"You think she blames you?" I asked, trying to work out that statement.

Mera nodded. "Possibly. What happened with Torin and me clued these fucks into the true-mate bond and what rejection can take from the pack. I managed to escape, but Sam had to go back without a mate like Shadow waiting in the wings to ease her pain."

"She doesn't blame you," Shadow said straight up. "I sensed her emotions, and she cares for you a great deal. I think she might just have a bit of a savior mentality."

Mera swallowed roughly, her eyes glassy. "Yeah, she definitely does. I was a complete stranger when she risked Torin's wrath to help me." She roughly wiped at her eyes before sniffling a few times and pulling herself together. "We need to help Reece now, but the moment we've dealt with the Desert Land's issues, I'm going to track Sam down and ask some very pointed questions. She might think she's doing the right thing, but she's really throwing her life away. If it's a simple matter of dealing with a megalomaniac alpha, well, we've proven more than once that we're capable of doing that. I want her to know there's another option."

"I don't understand why she didn't just tell you this in the first place," I said. "It's a simple issue that has a simple solution. There was no need for the suffering and secrecy."

Shadow released a low laugh, pitching his shoulder against the white wall as he waited. "Humans don't think like the rest of us. They're young and idealistic. And if they're even remotely decent, they always want to martyr themselves."

Mera glared and nudged him, not even moving him an inch. "Firstly, she's not human. But for the rest... you're probably right. I think Sam has spent her entire life feeling lost, like an outcast in her pack, and now she finally has validation. A place and purpose. Acceptance. All of which doesn't take away from the fact that very soon I'll be tracking her ass down to have a rather frank discussion."

Shadow inclined his head, straightening again to tower over us. "Simone first?" he checked, and Mera nodded, mood brightening a touch.

"Yes, absolutely. I don't think she'll be at the New Orleans meeting, because Torma wouldn't send all their shifters in fear. They've changed a lot since we restructured them, but their overwhelming arrogance remains."

Shadow's chuckle echoed down the hall as he once again wrapped arms around his mate. "These packs would have flourished with you as their god."

Mera pushed up on her toes, pressing kisses to whatever parts of his skin she could reach. "They flourished with you. You gave them wings and let them fly."

Shadow met my gaze over the top of her masses of red hair, and his expression... I wondered if anyone else outside of Mera, and now me, had seen him wear a look of such devotion.

This was not the same beast I'd gone up against over the years.

Mera had changed him.

She'd changed us all.

CHAPTER EIGHT

Mera's predictions proved to be true, with most of Torma filled with shifters going about their daily lives. We found Simone in their main shopping precinct, which was one long and wide street, lined on both sides with a variety of stores from homewares to cafes and even a large hardware store.

"Holy crap and fucking hell!" Mera squealed when she ground to a halt in front of a red brick store. "She reopened the bookstore."

Mera, like Shadow and myself, was a huge reader. Before finding out her true destiny, she'd worked in the only bookstore in Torma, which had been owned by Dannie, who had been secretly pretending to be a shifter. It turned out that Shadow's mom was the legendary Danamain of the Shadow Realm, and when too much power had gone to her head, she'd attempted to wipe all of our memories of her time in Torma.

This store had been one of those memories, but it appeared that now we'd disposed of her machinations, Simone had decided to give the store a new lease on life. The façade had changed, the red brick set off now by a bright forest-green awning framing a large window filled with fantasy and romance books, artfully displayed on wood shelving.

"Once Upon a Howling Good Time," Mera said with a laugh, reading the huge sign across the front door. "I love that she's giving it a good old shifter try at making reading fun again. Torma has never been known for their love of the arts."

Shadow cleared his throat. "Yeah, that's probably my fault. I designed shifters to be predators without taking into account that without culture and empathy as well, the packs would never evolve past the beasts from which they were born."

"They're not that bad," Mera snorted, rolling her eyes a touch. "But yeah, a sprinkle more book smarts would not have gone astray."

"I'll remember that," Shadow said drily, "for the next time I invent an entire race of beings."

Mera patted his chest. "See that you do." Then with a wink, she strolled her ass into the bookshop.

Shadow took a full minute to watch her walk away before he shook his head and rubbed a huge hand over his face like that would snap him out of the spell Mera had over him. He never looked my way, and I focused my eyes forward as well since there was an unspoken rule amongst warrior friends: We let each other have our weak moments, and we don't point them out.

Once we made it inside, it was to find Mera and Simone hugging and crying and rocking back and forth in the middle of the room. Bookshelves were to the right of them and a large, raw-timber serving table on the left. The room was filled with the scent of paper, parchment, ink, and... home. I would always find warmth and comfort in a room jam-packed with words and knowledge.

"Your belly is so big now," Simone gushed as she pulled away, her dark eyes lit up with what could only be described as true happiness. "You'd better not have this damn baby without me. I swear to fuck, Mera."

Shadow pushed in behind his mate. "That's why we're here," he said. "Mera has to leave the library for a few weeks, and she wanted to check in on you and drop off more parchment so you can stay in contact while we're gone."

Simone paused, some of her excitement dying as her hands on Mera's stomach stilled. "Where are you going? Should she be travelling in her condition?"

Shadow opened his mouth, but before he could say anything, Mera growled. "*She* is standing right here, and there's no condition. I'm pregnant, not dying. The baby shouldn't be here for at least another month or two, and I'll be safely back in the library by that time." Her gaze flicked toward me. "Back me up, Angel. I mean, women have been working in the fields right up until they squat to give birth. I can sure as fuck leave the library for a few weeks to help a friend."

Shadow wisely remained silent; we all knew they'd argued about the Desert Lands more than once, and since Mera had won, there was no point going over it again.

"Women have been giving birth in exceptional circumstances for millennia," I confirmed. "Especially on Earth, where often they lived quite primitively without the modern conveniences they have today. Despite the fact that childbirth has been one of the biggest killers of women for centuries—"

I cut myself off as Mera's eyes widen dramatically. *Shit.* Some of that factuality was probably not appropriate with her current situation.

"Which, of course, is not relevant to you at all," I hurried to fix it, "since you're a god. Our babies might be quite powerful, hard to grow and birth, but..."

Her face was super pale at this point, and I decided to just shut my mouth.

"You're going to be fine," Shadow said as he reached out and rubbed a hand across her lower back, soothing her in the way that only he could. "The most important part of what Angel said is that you're a goddess born of the Nexus. Practically indestructible. You will birth our child as easily as you snared yourself a powerful mate."

Mera's head snapped up as she glared at him. "Are you actually shitting me right now? What part of *everything that we went through to be together* was easy?"

Shadow didn't blink an eye at her sudden aggression. Even before pregnancy, she'd always had a streak of *don't fuck with me*, which I was fairly certain he loved. "Every single part of it was easy. Comparatively. We're fated to be together, but I would have chosen you and everything we went through even if that weren't the case. Loving you is the easiest thing I've ever done."

Mera's face softened as she let out a long breath. "It's lucky that you occasionally say the right thing." A small smirk crossed her lips. "And with that perspective, I guess loving you is also the easiest thing I've ever done."

Shadow's lips twitched, but he refrained from saying more. Mera also let it go, returning to Simone since we didn't have long. "This is the parchment," she said, handing it across. "Can you keep me updated on what's happening in the packs and if anything eventuates from this big meeting?"

Simone nodded, taking the paper and moving behind her counter to slide it into a drawer. "Of course I will. Now, take a seat so we can talk for whatever time you have left here. Tell me everything that's been happening since we caught up last."

Linking arms, the pair moved to the back of the shop where a few couches were arranged in a small reading space. Choosing a loveseat, they both started talking at once, and despite the words spilling from their mouths at a pace that should deny the ability to both hear and comprehend what was being said, somehow they managed it.

"I'm worried about Sam," Mera said after telling her what we'd learned in Clarity. "While it's clear that she's in no immediate danger, there's definitely some shady shit happening in her pack. As soon as Sam's ready to share with us, we need to help her wade through it."

Simone nodded, serious brown eyes locked on Mera's face. "Yeah, I've been worried about her for the same reasons. There's an undercurrent of darkness in her pack, similar to how Torma used to feel."

Corrupt alphas, the seed of evil that could send a pack into complete turmoil.

"I'm putting that alpha on my kill list," Mera muttered. "Those power-hungry bastards are the death of a true pack bond."

Shadow's chest rumbled. "You're sexy when you're plotting murder, mate."

Mera just shook her head at him. "You're no help, dude. You should be the one plotting murder. You're the goddamn Shadow Beast."

The rumble in his chest increased. "Firstly, don't call me dude. Secondly, if you want me to murder someone, you only have to ask once and it will be done." His voice lowered. "And thirdly, if you need me to destroy the entire fucking planet, it's done."

Mera's smile was so bright that it was blinding as she beamed and blinked back tears. "That's the sweetest thing anyone has ever said to me."

Only those two could turn murder into romance.

Shadow took a few steps to crouch down behind her chair and kiss her roughly. Even though it was only a kiss, Simone and I shifted uncomfortably because with these two, the chemistry burned so hot that right now I felt like I'd walked in on them right in the middle of sex.

Sucking in a rough breath, I turned and left the shop, needing a moment to compose myself. Through no fault of her own, Mera had me craving a life that was probably never going to be mine, a fact I needed to come to terms with and fast.

CHAPTER NINE

Once outside, it took me a few minutes to calm my racing heart.

It was so frustrating to be knocked by such strong emotions again, when I'd spent centuries learning how to control and manage every aspect of my physical being. I was out of control, and if I didn't get a handle on it soon, I was likely going to self-destruct in a very unpleasant manner.

I couldn't let that happen around Reece. I would not give him the satisfaction.

"Angel!" Simone called my name as she appeared in the street. "Are you okay?"

Releasing a slow breath, I prepared to lie, but somehow the damn truth came out instead. "I'm struggling."

Her dark eyebrows shot up and nearly collided with her equally dark hairline. "Oh, fuck. I have to say that's about the last thing I expected you to say, and I'm somewhat freaking out that you're being so open with me."

Simone and I had never spent much time together, our greatest bond being our love for Mera. But I appreciated her forthright response and decided to continue in the same manner. "Since my rebirth, my emotions have been awakened in a way that I never anticipated. I mean, I'm old—older than you probably think—and it took me a very long time to learn how to control every aspect of my being. Yet here I am, like a youngling again, unable to deal."

Simone took a step closer to leave only a few inches between us. There were no shifters on the street nearby, but she still lowered her voice. "How old are we talking here?"

Some of my angst died, and I couldn't help my smile. "Ancient. Trust me on that."

She rocked back on her heels. "Damn, girl. Older than Shadow?"

This time my smirk turned into a smile.

"Much older." Shadow's deep voice came from the front door of the shop as he stepped out with Mera. "She was the monster in the shadows before me."

I glared at him, hoping he'd shut up. "That was a former life. Now I'm just... Well, I have no idea who I am, but I'm hoping that I have a chance to find out."

Mera wasted no time hugging me, knowing in her own way that I was struggling, even though I hadn't told her in so many words. "It's going to be okay," she whispered as she pulled away. "I see a bright future for you, Angel. There's a reason you were reborn—a reason greater than the fact that I don't think I could have survived without you. We just need to be patient, and the truth will reveal itself."

Simone reached out and grabbed her hand, joining the three of us together. "Pregnancy has made you all philosophical. I like it."

Mera tightened her grip on her best friend. "It has, and with that in mind, I'm wondering if you're ready to tell me what happened between you and a certain vampire. I really hate when my *bestest* best friend is hiding shit from me and won't let me help."

Whatever joy and mirth had been in Simone's face vanished so fast it was as if someone had taken a cloth and erased it with a swipe. "I can't," she choked out, her voice rasping like she'd hurt her throat. "The compulsion makes it difficult, and until I figure out how to break it, the rest would be confusing."

Mera's lips thinned. "I need to kill Lucien, just stake the bastard right through the heart."

Simone coughed before shaking her head. "No, please. It wasn't his fault. He tried to help me, but some shady crap went down in Valdor. Now I just need to move on with my life, forget it even happened."

Mera still didn't like it, but she also didn't argue again. For today at least. "Yeah, I guess I can respect that. I just hate seeing you hurt with no way to make it better."

Simone hugged her fiercely, holding on like Mera was her lifeline. "I know you do, and I love you for it. But I promise," she pulled away, "I'm doing okay. I might even start dating again soon, and hopefully, that's the step forward I need to move past Valdor."

"Dating again is good." Mera nodded. "It would be nice to know someone else is looking out for you since your parents are humans living their shitty lives out in the real world."

Simone let out a rueful laugh. "Not like they were that interested even when they lived here."

"True dat," Mera replied with a sad smile.

Shadow cleared his throat, interrupting them. "In regard to dating, I would suggest we don't mention it to Lucien. He's got a temper when it comes to Simone, even if he won't admit why."

Simone crossed her arms protectively over herself. "He has

no right to even think about me let alone have a temper over it. He made his choice, and now I'm making mine. You tell him whatever you want, but make sure you mention that I'm doing fine. I have my own business, and there's a shifter I'm flirting with who I might even take a chance on. I don't need or want that vampire in my life."

Shadow just nodded, his expression remaining neutral, but I knew him well enough to know there were deep thoughts lingering below the mask.

Simone, done with this conversation, turned back to Mera. "How long can you stay? How long until I'll see you again?"

Time moved differently between Earth and the other realms. If we were in the Desert Lands for a few weeks, it could easily translate into two months in Earth time.

"We have a few minutes," Mera said quickly. "Should we grab some lunch? Baby is hungry."

That got her mate moving, and he immediately rushed us into a nearby cafe, which proudly displayed a specials board offering *beef stew, venison rump, and a whole rabbit spit roasted.*

Shifters hadn't evolved far from their beast forms, especially in their eating habits.

On the inside it was like every other diner I'd seen in this world: lots of booths, a red-and-white checkered theme, and a long bar that housed the drinks, sauces, cutlery, and a few bored looking shifters. As soon as they noticed our arrival, three of them rushed forward to help us into a booth.

"Mera!" one of the females with light golden-brown hair and large grey eyes exclaimed. "What are you doing here?"

Mera's expression didn't give much away as she said, "Hey, Greta, how're things? I'm just visiting Simone to catch up, and we're hoping to get some of that world famous stew."

Greta swallowed roughly, her eyes darting to Shadow and

then back to Mera when she couldn't hold the beast's gaze for longer than a heartbeat. "For everyone?" she squeaked.

Mera glanced at me, and I shook my head.

"Just two please," she said to the waitress, "and some water."

Greta hurried off then, a little unsteady on her feet. "This crap happens every single time Shadow walks among the shifters," Simone snorted. "One would think he was a god or some shit."

Shadow's chest lifted as his usual rumble of annoyance escaped.

"Don't worry, mate," Mera said as she patted his arm. "I'll protect you from the ladies."

His brow furrowed as he narrowed his eyes on her, but before he could comment, Mera was turning away, already occupied by her friend. "Jaxson is in NOLA at the moment," Simone said. "And together with the other three alphas, they're actually doing a really solid job of managing Torma."

"I didn't think it would work," Mera replied, just as the stew arrived. Greta placed two huge, white ceramic dishes on the table, followed by glasses of water. "More than one alpha seems like a recipe for disaster, but it appears that it's actually created a more levelheaded approach, a council that votes on decisions."

Simone, who'd already started to eat, took a second to swallow before answering. "Pretty much. Majority vote, and there's more pack voting going on as well. Since the Wolfe family was run out of the top job, it's been peaceful here."

Mera, now the one shoveling in spoonfuls of soup, just nodded. "Have you heard anything about Torin?" she finally asked when she came up for air.

None of us were surprised when Shadow muttered, "Should have torn his fucking head off."

"Not a peep," Simone said her lips twitching. "He's probably dead. The common cold kills humans apparently, and that bastard would get man-flu for sure."

Shadow looked pleased by this truth as he relaxed into his corner of the booth, making the large area look small.

"I'm going to track him down one day," Mera said. "I'm curious to see what he's chosen to do with his second chance— and whether Sisily decided to stick around or not."

"She gave up her wolf for him," Simone said with a shrug. "I think she's fairly serious about him."

Mera snorted out a laugh. "Her wolf was going no matter what she decided, but yeah, you're right, she was willing to sacrifice her shifter side. I can't think of a greater loss than that. Has to be love, right?"

Shadow scoffed, and it was clear he'd already had enough talk of the shifter who'd rejected Mera and set off the chain of events that'd led her to Shadow. In a way, they both should be grateful that Torin had been such a selfish shit, otherwise Mera's future might have looked different, stuck in Torma with that asshole forever. I also had a lot to be grateful for in that regard, and maybe one day I'd track Torin down and thank him for being a spineless sack of organs.

"We should leave now," Shadow said a few minutes later when the girls had finished their stew but were still chatting back and forth. "We must prepare to go to the Desert Lands."

I was already on my feet, ready for this next mission to be over and done with. As the ghosts of my past continued to hang over my head, I felt unsettled and anxious, two emotions I was not okay with existing within my energy.

Mera was slower to get to her feet, and not just because she had to maneuver her stomach out of the booth. It was clear she hated leaving Simone so soon after arriving. "It's always good-bye," she said tearfully.

"Do you want her to come with us?" Shadow asked, his eyes hooded at the sight of his mate's cry-face.

Mera's face screwed up tighter. "That's sooo sweet," she sobbed. "But I won't put her in danger. She's building a life here, and I stan that a hundred and fifty percent."

"I have no damn idea what stan means," Shadow growled, "but I do know that if you don't stop crying, mate, I'm going to burn this fucking town to the ground."

This only made Mera sob harder as she choked out, "It's a combination of being a stalker and fan. Super fan if you will." She actually started to calm here like she knew she was being ridiculous. "I don't think I even used it right, but gotta stay current."

Shadow's chest rumbled as he shook his head. "Sunshine, you're eternal. Words like *stan*," his face screwed up in mock horror, "will be gone before you blink a damn eye."

As Mera went on to list a ton more slang that she'd recently come into contact with, I found myself exchanging an amused stare with Simone. "Is she always like this?" Simone asked with a chuckle.

"Her pregnancy has been... interesting," I replied.

This set Simone off, her laughter filling the small diner, which thankfully helped Mera stop crying as she glared at us. "You assholes should try growing a Shadow Beast baby. It's hard."

Of that I had no doubt.

"It's going to be okay," Simone said, giving her one last hug. "We'll see each other again soon since I'd better be there when this baby comes. And while I'd love to go to the desert with you"—she shot Mera a fake-annoyed glare—"thanks for making that decision without even checking with me, by the way. But if I learned anything from Lucien, it's that I can't really play in your world. Not without getting hurt. In these life and death situations, I'm a liability. And you really don't need that in your cond—"

"Pregnancy," Mera interrupted with a scowl, but at least she didn't sound as upset. "And you're never a liability, but I would die if you got hurt... or worse. Just, write to me, okay. We'll stay in touch."

"Right back at you, bestie," Simone said softly before releasing a long, drawn-out breath. "Please stay safe. Keep yourself and that baby alive."

"We'll be there," I reminded her. "Shadow and I won't let anything happen to Mera or the baby."

Mera looked like she was trying not to smile. "*The baby* and Auntie Angel are still working out their relationship, but rest assured, we both know she loves us."

The word "love" made me as uncomfortable as it made Shadow, and even though Mera threw it around like confetti at a party, I never once doubted she meant it.

And she wasn't wrong. Whatever Reece had gotten them into, I would be there to ensure my family did not perish in the Desert Lands.

Never again.

CHAPTER TEN

Mera was subdued as we left Torma, but it didn't last long. Simone and Sam were the only parts of Earth she hated to leave behind, and I had a suspicion that all too soon both would end up in the library, one way or another.

Mera wouldn't put up with these goodbyes for long, and Shadow wouldn't put up with Mera's tears.

Once we'd left the hallway, returning to the Library of Knowledge, we found it bustling with even more Solaris System beings than had been there when we left. This was prime research time. As we passed the shelves, I began to mentally prepare myself for what was to come next.

Battle... again.

Battle in the Desert Lands ... again.

Reece... fucking Reece.

The real part I'd never be ready for.

"Gaster!" Mera shouted suddenly, thankfully distracting me. The constant thought and worry was getting a little overwhelming; I had no idea how beings did this all the time.

"We're going to be gone for a while," Mera said to the

goblin, who was staring up with a soft expression. "Is there anything you need from us before we leave?"

Gaster's smile was genuine, stretching across his wrinkled face. He might love Mera the most of all. "You take care of yourself and our youngling," he said gruffly. "We can't lose either of you."

Shadow looked pleased by these words, and I knew—because I felt the same way—that he would never begrudge having those who loved Mera around. All of us kept her safe. We were her family, and the goblin, who was more powerful than most would ever know, was a really fantastic ally to have on her side.

"I'll be with Shadow and Angel, and the others," Mera reminded him. "Not to mention I'm kind of a goddess myself, so I think it'll be fine. We'll keep you updated as best we can." She swung her head toward Shadow. "We can do that, right?"

Shadow nodded. "I can communicate with the library."

That satisfied Mera. "Perfect. I'll feel better knowing that if there are any issues here, we'll be informed quickly."

Gaster tilted his head, that smile never wavering. "I will keep your library safe, Mera Callahan. You do not need to worry so. Focus on what trials are ahead, and leave the rest to me."

She hugged him one last time, and then we were moving along the path again toward the dining hall. When we got closer, two familiar puffs of smoke spilled out of the shelves where they'd clearly been waiting for their bonded ones to return. Inky and Midnight wrapped themselves around Shadow and Mera, who disappeared into the black clouds.

The mists were original energy from the power that blanketed the Shadow Realm. It was near unheard of for any part of that energy to separate from the collective, and even less heard of for them to bond with another. Of course, Shadow and Mera made an artform out of proving the norm wrong, and it was nice to see them all back together.

"Midnight, I missed you so much," Mera exclaimed, reappearing as the dark cloud soared higher. "I thought you were staying in the realm."

"They're just back for a goodbye," Shadow said, also reappearing.

After that, their conversations went quiet since all of them could chat mentally. I wandered away to allow them this moment together before we left. My restlessness was growing, along with my anxiety, and since I'd never been prone to either of those emotions before, it was disconcerting.

In an effort to regain my equilibrium, I released my new wings, marveling once again at the flames sliding through their feathered lengths. After a lifetime with my previous wings and appearance, it was odd to experience change. Those of us who were long-lived didn't do change very well, especially when it wasn't only my wings filled with fire, but also my body.

Fire and passion.

If I talked to Mera about it, I knew without a doubt that she'd tell me I needed to get laid... and maybe she was right. This extra energy and *desire* had to go somewhere.

Sex was not a huge part of my life; in fact I'd only ever experienced it once before I'd turned myself into a damn robot. But I was a robot no longer, and with that, I was free to explore all of life's pleasures.

Like that thought alone dragged the fae out of wherever he had been hiding, Len appeared before me so suddenly I was forced to a halt. My eyes locked on his as I glared at his silvery features. "What the hell, Len? Are you challenging me to a fight?"

Approaching another supernatural that fast and without

warning was the human equivalent of throwing about fighting words.

Len's smile was slow, sweeping up the perfect planes of his face until it was near blinding. I knew that smile. I did not trust that smile. "I felt a vibe," he said suddenly. "A fissure and fire in the air, and... is there a chance you're in need of some assistance?"

Ahhh, so *fighting* wasn't the F word that had gotten him moving so quickly.

How he knew I was battling my sexual urges was beyond me since I wasn't one to allow my hormones or emotions to spill out physically, but there was a chance that this time I'd let it slip in my agitation.

"What exactly are you suggesting?" I said, crossing my arms, our bodies almost touching. I wouldn't back away from the fae, and he knew it. A fact he would use to his advantage. If he was intelligent, though, he'd also note that being within my arm's reach could be detrimental to his physical wellbeing.

"You're too powerful to bother with most beings in the Solaris System," he told me, those catlike eyes devouring me with their intensity. "Lucien is out since he's mentally *occupied*. Galleli does not date ever, and Alistair has his own specific tastes. Which leaves me."

It didn't escape my attention that he'd left Reece off the list of possibilities. He was smart enough to know better. He was also smart enough to know that there were not many outside of Shadow's merry band of assholes, as they'd been dubbed, that I trusted to be vulnerable with. Still, I hadn't asked for this conversation, and in all truth, Len was overstepping.

"My restlessness is not necessarily going to be eased through sex," I said bluntly, in no mood for games. "This is a natural process I have to go through after my rebirth. Sex would be a minor distraction."

Len arched a silver eyebrow. "I promise you, Angel, there would be nothing minor about it, and maybe regular sex is exactly what you need to work out this new"—he cleared his throat—"fire that has taken hold of you. We see more of Mera in you now. It's building in your eyes... your power. Even if you're not ready to admit it yet, you cannot hold back the flames of change for long."

My right hand swung out as I aimed high, grabbing onto the collar of his jacket so fast that I took him by surprise. Everything went white in my mind as my blood both boiled and froze. "You don't know me, Len. Do not presume that you can sense a weakness to manipulate, because it doesn't exist. I will face this change the same way I have faced all challenges in my life, without fear or restraint."

He didn't fight my hold, and as the shock in his expression faded, it was replaced by lustful swirls in his light eyes. "You are truly spectacular," he murmured, and there was a mingling of icy power between us—a moment of attraction, possibly, until both of us came to our senses.

I released him as quickly as I'd taken hold, and as his boots hit the ground, I realized that I'd lifted him in my rage. He was taller and heavier than me, but I hadn't noticed.

Len straightened his collar, still smiling that maddening smile. "Truly spectacular," he repeated. "We all know it and have wanted to approach you over the decades, but Reece never allowed us to look more than once. If he caught us a second time... Trust me, he made Shadow look like a friendly puppy."

Everything inside of me stilled. "What did you just say?"

That was the moment Len realized he'd screwed up, his pale features turning icier.

"He warned you about getting too close to me?" I choked out, rage and despair fighting for supremacy within me. "For centuries you all ignored me, even when we were in the same battles. I assumed it was because of my own personal shame. I accepted it and lived with the consequences of my actions, all the while working toward making amends. But now you're telling me that the reason I've always felt shunned, even among those I have never wronged, was because of Reece?"

Shadow and his friends had been treated as the supreme beings in this Solaris System for a long time. Everyone looked on them with envy, fear, and awe. If life had been different, I might have joined them—a thought I'd had more than once—but I'd been repeatedly rejected from their circle until eventually I stopped even trying. Then, for many decades we'd ignored each other until I'd become invisible.

Reece's punishment went too far—it was our feud, no one else's. To bring them all in on it... The bronzed god of the deserts appeared then, like my rage had called him. Swinging around, I caught sight of Len frantically swiping his hands in the air, attempting to warn Reece that my wrath was coming his way, but it was too late.

Reece had manipulated me, and for that, we were about to *have a little chat.*

Never again would he control me.

CHAPTER ELEVEN

He knew before he'd taken two steps toward me that I was furious. I hadn't spilled any energy, but my wings were pitched at an angle above that indicated I was ready to fight. Whatever peace I'd found from my blessing in the meadows, was long gone in the face of my oldest friend turned enemy. Reece, as always, upset every part of my equilibrium.

"It's time for us to head to the Desert Lands," he said, addressing the others, even though his eyes never left mine. The blue bored into me, attempting to strip me down, but I was too far gone to be affected by that look.

"How dare you," I said, my voice bristling with the undercurrents of my anger, even if the words never rose above a whisper. "You had no right to dictate who could and couldn't form a friendship with me."

The skin around his eyes tightened minutely. He was confused, but that would last all of two seconds before he figured it out. Unfortunately *for all of us*, this bastard was both powerful, attractive, and intelligent. The full package if, of course, you didn't mind the arrogant, controlling, *piece of shit* side of him that was part of the deal.

Reece's gaze flicked up and over my shoulder toward Len, and from my peripheral I saw the fae shrug as if to say *Sorry, it kind of slipped out.*

Returning his attention to me, Reece's expression gave nothing away. "You deserved what you got."

I slapped out with my energy, cutting through the protective layer of sand that always surrounded him. Most could not see it, the invisible barrier of red Rohami sand that was part of his natural defenses, but I knew exactly where to hit to bypass that security system.

He took a step back, jerking his head like I'd punched him.

"I accepted my punishment," I growled, moving closer, my power seeping from me for the first time, swirling around and around until it formed spears. "I lost that day too. I lost everything, and yet you have continued to hate me for so many years that I've nearly forgotten what it was like to be your friend."

His growl was annoyingly more impressive than mine, and then he was moving toward me fast. My energy-formed-projectiles released, and while he swiped most away like flies, a few sliced across his body, leaving wounds that healed almost instantly. It would take a lot more than I was throwing at him to truly wound the god, and I wasn't so far gone that I'd go there.

Yet.

"You've forgotten what it was like?" he growled again, his chest swelling as he stormed closer. He didn't stop as he swept me up in his powerful arms and slammed me back against a nearby shelf. The entire structure shook, books tumbling down around us, and despite the shouts of horrified goblins, neither of us looked away and no one approached us.

"I've forgotten everything," I lied, tilting my head and calling more power to my hands, the energy ready and waiting to reject his hold. "It was far easier than I expected. I'm sure you can say the same, since you've ignored me for a thousand years longer than you cared for me." I forced myself to hold his gaze, even as I wanted to look away.

He stilled, predatorily still, and after the galaxies flashed in his irises, ice followed, chilling me to the bone. "I've never forgotten a thing about you," he breathed, leaning in so our lips were almost touching. "Your taste. Your scent. The burning knife of your betrayal."

My eyes squeezed closed because I just couldn't do it any longer... stare into those beautiful blue depths.

"Lale," he bit out, and I couldn't ignore him when he used that name. No matter how much I wished I could. When I opened my eyes again, red filled my vision; his sand was surrounding us on all sides, preventing the others from seeing us or stepping in to break this up.

"You took everyone away from me," I said, an annoying tremble of hurt in my voice. Fucking hell, these new emotions were a pain in the ass. "I've been alone. No family. No friends. No goddamn hope. Your brother was injured in that battle; I understand that and know he was never the same until he passed. I get why you haven't forgiven me, but try and under-stand... I lost everything."

He didn't reply, but he was clearly confused by the impas-sioned nature of my speech. My newly reborn emotions had not been on display for him before now, and no doubt he had zero idea how to handle them.

Reece released me suddenly, and as he stepped back, I resisted the urge to rub my skin where he'd touched. His power continued to burn me, but I refused to show him how affected I was. "You've changed," he said, still staring at me like I was a mystery he needed to unravel. "Just when I needed the robotic warrior, you're back to being..." His words trailed off as he shook his head.

"Back to being what?" I pushed, most of my fury gone now. Learning the truth from Len had thrown me, but I was already at a place of acceptance. I really should have expected nothing less from Reece.

Deciding his answer didn't even matter, I simply gathered every ounce of my equilibrium and pushed through his power, exiting the sand barrier to find a furious Mera on the other side. Shadow was holding her back, and she was shouting, "If anything happens to her, I will legitimately break you into ten fucking pieces." Her eyes spat fire while tears traced her cheeks. "He's toxic for her—you know it as well as I do—and this is not okay."

Her protective streak was as large as the Solaris System itself, and it reminded me that I was loved now. No longer would I exist alone, stepping through the day without feeling a damn thing. No matter how hard these changes were, they were the best thing that happened to me.

"Reece is not her kryptonite, Sunshine," Shadow said, his eyes meeting mine over the top of his furious mate. "He's not toxic for her. And those two need to sort their shit out, or it will impact the rest of us and our ability to deal with whatever is happening in the Desert Lands."

Mera sobbed a few times, but she was no longer fighting him. "She always protects me, and I know she's struggling. It kills me that I can't protect her the same way."

My heart ached when I heard that. "Hey," I said softly. Mera's head jerked in my direction, and as she released her hold on Shadow, she raced toward me, dodging fallen books and scurrying goblins.

My wings were gone by the time she reached me, so there was only a round belly to get in the way of our hug. "Are you okay?" she asked breathlessly. "I could feel the energy spikes, but the sand was too thick to get through. Shadow thought we should give you both a moment."

Behind my back, I felt Reece's power die down, the sands returning to their invisible barrier around him. Oddly, he stepped closer to me, and I could almost taste the dry heat of his power on my tongue. When he stepped even closer, I was all but sandwiched between him and Mera.

"Angel and I are fine, Meers," he said in a soothing voice. "Don't stress yourself. We have some unresolved issues to work through, and it's best we do that before we head into this new situation. Once we're in the Desert Lands, I'm going to need us to present a united front. Desertlandians can sense weaknesses quite easily, and we have no time to deal with manipulations that could arise from that."

Mera pulled away to look up at him. "And have you sorted it out?" Her tone was short, and I was happy that she was still standing firmly on my team when it came to this situation. I turned as well to find that Reece wore his usual stoic façade, face void of any true emotion. "We're closer," he finally said.

Closer to murdering each other.

The thought thankfully didn't show on my face, and we were able to reassure Mera enough that we could move on to planning our next few steps. As the atmosphere calmed, all the others stepped forward, including Alistair, Galleli, Lucien, and Len. Everyone was suited up for the trip into the Desert Lands, except for me in my human clothes, but since I could call my armor when needed, there was no concern.

Reece, who was still standing far too close to me, got right to business. "Everything will be provided by the dynasties, so no need for supplies outside of weapons and energy stones." He looked around, catching our eyes. "There should be no immediate danger in this first part of our journey as we head to the Ostealon and attend this impromptu gathering of the dynasties. From here, I want us to start investigating the disturbance and figure out who's involved. Once we know that, we can question them about what's happening and hopefully get to the bottom of the real issue here."

"The issue of who or what is disturbing the sacred lands," Shadow added.

Reece nodded. "Exactly."

At the same time Mera asked, "What's an Ostealon?"

"It's our neutral ground," Reece told her. "A powerful piece of land that is owned by none and is a central gathering point surrounded by sand rivers, our main channels of transportation."

Mera's brow furrowed, and there was a flutter of confusion between our bond.

"You'll understand it better when you're there," I told her. "It's quite spectacular."

This brought a smile to her lips. "Despite the dangers, I'm pretty excited about this."

"We know," Len, Lucien, and Alistair all said at once.

Low rumbles of masculine laughter filled this section of library, but I didn't join in, far too stressed to find any of this funny. Returning to this world was always going to be a struggle for me. A torment I had to bear.

Something told me that after this mission, life as I knew it was never going to be the same again.

Chapter Twelve

The Desert Lands doorway was not one I'd stood in front of in years. Thankfully, I wasn't the first through today, with Reece taking that honor so he could direct the rest of us to the safest place to arrive. As the others moved into the swirling portal, Galleli and I were last. When it was my turn, I shivered at the feeling of *otherness* that always sprang up whenever my energy meshed with that of a foreign world.

Are you okay? Galleli sent warmth with his words, and it was comforting.

I'm oka—

The tail end of the lie died on my tongue as I was once again unable to push down my emotions. In the spirit of moving forward and growing up, I decided to be straight with him. *I'm struggling with this new reality. Struggling with my new energy, my new aura, and all of the emotions that are once again bouncing around inside of me without any place to go. I don't know how to get back to the equilibrium I used to exist in.*

There was a moment of silence as we moved forward into the doorway, the scent of desert and power filling our senses. It didn't seem that he was going to answer until I felt his touch on my shoulder. *You do not want to go back, Melalekin. There is nothing back there for you. No hope. No happiness. No love. This gift you've been given... embrace it. Fall into it. Stop fighting the inevitable because in the end, you're only costing yourself a second chance at a real life.* The ache in my chest was acute. *Your future is bright.*

His touch lifted, and I had to force my shaky legs to move forward again. There wasn't much in this world that could knock me like those few words had. *Do you truly see a bright future?*

He didn't hesitate this time. *Only if you can fight the darkness that holds you. It's up to you and whatever you discover in these lands. The ancients are not only calling Reece.*

With that portentous statement, he gently pushed me into the portal.

My thoughts were a mess as I crossed, and even though there had never been evidence that Galleli was a true prophet, I'd learned not to dismiss his words and feelings over the years. The events that transpired after might not end up a literal translation of his predictions, but I looked between the lines. Galleli was not one to be disregarded, but it did leave me more confused than ever.

Why would the ancients be calling me?

The swirls of the Desert Lands completely surrounded me, once again reminding me how truly ingenious the connections in the Solaris System were. When the mistiness finally cleared, I breathed in deeply, allowing familiar scents to fill my senses.

It shouldn't feel like it was only yesterday that I'd walked this world, but of course, my mind would never let me forget.

"Angel!" Mera called my name, and I opened my eyes to take it all in.

"Ostealon," I breathed, looking across the central hub of the

Desert Lands. The Ostealon's neutral ground was a wide-open plane, its sands a deep, rich ochre. Usually it was unoccupied but today was covered in a mass of tents, all with colors representing their dynasties.

I remembered from one of the other gatherings I'd been at that the large white tent, visible in the distance as it glowed softly against the golden sky under the mid-moon light, was where all the meetings and festivities would take place.

"You've been here before?" Mera asked, trying to see everything at once to the point I was worried her head was going to swivel right off her neck.

I nodded. "Yep. As Reece said, this area is a neutral land with large inlets to the sand rivers and almost zero dunes, which allows them to house thousands of Desertlandians during these meetings."

Reece took a few steps closer, bringing the others with him. "Correct, and I will explain the layout as soon as we've made our way to our tents. We're already drawing attention, and I'd like to get all the housekeeping done before we deal with the locals." Sometimes the way he referred to the "locals" of his world was almost as if he wasn't one of them.

The moment he led us into the bright bustle of this world, my memories returned with force. The dynasties were all dressed in the colors of their sands: golds and reds and blacks, depending on their territory. None of the dynasty lands touched each other, and everything here was on a large scale, with only the sand rivers and the great deep to connect them all.

It was a rite of passage to make your first ship, barge, or vessel to travel in—Reece had two or three back in Rohami. Or at least he had when I'd known him.

"How big is this place?" I heard Mera ask Shadow.

"It's huge," he said. "The Ostealon is the largest land mass in the deserts, but that doesn't mean any of the other lands would be considered small."

"They have a council?" Mera asked, her eyes taking in the multitude of colored tents that were temporary homes during this meeting.

"There are eight dynasties," Shadow told her, "and each are governed by a princeps who holds a monarch-type leadership. For the most part, they stick to their own lands, but on occasion they gather and speak on matters that impact the collective."

Mera nodded, her eyes still greedily drinking it all in. We were drawing some attention, as Reece had noted earlier, but when they saw we were with the desert god, we were left alone.

"They're all so beautiful," Mera breathed, a brilliant smile parting her lips. "I love the earthy colors, reds and golds and browns. It reminds me of the Nexus, and the Desertlandians glow against this backdrop."

She wasn't wrong about the locals, with their skin tones ranging from a deep bronze—like Reece's—to the darker browns of those closer to the Delfora. The eastern dynasties had the lightest skin tones since they were mostly bathed in half-moonlight. Whatever their territory, though, Mera was right about one thing: they were an unusually beautiful race, almost without exception.

When we pushed through many of the tents of black, gold, olive, and terracotta, we finally reached the red. The Rohami area was a fiery beacon in the wide-open ochre sands of the Ostealon, reminding me once again of that time so long ago that I took part in a gathering. It wasn't just the tents bringing me back either, but also the scent in the air: dry and earthy with rich spices and the thyreme flower. This flower had tiny purple buds that could spread out across the sands so thickly it created an illusion of a purple land. They were one of the few florae to survive in this dry climate, and its floral scent was one I'd never quite found an equal to.

Before I could fall further into the past, Reece called out that he'd found his tent, and I followed along with everyone, trying my best to stay here. In the now.

Rohami was a strong dynasty, with its relatively close proximity to the Delfora and an uncanny ability to produce offspring who had a little... *extra*. As we closed in on Reece's tent, I wasn't surprised to see it was about twice the size of most others we'd seen, with the large image of a *jackan* up top. The jackan was a beast that existed only in this world, and the closest thing I could liken it to was a hybrid with the head of a large fox and the body of a kangaroo. Its powerful hind legs allowed it to bounce through the thick sands and also burrow under them if need be. It was a predatory species, and one that Rohami had claimed as their mascot. After all, the largest and strongest warriors always came from this dynasty, as history had proven.

"Here we are," Reece said, placing his hand on the spikes on a panel just near the firmly closed tent flaps of the entrance. This was a security system that would allow only those with approved energy to enter, and since Reece was the last of his direct line, this tent was secure.

The technologies of this land were subtler than others, mostly drawing on the energy flowing under the sands and rivers. They used this power to turn the sands into many useful items, including buildings, glass, weapons, and ships.

For the most part, though, the Desertlandians lived simple lives, unconcerned with power.

And none had the abilities of Reece.

His connection to the sands meant they responded to his call. Even though the details of his birth were secret, everyone here revered and respected him. In this world he was considered a close second to the ancient gods.

Hopefully, that reputation alone would help us flush out the darkness. Now that I'd made it into the Desert Lands, Reece wasn't the only one feeling the imbalance.

Someone here had forgotten their history and what happened when one disturbed the Delfora. An oversight that could get all of us killed.

CHAPTER THIRTEEN

Inside the tent, the true size and opulence of it became apparent.

"They do nothing by halves here, do they," Len said, spinning to take in the sheer expanse of space.

"This is the main living and lounging area," Reece explained, waving his hand across the round area that was at least eighty feet in diameter. The sands here were covered in large, padded rugs weaved from the pamolsa leaves—one of the only tree-like plants that grew in the Desert Lands. It was a highly tradable commodity, and when used in conjunction with the sands, could be turned into many amazing products.

Atop the rugs were thick cushions weaved from strands of the olive-green leaves of the pamolsa. Inside was a cloudlike stuffing, spun through manipulating the sands of the east lands. There were so many cushions that as we moved through, we had to push them aside to be able to cross the lounging room.

"Everyone has a designated sleeping area at the back here," Reece said, pointing them out. Each of the sleeping areas had their own closed doorway, giving as much privacy as one could get in a tent.

"Spare clothes and some weapons should be in there as well."

I generally didn't bring changes of clothes since I could use my energy to clean mine and, more importantly, call my armor if needed. But for the others, this would be very helpful.

As everyone chose a room, I entered one and was unsurprised to see on the ground a huge version of the cushions outside. The bedding here was nothing like I'd felt in other worlds, and while I might not have slept that much before my rebirth, when I'd been here, I'd always found myself meditating in a supine position.

"Each of your rooms," Reece called out to us, "has a *githna* attached... a wash area. You should be able to figure out how to access the liquid, and you won't need any soaps because our underground aquifers are imbued with natural cleansing."

We all left the rooms to rejoin him near their entrance. "How does water work here?" Mera asked. "I mean, I know you probably don't call it water, but you know what I mean. You must have some sort of liquid to drink that hydrates you, right?"

"Right," Reece confirmed, "but it only exists deep under our sands. You will never find *liforina* above or see it fall from our sky."

Before Mera could ask another of the dozen or so questions that were no doubt lingering in her mind, Shadow spoke up. "Let's get settled in the lounging area, and then Reece can pull out his maps. A geography lesson on the deserts should calm some of the curiosity swishing around"—his deadpan stare turned in Mera's direction—"everyone's brains."

Mera smirked broadly before she clapped her hands in excitement. Through our bond I felt a spike in her adrenaline at the possibility of some new discoveries.

"I need to quickly rehydrate first," Alistair spoke up. "The dryness of this land and its air is already taking its toll."

Alistair had been born in the waters of Karn, and his skin was sensitive to heat and temperature. In most worlds there was enough moisture in the air to keep him functioning, but the deserts were not the same. We'd have to keep an eye on him because if his body dried out too much, he could die.

"Plenty of water in your room," Reece said, falling back on the more general term for liforina. "Take as much as you need."

Alistair slapped his friend on the arm before he ran a hand through his blue green curls, shaking them out like that would relieve his discomfort. As he disappeared, the rest of us returned to the lounging area to sit among the cushions.

I chose to sit away from Reece since the library incident still felt unresolved, not to mention being here was messing with my memories and ability to compartmentalize them. Of course, no matter how far away I sat, I couldn't escape his heavy gaze. At least he was distracted while he had to explain the basic layout of this world. His sands brought to him a large map that had been rolled up in a basket near the front door.

"This is the Desert Lands," he said, unrolling it easily, his sands holding it up higher so we could all see its full-colored glory. "The large land mass in the center with the ochre sands is the Ostealon—neutral territory." His fingers traced across from there, following the wavy lines. "As you can see, the Ostealon is surrounded by a complete circle of the sand rivers so that everything can flow to and from here as needed. For that reason, much of our bartering takes place here."

Mera leaned forward on her cushion, cradling her belly between both hands as she examined the map. "So those eight large lands around it are not connected by water but by *sand rivers?*"

It was clear that she couldn't quite wrap her mind around that concept.

Reece nodded. "Yes, we don't have rivers or oceans like you

might recognize on Earth. Just imagine depthless sand that you cannot walk across. It has tides and an energy flow, and is filled with many creatures that 'swim' through the layers."

"Like quicksand, only with a current," Mera said with a nod.

Reece grinned, enjoying the focus on his world. "Close enough."

"The rivers are their transport links," Shadow added. "They move fast, the sands sweeping in one direction on the left, and the opposite on the right. Only specially designed vessels can travel on them, and if you use anything else, you run the risk of being crushed by the currents and falling into the depths, never to be found again."

Mera swallowed hard. "That sounds... scary."

Reece's smile faded in a serious stare. "There's nothing for you to worry about. I have many safe and secure vessels for us to use if we need to travel around. Of course, they're in Rohami, but if need be, I'll have one brought here."

Looked like he still had a fascination with ships... it was nice to know some things hadn't changed.

"So, the red sands are Rohami?" Mera asked, her eyes on the map.

Reece pointed up to the northeast corner. "Yes, the red is the Rohami dynasty." His finger then moved across the other lands, working clockwise. "This is the Guardians, which is the closest to the Delfora; both have black sands." His finger moved again. "This is Shale with dark brown sands, Fret to the west with terracotta, Holinfra with dusky grey. Wanders are from the violet sands filled with the thyreme blossoms. Crani, sands of gold, and Yemin, the smallest land with its light orange sands."

"Eight dynasties," Shadow said as we stared at the map. "All controlling vast deserts and powers."

"Except for the Delfora," Reece said, tracing to the north-ernmost part of the map. "No one controls it."

"Holy fucking fuck," Mera breathed. "It looks like it's bigger than all the rest of the lands put together."

At this point Alistair returned looking refreshed, with damp hair and skin and wearing only a pair of yellow shorts, leaving the rest of his lithe body bare. He settled into a cushion near me, bringing the briny scent of oceans with him.

"The Delfora is massive," Reece confirmed. "And no Desertlandian lives there. Outside of the first flat section, the rest is completely forbidden to even step foot on. There are layers of security to stop anyone from just wandering through. Those who've dared to try without an invitation are generally never heard from again."

"Who invites you?" Lucien asked, genuine curiosity in his voice. If there was one thing all of these guys had in common, it was that they loved power. And the Delfora was a vastly untapped source.

Reece shrugged, broad shoulders lifting under the thick material of his black shirt. "It's mostly myth since I've never known anyone to make it deep into the lands."

Outside of his parents, of course, but he didn't want to tell that story.

"They believe it's the ancient gods," I drawled, dancing along the truth. Let that bastard sweat that I might reveal his secrets. "Giving the invitations. They might be buried and sleeping, but their power seeps through the land still."

Reece shot me a look, and I shut up. "The imbalance I feel didn't originate with the gods," he said with obvious reluctance. "But there's no denying that the Delfora feels different. A dark-ness lingers there."

That had my full attention. "What else resides there except the ancients?"

His gaze pinned me to the spot. "It is said that the ancient gods, who are guarded by the valley of the dead, are also the gatekeepers to a darker being."

An eerie silence descended over the room as we waited for his next words.

"In the deepest recesses," he continued, "far beyond any exploration, lies the namesake of the ancient lands: Delfora, meaning Death itself."

My choked gasp echoed through the tent, and with my back ramrod straight as I half got to my knees, I shook my head. "If that's true," I managed to say, "we could be facing another extinction level event. Akin to Dannie."

The ancient gods were one thing, but Death itself...

Reece and I had lived for a long time, and we'd fought many battles together, until the one that tore us apart. Only we knew the true implications of what he was saying right now—not just for this world, but all of them.

"How is this possible?" Shadow rumbled. "I know your land is an original, one of the first that many others evolved from, but are you telling me that Death, the very being who coined the phrase, originated in your Delfora?"

Reece looked grimmer than usual. "I don't have evidence, but I've seen and felt new tendrils of an ancient energy and feel it's best to warn you now of what we might be dealing with here." His eyes were hooded as he let out a deep breath. "The calling is stronger than ever from the Delfora, and now that we're here, I sense that once again someone is working to raise the gods."

"Every few thousand years this happens," I said flatly. "A select number of Desertlandians get it in their heads that they can control the ancients. We've had to battle over it before, and we lost too many the last time. But Death... that's an entirely new challenge I did not see coming."

"It was always a possibility," Reece said, his focus unwavering as it felt like he was just talking to me. "If Death does reside in the Delfora, then raising the ancient gods would almost inevitably lead to raising it as well. It's just that most don't know, or believe in, that fable. I didn't believe in it until these recent days, but now... I can just feel that there's more waiting out there."

Shadow's chest rumbled as he drew Mera closer, his hands protectively cradling her and their unborn child. He had a lot to lose, much more than the rest of us these days, and I knew that he would do whatever it took to keep the worlds safe. To keep Mera safe.

He wasn't the only one. "We need to figure out who it is and stop them from putting this into motion," I said, my energy shooting up as my adrenaline did. "Why are we wasting time in this tent? Or here at all? Shouldn't we be at the Delfora?"

Reece's voice was as icy as mine. "Because multiple dynasties called this random meeting, gathering all their power together. Members of those dynasties could be using this as a catalyst to form enough energy to break through the spells holding the ancients." His expression wasn't the only grim one at this point.

"So, whoever we're looking for is here," I mused, finally understanding his plan.

Shadow was on his feet in that same instant, Mera clutched in his huge hands—in his rage it appeared that he'd forgotten he even held her. "Mera needs to return to the library." The glare he leveled on Reece would have made a normal male cry. "You should have told us how serious the situation was."

Reece and Shadow didn't fight a lot, but when they did, the worlds felt it.

"I didn't know for sure," Reece said, almost sounding weary. "And in all honesty, I need your help. Not even I can deal with this alone. I knew Mera would never stay behind, and if this comes to pass and the ancients rise, the worlds will be absorbed by their greed. And if Death is truly a possibility... Nowhere is safe."

"They will all rage," I said softly.

Reece nodded. "Yes. I've felt their fury at being trapped for my entire existence. Not just their fury, but also the way they see no reason or logic. Nothing will stop them from consuming it all."

His words hung heavy in the tent, and even though Shadow's unhappy expression hadn't lifted, he didn't protest Mera's presence here again.

We all understood what Reece was saying: there was no safe place. Not when it came to ancient gods that could walk all the worlds.

Our only shot was to work together and prevent this from even beginning.

For in this case, the beginning could very well be the end.

CHAPTER FOURTEEN

The men left after this, accompanying Reece to officially meet the princeps and hopefully do some preliminary sleuthing. Mera uncharacteristically didn't argue with Shadow's request to stay in the tent and get some rest. I stayed too since I'd mostly only come on this journey to keep her alive.

"You don't usually do as you're told," I said, moving onto a pillow closer to her. She'd lain back at this point, her feet propped up as she crossed her hands over her stomach.

"Shadow has already given as much as he's capable of," she said with a sad half-smile. "I acknowledge the limits of my mate, and in this case, it wasn't worth fighting him when this visit is about shaking hands and talking politics. Better that he can focus on that and not worry about me, especially when they're hoping to flush out who we should be focusing our suspicions on."

"Once the actual gathering gets underway, we'll be out of this tent for most of the moon cycles," I said. "Best to rest now."

Mera nodded as she reached down to grab the sand-woven glass Shadow had left for her, filled with the slightly murky water of these lands. She took a drink, her nose wrinkling. "It has a weird taste but also reminds me of something," she said before taking another sip.

"To my knowledge, it's a lot like coconut water with extra minerals and electrolytes."

She sipped again, nodding a few times. "Yes. That's exactly what it reminds me of." After her next drink, her eyes met mine over the rim of her glass. "Now that the guys are gone, are we going to talk about what happened in the library?"

I'd wondered how long it would take before she brought up that incident.

"Reece and I have a very long history, you know that," I said with a sigh. "Len told me that the reason I'd been outcast from more than just Reece's life was because that bastard forced them all to shun me. I just... Dammit, Meers. There's just too much betrayal and anger on both sides."

Her eyes widened, brow furrowing as she mulled this over before shaking her head. "He can be such a bastard at times. Why can't he just get the hell over his grudge? You've told me bits and pieces, so I understand why he was initially upset. But it's been centuries. I'm sure you've more than made up for whatever happened."

"He doesn't see it that way," I murmured, staring toward the wall of the tent.

"Angel," she said softly, and I once again gave her my focus. "I'm your best friend and bonded family. I think it's time you tell me all the shit that went down between you two. Last time you just said family died and you bailed on a fight when you should have stayed, but I know there's more to it."

As much as I hated to relive the past, there was no way to avoid it while we were back here. Maybe it was time for Mera to know everything. "Reece and I met when we were both young," I said with a long exhale, "when the worlds were much younger as well. Our families were old friends, powerful beings, and we all enjoyed our friendship for many decades before our parents were killed in the same battle." I had to swallow a few times to find my next words. "After that, all we had was each other and one sibling each."

The burn in my chest was rising, bringing with it the despair I'd tried so hard to suppress.

"Many years after our parent's deaths, there was a war in the Delfora—the last time someone tried to raise the ancient gods." I didn't realize my hands were shaking until she reached out and took one, holding it tightly. Her firm pressure helped me keep my shit together.

"My sister and I came to fight, along with many others from Honor Meadows. This was an end-of-world battle, not my first and obviously not my last, but maybe the one that stuck with me the most."

"Sister?" Mera breathed, her eyes shiny.

"She died." Those two words stabbed into me. "She died in my arms, and I was alone. My family line all but wiped out."

Mera's eyes were wide and shiny as she pressed her free hand to her chest. "It's a vastly different world, right? When you realize you're walking it truly alone for the first time."

Young or not, she'd just hit the nail on the head. "Yes. It changed everything. Part of me died that day on the battlefield too—at the very moment my sister closed her eyes and never opened them again."

"Surely Reece could understand why you left after that!" Mera demanded, pushing her sadness aside in favor of annoyance.

"You have to understand," I told her, "that when my sister died, I inherited the mantle of my family's power. I had so much under my control that there was a possibility I could have ended it all where we stood. Reece asked me to stay, to fight with him, and I fled. His brother was injured some days later, and I heard that he was never the same until he died a few years after the battle. So, yeah, the battle was won, but not without many losses first."

"Angel," Mera breathed. "You were broken and grieving. I know that within your power you feel your family, so using it all then would have been like losing them again."

I buried my face in my hands, trying to comprehend her limitless empathy and understanding. If only I could have been so kind to myself. "I should have been stronger," I said, lifting my head again.

"Yes, you should have."

We both jerked our heads toward the doorway to find Reece crowding the space, his face hard and unreadable. I was on my feet in an instant, fury and pain warring inside of me as I desperately wished I had the power to make him disappear. Forever.

"Screw you, Reece," I rumbled, the vibration of my energy riding each word. "My power would have been lost, my family line gone, and I couldn't... I couldn't release them. Not when I knew that if you just kept fighting, you could beat them anyway."

I'd calculated the odds of them winning and gone with my gut.

Reece seemed almost stunned as he remained there, blocking the doorway completely to prevent any other from entering. "You were guessing," he finally said. "When you left, the battle could have gone either way."

"No," I shook my head. "I wouldn't have left you if I'd thought you were truly in mortal danger. Despite everything, you can trust me on that. But the truth is, you asked for too much in my grief. You pushed me when I was fragile and broken; don't be surprised that I shattered."

This was the moment, a chance we could move forward. A chance for Reece to stop punishing me for one knee-jerk reaction a millennia ago.

He examined me closely, and I found myself holding my breath in anticipation of what he might say next. "You were my best friend," he started, voice a low rumble, "the one I thought would stand by my side through everything. The way you stood by Mera. The way you sacrificed yourself for her."

He finally moved, stepping into the room—into my personal space so he could crowd over me. "I'd thought there was nothing I could be angrier with you for than what happened in the Delfora long ago, but it turned out, there was. Our last battle."

I blinked, confused by this rapid change of subject, and tried to read between the lines, as I often had to do with Reece. "You're mad about the last battle too?"

He was close now as he reached out to touch my face, only I jerked away before he could. "You died," he bit out, breaths harsh and broken. "You will never sacrifice yourself again."

Hot energy seeped from him as rage coated the tented area, and I could taste his earthy power on my tongue. He was on the edge of losing control, and I had no idea how to bring him back.

"Reece." This rumble came from Shadow, who must have come to check on us too. "Tell them what we learned and walk away."

The desert god ignored him, his hyperfocus remaining on me. We'd broken the dam after all of these years, releasing the emotions, and now neither of us knew how to stuff them back in.

CHAPTER FIFTEEN

Eventually Reece regained his famous control and got to the point of his and Shadow's return to the tent. "There's a celebratory dinner tonight," he said shortly. "We stopped by to give you the heads-up."

He was now looking anywhere but at me, and in some ways that hurt more, reminding me of the years he'd cut me from his life.

"I don't have anything fancy to wear," Mera said, spinning to Shadow. "I mean, unless you can conjure up the magic wardrobe here?"

Mera could create her own clothing if she wanted, but from what I'd observed, they'd mutually agreed that the wardrobe was Shadow's role.

"I can," Shadow said with a slow smile. "But it's not advised in the deserts. The energy here is unpredictable, and you never quite know what you're going to create if you overuse magic."

Like waking up some gods who were hellbent on destroying the worlds.

"It's official dress anyway," Reece said in his deep rumble.

"I'm having outfits dropped off soon so that you can wear Rohami colors."

Shadow crossed his arms, looking all broody and scary. "They will leave the clothes outside, so there's no need to exit the tent until we return."

"Yes, that's right," Reece said shortly. "They will not linger." The heat grew around him as well, and now the tent was akin to a sauna. "We need to get back into the mix," he said suddenly. "The unease in my energy grows stronger, and I think we should chat with the princeps of the Yemin dynasty. His response from before was definitely lacking some details."

Shadow nodded. "Yes, and we also need to focus on Rohami. Your land is the most powerful... and the most power hungry."

Reece didn't deny the truth of this. Everyone familiar with the deserts was aware of the dominant traits of each dynasty. Rohami loved their power.

"Is everyone in this world long-lived?" Mera asked.

Reece's smile was without the animosity he always directed my way. "We do have long lives by Earth standards. Many live the equivalent of a few hundred years, depending on how much energy they can absorb from the sands. But most are not eternal. Only a few of us with strong family lines can continue to refill the well of our lifeforce."

Before she could ask another question, he turned toward the main doorway. "We really should go now; time is running out."

Shadow, who was still holding his mate, leaned down and kissed her hard on the mouth. "I'll be back for you soon," he murmured. "Please stay in this tent and don't make me destroy dynasties to find you."

Mera fought a smile. "Only because you said please."

Shadow kissed her again; this one went on longer and I left

them to it. Standing between those two and the ice king that was Reece was not my favorite pastime. Moving into the bedroom I'd been assigned earlier, I headed straight for the bathing area. Not that I needed this sort of setup to clean myself, but I found great comfort in water. Many of the power layers of my land in Honor Meadows were surrounded by water, and if the opportunity to soak my woes away presented itself, I was always going to take it.

This quirk of mine was an oddity among the transcendents, but it was one that I'd claimed and accepted a long time ago.

The moment I felt Reece's and Shadow's energies leave the tent, I stripped away the "human attire" I'd donned earlier. Dropping it to the ground, since I wouldn't be wearing it again, I stepped into the glassed-off tub. The sand weavers were masters in this world, turning the various colored land into glass and weapons and household goods. This tub was mostly crystal-colored, with streaks of gold swirling in intricate patterns. Crouching down, I ran my fingertips across the swirls, following them to find they all led to a central point that was so cleverly hidden you didn't even know it existed until you were there.

As I marvelled at the desert art, I thought about how much I'd missed this world. Even after all of these years away, it still felt like a second home—I should never have stayed away for so long.

Shaking off the melancholy, I stood and hit a lever attached to some copper piping that extended high up the wall of the tent, ending in a spout designed to spray liquid down into the tub. From previous experience here, I knew this piping system would be planted deep into the ground, all the way down to where the *liforina* ran. As this "water" ascended, it would be heated by the land and sand itself since these deserts ran hot.

It took less than a minute before the warm, slightly cloudy

water ran over me, and I let out a low groan at the sheer pleasure of this cleansing ritual. Tilting my head back, I stood in silence, my mind busy while the rest of me slowed to a pace I could once again handle. My blood, my energy, the magic in my veins... I calmed it piece by piece, until eventually, even my mind was quiet. Which lasted all of two minutes before Mera's energy entered the room.

"I tell ya," she said breathlessly, "if I was into women, you would not be safe right now."

With a laugh, I opened my eyes to find her perched in the arched doorway, leaning against the frame, her face flushed and pupils dilated. Which had nothing to do with me and everything to do with Shadow and the state he'd just left her in.

"They've gone back to the meetings?" I asked, already knowing the answer but needing a conversation opener. It was too easy for me to sink into silence, and I had to stop doing that if I wanted my future to be different from my past.

"They have," she confirmed, "but they'll be back soon. Knowing Shadow as I do, it's going to prey on his mind that someone is leaving outfits at our door and that when we open it, we could be attacked because *obviously everyone is out to kill us.*"

"You love his obsessive possessiveness," I said with a chuckle.

Mera shuffled further into the room so she could take a seat on the small ledge along one side of the tent wall. "This doesn't make you uncomfortable, right?" she said suddenly, as if it had only just occurred to her. "I forget that everyone isn't as cool with nudity as I am."

A true laugh burst from me, and I had to marvel at Mera's ability to amuse me. "You are the most naked person I've ever met, friend." She shrugged because she was proud of that fact. "And it doesn't bother me at all," I said truthfully. "I'm too old to care about flesh and skin on display. It's just the vessel keeping our energy contained."

"You're always so covered, though," she said, no doubt thinking about my usual attire.

"We wear armor for protection, not because we're hiding our bodies. The last thing I'm worried about is someone catching sight of my breasts and having a moment over it."

Mera waggled her eyebrows. "Lady, your tits are totally worth having a moment over. Speaking of, I think you should use them and have some angry sex with that bronzed god. You two need to get it out of your systems."

My body tightened at those words, and the ferocity of that involuntary movement shocked me to the point I had to reach out and grip the side of the wall behind me to keep my legs steady. Memories crashed into me with the same force, and I found myself saying, "We've actually had sex before."

Now it was Mera's turn to almost fall off her chair. "What the hell, Angel," she near shouted. "How could you not tell me that? Was it amazing? It was amazing, right? I imagine he fucks like Shadow, and in that regard, you shouldn't have stopped at *once.*"

With that reminder, painful memories pushed through the lustful ones. "It was the night before my world ended. First time for both of us, and it was... amazing." That word didn't even come close to the truth of it. I'd experienced the sort of pleasure I hadn't known existed within my body and, for a brief moment, it had felt as if Reece and I were on the cusp of forming a true soul bond.

Until it had all been torn away.

Mera's face fell, her hand pressed to her chest. "The night before, Angel? Oh, I'm so sorry. That's so freaking sad."

It was. "My life was mostly about duty, with Reece being the one part that didn't fit the mold. Even our parents were allies due to their love of power and fighting, but we... we were true friends."

"A true friend you were secretly in love with?" Mera guessed.

I nodded. "Oh yeah, I was completely gone over him, but I also had no intention of messing with our friendship. The sex happened after a particularly hard day of battle, when we were both injured and needed some patching up. You know how it is when adrenaline is high and clothes are low."

Mera sighed. "I swear I've read this story in one of my paranormal romance books before, and it's my favorite kind. Please tell me there was only one bed and you had to share because, damn..." She fanned her face. "That's my kink."

My lips twitched. "There *was* a bit of a bed shortage."

She squealed before shutting it down in a flash, even as her eyes remained bright. "This is your second-chance romance, Angel. You have to give it another shot."

Second-chance romance...

"After a thousand plus years?" I said softly. "I think too much time has passed. I'm not sure I could live through having my Reece again—the warm, affectionate, arrogant, funny asshole who was my star in a sea of rocks—only for him to turn cold and brutal on me. The pain of that almost killed me once, and I had to robot myself to get through it. But there's no more robot, so it's safer just to do this mission with him, mend whatever fences I can between us, and then move on with my life."

Mera was silent for a long moment, and I found myself sinking down into the glass bath, my thighs blocking the drain so the water could fill around me. She eventually leaned forward, cradling her stomach. "I believe to truly move on, you need to wipe the memories of the past and create some new ones. Even if it's only one more night, it could change everything. Maybe then you'll truly be able to walk away."

I let her words marinate in my thoughts because there was sense in what she'd said. "Even if it could work, that Desert-landian hates me. Call me old-fashioned, but my preference with sex is to find a partner who's into me, right? Surely that makes the experience more pleasurable."

Laughter burst from her, shocking me into silence. "You can't be serious. Ever since you powered yourself up to fight Dannie, that boy has been obsessed with you. Sure, it's presenting as anger, but if you truly couldn't stand someone, you wouldn't stare at them like they were an oasis in the damn deserts. Shadow the Second has an obsessive personality to match my mate. Not to mention..."

I found myself strangely desperate to hear her next words.

"There's a fine line between love and hate, Angel." Her smile was knowing. "And with you and Reece, that line is so fine that it's barely existent. Don't let the past dictate your future. We are not doing that any longer."

The surprisingly philosophical ending to her advice reminded me of the words Galleli had said to me before we crossed into the Desert Lands. He'd told me I needed to fight the darkness that held me.

Two beings I cared about were giving me basically the same advice, and while they were both probably right, it was still easier said than done. The hate between Reece and myself was deeply entrenched, and it had been around far longer than our love had.

Maybe, in the end, the future would always be defined by the past.

Chapter Sixteen

I stayed in the bath for a long time, finding my moments of peace. Mera, who had dragged a cushion into the room, had fallen asleep at some point, and I let her rest while I soaked. By the time I emerged, dried off with my energy, and found a cloth to tie around my body until the outfits for this dark-moon event arrived, I felt refreshed. Ready for whatever lay ahead.

Taking a moment, I called some of my battle gear to my room, leaving the pieces lined up against one wall in case I needed them in a rush. Shadow had been quite right before about using foreign magic in this world, but I'd figured out the best way to touch the meadows from here many years ago, and as long as we weren't too close to the Delfora, my small ripple wouldn't upset the balance.

Polishing a spot on my bronze-and-gold breast plate, I was reminded that my best armor was still missing, lost that day we'd fought in the Shadow Realm. Usually, I could *see* my items in my mind's eyes, no matter where they were, but my death and rebirth that day must have broken my bond to that particular piece.

It bothered me because there were sentimental memories attached to that armor, but in the grand scheme of losses, it wasn't near the top, especially since I had plenty of other armor to choose from. All of my pieces were strong and durable and able to save my life during battle.

Checking on Mera again, I saw that small flames had seeped from her body and were surrounding her with their warmth. Her energy was stronger and more volatile than ever, and I wondered what this child's energy might add to our dynamic. I expected them to be powerful. Exceptionally so. But only time would reveal what else they'd bring into our lives.

Deciding that Mera would be more comfortable on the bed, I lifted her with ease, and the warmth of her fire cocooned us both without burning. She trusted me and so did her energy. Moving out of the bathing area, I transferred her onto the large pad in my room, adding a few cushions around her to cradle the stomach. She turned in her sleep, wrapping her arms around one cushion and lifting her leg over another, getting into the position she'd told me was most comfortable in her late stage of pregnancy.

Her breathing evened out again, and it was clear that she was tired. Her body was preparing to bring a god child into this world, and all of us needed to remember this as we moved through the mission. Mera's rest had to be a priority.

Leaving her to it, I decided to check if the outfits had been delivered. As I passed through the main lounging zone, my stomach rumbled, reminding me that I had to fuel that part of my body now. It didn't exactly impact my energy when I didn't eat food, but my body missed the taste and sensation of being full. Desertlandians did eat as part of their energy renewal, and I was sure that this event tonight would involve many of their delicacies. I'd never actually tasted any of them before, and I was beyond ready to finally know what I'd been missing all of these years.

When I reached the entrance it opened, and as I walked out, noise slammed into me. The tents were surrounded by energy, protecting and insulating them from the outside, and it wasn't until I stepped free that I was once again deep in the sights, scents, and memories of this world.

Forcing myself to compartmentalize, because there was no time to disappear into the past, I reached down for the large olive-green sack made from fronds of the pamolsa tree, which was sitting just to the left of the entrance. It was heavy, and that was all I needed to know about how formal this event was going to be. Full Rohami getup for all of us.

Just as I straightened to bring the items inside, a sweet, husky voice called my name—not Angel, but my warrior name. Not many knew that name since for centuries I'd been without a name or family, but now I had two names and a family I loved.

"Tsuma," I said with surprise, staring at the familiar Rohami woman. Older than me, she had been a close friend of Reece's family. One of the originals, powerful and strong, she had not physically aged a day since I'd last seen her many centuries ago. The long, orangey red strands of her hair curled to midback, her light brown skin was plump, showing no sign of line or age, and those gold-tinged eyes were as warm as ever. She'd been beautiful in youth, and the years had only increased her glow.

"I'm so surprised to see you here," she said as she bustled forward, wrapping her arms around me. I was surprised by the gesture since powerful beings didn't usually make physical contact with each other, and I wondered if Mera was somehow rubbing off on this world too. "Reece never mentioned that you would be at this gathering."

Tsuma spoke in her native tongue of Rohami—one of the first languages I'd learned.

"It was a last-minute decision, but it's definitely nice to be here," I said.

Her hands were still on my arms, and I fought the urge to shake them off. She was acting weirdly out of character, but it had been a very long time since I'd known her. My judgement of her character was uninformed. I'd changed, and maybe so had she. "I came by to see Reece," she continued excitedly. "Where are your wings? You look so different."

Her random jumps between talking points of conversation was much more how I remembered her, and no doubt I did look different standing here in a sheet of cloth, hair wild and streaked with red, no armor or wings. Very few beings had ever seen me like this.

"I recently experienced a rebirth," I told her, finally managing to move away so she was no longer making contact with my energy. "But the fundamentals of my power remain the same."

She chuckled, perfect white teeth flashing. "Yes, that is true. A few strands of fire in your hair did not change your insides."

This was only partly true because I would always be a stoic warrior type, but I was also no longer the robotic loner.

"You said you were looking for Reece?" I reminded her. "He's just gone out to mingle with the dynasty leaders before tonight's celebratory event. He should return soon."

She waved me off, the gold in her eyes dancing as she did what she'd always been excellent at: creating a sense of comfort and warmth. "Running into an old friend, such as yourself, confirms the push I felt to attend this meeting. I don't usually bother myself with this world's politics any longer, but somehow I knew this was going to be an important one."

"Right," I said, trying to read her, but she was holding her cards close to her chest. "We can catch up further at the dinner tonight. Will there be others in attendance from your family?"

She nodded. "Oh yes, Dally, Mirinda, Fleur, and Miver will all be there. Seeing all of you together... that will truly be something."

Those names evoked as many memories as this world did. Tsuma's children had always been at Reece's home in Rohami.

"What about Zena?" I asked.

That was when her smile faded. "Yes, she is here. I came to see Reece on her behest, actually. She's hoping he'll save the first dance for her tonight, but now that you're here..."

Some of her reticence in explaining why she'd been looking for Reece made sense now. Her eldest daughter, the very beautiful Zena, had always had a thing for Reece. I'd tormented myself over the years thinking of those two together, but from what I'd heard, it had never happened. Seemed as if that hadn't stopped Tsuma from continuing to try.

"Don't worry about Reece and me," I said shortly, a few flecks of ice seeping into my tone. "We are as we've always been."

Enemies.

While that wasn't strictly the truth, our lives no longer as black and white as they had once been, it would hopefully set her mind at ease.

Now I just had to endure whatever happened tonight because being back in the same room as my old life could be a recipe for disaster.

ONCE TSUMA LEFT, I found myself pacing the tent, wishing that Mera was awake so I could vent all these... feelings. How the hell did people live like this? With what felt like a damn bomb inside about to explode.

I should never have agreed to come back here; this world had always been destructive for me.

"Angel?" Mera appeared in the doorway, her face scrunched up as she yawned and rubbed her eyes. "I fell asleep?"

Thank the meadow's creator. She was finally awake.

Hurrying toward her, I found myself right in her personal space, which was so unlike me that there was no surprise when Mera's drowsiness vanished as her wide eyes locked on mine. "What the hell happened while I was asleep?"

I shook my head, reaching out to grasp her biceps. When Tsuma had touched me, it'd been uncomfortable, but it felt like second nature with Mera. "I collected our outfits, and just as I was about to return inside, an old acquaintance of mine from this world showed up." My words got faster and faster as they spilled from me. "I haven't seen her in centuries, but dammit, it was like no time had passed at all. I don't think I can do this. I can't be here."

At this point Mera looked like she was freaking out, no doubt because she'd never seen me *freaking out.* "Angel, slow down and take some deep breaths. You're having a panic attack, which is perfectly acceptable in these circumstances, but it's stopping the very rational side of your brain from func- tioning."

My breathing was rapid at this point, whistling through my teeth in harsh gusts, and I could not remember ever feeling or acting like this. It had to be some side effect of my rebirth, which was all well and good, but how did I snap out of it?

Mera pushed me down to the ground, spreading my legs apart, and when I blinked at her, she smiled. "Trust me."

I trusted her more than anyone in the worlds, so when she

put her hand on the back of my head and forced me to lower it between my parted legs, I didn't fight her.

"Now take deep breaths in and out."

At first, I couldn't comply, but as she started to count the beats for me to breathe in and out, I managed to slowly get myself under control, all the while cursing my momentary weakness.

For a second, I'd been the same Melalekin who had lost everything in these lands.

I refused to go back to that being, not now or ever.

Tonight would be a true test, and it was one I was determined to win.

CHAPTER SEVENTEEN

Mera sat with me for many minutes, letting me mentally beat myself up as I made plans for how I would be stronger next time.

"Stop that right now," she finally snapped, feeling the turmoil through our bond. "You're just so used to being strong that the smallest sign of weakness is abhorrent. I bet you never even anticipated how hard it would be to come back here."

I opened my mouth to protest because I had very much anticipated this being hard as hell, but she continued before I could say another word.

"I mean, I know it crossed your mind because you think about everything, but no doubt you felt that in your maturity you could handle whatever happened here. Banking on the fact that you're no longer the same Melalekin now that you've reborn into a new being—"

"I'd be annoyed that you know me so well," I interrupted drily, "but I kind of love that you do."

Mera shrugged. "Seriously, though, it's because of your rebirth that this is extra difficult for you to handle. In some ways, you're younger than me, especially when it comes to feelings. Your emotions are raw and new and fresh, and despite what you think, you're not a different being. Just a refreshed one. So, of course, coming back to this land, which is the epicenter of your pain, a pain you never really dealt with, was going to throw you."

She reached forward and wrapped her arms around me, both of us fitting together as best we could with her tummy. "You are still the strongest, most badass being I know," she whispered. "This is not weakness. It's inevitability."

This was the only point where I'd been confused in her speech. "Inevitability?"

I felt her nod against my shoulder. "Yes. You can only run from the past and old feelings for so long. Eventually, circumstances will force you to deal with them. You should probably be grateful you got to hide for as long as you did."

Resting my head against her arm, I thought on what she'd said. "I should have dealt with it many moons ago," I admitted, "because hiding and beating myself up did nothing except prevent me from truly living life. My eternal youth was wasted, and I almost died before I even got a chance to experience real joy." Now that the panic had passed, it was growing clearer to me. "I'm here to let go of the past so I can have a future."

Mera pulled away, clapping her hands as excitement lit up her beautiful face. "Yes. My girl is growing up."

"Patronizing, but I'll take it," I said drily, jumping to my feet.

Mera got up slower, taking my hand so I could help. "What does that mean for your next steps?" she asked, brushing back the long strands of her hair.

"It means," I said, feeling my energy bounce around inside me as Mera pressed a hand to her chest, no doubt feeling it too, "that we're going to get dressed for this ceremony tonight, and we're going to eat and dance. I will not stay in the shadows like normal. Life is too short, and I cannot continue to miss it all."

"Jumping straight in the deep end," she said with a nod. "I like it."

I was nodding too. "Yes, I know this is the best way for me to exorcise my ghosts. Tsuma took me by surprise, but I have a better handle on the sharp sting of these emotions now. I can handle the rest."

It might hurt... okay, it would *definitely* hurt since I'd have to, at some point, truly face my losses of this world: Leka and Reece. But if that meant I would be able to move forward and have a real future, I was more than ready.

Mera's face was creased in happiness. "I've been worried about you," she said, "and not in the normal way that I worry about my friends... but deeper. Maybe that's why the baby is reacting to your energy; they feel my tension around you and your future. Which is fading now! You're on the right path, and if I wasn't walking around with the spawn of a Shadow Beast inside me, I'd be partying it up with you. As it stands, though, with the merry band of assholes here, I'm sure you'll have plenty of company."

"We have all the time in the world for you to join me," I said, feeling my grin grow. "Once the baby is older. For this moon, I'll just have to party for the both of us."

I was fairly certain I'd never seen Mera this excited as she gripped my shoulders. "Okay, we need to get moving on prep. When was the last time you waxed? I wasn't staring at your vag before, but is there a need for maintenance?"

I'd spent enough time in the modern human world to know exactly what she was referring to. "We don't have the same *hair situation*," I explained. "There's nothing to maintain there."

Mera's eyes grew impossibly wide. "No hair? That's so weird! I mean, as a shifter I quite like a bit of body hair, you know, but I wasn't sure if it was the same for transcendents and other races." Her eyes traced over me like she could see under my sheet. "I mean, I've seen bits of you naked. I know we have the same body parts, but I never noticed the hair. Probably just figured you removed it. What else is the same or different? Do you have to worry about pregnancy and diseases?"

If there was ever a being with consistent sex on the mind, it was Mera. "Most of the evolved species of the worlds have similar parts," I said, amused. "The original gods are responsible for that. As for reproduction, transcendents are only able to create life with another of our kind. It's extremely difficult and rare, needing an infusion of light and energy."

"You can't have children with Reece?"

One question, cutting me to the core, but since I was all about dealing with these stronger emotions now, I forced myself to move through it. "No, there's no possible way. And we have no diseases to worry about either."

Before she could grill me for more information, the tent entrance opened, and Lucien stepped in. He paused at the sight of us before shaking his head. "You two better get dressed. Reece is going to be back in a few minutes to take us to the opening ceremony."

Mera all but bounced on the spot. "We've got to get you ready," she said in a rush, hurrying as fast as she could past Lucien. "This will probably be the only night here without fighting and drama and all the bloody bodies that our guys leave around, and I want you to enjoy yourself."

She leaned over to riffle through the bags that I'd brought inside, sorting out the outfits. As she pulled out the multiple bright red pieces, it was clear that their formal dress had not changed since the last time I'd worn it: red for Rohami with the jackan-beast somewhere prominent.

"Okay, someone is going to have to help me here," Mera said

blinking as she placed all the bits and pieces on the ground. "This isn't the little black dress I was expecting."

Both of Lucien's hands shot up in front of him like he was surrendering. "This is outside of my jurisdiction. I take women's clothing off; I don't have the skills to get them back on."

Mera threw a wristband at him, and he only laughed, moving at his vampiric speed to catch the object. "Now, now. Don't hate the player—"

"Don't you dare finish that," Mera interrupted, this time calling flames to her hands. "You and your damn human sayings. I will fry your ass. Don't push me."

Lucien's smirk never faded as he backed up a few steps. "Okay, preggo. Calm down."

Well, fuck. This idiot was getting fried.

At least zero universes existed where telling a pissed off woman to calm down actually resulted in her getting calmer.

The flames grew higher as Mera abandoned the clothing and focused her attention on Lucien. "You're already on my shit list," she snarled stepping closer, the flames nearly engulfing her. "I don't know what happened between you and Simone, but you broke my friend and that's enough for me to break you. Do you understand?"

Lucien lost all joviality, as he often did when Simone was mentioned. "I promise I did not dishonor her," he said softly but also quickly, as if he needed to get the words out. "She just... didn't fit into my world, and it wasn't ideal having her exist within the vampire community. Her safety was compromised there."

From my experience with Valdor, I couldn't imagine a situation where Simone would fit in. She was from Earth, a shifter, and to the proud upper echelons of Lucien's kingdom, she would be considered cattle. *Food.* Nothing more.

Lucien was powerful enough to protect her, and clearly he

had or she'd be dead, but knowing how willful Simone was at times... if she'd fought against his rules or restrictions, it would not have been pretty.

One day the truth would come out, but it wasn't going to be today.

Lucien took off in a flash, so fast that even I struggled to track his movements. Once he was gone from the room, Mera calmed down. "I need to birth this child before I murder all of our friends," she told me with a huff.

Compressing my lips, I worked valiantly to stop the mirth from showing on my face, but it wasn't to be. As soon as Mera saw me, a burst of laughter escaped her, and then we were both losing it.

"He took off so fast," she spluttered.

"Like his ass was on fire," I managed to say.

She laughed harder, half bent over. "It almost was on fire. My control is gone at the moment." With a shake of her head, she plopped herself down on a cushion, hands resting on her front. "I'm a fucking hot mess with this pregnancy. What is up with that?"

I didn't sit because we really had to get dressed or we'd be late, but I did crouch down to her level. "The combination of two godlike powers into one child was never going to be easy," I reminded her. "You're creating life. A being of pure power. Be easy on yourself and your body because, as far as I'm concerned, it's a damn miracle."

Transcendents were dying out as a race because we rarely produced young. At least, not anymore. As I'd told Mera, the process was difficult, and at times it felt as if the worlds had decided we were no longer relevant.

Mera's frustrated expression eased, lines smoothing around her forehead and eyes. "Yeah, if I think of it that way, I guess I'm doing okay." She waved me off. "Now get dressed so I can see how gorgeous you look."

With a chuckle, I straightened and made my way back to the scattered pieces of clothing. It had been a long time since I'd worn the Rohami traditional dress, but I remembered every piece. Pieces that were remnants of the past about to become beacons of the future.

Tonight was the first step to a new life.

CHAPTER EIGHTEEN

In the deserts, most of the clothing was made from a combination of different plant materials. A few pieces had to be imported from other worlds, but for the most part they'd figured out how to use their resources to create soft and durable materials.

The formal outfit for this event consisted of tight red pants, stretchy and thick, hugging my thighs and calves. Over the top was a knee-length, short-sleeved red tunic. It was also made of thick and heavy material, with gold stitching and a huge black jackan across the back. The front had a diamond-shaped cutout, exposing some cleavage. Unlike Mera, after years of honing my warrior body to limit its softness, I wasn't overly blessed in the boob department. But in this particular outfit, my size was perfect.

It was all finished off with a pair of black boots, which zipped up over my ankle and gave me another few inches of height.

"So, that tunic is literally never getting over my stomach," Mera said, holding up the pieces of her set. "And what are the rest of these *items* for?"

Grabbing a bracelet with thick gold links, I said, "This goes on your right wrist to show that you're unmated or left for those with a bond." Dropping it I moved to the solid band with a cut-out piece. "And this cuff is for your biceps. It doesn't matter which one since it's purely decorative."

"And this?" Mera asked, lifting some wispy red material.

"For our hair." I demonstrated how to curl it over my crown like a headband, then loop it through the long strands of my ponytail, allowing the rest to trail down my back.

Mera watched it all with wide-eyed fascination, and when I was done, twirling on the spot to give her the full picture, she let out a sigh. "With your new fiery coloring, you look just like an—"

"Angel," I interrupted with a laugh, since it was her favorite descriptor of me.

She wrinkled her nose and stuck her tongue out at me. "No, smartass. I was going to say you look like a goddess of fire and light—different than Shadow and me with our darker powers." She clasped her hands, eyes shiny. "You're so beautiful, Angel. Any male would be lucky to have a chance with you."

My heart squeezed. "Thank you. Your support means everything to me. I couldn't have made it through this rebirth without you." I was thousands of years older than Mera, but at times it felt like she was the rock on which I was growing my new foundation.

"Girl, I would literally not be able to exist in this world without you," she said, that sheen to her eyes spilling over. "When I thought I'd lost you—" She broke off and shook her head like there were no words to truly describe it.

I understood because the thought of losing Mera cut me just as deeply. It would be akin to losing another sister. Thankfully, that should never happen since she could be reborn in the Nexus, and for that, I was eternally grateful.

"We are going to be in each other's lives for a long time," I said, running my hand through the long length of the silky red material threading through my hair. "No more talk of death. Not tonight."

Mera nodded, wiping her eyes. "No more talk of death. Tonight is for living, and—" She broke off, looking around. "Weren't we in a rush? Where the hell are the guys? I'm starving."

That made two of us, and with her pregnant...

"They should know better than to leave you hungry," I said with a snort, before leaning down to grab her tights. "But first, let's see if we can fit you into this."

She groaned but didn't fight me as I helped her into the pants, which, thankfully, stretched up over her belly. The tunic, while more fitted, had fasteners under either side that allowed for adjustment. Some of her skin was exposed in the gaps at her waist, but she didn't give a shit. The bracelet went on her left wrist, the cuff on the same biceps, and by the time I'd adjusted her red scarf to wrap around her mass of hair, the others had finally arrived to collect us.

Shadow was the first one inside, pushing through the tent door and striding straight to Mera. His eyes traced across the red outfit, lingering on the exposed skin down her sides and the way her generous breasts were, as predicted, spilling out of the diamond cutout.

"We won't be at the dinner tonight," he drawled, his voice a deep rumble as a smoky scent filled the room. "I've made other plans."

From the glint in his eyes, it was clear what those other plans were.

But Mera was having none of that. "Dude, I just spent a damn hour getting my pregnant ass into this outfit. I will be going to the ceremony. I will be eating all the food. And if you try and stop me, I will strangle you with my fancy hair scarf."

She caught my eye and gave me a wink before returning her attention to Shadow, who was wearing a look of amusement. "And after you've eaten?" he pressed.

"You will dance with me," she said quickly, "and then you will take me back to our room here and strip this freaking thing off me."

"Deal."

He said it so fast that everyone laughed. The others started to get dressed in the formal attire as well, unconcerned about stripping off their regular boots and cargo pants. All except Reece, who was standing near the entrance, his gaze tracing over my outfit and lingering on the bracelet on my right wrist.

The wrist that advertised me as unmated.

A stormy darkness descended over his features, but before I could overanalyze that, I looked away. This moon, my focus was on fresh starts and having fun. Desert gods were not on the list.

"We'll head out in five minutes," Reece said gruffly.

The others made noises of agreement, most now taking their half-naked asses out of this room and into their bedroom areas to wash up and dress. When they returned, one by one, Mera and I got to take them all in. And by *all*, I meant my eyes were locked on Reece, unable to look away.

The men's outfits consisted of red pants too, only theirs were trouser-style with pockets. Their tunic was made of the same thick material and gold stitching, but the cutout was rectangular, exposing most of Reece's thick bronze chest muscles. His biceps were also on show in the short sleeves, a gold cuff around one, while the other was covered in marks—tattoos as Mera called them—made up of what looked like symbols of this world and a few I didn't recognize. It wasn't easy to brand the skin of those long-lived, but all of these guys had figured out a way to do so.

I'd never seen Reece's marks up close, since he'd gotten them after our time together, and I tried not to examine them now. No need to make it obvious that my fascination with him was as strong as ever. Lifting my eyes, I found a blue pair boring into me, and since I couldn't fall into those depths, I flicked my gaze up past his dark, shaved hair, pretending I was interested in the intricate arrangement of the tent's structure.

Why the hell did he look so perfect all the time with his stupid height and broad shoulders and cocky smil—

"Ready to go?" Len asked interrupting my mental berating when he appeared in the room. "I think I wear this outfit even better than the last time I had it on."

He propped both hands on his hips, looking confident as he swaggered forward. It was odd to see him in such a bright color when he lived and breathed his silver status, but there was no denying the glowing beauty of this fae. In fact, all of the males looked like the gods they were revered for across the worlds.

Mera hadn't been around long enough to truly understand the power of these six. Everyone either wanted to be part of this group or fuck their way through the six.

I'd been the only one sitting on the outside watching them rule it all, never for a second considering I'd one day stand among them.

It was a change I was still processing, but in the spirit of embracing change, I was walking into this moon with as much confidence as these males had.

It was my new beginning after all.

CHAPTER NINETEEN

Gatherings of this magnitude in the Desert Lands were rare, mostly due to the sheer size of the territories and the difficulty in coordinating travel through the sand rivers for thousands of Desertlandians. Not to mention managing the various feuds and issues between dynasties.

But when a gathering did happen, the grandeur of the event was absolutely breathtaking, from their young running through the sands to the traditional games taking place in designated tents. The energy was enough to make anyone feel alive, and it felt extra electric this moon, almost as if there was a higher connection and vibration of power zipping around the Ostealon.

As we walked through the various red, gold, and brown tents, the half-moon shining its golden light down on us, Len fell in on my right side.

"You look particularly stunning tonight," he said, staring ahead, but I felt his attention. "Red is your color."

"Red also suits you beautifully," I replied with a smile, the energy giving me a bouncy, euphoric feeling. "You should step away from the silver more often. I know it defines you, but it's not every part of you."

Len's flirtatious grin faded as he finally met my gaze. "You know and see so much," he finally said. We stopped walking then, having reached the large white tent that I'd seen when we first arrived.

"I see you," I said to Len, "and that's why we'll never have a random dalliance, no matter how much you temptingly dangle it in front of me. You're still searching, taking your journey to find a true mate. There's no room for me in that equation."

He turned away from me again, both of us staring into the entrance of the tent. He knew I was right, as any being of his age and intelligence would. The fae took spiritual journeys to find their mates, and even though Len's hadn't shown themself yet, I believed they were out there. One night of fun sex wasn't worth destroying that for him.

"My next journey is to be my last," he said softly, the true undercurrent of his lilting accent deepening. "Until then, I hold out hope."

Unable to help myself, I reached out and wrapped my hand around his, squeezing tightly.

"I will hope with you," I said, voice low but brimming with more emotions than I'd usually use. "If anyone deserves a true bond, it is you, my friend."

Just as he returned my hand squeeze there was a low rumble from behind us. Heat washed down my spine, and even though I recognized exactly who was standing too close, I still called on my weapons, spinning with my free hand to nearly slam the blade against Reece's throat.

He didn't stop me or defend himself, and it was only through my unparalleled control that I managed to halt my strike mere inches from his jugular. Furious blue eyes met mine, the swirls of energy moving faster in their depths.

"Always so quick to attack," he murmured in a harsh tone, pressing into me until the sharp edge of my blade sliced into his skin.

"Reece!" I cursed, sending the weapons back to my room in the tent. "Do you have a damn death wish?"

His expression now was unreadable. "Apparently I do," he said, and then with a sweep of his hand, he turned away, stepping onto the long white mat that led into the tent. The others followed him, but I found myself taking a second to find my calm. Clearly Reece still didn't want me forming friendships with his friends, but you know what? Screw him. No longer would he dictate who could and couldn't be in my life.

Len and I shared a similar pain in our family lines, similar loneliness, and we could always find common ground, which was the perfect basis for a real friendship. It would never be more than that, though, and if Reece had asked, I would have told him the truth. I didn't play games, but he'd given me no chance.

Which was always his way.

Releasing more of my hurt and anger, I pasted on my best happy face and strode through the wide open curtains of this tent. The thick white mat that had been in the entrance continued on into the main room, covering the sands and giving everything a sparkling clean look.

From where I stood, it was easy to see the four zones this incredibly large space had been divided into. Immediately to my right was a fenced area with multiple paddocks holding giant *rhjeta* creatures from the Fret and Holinfra dynasties. The scent was the first part I recognized, a pungent aroma similar to the stockyards I'd watched over in America, many decades ago. The rhjeta were not an Earth animal, but if I had to describe the scaly beasts, it would be as a dragon-lizard.

Mera and Shadow pushed over toward me. "What in the

worlds are they?" Mera asked, staring wide-eyed at the creatures.

"Rhjeta," I said. "They're desert creatures that can breathe fire and camouflage themselves."

"They're massive," she gasped as one moved closer to the fence nearest us. "Like someone crossed a beefed-up Komodo dragon with an elephant and got this." She waved her hand toward them.

Her descriptor was on point, from their brown, grey, and black scaled skin, which was thicker and armored down their spine, to the rotund bellies that nearly dragged on the ground.

"How did they tame them?" she asked, as two blasted fire at each other, their riders using shields to repel some of the heat.

"It's very difficult," Shadow told her. "Only a few have the skill, power, and control to bond with one. I've never known any except those in the Holinfra and Fret dynasties to even try. The rhjeta are a true danger in the deserts."

Mera cleared her throat, shaking her head a few times. "I really don't blame them for not trying. Look at their damn claws."

Front and back legs were topped with six-inch talons, not to mention the powerful tail that could easily crush a being. "Their teeth are coated in poison, too," I added, since their strengths should be discussed. "One bite and you'll be dead within minutes."

With a shudder, she turned away. "Let's not visit that zone just yet," she said in a strangled tone. "Or, like, ever."

Shadow made an amused sound, moving to stand right behind her so that no one in the massive crowds could jostle her. "Come on," he said, "the next section will be much more to your liking."

Leaving the rhjeta, we made our way into the dining area, which was set up with about a thousand round glass tables, woven from sands of all the different dynasties. The various colors made it easy to know where to sit.

"Hell yes," Mera cried, shaking her ass across the dining zone as we entered the area with red glass tables.

Each table was set with ochre dinnerware and glasses, made from Ostealon's sands, the land that joined them all.

"Is there allocated seating?" Mera asked.

"Sit at red for Rohami," Shadow replied. "Other than that, I think it's fair game."

Mera shrugged, continuing to look around. "Makes sense." She pointed to the third quadrant, bordering the dining area. "And what's that part used for?"

There wasn't a lot of structure in that section, but I could tell from the harder mat, where sand and pamolsa had been fused, that this was the zone for—

"Dancing," Shadow said.

A low, thrumming beat was already drifting from there, thanks to the Shale dynasty, which was renowned for their gifts in the musical arts. They didn't sing here; instead it was a combination of deep humming and the beat of drums built from the barrels of sand vessels that were no longer safe enough to take along the streams and rivers. I'd always found myself lost in their beats, and my body was already loosening up, the electric energy flittering within me.

"I see them," Mera called, distracting me from the music.

Turning slightly, I also found where our group was seated at a large red table close to the dance floor. We reached them a few minutes later, and when Shadow and Mera took the only two seats together, between Len and Alistair, I was left to sit in the only one that remained. Between Len... and Reece.

Forcing myself not to breathe too deeply or think too hard, I just sank onto the round, backless, cushioned dome. The music was stronger here, sending my blood pumping and head spinning as my connection to this land swelled within.

"Always the same," Reece said from beside me. Tilting my head in his direction, I found that my anger toward him was all but gone, swept away in this night. "Our music is in your blood. I never could figure out why you were so affected by the *hretun* drums."

"It reminds me of happier days and memories," I said, my words light.

Reece raised an eyebrow at me. "You were like that from the first moment you heard our beats and danced our dances."

This time I shrugged. "What can I say, it stirs my energy deep inside. Maybe I was born in the wrong world."

His jaw tightened, but he didn't snap at me for once. "Maybe you were. Or maybe you are more than one being."

Forcing myself not to react to such an insightful comment—I was getting them from all sides at the moment—I turned away once more and lost myself in the sights around me. It was a better alternative than facing the truth that I'd lost more than just Reece when I left the Desert Lands.

I'd lost a part of my true self.

CHAPTER TWENTY

Reece and I didn't speak again. In fact, it was extra-quiet at the table as everyone took in the sights of the room and waited for the food to be delivered. In the Desert Lands, they had a special system for the distribution of items, sending it on the backs of large—

"Sand turtles!" Mera exclaimed as the creatures slowly entered the space between tables, bearing trays on their backs. The trays were piled high with a variety of desert specialties, including a few deep purple *gry*, a native fruit similar to that of the cacti.

"They do look like those huge land turtles from Earth," Lucien said, tilting his head as he watched the dark green *yeth graba* meander down the lanes. Their shells were smaller than land turtles, which wasn't the only difference. The yeth had an exoskeleton, with a protective length of spiny protrusions down their heads and backs.

When a tray moved by our side, Reece reached out and lifted it, placing the five-foot length of brown pamolsa branch across the diameter of our table. Soon after, another tray with glasses of liforina showed up as well, and then it was time to eat.

Conversation after that centered around the food as more trays went past, and Mera asked a million questions about what each delicacy was. With anticipation brimming in my gut, I reached out to take a piece of gry fruit, wondering if the taste would live up to the sweet scent.

Reece intercepted me as I chose my piece, nudging my palm toward a smaller one on the right. "This one is riper," he said shortly before turning away from me to resume chatting with Alistair.

For a moment, I debated ignoring him and taking the original piece I'd been aiming for, but as I glared at the side of his face, I saw his lips twitch like he was expecting that response from me. Swallowing my stupid pride so I wouldn't give him the satisfaction of being right, I took his suggested slice, all the while knowing he'd won either way.

The thick, rough purple exterior had a slice in its side, so I dug my fingers in and pulled it all the way apart, exposing the bright magenta flesh. The pulp and seeds glistened, and the smell was mouthwatering, with both sweet and tart olfactory notes. Lifting it to my lips, I avoided the shell, biting into the flesh, and groaned at the first hit of flavor.

It was sweet, but as it danced across my tongue, heat followed. "Wow," I murmured, intrigued by the duality. "It tastes nothing like I expected but is strangely addictive."

Mera leaned forward and nodded. "Right? It's weird but awesome," She reached for a second piece. "Like a cantaloupe had a baby with a dragon fruit, and then cayenne sneezed on it."

I grinned around my piece as I bit into the flesh before dropping the skin into an empty bowl on the tray. Grabbing a towel that had been included with the table setting, I wiped off the excess juice. "It's fun to finally taste these foods. I spent years breathing in their delicious scents."

That caught Reece's attention, and he inclined his head my way. "It's a nice change to see you eat, rather than just play with your food."

"I'm all about change these days," I said with a smile, hoping to keep the mood light.

He didn't answer, but thankfully I felt no anger from him either. Which for us was definitely a win.

The music picked up as we continued to eat our way through the many dishes. I tried their broth—made from all the parts of the *junifer* plant, which grew multiple berries and had edible roots—along with some *butle* roast, which was a meaty dish from their only domesticated livestock bred specifically for food consumption. Most residents of this world did not eat meat, but for the ones who did, butle was their only option.

"Delicious," Mera said with a groan, a slice of the tender roast in her hand. "Tastes like prime rib, and damn, I've missed a good cut of steak."

Len laughed. "You might not be a shifter any longer, but you still eat like one."

Mera shrugged because what could she say? Girl liked her meat. In all ways.

When I was full, I decided to push my luck and see how far this amicability between Reece and me would stretch. "When you were out today, did you discover anything in relation to who is disturbing the sacred lands?" I asked him.

If my question took Reece by surprise, he showed no signs of it. "Yemin turned out to be fine, once we questioned them further, so Shadow and I focused on Rohami. For the reasons we discussed. There's an undercurrent in my land. Rohami and... maybe Guardians."

It wasn't surprising that those were the two suspect dynasties. Both close to the Delfora. Both infused with extra power. "Tsuma stopped by the tent today looking for you," I told him. "She was a little... off. Do you think she knows anything?"

Reece's eyes glittered in the arcs of light that reflected off the ochre detailing around us. "She found me too, and I declined her offer to dance with Zena."

Pretending I didn't care about that, I didn't even comment on it. "Did you not notice anything else odd about her? It's just... she hugged me, and Mera might have eased us into this touching thing, but it still struck me as *unusual*."

Reece shook his head. "I think Tsuma is doing her usual matchmaking, but other than that, she's been uninterested in politics for many years."

She'd mentioned as much, but the niggle of unease inside me wouldn't ease. Maybe that was the whole Zena thing, though. "Okay, so back to Rohami. Which families do you suspect?"

"Tattliner and Jorts," he said, lowering his voice. "They've both recently changed leadership, their elders aging out, and they want more power. They want to live forever and utilize the sands. They have means, motive, and opportunity with this gathering."

From what I knew, both of those families were midrange in the power hierarchy.

"Their elders' deaths would have created a power void they'll be hoping to fill," I said, thinking it over. "Are you saying both elders died at the same time?"

Blue eyes met mine. "Yes, which is exactly why those two clans are at the top of my list."

"And Guardians... You suspect them because they're so close to Delfora, able to move freely in the flats?"

He nodded, drawing in a deep breath as he stared across the tented area. "The ritual to raise the gods," his voice grew lower, "would require a massive burst of energy to get moving. Then someone would have to make it along the valley of the dead to cast a ritual upon the pillars that seal that land. It would take beings closely bonded to the Delfora."

Right, and if you couldn't have Reece for that job, someone from Guardians was the obvious next choice.

"Why are you already feeling unease in the Delfora if they've not yet started the ritual?" I asked, leaning in even closer as a few Crani crossed behind us, heading toward the dance floor.

"The ritual is not complete, but it could have started," he murmured, eyes nearly glowing. "I sense they have been in the Delfora prepping the area for this plan. Since I'm rarely here, they never expected anyone would know or feel, but I've grown more powerful... my connection stronger."

"They're not going to like that you've returned here," I whispered. "If what you suspect is true, you need to watch your back because you might be the only being who can stop them."

The smile that slowly spread across his face was not a nice one. It promised death on swift desert storms to whomever was disturbing the peace of this world. "They should fear me. I will get to the bottom of this, and I will stop them from whatever they're planning. When I'm done with them, not only will they not have the eternal life they're hoping for, they won't have any life."

Len leaned in from my left side, clearly listening in. "This is the best time to flush them out," he said. "Maybe we can just split up, create a sense of vulnerability among our numbers, and see who really wants to put a knife in Reece's spine."

"Other than Angel, you mean?" Reece shot back quickly.

I tsked. "You know I prefer the throat. You'll always see me coming."

He laughed, and the sound tore through my chest, leaving

me wondering if I was actually bleeding out on the dinner table. "Touché, Lale. You don't need to deceive to be feared."

I tried to laugh with him, but there was so little breath in my lungs I settled for a smile.

"When do you want to start this plan?" Len asked.

Reece sobered. "Not this moon. For this opening ceremony, we should focus on observing and keeping up appearances. The new-moon is when it will all begin."

Trusting Reece knew what he was talking about, I got right on board with that plan—tonight, I was still going to have my dance. Pushing to my feet, I moved around to help Mera up as well. "Dance time?" she said, already bopping to the beat.

"Yes," I replied, leaning toward her ear. "Battle starts tomorrow in the new-moon, which means I still have this moon for dancing."

"Woohoo!" she shouted, pumping her fist and drawing attention. "Let's get over there."

A new beat started, and now I was the one about to fist pump. "This is my favorite song and dance," I said in a rush.

Reece, who was on his feet as well, crossed his arms over his broad chest, drawing my attention to all the visible skin. "You still remember the *Deduna Lalita?*"

"Every beat and every step," I replied, managing to focus on his face again.

Before he could distract me further, I linked my arm through Mera's, and together we made our way to the hard flooring. We weren't the only ones there either, with many of the dynasties having finished their food already.

"Do you know all the dances?" Mera asked.

I shook my head. "Not a chance. There are hundreds, but I definitely know my favorites."

"I wish I could dance it with you," she said when we reached the edge of where the Desertlandians were already gathered. "But I want you to have so much"—she coughed, and I could have sworn she said *cock* before she cleared her throat and finished with—"fun. Have so much fun."

I barely managed to hold in my laughter. "You're the fucking worst," I said, "but I love you."

"I love you too." She gave me a shove. "Now go and enjoy your dance."

Stepping toward the crowds gathered for the Deduna Lalita, I let the familiar beat clear my mind and spirit. Reece had seemed surprised that I remembered the steps, but how could I ever forget? He had taught me this dance, as he had so many of their customs here.

He'd brought me into this world, and it was his fault I'd fallen in love with it.

Part of me would always belong to the Desert Lands, and this was my chance to feel it all. A chance I was not wasting. Even if I danced this alone, nothing was stopping me from entering the Deduna Lalita... The Long Dream.

CHAPTER TWENTY-ONE

The intro to The Long Dream went on for many minutes, giving everyone time to partner up. This was the sort of dance where dynasties mixed and mate-bonds were formed. It didn't really matter what partner you started with since you would switch every fifteen steps in a swirl of melody and beat.

Since I was displaying the "unmated" chain on my wrist, it took no time for a male in a gold tunic from the sands of Crani to step up and offer his hand. He had dark brown skin, deep grey eyes, and a long straight nose. He wasn't much taller than me, his shaved head almost equal in height to the red scarf across my crown.

"Would you care to partner?" he asked in his native tongue.

"It would be my pleasure," I replied.

His smile was broad, teeth slightly crooked but not unattractively so. When I took his hand, there was a slight flare as our energy collided, but other than that, nothing else sparked.

Desertlandians only touched during their dances, as cautious as every other world with sharing energy, and it was considered very bad form to draw on any of your partner's life-force while moving about the dance floor.

The Crani male swirled me closer, moving us into the starting position where we faced each other. Over his shoulder, I saw a broadly smiling Mera, and when our eyes met, she mouthed *hell yes* while waggling her eyebrows. There was nothing subtle about my best friend, but I didn't care.

Turning back to my new partner, I found his gaze locked on my face. Unlike when Reece focused his attention on me, the Crani's intensity didn't stir butterflies in my stomach or leave my chest tight and uncomfortable.

"My name is Hectar," he said, "and despite the fact that you wear the color of my least favorite dynasty, you're too beautiful for me to hold that against you."

That got a smile out of me as I switched my dialect to another that I expected he would know. "My name is Angel, and I'm just borrowing these colors. My heritage is Honor Meadows."

His eyes widened. "No wings?"

"Not anymore," I replied softly, and then thankfully, the beat started to pick up as the song moved past the intro. After that, there was no time for talking because if you lost focus, you'd lose your steps just as fast.

It had been more years than I cared to remember since I'd last performed The Long Dream, but my body remembered it like it was yesterday, falling into the song. Hectar's smile turned into deep laughter as he held me just a touch longer than needed before I moved on to my next partner, an orange-clad man from the Yemin dynasty.

We had no time for a greeting or anything else as the steps moved even faster, all of us twirling and spinning. Partners continued to switch, male and female alike. Desertlandians, like almost every world, had same-sex mating, cross-dynasty mating, and all other forms of love. No one was discriminated against because of it—we all respected the gift of a bond, no matter how it arrived.

As we neared the closing beats of the dance, my heart felt lighter than it had in a very long time, and one thing was growing abundantly clear to me: I was the one to blame for the sadness in my life. Reece might have shunned me, but that was only from his world. I'd been the one who'd shunned myself from the rest of them.

A new partner grabbed my hand then, and I noted that he wore the black tunic of the Guardians. Only the Delfora and the Guardian sands were black, and as I lifted my eyes to meet his, I had to blink at what was quite a stunningly sexy Desert-landian.

His skin was dark, only a few shades lighter than the black of his tunic, casting a striking contrast to the pamolsa green of his eyes. He was tall as well, forcing my head to tilt back to take in his features.

"Hello," he murmured, heat flaring in his gaze.

Strangely enough, there was a momentary stirring within me as well, a purely physical reaction in response to his unnatural beauty. We moved together in silence, but our bodies synced better than mine had with any other this moon. When it was time for him to swap out to the last partner of the dance, he side-stepped the Rohami male and swept me along, not missing a beat. I blinked at that but wasn't altogether unhappy to still be in his arms.

When he leaned in, a spicy scent, rich and earthy like the land itself, filled my senses. "Name?" he asked in a smooth, deep voice. Guardians were, in general, powerful due to their close proximity to the sacred lands, and this male was no exception.

"Angel," I replied. "Yours?"

"Darin."

By the way he said it, I got the distinct impression that most beings here would have reacted. That name meant something, only I had no idea what that something was.

His hold on me didn't waver as we continued to twirl. As the final beat trailed away, he spun me out of step, and I found myself much closer to him than was normal. His arm tightened across my hip before sliding over my back. Tilting my head again in an attempt to gauge his expression, a flash of red in my peripheral caught my attention, and that was when my interest in Darin waned

"Is there a reason Reece of Rohami is staring me down like he's about to stride over here and blast my skin from my body with his sand-driven powers?"

Darin's question barely registered as all of my focus was on the desert god. "We're enemies of a sort," I murmured.

"And yet you wear his house."

A chuckle choked from me. "It's complicated, but suffice it to say, he doesn't wish me happiness."

It was Darin's turn to laugh. "It's your lucky day, then, because I might just be the one Desertlandian in this room who doesn't fear Reece."

That allowed me to finally bring my focus back to him. "Who are you that you don't fear someone of his power and reputation?" I asked, moving back a step so we no longer touched.

There was a glimmer in his eyes as they widened minutely. "I'm guessing you're not a local."

"Honor Meadows."

He nodded. "Yes, that makes sense. The lack of wings threw me off, but I can only assume that you're not the typical transcendent."

I shook my head. "You could say that."

He settled into a smile. "I've always thought typical was

overrated." The beat of the next song picked up and he added, "Would you care to dance again?"

"I'm afraid I don't know this one," I said, noticing the other Desertlandians had fallen into a line, everyone in a line facing the same direction, before they all switched to another.

"Well, maybe a refreshment?"

I only hesitated for a beat before deciding that it could be worth exploring that flicker of heat I'd felt before. After all, this was my moon to let loose and start a new journey. "A refreshment would be nice," I said with a nod.

Just as I was about to move out of the way of the line dancers, a flash of sudden and intense heat burned down my spine. Darin's pupils flared as he looked over my head, and I didn't need to turn to know who was behind me. The rumble of Reece's chest rocked through me, and as I started to spin, ready to remind him that he could no longer dictate my life, a firm grip latched onto the base of my ponytail and scarf, tightening as he pulled me back against his body.

"Reece," I hissed out between my teeth. "You have exactly two seconds to let me go, or I *will* rip your arm off."

"Stay still," he growled, holding me almost immobile. He wasn't hurting me—this was a dominance move—but I didn't play those fucking games.

Just as I was gearing up to use my power, Darin pressed in on my front, leaving me sandwiched between the two of them. The guardian was almost Reece's height, and the sensation of being surrounded by powerful males actually dulled some of my anger.

A weakness of the flesh had finally gotten its claws into me.

"Don't push me, *god*," Darin sneered. "Angel is with me tonight, and I will defend her right to choose that."

Moving beyond their energies crashing into mine, I somehow found my independence again. Lifting up on my toes,

I slammed my head back, cracking into the underside of Reece's chin. As soon as his hold loosened, I spun and pummeled my fists into either side of his chest, aiming for the most vulnerable spots on his body.

Reece had no choice but to pull his arms into his sides and protect himself because I might be smaller, but I was far from weak.

Darin stepped in closer again, hands up like he was about to help me. Shooting him a narrow-eyed glare, I snapped, "Stay back. I defend my own honor." With one last spin I turned my body to slam my knee into Reece's side, knocking him out of my way.

Fury beat at me as I stepped out from between them and walked away. "Now you two can kill each other," I called back.

Cursing those sexy-as-fuck, dangerous-as-fuck, and annoying-as-fuck desert males, I never looked back as I headed toward the exit.

This moon was supposed to be a new beginning, but as always, it was off to a rocky start.

CHAPTER TWENTY-TWO

Mera made a move to intercept me, but I waved her off needing a second to cool down. Reece, once again sticking his nose where it wasn't wanted, was ruining the slivers of happiness I'd been desperately trying to bring into my life. What reason could he have for interrupting my time with Darin? Was this the same shit he'd been doing with Len? Could his petty ass really expect me to live alone for the rest of my long life?

I should have stabbed him when I'd had the chance. The next time he tried to interfere, I'd call my blades and he would be bleeding from places that weren't so easy to heal.

When I was halfway across the tented space, a swift wind rushed around me, grating over my exposed skin as the force swept me off my feet. It was such an unexpected attack that by the time I'd registered the hold, I was already shooting up hundreds of feet toward the peak of this giant tent.

Height and speed did not bother me or cause panic, and I already had my weapons in hand by the time I blasted out of a small slit in the apex of this structure. Fresh and surprisingly cool air hit me as I ended up in the now blue-tinged sky, half a mile above the Desertlandians who were reveling in the opening night festivities.

Breathing in deeply, I did not fight the hold. Ochre sands held me, and their fluidity was unaffected by my blades. I also didn't want to shoot my power into it, as two opposing forces of energy could create an explosion, killing innocents below. It was best to find some patience and prepare for who or what had decided to fuck with me now.

By the time the sandstorm stopped its upward sweep, I was ready in my favorite fighting stance holding my favorite weapons—curved blades. This pair were light and agile, responding to my every command and giving me the ability to come in from multiple angles to wound and kill.

The sand that surrounded me wasn't thick enough to obscure my vision as it continued to hold me prisoner, and when no one immediately appeared, I started testing the limits of this barrier. Taking a step forward, the sands followed, and even as I sprinted across the sky, the barrier of sand never left. Using my wings, I attempted to take flight, surprised when I was released to do so, but of course, the moment I tried to head for land, I was caught and flung back up.

I'd only known one being who could control the deserts like this, especially against my power and skill, so there was no surprise when an *asshole of a desert god* rose up through the tent. Unlike me, he was surrounded by his red Rohami sand, but it didn't matter since all sands obeyed his command.

"How dare you!" I snarled, racing as fast as I could, my wings sliding away because I didn't need them. "You have no right to remove my free will. Just because you're stronger here in your homeland, don't think I won't draw on my power and test that theory."

I'd originally decided there were too many innocents below

to use my power, but if Reece didn't release me soon, my priorities might change.

"We need to talk," he said shortly, remaining in a cloud of his sand, "before you make another mistake you'll regret."

If any statement was going to make me see red, it was that one. My speed increased, and when I was close enough for an attack, I returned my blades to the tent and threw myself forward. Hand to hand meant this would last longer.

Reece was going to feel the full brunt of my centuries-old fury toward him.

"You have taken too much from me already," I raged, slamming a fist into his side and cracking ribs with the force. Reece's jaw twitched, but he didn't move. He also didn't fight back. "I've had enough."

Every hit and curse and rage I sent his way he absorbed and healed until I was the very definition of insanity: doing the same thing over and over and expecting a different result. My attacks might be hurting him, but he was so powerful that the pain only lasted a few moments before it healed. If he didn't fight back, I couldn't use more lethal means, which meant... We were having this conversation.

Slowing my assault, I breathed heavily as I stared at him, deflated. "What do you want from me?"

He was a statue, the deep, midnight-blue light of the dark-moon just enough to showcase his godlike features. Staring at him as I was now, it was laughable to think that any other Desertlandian could ever come close to having the raw magnetism of Reece.

"Stay away from Darin."

Stepping into him, I shook my head. "You don't get to dictate my social life."

His smile was a little feral, matching the light in his eyes.

"Actually, Lale, that's exactly what I dictate. Until such a time as I say so, you do not touch, kiss, or fuck any Desertlandian."

As my body jolted, I wasn't fast enough to hide the shock on my face. "I will fuck whomever I want to," I managed to say, feeling the fire of our energies mingling in our close proximity. "You're just going to have to accept that my happiness is no longer yours to control."

His arms shot around me so fast that they were a blur. As they enclosed me tightly, I was barely able to breathe. "Don't push me, Angel," he murmured, and it didn't escape my notice that he used Mera's nickname for me when he was trying to emotionally distance us. Ironic considering how close we were physically.

Jerking my head away, I was just about to throw caution to the wind and rip through this bastard with my energy, when our eyes met. The galaxies buried deep in his irises started to swirl and build, and I felt my skin heat as I registered the roil of energy within me. "What are you doing?" I bit out. "Reece, you can't stir my power like this."

He leaned in closer, breath and scent brushing across my face. "You belong to me, Melalekin of the Honor Meadows. You always have. You will not go near Darin again, or the next time I won't just kick his ass... I'll kill him."

I was frozen in the simmering power of his command, recognizing the true threat in those words. "Was that why you took so long to get up here?"

Reece tilted his head, a cocky expression replacing his previously unreadable one. "Darin thought he was a match for me. He thought he was a match for you. I had to remind him that there's only one who controls all the desert elements here, and that one is me."

"You—" I spluttered. "You're a cocky fuck. Can't you just

be content with controlling the elements? Why do you have to control me as well?"

He leaned in. "You gave me your energy when we were new to these worlds, and it's time I took advantage of that."

Before he could say another word, I lifted my knee and shot it straight into his balls because, god or not, a good whack there hurt all males. Only this wasn't Reece's first trip around the block with me, and he shifted his lower body at the last second, leaving me to hit his thigh. Even worse, I ended up in a slightly more vulnerable position, with my leg locked between his. I could get free, but it would take more time.

"Work with me here," he said, his powerful thighs holding me in stasis. "Is it so hard to not touch another male while we're on this mission?"

I sucked in a deep breath. "Not that it's any of your business, but actually, yes, it is going to be hard because I have newly awoken needs."

Reece's hold grew tighter. "Needs..." he breathed, focus disappearing for a beat before he finally nodded. "I think I have a solution to that."

Before I could figure out what that solution was, he released my leg as his arm snaked around my back, lifting me higher. I barely got a "What the actual fu—" out before he slammed his lips to mine.

He got me for a beat, the feel of his heat and the scent of his body, but before I could register how damn good he tasted, I jerked my knee up again, managing to connect with the part of him I'd been aiming for before: his balls and the now obvious, hard length of his cock.

Hard? Reece was hard...

"Lale, what the fuck?" he groaned, crumpling a touch but not releasing me.

"*What the fuck?* is right," I yelled back. Apparently this was the sentence of the night for both of us. "Why are you kissing me?"

My body was on fire, near trembling at the sensation of that kiss. I remembered the first time our mouths met and how it had near destroyed me. That day I'd been young and naïve, desperate to have whatever part of Reece I could. That woman no longer existed, and now... now he had to earn this moment.

He recovered quickly, and this time when he lifted his head, there was fire burning within those galaxies. "I will fill your needs," he said in a low, hypnotic rumble of words. "While you're in the deserts, there will be no other that touches you. Only me."

I'd never thought that an arrogant, possessive statement like that could break down my walls, but when my body tingled, flutters of arousal settling between my thighs, I gave real consideration to his proposal. Logic had always been a strong asset of mine, and this time was no exception. "Why should I agree to this? You hate me, and I don't want to be used."

Reece laughed, shaking his head. "We are too old for hate now, Lale. Let's look at this as a way to rebuild our relationship. A way to repair old bonds and... move forward."

Exactly what Mera had said, and dammit, it was so tempting.

Sex might be messy, but in the end, I would take any means of destroying the lingering anger between us and the last tendrils of Reece's feeling of betrayal. Our attraction was undeniable, energies all but clashing as fire raced through my veins. The ache in my body was stronger than ever, and when my hips shifted involuntarily, I felt the damp heat between my thighs. My body clearly wanted everything this dominant male could offer.

Before I could second-guess myself, I took a leaf out of Mera's guide to life and threw caution to the wind. Pushing up and forward, I wrapped my arms around his neck and jerked him closer, my mouth on his. This time when he opened his lips, our tongues collided.

Urgency built in seconds, his hands slipping down my body to strip away my tunic, his energy helping with that. My nails scratched him as I tore through his tunic, ripping it at the seams, needing to feel all of him. Our pants somehow disappeared, and when his hard cock fell into my hand, already pulsing, I tore my lips from his and moaned.

It hadn't been like this our first time when Reece had taken it slow, both of us learning our way through sex. This was different, urgent and fierce... and exactly what I needed. Reece lifted me so I could wrap my legs around his waist, bringing our naked bodies firmly together. His hands landed on my ass as our lips met again, and with one sudden thrust, he was pushing into my wet heat. My tight muscles held him for a moment before the burn of pleasure and pain had me jerking against him, needing to feel his full length.

Some of the sands holding us up moved behind me so that I was resting against a wall of red and ochre while Reece slammed into me. "Yes, fuck, don't stop," I moaned, needing this hard, punishing sex. Fury and frustration and tension built deep in my body, swirling and expanding as I clawed at his back. When I couldn't take it any longer, the pressure exploded, and I screamed my pleasure, feeling grateful that we were well above the land, hidden by the sands.

Reece didn't stop there, though, changing his rhythm so he could move slower but deeper, sending spikes of new sensations into my center.

"Lale," he groaned, movements more jagged before he dropped his head and growled against my skin. "No one touches you," he bit out, "no one sees you naked. You belong to me until I say different."

The second round of pleasure that had been building within me exploded, and I cried out, voice hoarse as my vision darkened for a beat. Reece lifted me higher as he thrust, and I was so turned on that every time he moved my pussy made a wet sound. A sound which, until this moment, I had not realized would be so damn sexy.

"Do you agree?"

I had no idea what he was talking about, my well-fucked brain slower than normal. "Agree with what?"

He didn't waste a minute. "While you're in the Desert Lands, you belong to me, Lale."

The meaning behind the words finally registered, and with that, I barely managed to hold onto myself.

Belong to him? Wait... what the hell was happening here?

CHAPTER TWENTY-THREE

"Wait—" I had to clear my throat because there was no moisture in my mouth—it was all in my vagina apparently. "Isn't this an indication that I agreed?"

His expression darkened, but he didn't stop moving within me. A decidedly unfair way to have a debate. "I need you to say the words," he said softly. "Our time here is a chance to lay the ghosts to rest. To move forward. But you need to be all in."

"How would it work?" I asked, proud my words were somewhat clear.

Reece changed our angle, the sands allowing him to place me horizontally so he could thrust harder and faster. Logical thought was fading again, and I knew this bastard was doing this on purpose. "While we are on this mission in the Desert Lands," he rasped out, answering my question, "you will come to me and only me to fulfill the needs of your body. New or dark-moon, it does not matter. Another man will not touch you, and you will not touch yourself."

I was shaking my head, but he growled and cut me off before I could get a word in.

"Nonnegotiable. I've been obsessed with you for years, Lale, and the longer I ignored it, the worse it grew. So for now, your body, your pleasure... and your fucking pussy belong to me. At least until we get this out of our system."

As if to prove his point, he allowed the sand to take all of my weight and used his hands to trace across my skin, fingertips swirling over my nipples and down the muscles of my abdomen before he reached my clit. His strokes there were firm, moving in time to his thrusts, and I was too far gone to do anything except moan and try not to fall into the spirals of my impending orgasm.

"Agree, Angel!" he said on a groan. For all of his control, he was affected too, and that was a powerful feeling.

"I know what you're doing," I bit back, desperate not to come but knowing I was literally a second from being sucked into the abyss of pleasure that was coating me like endless space.

Reece snorted out a rough laugh. "I doubt that very much."

This response took me by surprise, and my lack of argument spurred Reece on. His body got harder and hotter, every part of him seemed to grow larger as he dropped his head down to wrap his lips and tongue around my nipple. I screamed, unable to stop the orgasm no matter how much I wanted to.

This time, though, he came with me, cock jerking as I felt the hot explosion of his power and essence inside. We rode out this orgasm for a long time, an impressively long amount of time, and I allowed myself to truly consider his proposal.

There were flaws to the plan, so many ways it could go wrong, but after years of missing Reece and wishing for a way to repair the broken bonds between us, I was tempted to go *all in*. "There's a chance this could work," I said when I could finally talk.

He lifted his head from the nipple that he'd claimed a moment ago.

"A great chance," he said.

I nodded. "Even if it is hate-fucking, it's a way to cleanse us of our anger and give us a second chance at friendship. But we're going to need some ground rules."

Our bodies were still joined, neither one of us ready to move away. And I clearly had his full attention.

"We cannot get emotionally attached," I said bluntly. "At the end of this, we both have to walk away." His brow furrowed, but I pushed on. "I will not touch another, but I expect the same from you while this agreement is in place."

"Done," he said without hesitation.

I took another deep breath. "And I think it's best that we don't get our friends involved. This is just between us."

His gaze darkened, and I could feel the rumble deep in his body, which was still intimately entwined with mine. That last rule wasn't sitting right with him, but I pushed on anyway. "This lasts as long as we're in the Desert Lands, and then... we let the past go and allow ourselves a different future."

His eyes seared my soul. "Okay, Angel. If you want rules, we can have them. As long as you remember"—his power slid along his hard cock and into my pussy, sending vibrating shocks of pleasure through me—"that as long as we're in the Desert Lands. No fighting. No anger. No enemies."

Those words were branded in my energy now, filling my mind and overwhelming my senses. Reece, jaw tense, finally nodded and in the same breath drove forward again, sliding inside of me in time to the pulse of his power.

My body was already arching up, unable to handle the sensations. "Did you not come before?" I moaned, confused by how damn hard he still was.

A low, dark laugh escaped. "I can remain hard for as long as needed, through as many *hate fucks* as you require." His lips twisted over those words, and I briefly wondered why before he growled, "Enough talking."

After that I forgot everything except living in the moment. Up until this point I'd been somewhat submissive with Reece since sex was not an expertise of mine, but I was done with that now, wanting to take back some control.

Tightening my legs around his waist, I adjusted the position of my hands, preparing to move. Reece figured out what I was doing a split second before I shifted, and even though he attempted to counter—to keep me locked under his grip—he was too late.

Spinning our positions, I used a cross-armed hold to keep him pinned under me, and despite my disadvantages of size and reach, I managed to slide onto his body, riding that hard length as I chased my next orgasm.

"I am not submissive to you, Reece," I rumbled against his mouth, then bit down on his lush bottom lip, drawing the flesh into my mouth and pressing hard enough that if he hadn't been a god with a god's strength, I would have broken his skin. "If this is going to work, it has to include mutual respect."

We were talking—okay I was talking and his eyes were darkening—and yet neither of us missed a beat in the fucking. My lower half was a mass of raging energy, an orgasm so close, but this time I refused to allow myself to fall into that pleasure. Not until I had my answer.

Reece's powerful body surged up under me, his control over the sands giving him the angle needed to slam into me, and as I came down to meet him as well, there was a tremble in my thighs that told me I was going to explode very soon.

"Dammit, Reece! Meet me— Holy fuck," I choked in some air. "Meet me half... way."

"All the way, Lale," he murmured, his voice as hard as the

cock driving into me. "I don't do anything halfway, which you'll find out very soon."

I couldn't stop the cry spilling from my lips as he sent me over the edge again. I knew I'd lost that round, but I wouldn't beat myself up over it. There were going to be many more rounds.

A fact that filled me with both anticipation and dread.

Hate-fucking or not, I had to be able to walk away when it was all over.

I'd already left a broken heart in this desert once before, and I couldn't do it again.

Whatever happened between us, I needed to protect myself.

It was the only way to keep my reborn world intact.

CHAPTER TWENTY-FOUR

By the time I was coming for the fourth—*fifth?*—time, exhaustion had its hold on me, and despite my attempt at dominance, the desert god was just too powerful for me to best.

At least not this moon.

I might still have my seat on top, but we both knew who held all the control.

His eyes darkened as the stars and planets swirled in their depths, and when he finally came again, the fire that burned between us soared higher. It felt like the flames that had been burning under my skin for months were finally freed. I had no physical fire like Mera, instead mine was an internal Nexus flame that never went out.

In the midst of my pleasure, my wings sprang free without any command from me. As I collapsed onto Reece's chest, his arms closed around me, and I felt him stroke my feathers. Almost as if he needed to reassure himself that I was really here with him. Of course, that moment was over as quickly as it began when his hold loosened and he wrapped his hands around my biceps, lifting me up and off him. My wings retracted in the same beat.

It took forever for that slow slide of his cock to leave my body, and as he'd stated earlier, he was still hard. Veins pulsed up the sides, leading to the thick head, which was darker than the rest of him. The evidence of our pleasures glistened along the length, and I was tempted to lean over and run my tongue across him because, apparently, I was just fucked up like that when it came to Reece.

Fucked in all ways.

"Keep looking at my cock like that, Angel, and you will be riding it again."

That warning snapped me out of whatever trance I was under, and I shook my head to clear it while pushing myself up to stand on shaky legs. A quick glace around told me that my tunic and pants were nowhere in sight. Actually, even Reece's clothes were missing.

"You tore them to pieces," he said drily, noticing my search.

Closing my eyes, I was hit with memories of the frenzy I'd felt. I'd been out of control, filled with burning need. Need that was rising again, until I managed to push it away.

"No one can know what we're doing," I reminded him once I got myself under control, "which obviously means we can't wander into the tent naked and covered in the fluids of... yeah."

His smile was slow, gaze lingering on my mouth before it slowly rose and trapped me in its intensity. "I enjoy seeing you covered in my essence, Lale. Maybe I will keep you like that."

Before I could shout at *this frustrating god* one more time, his sands tightened around us to form a heavy barrier, blocking my view of the deserts. No one could see us cocooned like this, and I'd forgotten how safe I felt enveloped in Reece's power.

I'd forgotten a lot of things or, at least, convinced myself that I remembered incorrectly. Like the spice of his taste, how it drew me in and addicted me. Made me want him again, even though I was barely standing from the last sex session.

My clarity after the fact forced me to recognize just how much trouble I was in, but even with that knowledge, I would not break our deal—mostly because I didn't want to and a small part because I would not give Reece the satisfaction.

I would get through this without growing attached. I would use this as a cathartic exercise before I released him forever.

Turning away from the intense male, I tried to find some space in the tight bubble of sand. As I stood, a slow, hot drip of cum made its way down my inner thigh, and I wondered—despite his words from before—why he hadn't cleaned us up.

This was his essence, his lifeforce, and usually, when eternal and powerful beings had sex, we did not allow the aftermath to remain for long, lest it be contained and used against us. Or so I'd heard.

But Reece was making no move to clean either of us. "Do you want me to use my energy to destroy what remains of our power?" I asked, breaking the silence as I waved my hand toward my slightly parted legs, in case he mistook my intentions.

His heavy gaze traced across and down the junction of my thighs. "No," he rasped, and then as he took a step toward me, the sands tightened even further before the mass started to move us. It was a quick jolt that sent me forward; Reece caught me before I could catch myself. I didn't fight his hold since we had made this deal, and if nothing, I was a transcendent that kept my word.

"No?"

The hands on my arms tightened. "No. It remains until I say differently."

What in the...? "Are you out of your fuck—"

He all but lifted me into him, a deep rumbling sound in his

chest. "I already told you: I want you to wear my essence. I will clean you when we reach the tent, but until then..."

I stared, unblinking, up at him, finally understanding why Mera called him Shadow the Second. The Desertlandians weren't usually so animalistic and possessive in their claiming. What he was doing now—*this marking of his territory*—was a beastlike trait.

For a brief moment, I was tempted to challenge his hold, but the logical part of my brain reminded me that I had agreed to his rules. Rules which included allowing him to claim my body until we were done. It was counterproductive to be fighting him all of the way.

Come on, Melalekin. You want this.

And there was the other part of my mind, which wasn't so logical. The less logical side was where I acknowledged that while this was a new experience for me, surprisingly... I did want it. The very possessiveness I'd always enviously watched between Mera and Shadow was front and center, claiming me in almost all ways. It appeared that I'd finally found a growling, demanding, sexually dominant asshole of a man.

I'd gotten my wish, even if it wasn't quite in the way I'd anticipated. But still, I'd take it for now, and as long as Reece didn't step over the line, maybe... just maybe, I'd even enjoy it.

He released my arms as the cloud of sand slowed its arc, descending for a few seconds before it came to a halt. I had no idea where we were until the barrier faded from around us, leaving only the platform below our feet. Familiar tent flaps came into view, and now it was clear how Reece planned on getting us cleaned up and unseen by our friends.

He stepped off the platform first, and I went to follow, only to have him reach out and wrap his hands around my waist, pulling me into him once more. "If you're naked, you're mine," he said near my ear, the hot brush of his breath over sensitive skin sending a shiver across my body.

He didn't wait for my response, and I honestly had no idea what to say to that. As he walked us inside the empty tent, our bodies remained flush, and the friction of our movements against my naked flesh...

Two seconds ago I would have sworn that there was no way I could have sex again tonight, but right now, I could call myself a liar.

Reece entered his bedroom, which was the largest and most opulent in an already luxurious setup. When we reached his bathing area, the water started before he got to the glass tub, and by the time he stepped under with me still firmly in his arms, the warm water was at full stream.

My eyes closed as I tilted my head back; the dual pleasures of a shower and Reece's skin had me existing in a perfect moment.

"Some things never change," he murmured, and my eyes flew open again so I could see the expression that went with that statement.

His eyes were hooded, features shadowed as his skin appeared even darker than usual, his power riding him. "You've always loved the liquid lifeforce of a world," he murmured. "Even when your wings were a deterrent, you figured out how to swim, and you've never looked back."

My wings were designed for air, lacking the protective coat that winged creatures of the water had. For years I'd fought against them as they dragged me under the lakes and oceans of various worlds, until eventually they'd either adapted or grown strong enough to handle swimming.

"You remember so much," I noted, not sure how I felt about that. My voice lowered. "Sometimes I wish you didn't. There are parts of our past I'd really like to forget."

Like my betrayal and his hatred toward me.

Reece crowded in, pushing us both under the steady stream until it coated my hair and face, which distorted my view of him when he said, "I wish that too, Lale, but what's done is done. We cannot change the past, only the future."

For Reece, that was almost a positive statement, and before I could say another word, he cupped his hands and gathered the liforina. He rubbed the water between his hands, and I noted that there was a slight bubbling as if he was activating the cleansing properties.

As he moved that liquid toward me, I quickly said, "I can do it!"

He snorted out a laugh. "Not a fucking chance, Angel. As I said before, when you're naked, you and your gorgeous body belong to me."

The dueling nature of my feelings over that statement was intense, but I couldn't just let him control and dominate every part of me. "Listen, asshole," I bit out. "I can try and work with your dominant nature because we made this deal and that includes me accepting who you are, but for the love of warriors everywhere, don't forget who I am. You can only push me so far—"

His hands slipped between my thighs, and as the friction of the water and his fingers hit my pussy, I actually jerked into him. Before I could recover, he stroked me again, moving deeper. Panting, I tried to back away, only there was nowhere to go. I mean, I could have exited the tub, but... let's not get too dramatic.

"I'm going to clean you now," he said in that same low, soft, don't-fuck-with-me voice. "I want you to stay completely still, or our friends, who are about to walk into the tent, will hear your screams."

My eyes were spitting fire at him, but since I was the one

who'd decided this had to remain a secret, I couldn't break that rule in the first few hours of our arrangement. Going as still as I could, I focused on breathing in and out as Reece ran his finger along my slit, parting my folds so he could push one finger and then a second inside of me. He had big hands and knew what to do with them as he slid deeper, curling his finger at just the right angle that intense pleasure shocked me into almost crying out. I caught the sound a second before it left my mouth, and as his smirk grew, I wished I could punch him.

Of course, I was too busy trying not to scream while keeping my legs from collapsing under me. Which was not at all helped when Reece brought his other hand in to "clean" me as well, those fingers tracing across my clit.

Fuck. I murmured his name, feeling the loss of control storming toward me, and just when I was about to come, he increased the pressure. I let out a silent scream, my mouth opening as my head dropped backward, the energy reverberating within me almost sending me to my knees. Or it would have if Reece's hold hadn't kept me standing.

After what felt like centuries, the orgasm finally died down to a manageable level, and Reece slowed his strokes until he finally slipped his fingers from my body. As I trembled, hands still gripping the wall like it was my lifeline, he turned and stepped out of the bath, the burst of his power all I felt before he was dry, dressed, and gone from the room.

Leaving me a hot fucking mess—*a satisfied hot mess*—who had gotten myself in way over my head.

CHAPTER TWENTY-FIVE

After Reece's energy disappeared from his bedroom, I wondered why he'd left without taking a final pleasure for himself too. He'd been hard, those veins pulsing along his shaft, and it felt strangely generous for a male who was just "hate-fucking" to get me out of his system to do that.

I mean, I wasn't a complete idiot... I knew our feelings were more complex than just "hate," but it had been the defining emotion between us for too long to ignore its influence in our newly formed agreement.

Deciding I was going to drive myself crazy if I pondered his every move during our time in the deserts, I let it go for now and finish cleaning my skin. It didn't take long, and determined to get out of Reece's bedroom before anyone noticed, I left the tub and dried myself off with a little energy. Thankfully, when I emerged into his room, there was a set of clothing sitting on Reece's bed. Another generous act for the broody god.

Shrugging on the tunic and pants, which were an exact match to what I'd worn earlier, I ran a hand through the tangle of my hair, smoothing it out with a hot brush of energy. By the time I emerged, there wasn't a single sliver of evidence that anything had happened. And even better, no one was in the lounging area to see me sneak from his room.

But... wait, Reece had said they were entering the tent earlier. Sending my senses wider, I found that none of them were here at all. Had Reece lied to me about the others returning to keep me quie—

An explosion of energy rocked through the tent, slamming against my own protective wall of power. Reacting on instinct, I called my weapons, then my armor in the next beat. If the sound of the attack could penetrate the silence of this tent, it had to be close.

Tapping into my bond with Mera, I was relieved that she felt somewhat calm and in no pain. She was my priority, and it pissed me off that I'd lingered longer in that bathroom, caught up in lusting over Reece, while she was possibly out there in danger. If anything happened to her because I had newly awokened hormones, I'd never forgive myself.

Outfitted and ready for battle, I sped across the pillows and burst out the entrance. As I rolled free and leapt to my feet, the true scope of the commotion hit all my senses, and I was prepared for an impending strike.

The dull blue shine of the dark-moon was enhanced by fire, no doubt courtesy of Shadow and Mera, as many of the tents around ours were burning. Smoke obstructed my view, but I could hear the battle and smell the energy in the air. Coordinating energy. This was more than just a random attack... it'd been planned.

Needing to move closer to the heart of this battle, I stepped into the smoke, senses on high alert. Even without sight, I was hardly vulnerable. I heard the swish of a blade a second before an attacker came into view. Shifting my stance to the left, just enough for the weapon to slide past me, I was now facing an assailant clad head-to-toe in a black bodysuit. Taking advantage of our close proximity, I struck out in two quick blows, aiming to mortally wound them, only to find my blades glanced off their suit.

My weapons were ancient and power-infused, so the only way that could happen...

Through the smoke, I focused on their suit, noting the distinct glint as it was illuminated by sparks from a nearby fire. Dammit. This was not just any outfit, but one enforced with the armored shell of the *deker beetle*—a furious desert predator, even if it was only a few inches wide. Its shell was nearly impenetrable, and this asshole had taken advantage of that by securing thousands across their suit.

Not that it was going to save them. I was trained to spot weaknesses and had already noticed a few spots where the shells weren't perfectly overlapping. Releasing my curved blades, I sent them back to my room in the tent before reaching out to the Honor Meadows to bring forth a different set. These were my *skintas,* thin, almost circular blades with a fine, needle-like tip.

The suited figure jerked back as I struck a second time, my skinta sliding between two shells right near their ribs; a deliberate choice to attack their dominant sword-arm side first. As I jerked my weapon free, I was satisfied to note that the injury had already caused them to lose strength, their sword dropping a few inches.

They compensated by roaring loudly and switching their blade to the other hand, attacking with a surprising level of ambidexterity. Most well-trained warriors were good on one side and adequate on the other, but this one was good on both.

We struck and parried, metal clashing as we danced, and all the while I sent my senses out to make sure Mera and my friends were okay. From what I could tell, there were at least a dozen darkly shrouded attackers, but it seemed that all of us were holding our own and that was a relief.

Focusing all of my attention on my opponent now, I picked up speed, ready to finish this. Exploiting more imperfections in the suit, I sliced out in three quick thrusts, cutting into their right shoulder and left thigh and slicing a deep gouge near their cheek. At this point their strength started to wane, and with one last lunge forward, I flicked the tip of my weapon up under the neck of their disguise, hoping that the small slip of material there was the key to unmasking them. They tried to back away, but there was not a hope in hell of that happening.

These assholes had attacked my friends. My family. My pack.

With a deft flick of my wrist, I got enough leverage in the material to slide it up and over their head. Long black hair came into view first, thick and lustrous as it burst free from its confines. It was followed by a familiar face.

"Zena!" I spat. "Are you fucking kidding me?"

Tsuma's daughter glared up at me. "You have no idea what you've stumbled into here, Melalekin. You should have stayed on your world because now you'll die here just like your sister."

My blade was at her exposed throat in a heartbeat, and she never blinked an eye, clearly prepared to die. "Why have you attacked us?" I demanded.

She shook her head, a dark laugh spilling from her lips. "Always the last to put the pieces together."

She was goading me. It was a classic move to get me to lose control and do something stupid, but even with my rebirth, I was too well-trained to fall for that. I also had a very good idea why they were attacking us: my suspicions of Tsuma were correct. But it never hurt to see if she would reveal additional information.

Pressing the blade deep enough to break skin, I smiled.

"Spell it out for those of us too stupid to put it together."

Her eyes, dark pits of midnight green, spat fire at me, but there wasn't much she could do. "You don't belong here Melalekin. You don't belong with Reece."

Again she was trying to distract me, and I'd be a liar if I didn't feel a pang at that jab.

"Angel," Mera shrieked, appearing through the smoke, fireballs in her hands as she glared down at Zena. "Who is this bitch, and how do we kill her?"

Zena's eyes widened, and I was fairly certain she had no idea how to take the heavily pregnant redhead who was literally holding flames in her hands and casually talking about murder.

"This is an old family friend of Reece's actually," I said shortly.

Mera snorted. "My god, he has horrendous taste in friends. We should still kill her; he won't even notice."

I tried not to laugh, lest my prisoner think I was weakening. "Reece would want you to remove the blade, *lunta*," Zena sneered at me, insulting my heritage with that Desertlandian slur.

Kicking out, I slammed my boot into her side, and even with the protective shells, her forehead wrinkled as she winced.

"Firstly, I won't remove my blade," I said softly, infusing into my tone every ounce of the deadly intention I felt. "Secondly, if you insult my family one more time, I won't wait for Reece to finish the job. I'm giving him a moment because I know your family was important to his, but my patience is very thin."

Her bravado was all but gone now, the light brown of her skin paling to the point that she was turning splotchy.

Mera laughed, her fire fading away as she relaxed by my side. "And that's why you don't fuck with my best friend."

Taking my eyes from Zena for a beat, I met Mera's warm

gaze. "How is everyone else? Do they have it all handled?"

"Of course they do," she shrugged. "These dumbasses vastly underestimated us; most of them weren't even armed. Shadow rounded up three of them, Reece a few others, and you've got ass-eyes here, who looks like she swallowed an entire lemon with that sour expression."

Her observation was acute. "This one is well-trained," I said, keeping my voice even. "Wearing protective shells."

"None of the others have that." Her statement confirmed what I'd been guessing—Zena was the leader of this little attack. But did her orders come from Tsuma?

"Did you find out exactly what this is all about?" I asked. "Is everyone from Rohami?"

Reece stepped out of the smoke then, his gaze running over me so fast I doubted anyone else would have noticed. I wasn't sure if he was checking me for injuries or just checking me out, but either way, heat blossomed in my chest despite our current situation.

"There are members of almost all the clans," he said flatly.

"They're part of whoever is attempting to wake the ancient gods?"

He nodded, looking grim, and whatever lust I'd been feeling faded under the worry of that statement.

"None of them are the leaders or higher-up family members," I said softly, having already felt their energy.

Reece's lips thinned; his brow furrowed. "I know. This attack was either a distraction or a ridiculous attempt to cast suspicion onto lower members so the higher-ups could continue on with their task."

"We need to get them to talk now," I said in a harsh bark. "We need to know what their plans are and why this gathering was called."

Before it was too late.

CHAPTER
TWENTY-SIX

Reece, ignoring the blade I still held against the throat of one of his oldest friends, reached down and hauled Zena up. He used one hand, wrapping it around her arm and right shoulder, and even I was a little impressed by that display of strength. "The others are inside so we can question them," he rumbled. I'd only heard him this pissed a few times—usually directed at me. "They'll tell us everything before we're done."

Zena dropped her head back and laughed, the sound tinged with a touch of mental instability. "You're too late. We've set forth a ritual from here, using energy from all the dynasties. Then, in six or so moons the first power moon in centuries will rise. Twins. This is the moment we've been waiting for, and it's finally our time to rule it all."

Reece paused halfway in the open door to his tent, Zena still effortless held in his grip. "If you have the power moon, why did you bother with the ritual from this gathering?"

I interrupted before she could speak. "What the hell is a power moon?"

It was rare that I didn't have at least an idea of what

someone was talking about, especially when it came to power. Power and the Desert Lands were somewhat expertise's of mine.

He briefly met my gaze. "I've only heard of one, just a few months before I was born. It's said that for a brief moment, the moon splits into two and fills our land with primal energy. It's a time of new awakenings and rebirths."

Deep in his eyes, those galaxies swirled, and I read between the lines. Just before his birth... Was that how his parents had been able to conceive in the Delfora?

Reece continued inside, and as I went to follow, Mera grabbed my arm. "This power moon is bad, right?" she whispered.

Swallowing hard, I sought words to explain when I didn't completely understand myself. "I've never heard of or read about this moon," I admitted, annoyed by this fact. "But in theory, if what Reece said is correct... Yeah, that's the sort of event that can bring about world-ending change."

Mera let out a deep sigh as we entered the lounging area to find Shadow and the others standing before a line of Desert-landians. Each of them was on their knees, held down with Reece's sand, and they had been unmasked.

I recognized a few of them, including Dally and Fleur, also Tsuma's children.

Edging my way closer to the group, I kept my weapons at hand because we had no idea what tricks these assholes had up their sleeves. It made no sense that they'd attacked us as they had, especially Reece. Among the sands, he was near unbeatable.

"Your princeps have been called," Reece said, walking along the line. "Might as well confess now, and I can see if the council will spare your lives."

A threat that would work only if the princeps weren't all in on it.

No one said a word, each of the prisoners staring ahead with blank expressions. Zena had even lost her anger, focused on the tent wall. Shifting around Reece, I moved as close as I could without putting myself in striking reach. Not that I was worried about an attack—we far outpowered them—but I didn't want to kill anyone before we got our answers.

"It's not adding up," I said in a low voice as I mulled it over.

Reece heard me, and I could feel his heat sliding down my spine as he pressed closer. "What are you sensing?"

"They're not worried or trying to escape. All of them are just sitting and waiting like they knew—"

"I would call for their princeps before taking any action," Reece finished in a growl.

I nodded. "Yes. More and more this is looking like a distraction."

Zena's gaze finally left the wall, lifting to focus on us, her lips tilting into a smirk. "Always too slow to stop the inevitable from happening. While we have been keeping you busy, our parents ensured that all the gathered energy was set into motion, building below the sand rivers. It will continue to build as they head toward the Delfora, shrouding them until the very moment they need to arrive in the sacred lands. It's a flawless plan, and there's nothing you can do to stop them."

"Is the gathered energy just to hide their progress toward the Delfora?" I asked. "Or is there more that it's needed to achieve?"

Her eyes were laughing at me as she preened, arrogant in her supposed success. "Even with the moon, we couldn't get through the valley of the dead without a boost of power—power from all the dynasties since all of our dead guard the burial grounds. This was an easy solution."

I wasn't the only one who fell silent as the true implications of that hit us. The Delfora was well protected, but there were ways to counter it. Ways Tsuma had clearly put into effect.

Reece was furious, the heat coming off him near inferno level. "For this, you and your family will die," he said without inflection, despite his fury.

In response, Zena just laughed again, and some of the others in the line joined in.

"What an annoying fuck," I heard Mera snipe. "Can we kill her now and save ourselves the trouble later?"

Shadow laughed, a rumbling sound of darkness. "Patience, Sunshine. She will get what's coming to her."

Reece lowered himself, crouching in front of Zena, and for a second, a flash of longing passed over her face before she covered it up with another blank look.

"Why would you betray our dynasty? Our people?" he asked her, his sands spilling out and surrounding them, heat building as they did.

She cleared her throat more than once. "We applied for extra energy sources," she finally said. "Over and over. When you didn't take the role of princeps, it should have gone to us. To mother. But she was always denied. Eventually, we decided to stop asking and start taking."

Reece released his next breath in a slow hiss. "Your family is very powerful, and the reason you've been denied more is that it would shift the balance and equality of our people. Not to mention, your love of power makes you a terrible candidate for princeps. Which is why I voted against your family every time."

Her gasp was loud as she pressed a hand to her shell suit. "You voted against us? We thought you were the one vote we had in our favor."

Reece didn't bother to sugarcoat it for her. "Family friend or not, power corrupts within your aura. You are not worthy."

Zena tilted her head back, looking like she was about to start yelling.

"Shut the hell up, Z," Dally, her brother growled, shutting her down. "You've already given the bastard god too much information."

Reece didn't respond to the insult or even acknowledge that another had spoken. He simply rose and turned to the rest of us, indicating we should close in ranks. I sent my weapons into the bedroom as I joined the others, moving away from the line of Desertlandians on their knees.

Reece's sand power formed a wall between them and us. "As expected, this entire event was a setup from the start," he said, "and it seems we are now on a countdown to the power moon. We must reach the Delfora before then and ensure this plan never comes to pass."

"How do we know which of the princeps are in on it?" I asked him.

His expression darkened further. "My sands are out gathering information, but now that I know what to look for, I can see the energy sources running through the Ostealon. It's clear who has had a hand in this, and from what I can see, none of them are princeps. These are all lesser members wanting to step up in power."

That was why Tsuma had touched Reece's tent, when she'd been there. She'd been marking the spot, preparing the power to span out from all the dynasties.

"I've felt no pull on my energy," Shadow said at a dull roar, his rage palpable. "None on mine or Mera and the baby." His eyes turned to his mate. "Right, Sunshine?"

"Right," she said quickly. "I feel great, and the baby is kicking the shit out of my internal organs as usual."

"Their plan is subtler than that," I said, piecing it together. "As Reece said, unless you're looking for it, you wouldn't notice the network now joining all of us together. The Ostealon is a central gathering spot where all the desert rivers converge. From here, they could send the power straight to the Delfora and no one would feel anything until it was too late."

"I've cut the ties now," Reece said in a huff, "but the energy has already started to swell within the rivers. It will be enough to get them through the Delfora and hide their path. We would be wasting our time to follow. Instead, we must get there first."

"They didn't count on all of us being here," Lucien said, his fangs extended as adrenaline from the previous fight still raced under his skin. "They know we can stop them, which is why this battle went into play—a distraction so they had a head start to hide and get moving."

I stilled, my eyes meeting Reece's. "There's still time," I said. "We just have to get to the Delfora before the power moon."

"We need to hurry then," Len said in a rush, and I noted he was once again dressed in his silvers. "Even though I have no idea how these morons think they can control ancient gods when they wake them."

Or Death, if it came to that.

Myth says that until the gods are at full power, they will be beholden to those who drag them from the sands.

We all looked at Galleli, letting those words marinate. Tsuma had to have a plan for the gods, and whether she was fighting in a class above her own or not, the fervor for power had already warped her mind past the point of return. She was more than prepared to risk life as we all knew it for a chance at godlike-power.

"We can't let this happen," Alistair said softly, his skin

looking dry even as his eyes were bright. "It will not just impact this world, but all of them."

Mera sighed. "Not like we can ever just have a regular disaster. Nope. We always have to have the sort of disaster that ends life as we know it."

She pressed a hand to her stomach, and despite the sarcasm in her tone, we all saw her fear. We felt her fear. Each new member of our family was another member we had to keep safe.

"We still have time," I said again, voice stronger than ever. "We can get there first. We can stop them."

I wasn't usually the cheerleader type, but hope and purpose were powerful motivators.

"I agree," Reece said, backing me, much to everyone's surprise.

That was the point they all appeared to notice our lack of trying to rip each other's heads off. "We reached a truce," I said in a rush, needing a temporary explanation, "until we sort out the shit going on in this world."

Reece nodded. "There's no time for internal battles. Our only chance for success is if we all work together."

"I agree," Shadow said shortly. "And we all will, except Mera."

She swung on him like a boxer ready for the fight of her life. "Excuse the fuck out of me? What did you just say?"

Shadow didn't bend an inch. His mate might be able to get what she wanted out of him most of the time, but now that we knew how dangerous it could end up being, he was unmovable. "Ancient and dangerous power and spells are in play here," he told her in his low rumble. "We have a child on the way, a powerful child, and the ancients might be able to utilize that pure energy for the final stages of their awakening."

Mera opened her mouth, eyes spitting flames, but no words

emerged. She wanted to argue, that much was clear, but she couldn't. Finally, she turned to me. "Is that true?" Her trust in me was unparalleled. I hated the thought that we were about to be separated, but the truth was, I had to agree with Shadow.

"There is a good possibility," I told her. "Doing the calculations, I'd say there's a seventy percent chance they would take you and your baby. A growing god-child is filled with the energy of creation. An energy that fades as we age, but in those first few years, it's a remarkable power."

Mera's face crumpled, and I barely held myself together as I pulled her into a hug. "I'm so sorry," I whispered. "I don't want you out of my sight, but if anything happened to you or the baby, it would destroy us all."

A single sob escaped before she drew on her strength, pulling away from me and looking perfectly calm. "If it was only my safety, nothing would stop me from being with you on this mission. But I'm a mom now, and I have a responsibility to this baby."

Shadow wrapped her up from behind, and my hands fell away as he pulled her closer. "I will take you to the library, reinforce the security, and bring Inky and Midnight back. Along with Gaster, you will be as safe there as anywhere in the Solaris System."

Mera nodded, her face still set. "As long as you keep me updated as many times a damn day as you can."

"All day, Sunshine," Shadow said in that tone he reserved just for her. "I will also close down the doorways to the library to ramp up the protections. It should all be over before you know it."

"Doubt that," I heard her mutter, but she didn't argue again.

This fight was not to be hers, but for the rest of us, it was a different story.

We were now in a race against time, once again set to save

the worlds or die trying. The odds of that were ones I refused to calculate, even though deep in my heart I knew the truth.

There was a possibility that not all of us would survive this mission.

CHAPTER TWENTY-SEVEN

None of us did goodbyes well, but we all took the few extra seconds to hug Mera. Lucien, Len, and Reece all whispered their goodbyes. Galleli was a silent exchange, and Alistair went last. I didn't like the look on his face as he held her tight.

Fuck the statistics. I could not lose anyone to these lands... not again.

When I was the only one left for a goodbye, Mera threw herself at me. "Please don't die," she said into my shoulder. "Promise me. The Nexus is too temperamental for us to trust that we'd return that way again."

"I promise," I replied without hesitation. No part of me was leaving this world again. "I'll be back. I've got a baby to spoil and eventually win over with chocolate."

Mera chuckled through her tears. "Yes, remember that. You're going to be the favorite aunt who lets my beast-baby get away with everything."

It was a future I was desperate to have. "You know it."

Shadow stepped in then. "I'll return her to the library, get everything in place, and then meet you wherever you are on the journey," he told Reece as he wrapped Mera in his arms.

"Can you just doorway everyone to the Delfora now?" Mera asked him.

He shook his head. "No, it would take all of my power and more to open a doorway close to the Delfora and transport others. I could take myself there, but no one else."

And we all knew the beast couldn't defeat Tsuma and the others without Reece.

"There's no rush," Reece reminded her. "We can't stop them until they arrive in the sacred lands, which could be no earlier than the approximate day of the power moon. Best we save all of our energy and not fight the deserts on our way to the Delfora."

He turned to Shadow then. "We would understand if you decided to stay with Mera. I can call for you if it looks like we need the help."

That offer was very tempting to Shadow, as was obvious by the dark burst of power that shot around us. If there was one thing this beast hated, it was not being close to his mate.

"I need to be here," he finally said. "I need to make sure that this danger to our family does not come to pass."

Reece nodded once, and in the same beat, dropped the sands that had been forming the wall between us and the others. They were all in the same spot, held down with more of his energy.

"While Shadow is gone," Reece said, voice much colder now that we had an audience. "We will gather supplies and find the fastest vessel. We need to get onto the eastern stream before this new-moon."

Mera all but pouted. "I wanted to see the sand rivers the most. There's not even any danger this far out from the Delfora. You said you can take yourself closer, right?"

She turned her sad eyes to the ground, and Shadow groaned, rubbing a hand over his face. "Two hours, Mera," he eventually bit out. "I will give you two hours on the vessel and then we head to the library, no more arguments."

Her head jerked up, and somehow she refrained from bouncing on the spot. "That would be wonderful," she said sedately.

With a shake of his head, Shadow leaned down to kiss the hell out of her. As I turned away from them, a hand brushed across mine. Reece's energy slid into me, and I had to clench my thighs to ease the fire his touch sent spiraling through my needy body. Our gazes met, and there were promises in those endless depths. Promises I really needed him to keep.

But first... Reece's sands swept up the prisoners, encasing and lifting them so he could move the lot at once. For the first time since being captured, they started to fight, and knowing it would strain his energy, I placed a hand on his shoulder and shared my power.

"I don't need your—"

I cut him off. "I know you don't need my help, but you're still getting it. You have to be at your strongest going into this mission. So shut the hell up, take the help, and let's get it done."

We might be fucking, but I would not hesitate to smack him upside the head when he needed a wake-up call. He wanted to argue, I could tell by the flare of heat in his eyes as he narrowed them.

When he leaned down, I expected one of his usual harsh retorts. "You're lucky that we're not alone, Angel," he said instead. "Because you would learn to do as you're fucking told."

I laughed in his face. Who the hell did this moron think he was? "Listen up, Desertlandian," I said, not bothering to keep my voice low. "You will never tell me what to do, and I will never blindly obey. Take my damned help and stop being a juvenile. You're too old for that shit."

I heard a harsh intake of air from nearby—Len I was fairly sure—and I also felt Shadow press in closer, no doubt anticipating a fight that he would have to break up. Despite our declaration of a truce, they all knew how hard it was for long-standing grudges to truly end.

Reece's breathing grew heavier as he used his sands to move me away. "I'm not fighting with you, Lale. You need to save your strength." Despite his annoyance, the push of his energy was gentle, and I decided not to bother again because this was wasting time.

Turning my back on him, I made my way to Mera, grateful she'd be around for a few more hours. She slid her arm through mine. "Are you two actually getting worse in this attempt at a truce?" she asked in a whisper, as we watched Reece's sands sweep the prisoners out the door.

"We're doing our best," I said, memories of our sex high above the Ostealon filling my mind. Reece's best had near killed me. "Truth is, being here and heading toward the Delfora for battle has memories rising and tempers flaring. Reece's controlling nature also appears to have really amped up in the years since we stopped being friends. He's forgotten that he's not my superior, even in the Desert Lands."

Mera squeezed my arm. "Yes, exactly. You're Angel of the motherfreaking Honor Meadows. You're a legend. And you're not going to be defined by the past any longer."

She always had my back, and I must have done something right to have a being like Mera in my life. "Thanks, friend," I replied softly.

At this point everyone was following Reece and Shadow out of the tent, so we did as well. Outside was still very dark, the new-moon quite a few hours away. The group of prisoners were visible off in the distance, Reece's sands holding them above the tents.

"So, how long do you think until our bond moves past what it is now?" Mera asked randomly after we had left the red tents and were halfway through the gold. "Like, at times I can hear you in my mind, but then it's gone and our bond is barely a blip in my chest."

Through our joined arms I felt her energy and that of the unborn child, muted but steady. "Increases in power or stress can amp up the connection," I told her, explaining how we'd heard each other's thoughts before. "But it's like a wave; after the peak, there's an inevitable fall. As the years go on, though, the waves will calm and we won't have so many ups and downs. Eventually, our bond will be strong and unbreakable. No matter where we are, you will be able to feel and talk to me."

She made a pleased sound. "Good to know. Is that when we'll become twin souls?"

Ever since I'd mentioned the term, she'd been curious about it. "It's the strongest bond in the Honor Meadows," I explained. "The birth of transcendent twins is as rare as any birth in the Solaris System, and it results in a bond with shared powers, a mental connection, and a plethora of other strengths. It's also a bond we can almost replicate when we connect in the way you and I have. In the next few decades, we will find our twin compatibility."

Decades no doubt sounded like a lot to a youngling like her, but she'd come to find that it was barely a blip in time.

Mera let out a happy sigh. "After years of being alone, it's still astonishing to me that I'm now bonded to you, Shadow, and Midnight. Beings I can literally feel in my chest and even talk to in my mind. The concept should freak me out, but for some reason, it doesn't. I feel... safe and protected."

"You are safe and protected," I said, the words more forceful than was probably needed in casual conversation. "All of us would give our lives for you."

"I have to live for my child," she said, pulling me to a stop amid the brown tents of Shale, "but know that I would give my life for you as well. This bond doesn't just go one way. Promise me again"—she swallowed roughly—"promise that you will do everything in your power to come back to me. You and Shadow and all of our family. Bring them home to me, Angel."

"I will do everything in my power," I said, sealing my words with energy. There was a thrum in our bond, and both of us pressed a hand to our chest.

"It feels stronger," Mera whispered.

"It does," I confirmed as tendrils of her lifeforce ebbed into mine. "I think I'll be able to sense you in the library and know if there's anything wrong. Or if the baby is coming."

She narrowed her eyes. "Girl, do not even mention this child coming into the world while you're all stuck in the Desert Lands fighting the freaking gods. Nope, they will do just as their momma tells them and stay inside until we're all back together as a family."

She stomped her foot to reiterate her point, but we both knew that there was nothing she could truly do to stop this impending birth. The race to the power moon wasn't the only race we were in.

At this point, a few Shale Desertlandians exited their tents, wondering at the noise. Ignoring their stares, I dragged Mera along again, hurrying until we caught up to Galleli, who brought up the back of the pack.

All of the princeps and powerful families are meeting in the main tent now, he told us. *Reece said it's best to let them know what is happening so that we can get the supplies and permissions we need.*

"Yep, the East River will require permission," I said,

remembering that from my time here. "It's the fastest and most direct route to the Delfora but is also guarded."

And the last thing we needed was to waste time fighting Desertlandian warriors.

"I'm near peeing myself with excitement to see how this transport system works." Mera said in a higher pitch than normal. "Rivers of sand are not easy to imagine."

There are dangers to it, Galleli said, *But it's an experience. I just hope that the stolen power set in motion already doesn't stir the tumultuous streams too much before we make the Delfora.*

"It will take days to build," I said shortly. "But I imagine it's going to be rough going by the end."

Luckily, Mera would be gone at that point, and the rest of us would manage the swells.

"It'll be fine," Len called as he fell back to join us. "Not much can best our family. Not when we're together."

Mera let out a huff, and I knew she was once again pissed about our inevitable separation. She might understand the reasons why, and even somewhat agree with them, but that didn't mean she liked it.

None of us did.

CHAPTER TWENTY-EIGHT

When we reached the huge tent, all of the princeps were in attendance, along with many powerful families from various dynasties. Except, of course, for Tsuma and whoever else was already in a vessel on their way to the Delfora.

We all met in the middle of the dance floor; the sand-bound prisoners positioned above our heads. "Why have you summoned us?" a male from Fret dynasty demanded, hands on his hips as he glared in Reece's direction.

The response was a whoosh of energy as Reece withdrew his power from around the captives, allowing them to tumble to the floor. A few of them groaned as they sprawled on the hard surface, but Zena and Dally wasted no time, bouncing to their feet, ready to fight again. That was until they realized they were surrounded by powerful dynasty members.

"We were ambushed by these traitors tonight," Reece said calmly, even while red sands whipped around him in a heated frenzy. "And while interrogating them, we uncovered a plan to raise the ancients' gods in the sacred lands."

More like *confirmed what we'd already expected*, but these leaders didn't know that.

The silence after his statement was heavy.

"Impossible," the Yemin princeps finally spluttered, rubbing a hand across the chest of his orange tunic. He was a tall, thin man with a completely bald head and arresting golden eyes. I'd met him once, but his name was evading me at the moment. "Those gods cannot be woken. No one can even make it past the securities, not without a massive source of energy, and since the most powerful of us are all here"—he waved a hand around — "who else could there be?"

When Reece focused his full attention on the princeps, the Yemin male took a step back. "Nothing is impossible with the right planning," Reece said, his tone indicating he was about done explaining facts to stupid fucks. "This entire gathering was a plan to tap into the collective dynastic powers and use them to set this all in motion. They've already sent this power toward the Delfora, and it will keep building until"—his voice lowered ominously—"the power moon."

There were gasps all around, but Reece didn't let that deter him. "In half a dozen new-moons, a twin will form, and with that, there will be more than enough power to wake the ancients."

Panic and disbelief were now the most prominent expressions, but no one argued again, knowing that Reece was not only not prone to exaggeration, he also had a connection to the Delfora.

"Tsuma was the one to suggest this meeting," Yemin finally said, his body drooping, "after decades of staying out of our politics."

Color us all surprised by that revelation.

"So, where are they now? Why are you here and not stopping them?" Those questions came from a tall, voluptuous Crani female whose gorgeous brown skin was highlighted by the gold of her dynasty. She crossed her arms over her ample chest as she glared at Zena. "Have you interrogated these traitors fully?"

"We have enough information," Reece said quickly, "and we are about to take off after Tsuma to hopefully make it to the Delfora before they do. There's no point tracking them along the river they've chosen, because their gathered energy is shrouding their path. It would be a waste of time to follow them. Our only shot now is to take the fastest vessel we have and get into the East River."

I had no idea of the dynamics on this world these days, but it stood to reason that many Desertlandians in this tent were not allies. And almost all of them could be stubborn bastards for no reason other than they were powerful enough to do what they wanted. With that in mind, I was prepared for the sort of backlash and refusals and arguments that could take hours to resolve. Hours we did not have.

"We cast a vote," the Crani princeps said, her voice rising up. "Those who agree to Reece's plan, raise your hand now."

To my utter shock, almost every hand I could see went into the air.

Crani nodded. "That's a majority. Do you need anything else?"

"Supplies—" Reece started to say before a familiar male stepped to the front of the leaders, all but interrupting.

Darin's eyes were more intensely green than they'd been when we danced. He bore no obvious injuries from whatever had happened between him and Reece earlier, but with advance healing, that didn't mean much.

"Did you want something?" Reece asked shortly. "We're on a tight schedule here, what with trying to save the damn worlds."

Darin's lips tightened, but he didn't bite. "As the princeps of the Guardians, I request that I and my Desertlandians be allowed to go on this journey also."

"No," Reece said in a hard snap of that one word. "I trust my family only." He waved a hand toward one of the prisoners, who was standing with the others, waiting for their punishment. "We were attacked tonight by a Guardian."

Darin's brows bunched heavily as his expression grew darker. "They will be dealt with in the harshest of punishments. But don't tar us all with the same brush. Rohami stand with the traitors as well."

Reece's expression indicated that he'd kind of hoped Darin wouldn't notice that.

"We are Guardians," the princeps continued, "and generally the ones who stand between the sacred lands and the rest of the worlds. I won't fail at that again. You don't know what you're up against. You need us."

Reece barked out a harsh laugh. "I could kick your ass all day every day and you know it. This is not my first battle in the Delfora, and no doubt it won't be my last. We do not need your assistance."

Darin's let out a curse in their native tongue. "The sacred lands are our responsibility," he repeated.

Reece shook his head, and it was clear he would not budge on this.

"What if I take another vessel?" Darin changed tact. "We would stay behind yours and be backup only. You can't argue with that."

Reece wanted to, but with all the princeps and Desertlandians watching him—not to mention the metaphorical countdown clock ticking—he must have decided to try and be a team player. "Do not get in my way," he warned Darin. "And if you betray me in any way, I'll wipe out your entire dynasty."

A few gasps and whispered words followed that threat, but Reece and Darin were too busy locking eyes to notice any of it. At this point I was the one ready to kick some asses because we were wasting time in this redundant pissing contest.

"I accept your terms," Darin finally said, breaking the tension by turning to a redheaded female beside him. "Ready our vessel and warriors. We set sail immediately."

Without a glance our way, she hurried off, followed by the other Guardians who'd been in attendance. "I'll meet you at the East River," Darin said, and as his gaze met mine, I wondered if this princeps was playing games or not.

He didn't wait for a response, striding after the others from his dynasty. "You should hurry too," the Crani female said. "We cannot allow this to come to pass."

"We'll need supplies at the docks," Reece said, before jerking his head toward the traitors. "And if you get any new information from this lot, send word on the sands."

"We will," she murmured, her pink lips tilting in a harsh smile. "There'll be no more secrets between them by the time I'm done."

This satisfied Reece, and then it was time for us to leave. The rest of us hadn't spoken during the impromptu Desert-landian council meeting, and that silence continued once we were outside. With the warm winds having picked up a little, I felt the power surging much stronger than it had been when we first entered.

We needed to get to those docks as soon as possible.

Reece led us to the northern point of the Ostealon, toward the largest docking stations and our best chance of a speedy vessel.

"Will they have the ship and supplies already?" Mera asked, finally breaking this silence we'd been in.

At this point we'd reached the glass fences of the yards, the security at the helm of the gates opening them for us without question. Someone had sent word already, making it all much easier.

"We will take whatever ship we deem the best," Reece said. "And I assume the supplies will make their way onboard at some point." Despite his words from before, he clearly trusted the Desertlandian council to follow through on this promise.

As we passed through the gates, the guards dressed in ochre tunics, saluted Reece with the traditional fist to chest and then out in front. He returned the gesture, and from here, we were in the shipping yard with its sand bay—the quieter stream before the river systems.

This was the point Mera lost her shit. "Oh my fucking demons," she cried, grinding to a halt and clutching her stomach.

"Sunshine!" Shadow barked, reaching out to snatch her into his arms, but she sidestepped him before he could.

"No, no, no no," she said in a rush, waving him off. "I'm not in labor, I'm seeing sands move like water for the first time."

Shadow, who appeared to be having a stroke, if the pulsing vein near his temple was any indication, let out a rumble loud enough to shake the ground.

Mera realized at that point that she'd actually scared her mate half to death. "Sorry, babe," she whispered, stepping back to hug him. "I got caught up in the moment."

The beast was beyond words as he held onto her like she was his life raft in the streams of sand. "We'll meet you at the ship," Reece called since these two—about to be separated during a dangerous time—clearly needed a second.

The rest of us made our way onto the docks. The ochre and gold sands swirled and pulsed about three feet below our platform. It had been a long time since I'd seen a sand river, and as

I stared into the tumultuous depths, I felt a ridiculous sense of home.

"Missed it?" Reece's warm drawl reminded me that he was the bastard who'd stolen this stream from me. For a beat I was tempted to push him in, only there was no time for pettiness.

"Not for a second," I said baldly, meaning not one word.

He called me out straight away. "Liar. The circle around your iris darkens to a deep pink when you're sad. No matter how well you've schooled your face, I can always tell."

Dammit. This fucker. "You don't know me anymore," I snapped, feeling trapped. "Don't presume you do."

I strode away, but I heard his last words. "I know everything about you, Lale. Everything."

Whether that was true or not, the real question was... how the hell could I survive multiple moons on this ship with him?

CHAPTER TWENTY-NINE

The rivers of the Desert Lands varied in colors. The ones that led off this fast-moving sand waterway were ochre like the Ostealon. As we crossed the docks, moving to where all the big, golden vessels waited, I noted that the swishing and swirling of the sands below was growing stronger. Generally, this part—the bay before the rivers—should be relatively calm, but this moon it was wild.

Tsuma's stolen energy was already stirring the tides as it swelled deep in the power that ran below the deserts. As we all stared, a creature leapt out of the sands as if trying to escape their new fury.

Mera and Shadow had caught up at this point, and my friend almost fell off the docks at the sight of the dark red, heavily boned beast diving deep. "What was that?" she gasped when Shadow caught her and pulled her back. "It almost looked like a skeletal dolphin."

"It's an *echinat*," Reece said, his gaze focused on the vessels as he used his years of expertise to find the fastest and most stable ship for this mission. "It's scary to look at but is harmless."

"It has no external flesh," Lucien explained, leaning out

from the docks too. "I remember the first time I saw one in a sand bay near Reece's home; I near jumped out of my damn pants."

Even Reece managed a laugh, despite his focus, as he pushed us further into the shipping docks. "The bony exoskeleton protects the internal components. So it looks like a skeleton, but that's just the shell."

Mera's eyes grew wider as she tried to lean out from the ochre dock again, its compacted sands holding her with ease. Shadow didn't care though, reaching out to grasp onto the back of her tunic to keep her from tumbling forward. "Not too close, Sunshine. If we're lucky, one will jump while we're travelling."

That seemed to mollify Mera, who fell back into line behind the rest of us.

When we were about halfway through the hundreds of ships, Reece ground to a halt. "Oh, yes," he said softly. "I was hoping she'd be here."

Peering around him, I saw a huge vessel, tinted both red and gold, indicating this was a Rohami ship. "The Odessa," he told us, "is one of the fastest ships in the world, and since I have full permission to use whatever is available... let's get onboard."

"Like you care about permission," I muttered, thinking of all the shit I'd seen him get away with over the years.

My words had been too soft for most to hear, but when his lips twitched, I knew he'd caught my comment. But... whatever. It wasn't like he was unaware of my thoughts toward him. I did manage to keep further comments to myself, though, as I followed him down a ledge designed to give us access to the side of the ship.

I'd been on a few of these transports before, but nothing the length or breadth of the Odessa. When Reece stopped about halfway along the dock, he said, "This long, sleek shape is how she's so fast. But with the addition of a slightly deeper hull, we can plow through the more treacherous conditions of the East River."

"Especially once that energy really swells into full force," Len added, his concerned gaze on the rowdy sands edging up the side of the docks.

"How do we get onto it?" I asked.

From what I could see, the ship was anchored by two streams of energy, one off the front and another at the back. I could use my wings and ferry everyone over, but there had to be another way for the wingless Desertlandians.

"We use this platform," Reece said, leaning down and retrieving a large board I hadn't noticed hanging over the side of the dock, attached through energy streams like those holding the ship.

The platform was heavy and solid, made from the same hard material that had lined the dance floor in the main tent, and Reece showed no strain as he spun the long length around and placed it into a small groove etched into the side of the boat. The other end landed on the dock itself.

"All aboard," he said, jerking his head to indicate we should get moving.

Since I was the closest, I hurried up the platform, adjusting my stance to move with the sands lifting the ship. It was an odd sensation as my center of balance shifted constantly, but I figured it out fast and, in no time, was up on the deck. Moving out of the way, I marveled at how the pamolsa oil and sand created a waterproof but nonslip surface, the shiny length filling this level of the huge vessel.

This world might prefer its lack of "technology" but that didn't make them primitive.

The others followed until we were all onboard. Reece was last, then he lifted the platform to store it against the inside railing of the Odessa so we could use it to disembark when we arrived.

"This is incredible," Mera said, widening her stance so she could balance with the movements of the sands. "I can't believe it's sand; it feels like we're on water."

"Magical currents," Alistair said, his eyes brighter as he stared over the side. "I've always wanted to swim in its depths, but these main rivers are way too tidal. It's easy to be pulled into the unknown."

"I know some rivers that you'd enjoy swimming in," Reece told him. "I'll take you after we save the world."

"Again," half of us chorused.

The desert god chuckled, despite his grim mood. "Yep. Again."

Len, his coat extra silver in this world built of many colors except that one, stood in the center of the main deck. "How do we get the supplies?" he asked. "I don't like the feel of the energy. We need to get moving so we're past these first port tides as the power swells."

Reece tilted his head to stare into the sky, the dark-moon casting no more than a sliver of light. "There's nothing yet," he said. "We should prep to leave; the supplies will just have to find their way to us."

"How can we help prep?" I asked.

Reece shook his head. "These ships all but sail themselves, with a little help from the engines, of course. You all stay here, and I'll get us moving."

His sands flashed red around him, visible as they took off to cut the power cables holding our commandeered vessel. As soon as that happened, the ship began to move more dramatically, giving us a very good indication of the increased volatility in the underground power streams.

Reece, despite the swell, strode with ease to a set of stairs that led up onto a higher deck. Until that point, I'd thought that was more of an observation level, but apparently it was where he controlled the ship from. Within minutes, I heard the powerful thrum of engines from deep below us, and with both skill and speed, Reece backed out of the docking area and moved past other ships to enter the main bay. From here we'd sail toward the East River and hope like hell the supplies showed up before Tsuma's spell turned these rivers even more treacherous.

Once we got into the widest section of the bay, I moved closer to the front of the ship. I'd never traveled from the Ostealon before, and it was quite impressive to see all the rivers spanning around on all sides, leading to basically every land in this world.

"This is the junction," Reece called down to us, voice loud over the sound of the engines. "Each of these rivers leads to a different land or dynasty. East River will take us past Rohami and into the sacred lands."

The whirring of the engine eased as our forward trajectory halted. "I'll give them a few more minutes for supplies," Reece said. "We need water for Alistair at minimum."

The Karn native waved him off, but all of us could see the dryness in his skin and the droop to his shoulders. If it were up to me, he'd be leaving with Mera because the deserts were only going to get drier the closer we got to the Delfora. However, since I doubted Alistair would appreciate my advice, I remained silent while vowing to keep an eye on him.

Once the vessel was as stationary as it could be at the junction of the rivers, Reece left the top deck and made his way back to where we all stood. He settled in at my side, both of us watching the rivers.

"That one leads to Rohami," he said, pointing at one to the left of us. "And that one—"

He was cut off by a loud shout, and all of us spun in time to see another ship approaching, one that was black in its coloring. Darin had caught up to us. It took them another few minutes to draw close enough for us to see the dozen Guardians on board. "They have our supplies?" I guessed since nothing else had arrived.

"I would assume so," Reece said with a sigh.

Darin's vessel stopped with about twenty feet separating us. "We have your supplies!" he shouted, confirming it. "Can you send someone across to get them?"

Reece moved closer to the side of the Odessa. "Just throw them over," he called back. "We need to get on our way."

That wasn't just him being difficult. Already the winds and tides were picking up, and I felt the swelling of power under our ship. Tsuma's gathered energy was really kicking in now, and if we didn't get moving, we'd be in trouble.

"I can go," I said in a rush, my wings popping out without another thought. "It shouldn't take more than a second."

"Great idea," Mera said, just as Reece snapped, "No way."

Everyone looked at him, and I hoped the pointed stare I shot his way reminded him that our incognito arrangement was in danger of being blown to pieces.

"We don't know if we can trust them," he finally added. "Do you really want to risk Angel to a possible attack?"

Mera crossed her arms. "Dude, Angel could wipe the floor with those assholes. Fuck, she could do it with her arms tied together."

Now I was the one smirking, daring him to argue with that. I mean, it possibly wasn't true—I didn't know and hadn't had a chance to assess the power of Darin and his men—but if Reece talked my abilities down, he'd be handed his ass by me. And then Mera would step in.

"Fuck," he growled. "Okay, but I'm coming too."

I moved to join him near the side.

"Do not linger," he murmured darkly. "Over and back, or I'll deal with Darin. And we both know what happens *after* he touches what's mine."

Holy meadows. Shivers wracked through me as I remembered the dance he'd interrupted and the events that had gone down after it. His powerful body driving into mine...

Swallowing my arousal, I forced myself to act normal. "No idea what you're talking about," I managed to say, spreading my wings wide as he gathered sand around him. "Must not have been that memorable."

I was gone before he could reply, and even though poking the sleeping sand dragon wasn't the smartest idea, I finally understood the thrill Mera always talked about when she was dancing on the edge of danger with her Shadow Beast.

And with the possibility of being destroyed in the Delfora in six moons, there felt like no better time to risk it all.

CHAPTER THIRTY

s we crossed the short distance to the other ship, the sky was already lightening. The new-moon was nearing, its bright red curving out of the edge of the bluer dark-moon.

Darin waited for us, his second-in-command to the right, both standing in what I had dubbed the "ship stance," slightly wider legs with hands on hips as they stared out across the horizon. Something told me we'd all be doing a lot of "ship stance" over the next few days.

"Welcome," he said, when I landed on the deck and tucked my wings away. "Nice to see you again."

I smiled, but when he stepped to my side, closer than was necessary, I found myself moving out of his way and striding to the center of the deck. Reece, looking pleased for once, landed beside me, his sands disappearing.

"Where are our supplies," he said to Darin as way of greeting.

The Guardian was no longer smiling, his expression blank as he stared at Reece, and I recognized the start of two males about to lose their minds in some stupid dominance contest.

Ignoring them completely, I turned to his second in command, the redheaded female he'd sent from the tent before. "Where can I pick up the items?" I asked her.

"This way," she said shortly, making her way toward the back of their ship.

She wasn't particularly friendly, but I didn't care. I wasn't here to make friends.

As we crossed the deck, I noted that their ship looked wider and larger than ours, which would be useful in some situations but not when speed was of the essence. Thankfully, we had first passage, so they wouldn't slow us down. The redhead left me in a small storage room near a set of stairs that led down into their ship, and I wasted no time grabbing up a couple of the white bags inside.

Reece showed up a second later. "That's enough," he told me. "My sands can carry the bulk. You just get back to our ship."

Wanting to argue with him because he was pissing me off with his moods, I spun, only to find he was much closer than I'd anticipated. Normally I would have felt the heat of his sandy protection, but at the moment those protections were busy gathering bags. Our eyes met, and before I could say a word, his arm went around my back to pull us together with enough force that I actually let out a low gasp.

As I arched against him, he let out a low groan. "Dammit, Lale," he murmured, clearing his throat. "Soon."

He released me with a muttered curse, and needing some space, I stumbled forward on momentarily weak legs before reaching out to gather bags again. As I passed the desert god, he shot me a look that promised to finish what had been started in here, and I was feeling every inch of his touch by the time I emerged onto the main deck.

Darin, who stood near the storage room waiting for us, wore

an unreadable expression as he held out a hand. "Do you need some help?" he asked.

I shook my head, frustrated for so many reasons. "I'm stronger than I look. Don't underestimate me."

He held up both hands, expression softening. "My apologies. I was taught to offer assistance whether it's needed or not."

In the Honor Meadows that would probably get a being killed. But Desertlandians were different, and I had to respect that while in their world.

"Cultural differences," I offered in an attempt to not be a bitch. My wings sprung free as I shot a small smile his way. "See you in the sacred lands. Safe travels."

"You too," he said, inclining his head.

I pushed up off the deck and took to the sky, the four bags held tightly in my grip. During our absence, the two ships had drifted further apart, and from this vantage point I could see it would take extra time for Reece to get us back into position to take the East River.

Once I was over the main deck, I dropped down near Mera, Shadow, and Lucien.

"Was everything okay over there?" Mera asked me, moving to my side.

"Yes, perfectly fine," I said, placing the bags on the deck. "Judging by the weight, and the amount I left behind, we have at least six or seven moons worth of supplies. It should be more than enough."

Shadow used his energy to unwind the ties at the top of one, and as he looked inside, he nodded. "There's food and water, along with energy pods."

I peered around him to see the dark green seeds, each about the size of my palm. "The energy pods grow only in Faerie," Shadow explained to Mera, "but they're probably the most trad-able commodity between all the worlds."

Powerful energy boosters, I'd never needed to use them before since I could always gather energy from the land itself. My rebirth did change my need for more than regular energy, though, so having the pods as a boost if needed would definitely be useful.

"We should save those until right before we hit the Delfora," I said.

"Good idea," Shadow replied, shifting them into a small bag, even as Mera reached down to grab one.

Turning it over in her hand, she examined it from all angles.

"You split there," I said, pointing to a nearly invisible line along one side. "Eat the seed inside the hard shell."

"It looks like a green mango seed," she said, running her thumb over it. "But it feels fuzzy, like a peach skin. So weird, but I really want to try one."

"Maybe not while pregnant with a god baby," I suggested. "They can have an unusual effect on the energy of some beings, especially ones with an already complicated power base."

Mera let out an exaggerated sigh. "Could there be a more accurate description of me than *has a complicated power base?*"

I had to laugh because her powers would be nothing on her child's. Reece landed on the deck a second later, the sands bringing the rest of the bags with him. There must have been a few more hidden away because I counted many more than I'd originally noticed.

"We have clothing, food, medical, and a few weapons," he said. "Looks like they gathered everything they could in the short amount of time, and now we must leave."

Mera dropped her seed into the bag just as a particularly large swell of the sand rocked the ship. Being as off balanced as she was these days, she almost face-planted, but Shadow and I both caught her. Once again, I was reminded that Mera didn't need me the way she had when we originally met. Back when Shadow was her enemy.

He now held the number one place in her life as her protector and closest friend, and that was totally okay. That was the way it was meant to be, and it didn't lessen my bond with Mera—a fact that had taken me a while to come to terms with.

"Holy shit, thank you!" Mera exclaimed, holding onto Shadow. "I'm not used to the extra thirty pounds up front."

Lucien, who was crossing from the back of the ship, let out a bark of laughter before clearing his throat. Mera pointed her finger at him. "Shut it, vamp. It's thirty pounds, and I won't hear another word about it."

The vampire's smile was wide, fangs visible. "I was going to say that you don't look like you've gained a pound over twenty. And you're always beautiful."

Mera narrowed her eyes on him. "Nice save," she finally murmured.

By this time, Reece was back on the upper deck and the powerful engines were kicking in again as he got us on track. It was clear he'd spent a lot of time on these ships, and we were in the best hands to get us safely to the Delfora.

"As cool as this is," Mera said as we all started to move the bags into our storage hull so they wouldn't scatter as we sailed, "Are you all really sure that we shouldn't be going faster? Even if it's not the doorways, what about wings or Reece's sands?"

Shadow crossed his arms. "Both possibilities, but why drain power when there's no point in rushing? Not to mention, we have no idea what an influx of power usage near the Delfora could set in motion. Everything is out of balance with Tsuma's gathered energy ritual."

Mera nodded. "Right, right. I forgot the part where we'd

just be twiddling our hands in the sacred lands until Tsuma and the others showed up."

With a whoosh of wings, Galleli landed to join us on the main deck. *It will be in our best interests to reach the Delfora at the same time as Tsuma,* he said. *Staying in the Delfora for too long would crush our powerbases as we battle the energy swelling there.*

With those words, our ship surged forward, the roar of the engines louder than ever as Reece put all the power into moving us onto the treacherous East River. Apparently the fastest and best path in our current predicament.

We were finally on our way.

CHAPTER THIRTY-ONE

The Odessa lived up to her reputation, slicing fast and smooth through the junction and into the East River —which was the point it all got hectic.

"Whoa," Mera said, lurching forward again, Shadow's hold keeping her standing. "Has the gathered energy gone haywire or something? Everything feels much choppier here."

Moving forward gingerly, I made it to the side railings, holding on as we lurched to the right. "This part of the stream is naturally turbulent, and with the energy ramping up, I can feel it pushing us along. It's going to keep building as we move until it becomes a veritable tornado once we reach the Delfora. That's why we had to get out in front of it and hope our speed keeps us that way."

Mera pressed a hand to her mouth, looking a little green. "These rivers have streams of power under them? Is this what causes the sand to move freely and be both buoyant and tidal?"

I nodded. "Pretty much."

"The Desertlandians could not move about easily if not for these channels," Shadow told her. "This world is huge, actually

much larger than Earth, and there's no form of airborne transport, just their legs and ships."

Reece shouted out for all of us to hold on, and as the ship
sped into a wider part of the river, the sands whipped up higher
on the sides. Moving closer to Mera, I helped Shadow keep her
propped up between us.

"Will it be like this the entire way?" she asked, her voice
barely audible over the winds that roared around us, the sky
bright as the new-moon filled it with warmth and light.

"Nope," Shadow said, "because you'll be safely in the library
in a few hours and won't have to deal with any further
turbulence."

With a wrinkle of her nose, she glared up at him. "Come on,
mate. There's clearly no danger in me staying a little longer... I
mean, outside of me spewing up my fucking intestines. I really
want to experience the rivers, at least until the danger is closer."

Shadow breathed deeply through his nose, and in an
attempt to hide my smile, I turned my head to take in the
breathtaking sight of the Ostealon as we left its sands. A few
desert birds, *penticarlo,* flew by as well, battling the winds as we
were, but there was no other sign of life.

"I know what you're doing, Mera Callahan," Shadow
rumbled.

"I have no idea what you're talking about," Mera shot back.
"My logic is sound, and you know it."

His next breath might have been deeper than the one he'd
taken a moment ago. "Once again, your logic isn't the same as
everyone else's logic. One could say that you are actually using
that word completely wrong."

Mera shrugged. "I'm the only native English speaker, so it
seems that, once again, *logic* dictates we trust my judgement on
this."

Before she could sass him again, his height shot up as he

lifted her into his arms and strode across the deck, then they disappeared into what I could only assume were cabins below. No doubt it was safer for her down there until this river evened out, and Shadow would spend his time wisely by distracting her before reiterating that Mera was getting her ass back to the library, as previously decided.

Despite knowing it was safest for her not to be here, my money was on Mera somehow making it to the Guardians. Like he'd read my mind, Len glided smoothly—despite the rocking of the ship—to my side and said, "Five sacred gems that Mera makes it four moons before Shadow convinces her to leave."

I snorted. "Five boosts of power that she makes it all the way to the Guardians. I would say the Delfora, but since Shadow can't portal from there, Guardians is the farthest point."

He pondered it for a moment. "Shadow is too stubborn to let her get that far. I'll take that bet."

Compressing my lips to hide my smile, we shook hands and sent out a sliver of power with it to seal the deal. I didn't bet often, and generally never with my family line of power, but I knew my best friend very well. Mera might not be the oldest or most powerful of our group, but she made up for that with extra stubbornness and *logic* as she put it.

Getting her way despite her lack of experience was one of her superpowers.

Reece shouted out then for Len, and as the fae turned to stare up at the higher deck, I had a brief thought that once again this desert asshole was trying to dictate the friendships in my life.

"Looks like Reece needs a dash of silver-city powers," Len said, meeting my gaze. "I mean, it sounds like the sort of energy he could have gotten from anyone, but who am I to expect an ulterior motive to get me out of this spot."

"Stop right there," I warned him. "Do not finish that thought."

His laughter was light and infectious. "We both recognize the flaws in our Reece."

"Wouldn't let him hear you say that," I muttered, turning back to the view as the fae drifted away, his laughter lingering longer than the feel of his energy.

Reece would object to the knowledge of "flaws" because he had spent so many years perfecting his "god" aura. And when one was a god, there was no room for faults. With his family and mine gone, there was no one left that knew the Reece from his earlier years. The Reece who didn't talk until he was near five. He'd choose his words so carefully at that time that I cherished each and every one. They also wouldn't know that we'd both cried that same year when I was torn away and sent to battle training, resulting in us being apart for many moons.

Reece was always so careful with what he shared with the world, but when he opened his heart to you, it was like winning the most precious prize in the Solaris System. Hence why I'd been so broken when I lost all of that through my own stupid fault.

Turning from the deserts, I looked up to where Reece stood, Len at his side. For once, his eyes weren't locked on mine as he remained statue-like, staring out into the horizon, illuminated by the red light of the new-moon. He looked relaxed, calm even, guiding us down the river, his dark beauty surpassing even that of the deserts.

As I stared at him, caught between the past and the present, I recognized a fundamental truth: he wasn't the only flawed one. And it wasn't only his pride that kept us enemies.

I'd more than played my part, never even trying to repair the damage of my decision that fateful day. I'd made amends with everyone except for Reece, and now it was up to me to ensure that our plan worked. Because I couldn't go back to being his enemy.

I jolted as he turned suddenly and met my gaze, as if he'd felt my eyes on him the entire time. A long, silent moment passed between us, and while his thoughts were hidden, for once there was no apparent anger. If anything, his stare set off a twinge of memory inside me, reminding me that at one point in time, Reece and I'd had a bond too. One long neglected, now built of broken tendrils and burned bridges.

When he turned away again, I sagged into the railing, my heart pounding hard.

So much of our life together I'd suppressed, but that was not to be my fate any longer.

Reece and I... we were as inevitable as the desert winds. Or his sand protection. Even when you couldn't see them, they were always there, pushing us on our course.

A course that was, for once, moving in the same direction... If only we could manage to avoid the storms.

CHAPTER THIRTY-TWO

The next few hours were rough to say the very least. Whatever energy had been building below reacted to us leaving the Ostealon, and at some points, we were forced to cling to the sides to keep from being thrown overboard.

"I think we know why this is not a regularly used route," I groaned to Alistair, who stood near me at the back of the ship.

He turned from where he'd been gazing into the sands below, and as he straightened, he lifted a glass container of liforina, tipping it over his head for the second time in ten minutes. "The power is making it worse, but this part of the East River is definitely wild without any help. It cannot be tamed."

Hence why he'd been fascinatedly staring into the depths for hours. Alistair was well known for attempting to tame the strongest and angriest waters. He did so with little regard for his life because this was how he actually felt alive. Unlike the rest of us, he was not eternal, even if his warrior race was still very long-lived. It was the knowledge that he would eventually die which had him embracing life to the fullest, living like he might die tomorrow.

"Is it getting drier?" I asked when he dumped a second bottle on his head, the patches on his skin easing as he absorbed the liquid through his pores.

His expression was grimmer. "Yeah, the air is drier here than back near the Ostealon. There're fewer aquifers, and that makes the air and sand itself more arid."

"You know the Delfora is the driest of all, right?"

Alistair met my gaze, and there was a soft determination in his expression. "I know, but I still can't allow my brothers to take this journey without me."

I really wished that, just this once, he would. "Make sure that we always have enough liquid for you to hydrate," was all I ended up saying.

He smiled, those expressive eyes warm, and I was reminded of how kind he could be. For a warrior, Alistair had a surprisingly soft demeanor. "It will be fine; don't worry about me."

And yet I did. I worried about all of them now, fussing about like a damn mother hen looking after her flock, all the while knowing that Reece waited in the wings, ready to sweep them out from under me. My very own wolf in the henhouse.

Refusing to think about that Desertlandian again, I focused on the changing sands, noting that there were some reds mingling with the Ostealon's colors now. We were edging closer to the Rohami sands, and knowing I had questions that needed answers, I left Alistair and stumbled my way across the main deck toward the upper level.

At first, I made almost no progress against the roll of the ship, and while I was tempted to use my wings, the strength of the winds here would send me into the sky, draining my energy as I fought to return. Eventually I decided to tap into my energy stores, sending a jolt down into my legs to stick my boots to the deck.

With that assistance, I managed to cross the area, and as I reached the stairs, I released the magic and used the smooth, glass-infused railing for assistance. As the energy I'd used seeped from me, it didn't return to my center; instead, it soared into the world to rejoin the collective.

We'd all taken a shot at explaining how this worked to Mera, but in truth, it all boiled down to a few simple facts. One: Magic was the ability to harness the natural, free energies of any world. Two: If you knew how, you could take that energy and transform it into whatever you needed, be that endurance, strength, transfiguration, or teleportation. Three: Once the free energy has been taken and used, it would release back into the world, unless you figured out how to harness it again, which most beings could not do without destroying themselves through a form of energy blowback.

All of my "used" family power would now be in the collective of the Honor Meadows, recycling itself to be sent out again, part of the lifeforce that kept our world functioning and spinning. That collective was shared in small increments every wet season, but it took a long time to rebuild it and it was never quite the same. Many of the layers of my world had been formed by members of my family, and once they were lost, there was no return.

When the layer was gone, so was my last connection to them.

Halfway up the stairs, the ship did a particularly strong lurch to the left, but I kept my feet by gripping the side rails. When we evened out again, I used my natural speed and hurried up the last steps as fast as I could. On the top deck, the winds were much stronger, but the views more than made up for that with a stunning vision of rivers and deserts spanning out for miles.

I could see many colors, from the ochres we'd left behind to the pale oranges of Yemin far off to the east and the reds of Rohami coming up to the north-east. And straight ahead was our final destination, too far away to see yet, but I knew the Guardians and Delfora were waiting out there for our arrival.

Reece was alone on the top deck, and even though there was no chance he didn't hear me stumbling over, he never turned my way. Was there a chance that even with our new arrangement, and that mind-blowing sex, he was actually acting colder?

"Hey," I said, almost falling into him but, thankfully, catching myself last minute. "Smooth sailing so far." I really hated small talk. It was a waste of my time and energy, but he had me so off-kilter and out of whack that here we were.

Reece still didn't look at me, completely focused on the destination in front of us. "It'll calm down soon. We're almost in front of the natural energy of Ostealon, which is mixing with Tsuma's spell. At that point our speed will decrease until the power below us builds again, but at least we'll be able to walk about without face-planting."

He still wasn't looking at me, but he was talking normally, so I went with it. "Does this stream cross through any other dynasties?"

"Not really," he said. "It leaves the Ostealon and spends most of its time in the deep sands, but you will catch glimpses of Rohami in the distance. The Guardians is our first land destination before hitting the Delfora. I'd estimate at our current speed, and considering it will slow once we get away from the heavier currents of the East River, it'll be about five moons."

We didn't have much of a window to make it to the Delfora before the power moon, but if that was the case, Tsuma wouldn't either. She only had a short head start on us, and we were on the fastest river. The East River was only for princeps normally, and Tsuma would have drawn attention by using it, so we had that advantage.

"Okay," I replied, any other questions forgotten in this awkward energy between us. Needing to escape, I was almost back to the steps when he finally released the wheel and lever he'd been using to guide us and called my name.

When I looked over my shoulder, he was in a strong ship stance, looking unaffected by the currents. "How's Mera?" he asked.

Was he the one making small talk now? And why was I relieved not to have to leave just yet? "She's miserable and trying to rest," I said. "Shadow is working on convincing her to leave, but she insists that she hasn't seen anything yet and they need to wait until the sands calm so she can experience the true majesty of your world."

A fraction of his rigid demeanor softened. "What are the odds that she stays on this ship until we reach the Guardians?"

That got a smile out of me. "Len and I have a bet going. My power is on her making it to the Delfora. He thinks she'll be gone in a few moons."

"Len should know better than to bet against you," he said, his voice dropping lower as he took a step toward me. He seemed unconcerned about leaving the steering apparatus, which was explained when his sands turned visible and streamed out from him to wrap around the wheel. Of course, as he took another step forward, the damn boat lurched at almost a forty-five-degree angle—*was it his sand's first freaking day steering a boat?*—but he didn't falter, solid as a desert cliff.

He reached me in a single breath of time, crowding his big body into mine.

"What are you doing?" I murmured, tilting my head back to see his eyes and whatever emotions they held.

Reece leaned down to brush his lips across my cheekbone.

"Stay away from my friends," he murmured as his power tingled into mine.

I swallowed hard as anger and arousal slammed into me. "You have got to be kidd—"

"You know the damn rules." He cut me off. "This"—his hands swept down my shoulders, and since I'd removed my armor earlier, he had free access to cup my breasts, thumbs brushing over the nipples that were ready and standing at attention under the tunic—"is mine."

I had to swallow again because this drier air was getting to me... Yep, it was definitely the air.

My voice was husky. "It was just a bet."

His hands slid down my stomach, slowly making their way to the junction of my thighs. He pressed against my clit, sliding his fingers across the throbbing bundle of nerves. "That's the only reason you're both walking around. Unpunished."

I managed to snort out a laugh, desperate for casual disdain. "Oh, right? And how would you punish us?" This fucker had another fight on his hands if he thought he could control me, even if his current actions were turning me into a quivering ball of need.

"Len would learn the hard way not to disregard my orders," Reece said calmly, "and you would be tied to my bed until you remembered the rules of this agreement."

I opened my mouth to blast him, but my body was already on fire at the thought of being under his control like that. As much as I was strong and built for battle, there was a part of me that craved a moment to release that control. To give myself to the pleasure I knew Reece would bring to my life.

With a shake of my head, I knocked his hand away, ignoring the parts inside me screaming to let him do *whatever the hell he wanted*. "You can try, asshole," I managed to say without sounding like a breathless fool. "Try and see what happens."

"Flirt with my friends and see what happens," Reece shot back. "You know I don't share well, Lale. You've known me longer than almost anyone else in the worlds. We might have ignored it for a time, and others also might have forgotten, but you were mine before anyone else's. And for now, I've reinstated the old rules."

He returned to the wheel, leaving me there frozen like the very fool I had been trying not to be. *Others might have forgotten.* It wasn't just others... He was talking about the bond that, until just recently, I'd also forgotten. A bond that he'd blessed in front of their higher energies, and that meant something. Desert Lands claimings were soul-deep bonds that tied powerful mates, families, and... even friends together.

I've reinstated the old rules.

Holy shit. What were the old rules? I didn't remember the rules of these bonds, having been so young when it'd happened. No doubt they'd been written somewhere... probably at the time of the early Desertlandians. The time of the ancients.

"What are the old rules?" I asked his back.

Reece lifted his head higher, those broad shoulders blocking my view of what lay ahead. "You'll find out soon. They're written in the Delfora on the stones of my ancestors."

I waited for him to continue, but there was nothing else said.

Six moons. I would have to wait six moons to find out what that meant, and part of me wondered if my life would ever be the same.

CHAPTER THIRTY-THREE

We spent the next couple of moons in turbulent sands, but when we left the narrower section of the East River, everything evened out. Mera finally made her way back up to the main deck, looking relaxed and rested, despite the rough trip so far. She wore stretchy black tights, a long white shirt, and flat-heeled ankle boots. Her aura gently swirled around her, feeling stronger and more intense than ever, and I had a sense that this baby would soon be ready to enter the world.

"Hey," I said, crossing to her side. "How are you feeling?" I'd been checking in on her periodically, but since Shadow was keeping her occupied, I'd probed through the bond first before knocking on their cabin door lest I find them both... busy.

"Feeling fantastic now," she said with enthusiasm. She nudged me toward the side of the ship, and we stared into the darkening sky where the blue of the dark-moon had replaced the reds and golds. "This is absolutely spectacular, right?"

Vast understatement. There was no comparison to the beauty of the deserts. We were not quite in the deep sands yet, so off to the east we could see the reds of Rohami spanning out like a giant sunset. There was no sign of life since that massive land was no more than thirty percent populated, and the only sound was the whirring on the energy engines below.

When Mera'd had enough standing, we made our way to a small bench tucked in along one side of the hull, taking a seat to catch up. "How's our baby doing?" I asked.

"Baby is as active as ever." She laughed and somehow groaned at the same time. "Kicking me with enough force to bruise some ribs."

"Sounds about right," I said with a chuckle. "It's a god baby, after all."

Mera groaned again. "Don't remind me. Shadow's been trying to get me to leave all day, laying on the guilt." She lowered her voice dramatically. "*They'll hurt you for the baby's power* and *you have another life to consider,* in between him using his damn tongue as a weapon to cloud my mind."

"That also sounds about right," I said with another laugh. "Surprised he's let you out of arm's reach to sit here with me."

She wasn't out of his sight, though; Shadow and Reece were on the top deck, cutting imposing figures across the darkening horizon. The friends were chatting, but it was clear where both their focuses were: right on this bench.

"He could be here in a heartbeat and we both know it, so I'm never really out of his arm's reach."

I turned back to Mera. "Doesn't that bother you?"

She shrugged. "You know, I thought it would, but I actually want to be with him all the time. He gets me, and I feel complete when he's nearby. In the end, Shadow can roar and throw fire and act like a possessive Neanderthal, but we all know I have the true power. He loves me, and I've never known another who'd work so hard to give me everything I've ever dreamed of or desired. What woman wouldn't want to be worshipped by a dangerously gorgeous asshole of a man?"

Her words twirled through my mind, round and round, filling every thought as I tried to understand. A few moons ago I would not have been able to at all, but now... maybe I did get it. "I never thought I could exist like that," I told her softly, my gaze finding Reece again for a beat, "but since my rebirth, there's a part of me that feels empty. A part that craves the connectedness I see between you and Shadow..."

"But the independence you've clung to for centuries rejects the idea, making you feel like you'd be weak to allow that into your life?" Mera took a fairly astute stab at the thoughts I hadn't expressed. She pressed a hand to her chest. "I feel your battle here. In your energy. I know that you're dancing around something with Reece, and I'm here to tell you that it isn't a weakness to give yourself to another. It's a strength to trust them in that way. It's a strength to follow the instincts of your body and not deny what it needs." Her lips tilted into a smirk. "And it's definitely a strength to orgasm as many times as you did the other night and not have a heart attack."

I jerked as my wide eyes met hers, and she lost her shit, laughing so hard. "Oh my gods!" More laughter. "Come on, Angel. You completely forgot we were bonded, didn't you."

Shit. It wasn't that I'd forgotten, but I had expected her to shield like I did. "You're not supposed to know. Our deal was very specific."

At this point it was lucky she was a goddess who didn't really need oxygen to breathe because she was laughing too hard to take a breath. "Girl!" she gasped before shaking her head until eventually she calmed. "Did you really think I wouldn't feel it when you were in the midst of something so intense? Don't you feel Shadow and me?"

I was so used to blocking her now, and it had been my mistake to assume she was doing the same. "Not anymore," I said with a shake of my head. "I've trained my energy to block you the moment I feel your lust rising. It happens without thought now, so I don't catch the sexy times."

Mera pressed her lips tightly together. "You must block me a lot then."

"It's pretty much constant." My laughter finally spilled out as I leaned back into the wooden bench, feeling strangely more at peace now that Mera knew. "I don't even know how it happened," I murmured.

She snorted. "Well, when a warrior angel and a broody desert god are hot as fuck, sometimes they end up with the big coc—"

"Shut up," I spluttered. "I know *how* that part happened. What I meant was after all the centuries of anger and hate between us, it's odd that he's chosen now to claim me in the hope that we can quench the fire between us. Fires of hate as well as lust."

Mera sobered, eyes darker than usual. "I was the catalyst, throwing you two together in a way you could no longer ignore. And once you open the gates, even if only a touch, the energy trickles through until it turns into a flood. You've just reached the point where neither of you can close the gates any longer."

"You're awfully intuitive for someone so young," I said, reaching out to grasp her hand. "Guess it's the old soul you possess."

She gave my palm a tight squeeze. "It's easy to look in from the outside. I'm not as close to this as you and Reece. I just think that you two insisted on ignoring the truth while you were super pissed at each other. The truth that, in the beginning, there was love. Reece is kidding himself if he thinks he can fuck you out of his system. You're both kidding yourselves."

Part of me hoped she was right, but I'd learned the hard way with Reece and hope. "I guess only time will tell," I conceded. "We're giving this a shot, and when the dust settles on this battle, we'll know the truth. We'll move on."

"Sure, sure," Mera chided. "I'll place a bet on that *not* being the case."

I glared playfully, hoping she didn't bet anything too important on this relationship. It had been days with barely any contact between Reece and me, and I sensed that he was preparing himself for our inevitable parting. I should be doing the same, only I couldn't manage to distance myself like I had in the past. As Mera had said, the floodgates were open.

"Dinnertime!" Len shouted across the decks, and at that, Mera jumped to her feet.

"I'm freaking starving," she moaned, clutching her belly. The swollen section looked as if it was larger and hanging lower than it had been a few days ago, and as she hurried off, I hoped that I could be there when her baby arrived. I had never seen young born, and it felt like the sort of life-changing event I'd regret missing.

Especially since I'd never have it for myself.

I trailed Mera down the stairs into the main cabin, the guys leaving their stations to follow as well. We'd all gotten into a bit of a routine here, Reece steering, Alistair perched on the back deck communicating with the sand creatures while dousing himself in liquid, Galleli flying above when he could to scout ahead, and Len and Lucien moving back and forth across the main deck, clearly bored out of their minds.

Every dark-moon, though, we all ate together, family style.

Most of us were used to being alone for long periods, but this new tradition of eating at the long pamolsa-and-sand table was growing on all of us.

The dining section was the stern of the lower cabin, with the bow taken up by small cabins, a bathing area, and a galley with fire burners and liforina stores. The galley and each of the cabins had a round window, giving a glimpse of the deserts and sands beyond, but other than that, the only lighting in the lowest level came from desert lanterns, their heatless fires burning high.

Len, who had been our unofficial cook so far, was already at the table when the rest of us arrived. Dishes were laid across it, each with a similar array of food to what had been at the opening ceremony of the dynasty gathering. Mera was the first to sit, looking around expectantly. Her narrowed eyes urged the rest of us to get our shit together and sit so she could eat. I slipped in on her right, leaving the left for Shadow. Lucien was at the head, Len across from Mera, Galleli across from Shadow, and Alistair on my opposite side.

Reece took the other head of the table, which put him on my right, and as the blast of his power mingled with my own relatively cooler energy, I focused on the food. One hunger sated was better than none. "Your sands appear to be getting better at steering a ship," I said, hoping for normalcy.

"I've upgraded them to a full license," he said with a smile.

I blinked. "When you joke with me, it really messes with my head."

"Ours too," half the table chorused, and I caught Mera's smirk, which reminded me that we were not supposed to make our new arrangement public knowledge.

Turning away from Reece to focus on the food, I chose some gry fruit, having really developed a taste for it. After giving Mera a ripe piece, I placed another two on my plate. Shadow added some more foods to Mera's plate, taking care of his mate, and all too soon she had more nourishment in front of her than two goddesses could eat.

Shadow's protective instincts were stronger than ever, and I had a sense that when this baby was born, daddy beast was going to be a right pain in the ass.

"Here," Reece said, distracting me. I looked down to find that he'd made me a *yert*, the Desert Land's equivalent of a sandwich, filled with fried vegetables that grew under their trees. "You're not eating enough."

I blinked at the food, having no idea how to react to this gesture. He was acting like Shadow, and even if my first instinct was to reject it, expecting an ulterior motive, I decided it was time for us to change the narrative. "Thank you."

His eyes widened, a flash of surprise slicing through them, but he didn't question my compliance. Instead, we ate together in a comfortable silence with only occasional small talk around the table. There was proper nourishment for all of us in the supplies, including even the plasma beverage Lucien needed to renew his energy and the algae-type greens that Alistair consumed. Shadow didn't eat, but he still sipped on his favorite drink: a blend of Earth's finest whiskeys with some faerie spice to give it a kick.

It was a freaking picture-perfect family scene, and I knew that this was the calm before the storm. My senses were twitching, telling me that we were moving toward a disaster, and no matter how prepared I was, I couldn't keep this ship from crashing into the rocks and scattering all of us into the deep sands.

Lost forever.

CHAPTER THIRTY-FOUR

By the time dinner was done, Mera had once again convinced Shadow that it was too late to journey back to the library and that they best discuss it again in the new-moon. Len and I exchanged an amused glance, even though he was dangerously close to losing this bet.

Reece let out a huff as he got to his feet and swept out his hand to clean away the remaining food and dishes, sending everything to the galley. Without looking my way, he left, his broad shoulders disappearing from the cabin.

Len sidled closer to me, just as I was rising from the table "Should we relieve him for the night?" he asked.

My knee jerked into the table in an uncharacteristic show of incompetence. "What?" I managed to say.

"Relieve him of steering duty," he said slowly. "It's been a few moons, and I haven't seen him use a cabin once."

Oh, right. "From what I know, he's been leaving the sands in charge if he needs to rest, but I'll check in on him." In my flustered state, my words were rushed. "You all get some sleep. We'll wake you if there's any issue."

No one argued since a sense of frustration and mild fatigue

had started to filter through our energy after a few moons stuck on this ship. One by one they left the table, heading to the bedrooms, until only Mera and Shadow remained. "See you in the morning," Mera said with a smirk, "after you check on *relieving* Reece, of course."

"Shut it!" I mouthed, and she just chuckled like the maniac she was.

Even Shadow looked amused, and it was clear that he knew as much as his mate. There were no secrets between them, which was exactly how it should be. Truth be told, as I bid them goodnight and made my way to the deck, I really hoped this night would include some relief. Our time in the deserts was coming to an end soon, and so far, our bargain was going sadly unfulfilled.

When I hit the higher deck, I felt the brush of Reece's power, but everything else was calm. Such a vast difference to the previous moons. The breezes barely even ruffled the strands of my braid, and the light black shirt I wore tucked into my cargo pants was more than sufficient to protect me from the sands.

Crossing the deck, bathed in the blue rays of the dark-moon, I approached the bright spot that Reece appeared to occupy. He looked otherworldly, his energy giving him a glow so obvious he almost didn't seem real. Even here in his dominion, he was noticeably... more.

My footsteps were light as I got closer, wondering at the reception I would receive. "Do you need us to tag in and keep watch—" was all I managed before he spun and scooped me up.

On instinct, my legs went around his waist as he hauled me close, and I was already lifting my head, ready for the slam of his lips on mine. Reece did not disappoint, his tongue sweeping across my lips and demanding entry. I complied because I felt like I would explode if I didn't taste him... if I didn't feel that surge of his power colliding with mine.

Sand swept us up, and I wondered if we would once again be high and hidden from the world.

"The other ship is too close," Reece grumbled against my mouth before dragging out another long, delicious kiss, his left-hand tightening on my ass to almost painful levels. "We will seek privacy elsewhere."

I hadn't seen Darin's ship for days, but now that we were in the slower currents, it seemed that he'd caught up. There was no time to think about the journey though, for tonight was about Reece and me and the sparks of fire igniting between us.

His sands lifted us higher, zooming us across the river in the direction of the red land visible far off in the distance. "Will they be okay on the ship?" I gasped between kisses, my brain spinning as I sought to remember the others. "I didn't wake any of them to steer."

"The ship is safe," he said, lifting his head so his eyes could stare into the core of my essence. "I would never risk them. Now, forget everything else, and focus on us. This is your only need to be filled."

Need. He couldn't have picked a more accurate word, and I was instantly reminded of the conversation I'd had with Mera a few hours earlier. It wasn't weakness to give into the demands of my body. I could do this and be a warrior. It was time for me to stop stereotyping myself and just enjoy the ride. In all ways.

Living in the Desert Lands with Reece had been my child-hood hope and dream, and we should never have let ourselves fall apart as we had. It was time for a new future.

Maybe... even some hope.

"They'd be happy, you know." The words slipped out as memories of the past filled my mind. Maybe it was the red sands or the new knowledge that there was a tattered bond between Reece and me, waiting to be finally dashed or fully formed, but either way, I was stuck in the past for a moment.

"Who would?" he asked as he followed my line of sight into the endless Rohami sands we approached.

"Our families."

Pulling my gaze back to him, he lowered me to his sands, and I wished I hadn't said a damn word. We were supposed to be keeping this casual... unemotional. Reminding us both of our past and the love we'd shared was the surest way to remember the betrayal and pain too.

Not a healthy path in moving forward or changing our narrative as I'd previously hoped.

Reece didn't answer, and as I sought a subject change to get us back to the sexy vibe we'd had before, he reached up and brushed his hand across my cheek. "They loved you," he murmured. My throat grew tight at the emotion in his tone. "Mother always told me that you were the epitome of honor and strength. She told me I was the lucky one to have you, and I think that's why I took the betrayal so hard."

I didn't have to ask for clarification on what betrayal.

"Guess I ended up being a disappointment," I conceded. "But for what it's worth, I loved them too. I loved your entire family and considered them mine as well." Despite their flaws, and fascination with power, his parents—and mine—were worthy of our love.

Reece, wearing an oddly blank expression, shook his head. "You wouldn't have disappointed them, Lale. They would have understood your choices that day. I expected you to carry us all in a fight that wasn't even yours. A fight where you lost Leka. I should have tried harder to understand, and I'm the reason we spent so many years apart. If I could go back..."

Every part of me was screaming in both sorrow and joy, the emotions mixed and mangled together until I was a mess.

Reece had finally given me the grace I'd been desperately craving as I'd punished myself through the years in failed attempts to make amends.

In the end, our world had never been made up of black and white morals, good and bad deeds, or betrayal and hate. There was more than one side to a coin, and acknowledging that might give us a shot at finally moving forward.

"We can't go back," I reminded him. "So, let's not waste this chance to move forward."

Our gazes locked, and the flames burning deep in the galaxy of his power warmed me to my core. "My sentiments exactly," he rumbled.

I lifted my head and initiated our kiss, and once again I found myself off the ground, legs around his waist as I arched into him. His left hand slid up my spine to tangle in the strands at the back of my braid, pulling my face into his. Reece kissed with the sort of intensity that could destroy worlds. It near destroyed me, so I was most certain of this fact. Opening my mouth, I let his tongue stroke across mine. The more I tasted him, the more I wanted, and with a groan I wrapped my hands around his neck, pulling our bodies as close as was possible.

By the time Reece's sands began to descend, I was breathing heavy, my lower body aching. This was the point where I was ready to claw his clothing off. "We need to be naked," I muttered, feeling put out that I wasn't having an orgasm already.

Reece's husky laughter didn't help the situation. "You've been spending too much time with Mera. Patience... You should have learned it by now."

Oh, was that right? I arched my back and ground against him, feeling the strain of his hard length through our clothing. Reece's eyes darkened to midnight, the flash of stars and galaxies brighter than ever, and I knew my expression was smug as I smiled.

His growl was impressive. "Yeah, you're right. Fuck patience." Hot sands washed over us, and within a beat, I was completely naked. As my breasts fell free, Reece leaned over and closed his mouth over my right nipple, teeth scraping as he applied pressure before he swirled his tongue across the peak. By the time he moved onto the left, I was groaning, both hands gripping the back of his head.

Even though I loved his warrior look, with closely shaved dark hair, at this moment I wished he had something for me to grip. When he lifted his head, I met his gaze, my panting breaths loud and shallow.

"No more patience," he repeated, lowering me to my feet. My legs took a second to hold me up, but once I found my equilibrium, I was able to stand and look at where he'd taken us.

"This is the outer territory of Rohami," he said, grasping my hands and sliding his fingers through mine as he led me toward what looked like a sand dune rising about thirty feet above the flat plane.

"Why did you choose this area?" I asked, looking around for an answer.

His grip tightened as he pulled me forward. "I found a grotto."

My feet ground to a halt, and for a beat I wondered if I'd misheard him. "Sorry, what did you say?"

He'd stopped with me, turning fully to face me. "It took me nearly a hundred thousand moons, but I finally found one."

Staring wide-eyed, I opened and closed my mouth. "It's a myth."

In the Desert Lands, grottos were their version of an oasis, the fable of finding paradise in the middle of the desolate sands. In this world, it was said that they existed below the plains, but no one had ever found one to prove this tale. When we were young, Reece had told me of his plans to find one of these gifts that the ancients had supposedly left, even though none had ever achieved this task.

I should have known that if anyone could discover a grotto, it would be Reece.

"I can't believe you actually found one," I said, shaking my head as excitement pushed through my shock. "We spent so many moons making plans for what we'd do with all the treasures."

He leaned down and pressed his lips to mine, a completely impromptu kiss, and it rocked me in a way that was unexpected. Pulling away, breathless, I asked, "How did you find it?"

Reece shrugged, his eyes still focused on my mouth. "I've had a lot of time on my hands, not to mention the sort of determination that's gotten me through rough days."

That sobered me up somewhat. I hadn't been with him for the rough days—no doubt I'd caused more than a few of them. "I should have been here when you found it," I whispered, drawing his gaze up to meet mine. "I missed that moment."

The tilt of his lips was barely visible, but he didn't look unhappy. "You're here this moon, and we can finally fulfil our plans."

Plans... "Who knew those plans would one day include naked body parts and multiple orgasms," I joked, needing a break from the heavier emotions.

"I knew," he said, with a low laugh that stirred power deep in my chest. "This has been destined for a long time, and since I've never brought anyone to this spot for fear it would be stolen or corrupted, it looks like all my boyhood dreams are about to come to fruition."

A sense of relief filtered through me at the knowledge that

no one else had ever come to the grotto with him. This was still a chance to experience it all with him. A first for both of us.

Before I could say anything else, he released my hand, moving closer to the dune. He spent several minutes searching the grounds closely. "It shifts every moon," he explained, brushing away some sands. "And I haven't been out here for a long time, but it's usually..."

He trailed off as he leaned down further, dusting off another layer. Even in the dark moonlight, I could see what looked like crystals embedded in the red sands. "You won't believe the color of the sand below," he said as he looked up, our gazes meeting. "It's unmatched anywhere on the surface."

I found myself crouching closer, and as I did, I felt his power moving deeper and deeper into the land. "What exactly are you doing?" I asked.

"Seeking permission to enter from the sand below."

I pressed my hand to the ground near his and almost gasped at the undercurrent of power. The Desert Lands always had a flowing well of energy that could be tapped into, but this was something... bigger. As I moved my hands a few yards to the right, all I felt was the normal Rohami power.

"The doorway is contained within a very small sliver of sand," Reece explained.

"Hence why they're near impossible to find."

He nodded, before lowering his head again and continuing to ask permission. In minutes, the sands started to shift and move below our feet, followed by a distinct rumble. Reece jumped up and all but dragged me back a few dozen feet. "I've only found this one," he said as we both watched the sands drop away from the land until what looked a lot like a doorway into the ground formed, "but I believe more exist."

All the lands here were equally powerful, and it made sense that Rohami wouldn't be the only one to benefit from a grotto. The rumbling eased as the sands completely split the earth where Reece's hand had been pressed mere seconds ago. The gap continued to widen until eventually the deserts were once again peaceful, except for this new opening with twinkling lights highlighting a path under the sands.

I was about to see a grotto with Reece, and for a beat I wondered how this was my life.

CHAPTER THIRTY-FIVE

If Reece hadn't been confidently strolling into a giant *hole in the land,* I would have been more cautious in my approach, but trusting his experience with this grotto, I followed, naked and quietly anticipating what I might see in this place of myth and legend.

As we descended many steps, leading even deeper than I expected, the lights highlighted the red sands. I couldn't see what lay below from this angle, but I noticed that as we moved into the grotto, the reds were changing tone, growing lighter until...

"Silver," I breathed. "The sands are pure silver."

"Yep," Reece's deep voice filtered up from where he was a few steps lower. He turned back to me, and I noted that his skin looked darker under the silver. His eyes bluer and more intense too. "These sands hold properties unlike anything I've ever experienced. Not just in this world, but all of them. It's true power, original power, but it can never be removed from the grotto."

"You tried to remove it?" Of course he'd tried to remove it.

He nodded, that cocky smile reappearing. "Yeah, you know

how I like to best whatever challenges come my way. I've tried to take this power out in so many ways I lost count. It didn't matter, though, because by the time I reached the surface, not a speck of silver remained with me."

"You're lucky the grotto continues to allow you entrance," I said drily, shaking my head.

His laugh echoed through this stairwell. "I think it enjoyed my attempts. A familiar game we play."

He returned to his descent, and after what felt like a mile into the core of Rohami, we stepped out into a field of silver sands, and I finally found myself in a grotto. For a beat, before I visually took in one part of this hidden secret, I closed my eyes and let the energy fill me up. That was when I truly understood what Reece meant by this grotto holding power unlike any he'd ever felt.

At first it didn't flow easily with my essence, the ancient tendrils of the silver sands cold and foreign, but within seconds, it turned more comforting. Comforting and incredibly intense. A soft chuckle escaped me. "Feels odd that I'm naked now," I breathed, holding my hands out to twirl my fingers through the power.

"I like you naked," Reece said, closer than before. "And I plan on keeping you that way for as long as possible."

Despite this sort of possessive statement bothering me earlier, here, surrounded by silver sands, his words struck a part of me deep inside. A part that had been owned by this damn male for centuries. As my eyes opened, I found Reece before me, looking right at home in the land of the ancient gods. "You're not naked," I said, my voice breathless. "Which if you ask me, is a touch unfair—"

In one smooth motion he pulled his shirt off, and whatever I'd planned on saying next faded into the silver sands. Rich bronze skin draped over firm muscles filled my vision.

Reece let out a low laugh. "As much as I'm enjoying this moment, it might be best if I leave my pants on until you've seen more than the front entrance."

Dammit... he was right. If he were naked, even a magical grotto would pale in comparison. "I'm naked though," I noted, forcing my eyes to lift from the writing across his lower abdomen in a script I couldn't read. "Am I not a distraction?"

His answer was to sweep me into his arms, and with a growl he buried his face in my neck and bit into the flesh there, sending trills of pleasure straight to my center. "The only reason I'm not buried inside of you right now," he murmured, tongue caressing the bite mark, "is because this is your first chance to see a grotto, and I won't take that away from you. There's plenty of time for the rest..."

At this point I was dead. Just fucking dead as his words and aura caressed every damn sense I possessed. Before my soul followed me into the grave though, Reece set me on my unsteady legs, and off he went into the grotto. As I followed him across the soft sands, silver spreading out around my bare feet as I walked, I leaned over to touch it. It was silky, much finer than the sands of Earth, and the energy coursing through it was intense.

"I see why you've never advertised this find," I said as I straightened, the sand falling from my hold. "It's addictive, a true shot of power from what feels like an original source. One could grow used to having it."

He nodded, and for the first time since entering this cave, his expression turned serious. "In my darker moments, I found myself lingering here, unable to leave. If it wasn't for my own powerbase and the strength of my friendships, I feel that I might have lost myself to the thrall."

"Why did you bring me here when you didn't bring Shadow and the others?"

His furrowed brow remained. "Multiple reasons."

I thought he was going to leave it at that, but before the disappointment could even well up, he continued. "One, this was our adventure together. Despite everything, it felt wrong to ever bring another here. Two, none of our friends have the bond to the deserts that you and I have." He let out a low breath. "And three, you have shown time and time again that power doesn't addict you. You are in possession of arguably one of the strongest power sources in the worlds, and you never abuse that gift."

This was the caring side of Reece that I'd lost, and it had almost killed me when it happened. "In the Shadow Realm was the only time I've powered up past my normal means in centuries," I said softly.

A smile cracked his stoic stare. "You were lit up like a damn goddess. Shocked my old system a touch."

"I could tell," I replied drily. "You broke a centuries-old standoff to remind me that I'm a shitty, weak warrior."

With an exhale, his head dropped, and I had to blink and make sure I was seeing that minute display of shame correctly. "It's my turn to apologize," he said. "I acted like an asshole, and honestly, you didn't deserve it. It was just seeing you there, so fucking powerful and perfect—ready and determined to do whatever it took to save someone you loved—triggered the hell out of me, and I couldn't let it go."

Closing the distance between us, I put my hand on his arm. "We're moving forward," I reminded him, "healing the scars of the past so that we have a different future."

His voice lowered to a gruff whisper. "What if I don't want a different future?"

Now I was the one triggered. "I—I don't understand. You want us to remain enemies?"

With a rough shake of his head, he growled. "No, that's not

it at all. Let's just survive the next few moons, and then we can talk."

He was driving me crazy with his back and forth, but I couldn't argue with his statement. We were possibly going up against the ancients in a few moons, so there was no point worrying about the future until we were sure we had one.

Forcing myself to focus on our surroundings again, I nudged him in the side. "Okay, then. Show me around."

With all the distractions—aka Reece not only half-naked but also emotionally opening up to me—there was no surprise we hadn't made it far past the bottom of the stairs. As we powered on, that loose silver pathway expanded into a huge, round space. The walls and ceiling, high above, were as silver as the sands below. This ancient grotto was literally lined in power.

At first, the bright twinkling of the sand blinded me, but as my eyes adjusted, the most incredible vision appeared in the distance. "Liforina," I cried, almost bowling Reece over in my excitement. "There's water down here."

His laughter followed as I raced across the loose sand to reach what looked like a shallow lake lapping against the shore. "These are power-infused hot springs," Reece said as he came up behind me. "If I'm seriously injured, it only takes a few hours in here to return to full strength."

I was already naked, so there was literally no reason for me not to enter the warm spring. It didn't look very deep, even though the water spanned out for many dozens of feet in all directions. As the heated liquid surrounded my muscles, I could feel it seeping into my energy, merging with it to repair any imperfections it felt.

I continued out, finding that it never got deeper than my thighs. After moving toward the most northern tip, I sat with my back against a hard silver wall, and the water leveled out just under my chin. Small bubbles flowed around my legs, the current helping to heal and soothe me.

From this position, I was able to see that this grotto was a simple space: the sands, this water, and some plants dotted about high on the shore. My sight of anything else was cut off as I focused on Reece, who had followed behind. He was naked now. The water lovingly caressed his thighs, which meant I had the most delightful view of every part of the desert god. Especially the hard length that was drawing my gaze.

When he stood before me, I attempted to breathe normally. "It's not found anywhere else in the worlds," he said.

"I know," I replied quickly, sure that his dick was absolutely one of a kind.

He laughed, and I jerked my head up, realizing I'd been a little cockmerized, as Mera phrased it. "The trees that grow here," he said, as he dropped down to sit at my side. "And the other flora. None of it is found anywhere else, and they can't be removed from the grotto either."

Right. Plants and trees were the unique wood he was referring to.

As our skin pressed together down my right side, I fought to stay on point. "Do the plants have any special magic?"

I jumped as his hand slipped across my leg under the water, a smooth movement I hadn't expected. "I think that this entire ecosystem," he said slowly, his finger tracing up my inner thigh, "is what makes this oasis so unique and special." When he hit my center, he parted the folds and slipped across the swollen flesh there. "We're already reaping the benefits, which you'll really understand when you leave."

He slid his finger inside of me, and despite the water, there was no resistance. I'd been turned on for so long that I was more than ready for him. Tilting my hips, I moved against his touch, needing more. A second finger joined the first, and we both groaned. "How long have you been wet for me?" he rumbled, turning his head so his lips could caress along the skin of my cheek and down to my lips.

"I'm not sure I've stopped aching since the last time at the gathering," I admitted, crying out as he moved his hand faster, fingers pumping in and out of me while his thumb circled my clit. Within seconds, the pleasure from my sensitive nerves had me hurtling toward an orgasm.

"Tell me, Lale, did you find release without me? Over these many years?"

Even through the fuzziness of my brain, I growled at this fucker asking me questions like that when he was in the middle of controlling my body like a puppet master. With his intense gaze on me, I wanted to lie and tell him I'd moved on many times over the long years, but the truth was, in my robotic state I'd shut down every part of my body.

Punished myself in all ways.

"There has been no other," I gasped, my breathing faster than ever as I lifted my hips higher and all but rode his fingers, greedy for his touch.

Greedy for the emotions he was returning to my world.

Mera had started my metamorphosis with the fires, but Reece... he was a damn rainbow, exploding color all over me. No matter what the next few days brought, one thing was for certain: I could never go back to my black-and-white existence.

CHAPTER THIRTY-SIX

It took me a few seconds to realize that Reece had frozen at the answer to his question. His fingers were still buried inside me, his naked chest still pressed to me as his other hand pulled me close, but the rest of him was still. Not to mention the full dilation of his pupils in those wide eyes. "Never?" he breathed harshly.

"I was a robot, Reece," I got out, just as breathless, thanks to an impending orgasm. "I refused to feel or want for anything except my duty as a warrior. With the power I controlled, letting myself feel all the pain would have been disastrous."

His shock was fading as a spark of satisfaction burned through his expression. Without moving his fingers from inside me, he used his other hand to lift me in the buoyant water and move me onto his lap. I ended up straddling his thighs, leaning back just enough so that he could continue thrusting his fingers inside me. "You have always belonged to me, Lale," he murmured, shaking his head.

I groaned. "Don't get too cocky. I'm awakened now, and I won't be a robot ever again."

The growl deep in his chest caught my attention, and he

went from shocked to possessive to pissed in a mere second. "You are mine until I say so," he said as that growl deepened, "We made a deal, and you can't back out of it."

"Until—" I tried to catch my breath. "Until we leave the Desert Lands."

The swirls in my stomach moved faster, desire slamming into me as I got closer. My fingers had been digging into his shoulder for leverage, but wanting him to feel what I was, I slid them lower and wrapped them around the hot shaft that was between us.

"It'll be well beyond the deserts," Reece finally murmured, but I couldn't focus on his words with those damn fingers destroying me, gliding deep inside as my muscles contracted around him. Leaning forward, instinct took over as I tightened my grasp on his cock, fingers managing to get about halfway around his thick shaft.

Reece jerked against me with a groan. "Lale, fuck. You have a firm grip."

I was strong, and worried I might hurt him, I was about to loosen my hold when he groaned again. "Don't stop... I like it."

Well, okay then. Stroking him, it was a balance between giving Reece pleasure and not coming myself. A balance that was failing as I felt the tremble in my thighs. Denying my orgasm had it building up to the sort of intense release that might just kill us both.

Reece leaned forward. "I need to taste you," he murmured against my lips, and I could tell he meant more than just a kiss.

"Only if I can reciprocate," I replied, desperate to know what he tasted like.

His fingers eased from me, and I tried not to whimper as he stood, lifting me at the same time. As the warm waters fell away, leaving not a trace of moisture on our skin, I wished we could stay here in their powerful and soothing embrace.

Reece noticed my disappointment. "I can't control these sands," he told me. "So, if we want to breathe, we need to do this on land."

Fair point and thank the fucking gods he was already striding through the shallow waters, powerful thighs eating up the distance until we were soon on the loose silver sand. Here, he slowed and lowered me to my back; the silver surrounded me as hot and soothing as the water had been.

Even better, it didn't get all over our skin and between us. It just stayed in its current position, cushioning my body, letting us enjoy all the naked skin on display. Reece leaned over the top of me, mouth wrapping around my right nipple. Lacing my fingers behind his head, I held on until he was done.

As he lifted his head, hooded eyes met mine. "I want to know everything that gets you off," he rasped. "I want us to figure it out together."

Yes. Yep. Yeah. Totally. I could agree to that. "Better hurry up," I managed to say. "We'll be in the Delfora soon."

That hooded gaze did not ease. "Challenge accepted," he finally murmured.

Before I could take another breath, he reversed our positions, rolling me so that I was on top, and he was now sprawled out in the silver. "What do you want to do now, Lale?" he asked in his husky drawl. "Tell me exactly what you want."

I swallowed roughly. "I want to give you pleasure."

His laughter was dark and seductive, the sound curling around me. "I want you to tell me what you want from me. In detail. Do you want my tongue in your pussy? Would you like to fuck my mouth? How many orgasms?"

It was my turn to stare at him like a stunned lunatic because it almost sounded like Reece was giving up control... to me?

"Limited time offer," he added, sensing my shock.

His hands were on my hips as I straddled him, his firm hold biting into my skin. "I want to taste you while you taste me," I told him, needing a release soon.

He lifted me higher to spin me around so I was now facing his erection. "Back up, Lale," he said, voice strained.

Reaching out for the heavy cock lying halfway up his stomach, I held onto it while wiggling myself backward until my ass was in his face. As I did, his hard length jerked against my hold, precum beading on the end. With more confidence, I kept moving, and as I settled my knees into the sands on either side of his head, his tongue slid across my aching pussy, lapping up the moisture there. I rocked into him and groaned, "More."

Reece returned that with a groan of his own before he wrapped his arms around my thighs and pulled me right onto his mouth. "Tell me what you want," he demanded, breath hot on my quivering flesh. "In detail."

At this point I was desperate. I'd been close to an orgasm too many times, and I needed the final release. "I want to ride your face," I got out. "I want you to fuck me with your mouth and tongue."

His mouth was on me so fast that I almost jumped. As he lifted me to change my angle, he slid his tongue across my ass and down into my pussy, sucking all of my pleasure into his mouth. His cock jerked again in my hand, and he was harder than ever as I leaned down his body, needing to know what he tasted like.

My head spun as my body trembled. It was difficult to focus on his cock with his tongue destroying me while his fingers slid into my entrance. I cried out as I wrapped my lips around the head of his cock and a hot, salty power exploded in my mouth. Reece tasted like life and energy, and I marveled at the low groan he let out when I sucked and caressed him.

His grip on me tightened, and as he continued to pump two

fingers into me, I rocked against him, which also rocked his length into my mouth. He was too big for me to take much more than a few inches, so I used my hand as well, the movements jagged thanks to the dozens of sensations hitting me at once.

The tight curl of pleasure swelled until it couldn't be contained, and I let out a low scream as I came, my body jerking hard and fast. Reece did not ease up, sucking my clit into his mouth and swirling his tongue across it with enough force that I came again instantly and almost as violently as the first time.

As I shook, his dick popped out of my mouth, but I was too far gone to find it again as I rode out the full orgasm. It took a long time for me to breathe and think again as my body all but collapsed on top of his. For a second, I relaxed into his heat, right until he was teasing my clit again, and I realized I'd fallen behind on giving pleasure as well as receiving it.

Able to focus a touch more, I leaned forward and wrapped my hand and mouth around him again, working this time to relax my jaw and take in even more of his length. I had no experience in giving head, but I was a quick learner, focusing on the actions that made him groan the most—a great plan until he was, once again, working my lower half into a frenzy, both hands wrapped around my thighs as he parted my folds to swipe his tongue full length, over and over.

He groaned when I focused on his knob, rolling my tongue across the slit at the tip, his taste filling my mouth. "Lale, fuck," he said, and the sound of his raspy voice was enough to spur me on, filling me with determination to give him pleasure. Relaxing my jaw, I managed to take another inch, and just when I had a good rhythm going, my body rocking against his mouth while I took him into mine, Reece tightened his grip on my inner thighs and pushed his finger inside, coating it in my pleasure. Almost immediately he removed it, and just as I wondered why, I felt his touch slide a little higher than before.

Now, as I'd told Mera, many of the beings in the Solaris System had a similar anatomy to shifters and humans as all of us had been created from a single source. Most of those beings found pleasures in multiple parts of their bodies, but it'd never occurred to me that I would.

When Reece's fingers, lubricated in my arousal, slid across my ass, pressing into the entrance, I paused. "What are you doing?" I rasped, my voice a husky mess after those screaming orgasms.

"Figuring out what you like," he murmured, his mouth still working my vagina while his fingers were exploring *wherever the hell they wanted,* apparently.

"Uh, I'm not sure—" He pushed one finger inside me, slowly, and *holy mother of the moons.*

I was rocking before I even registered it while his tongue worked my clit, and the speed of another impending release shocked the fuck out of me. As his finger moved slowly in and out, the muscles there loosened, allowing him to slide further inside, stimulating a ton of nerve endings in a way I'd never experienced. It was a different pleasure stemming from a part of myself I'd never explored, and as I arched further into his touch, I realized that this arrogant bastard might know exactly what I liked.

"Reece," I choked out, moving against him, needing more as I chased the pleasures unfurling. This was going to be a total release, and I might finally understand human's fascination with ass play.

Unable to do more than hold on and enjoy the ride, I gripped the side of his stomach, nails digging in as his finger moved faster in time with the strokes of his tongue on my clit. The orgasm this time exploded from deeper than I'd ever felt, and I might have passed out for a few seconds because the next thing I knew, Reece was flipping our position, that hard length I'd tasted only minutes before slamming inside of me in one swift move.

As he stared down at me, lips full and glistening, he groaned. "You're the most dangerous creature in the worlds," he said as he lifted his body to slam his cock into me again, a heavy thrust that should have sent us up the sand. Only this was no ordinary sand; it held us in place, adding force to his strokes.

I'd already come three times in quick succession, and in theory it should take longer for another. But as Reece leaned over, kissing me—I could taste myself on his lips—I found the buildup already growing. "I'm going to come again," I cried, slightly frustrated at not being able to drag it out a little bit longer. "Do you have to be amazing at everything?"

"Yes," he shot back, lips quirking into a teasing smile, even as his body destroyed mine with the powerful strokes. "You've spent years denying your passions, and now your body is taking advantage. You should listen to it."

"Oh— I'm— I'm listening."

The speed of his thrusts increased, and as his length buried deeper each time, I dug my nails into his skin. When he lowered his mouth to my nipples, my hands fell to the side, clawing into the sand to find the traction I needed. Silver energy rose to join the strength of Reece's and mine, imbuing us with the power of the ancients.

As I had that thought, my body lifting to meet each thrust and Reece reached down to slide a finger across my clit. My energy expanded while darkness danced across my vision, the release flowing through me in sharp, jerking motions that had me crying out and holding onto the sand like my life depended on it.

Reece's roar joined in with my cries, and I felt the swell of his cock and power, his thrusts jagged as he rode out the end of his orgasm. "Damn," he whispered against my neck. "The power of the grotto is not to be underestimated."

Truer words had never been spoken, only it wasn't the grotto that one should never underestimate.

It was Reece.

CHAPTER THIRTY-SEVEN

By the time my head stopped spinning and the last tremors left my body, Reece had moved us back into the hot spring. As I relaxed into the swirling depths, I sighed at how good the water felt against my sensitive skin.

Reece remained silent at my side, and I could swear he was already distancing himself. "Why haven't you asked me about my sexual partners overs the years?" he asked out of nowhere, when we'd sat in silence for too long. "I asked about yours because I was tempted to murder any who'd touched you, as irrational as that is... But you never asked about me. Do you not care?"

My chest ached with dueling emotions. "We only have a few more days in the deserts. Is there really enough time to discuss the many females you've been with?"

Reece was silent, and it was clear my attempt at humor had fallen flat. Time to try the truth. "I really don't want to know," I admitted.

This got his full attention. "You're jealous?" he asked, gaze stripping me to my core. "Melalekin, who's had males from all the worlds chasing her from the moment she could wield a sword, is jealous of attention I've had?"

"I'm not jealous, you arrogant asshole" I shot back, lying to save face. "It's just not worth discussing."

Reece let out a cynical laugh. "I want you to be jealous, Lale."

I blinked at him, unsure what he was saying. "Clarify, please."

"Jealousy means you care," he said softly, wrapping his arm around me and bringing back a touch of the closeness we'd had during sex.

With a long breath, I pushed my pride aside and said, "Even as a robot it was torture thinking of you with other females. I'm not sure I could have seen that and not killed you both."

Reece didn't show an ounce of concern over my threat to murder him. "There have been no others, Lale," he finally said. "I was angry for many years, but when it came to females, none compared to you. No matter how much I tried to destroy our bond, it never happened."

I'd been shocked by much that had happened between us in the Desert Lands, but this was the moment my heart finally seized in my chest. "You—You—What?" I cough. "You haven't had sex in centuries?"

Reece shook his head. "No one could satisfy me, so I didn't bother. My hand was better company."

Still gasping like a fish out of water, I managed a sob. "You're not like that with me. You clearly love sex and foreplay..." I groaned. "The foreplay is... damn."

His laugh was strangled. "That's with you, Lale. It's always been like that with you. I was a fool to ever think I could hate you out of my life."

I had to press a hand to my chest to keep myself together.

"You gave it a solid shot," I finally said, and needing relief from this conversation, I stood. "We should go."

Reece didn't argue, rising with me. We were quiet as we strolled onto the sand, my body and hair dry before we got out of the springs. Nothing from this grotto would leave with us, not even a bead of moisture—a prediction proven as we stepped out of the silver sands and back onto the red of Rohami and I looked down my naked body to find not a speck of silver remained, even on my feet. He was also right about the loss of energy hitting me like a ton of bricks.

"Fuck," I groaned, half leaning over with my hands on my knees.

"It'll take a few minutes," Reece said from nearby as I closed my eyes in an attempt to keep it together.

For many long seconds I felt powerless, but then the natural ebb and flow of my energy base returned, and I was once again able to breathe deeply and focus.

"Wow, that was intense," I said when I could speak. "You were right not to bring others here. One could easily lose themselves to that feeling of invincibility."

It had only been when I'd stepped outside that I'd truly felt the loss of power, followed by a need to return to the grotto.

"You handled it exactly as I'd expected," Reece said. "Strongly and resiliently."

For a beat, a sense of comfort settled between us, and I hoped that this time, it would last longer. In truth, a huge part of me was still completely stunned by his confession in the grotto, and for once, reading between the lines took me to a place that I wasn't ready to go yet. A place with too much hope. "Let's head back to our friends," I finally said. "With any luck they haven't floated off course."

His smile was warm, and I pushed into him, feeling the sands of time slip away from us. We were already so much closer to the Delfora, and with that, the uncertainty of our future felt stronger than ever.

"The Odessa is on course," he said, "heading for the Guardians." As he tipped his head back, his strong jawline was the only part of him visible from this angle. "I feel the call of the sacred lands." His murmur was filled with power. "It's louder than ever. It won't be long before the calm rivers grow wild again and we're fighting for our lives."

Pushing my body as high as I could without unfurling my wings, I sent energy into the world until I too sensed the tugging tendril of darkness deep in the north. "I feel it," I told him, "the rising tide of power and anger of the lands."

There was no reason for me to have any connection to the Delfora or the Desert Lands in general—I was not born of this world like Reece. But there was no denying that I could feel the call too.

Neither of us questioned it. The reason would show itself when the time was right. Whether it was the bond we'd created in our youth or something more sinister, I would face it the same way I had vowed to face everything since the time of my weakness here: head on.

With nothing more to be learned in Rohami, Reece pulled me against his chest, and as his sands surrounded us, I marveled at how much control he had over the dominating power of this world. All the sands except that of the grotto.

Made me wonder what a being who could control the silver sands might be able to do. What power could they manipulate for their own means? "Do you think the ancient gods, or maybe even Death itself, were the ones who created the grottos?" I asked as he lifted us into the air. "Can they control the silver sands?"

If the jolt in his energy was any indication, that question did not sit well with him. "We'd best hope not," he bit out. "If we fail in our mission to stop them from rising and they can use the silver sands, we're all doomed. I have nothing that can stand against that strength. None of us do."

Reece used a tone that I'd rarely heard from him. A tone that said he was unsure about the future... unsure we had enough power to win this mission.

For a brief moment, I sensed that we were thinking the same thing: Was this the battle we'd join our brethren in the sands? Our bones added to the valley of the dead, never to walk the worlds again.

CHAPTER THIRTY-EIGHT

Reece and I journeyed back to the ship, re-clothed ourselves from the spares in the supplies, and finally got some rest, but after that moon there were no more chances for dalliances in the desert. The next few moons were a battle with the sand streams again as Tsuma's rising power mixed with the treacherous deeps, sending all of us to the edge of losing our minds.

"It's time for you to go now," Shadow told Mera in the dining area on the eve of us making the Guardian's lands. "We have delayed for you to see the Rohami sands, observe an echinat jump in *all its full skeletal beauty*, eat the food supplies *because there are starving children in the worlds,* and now you have glimpsed the black sands of the Guardian dynasty. That's it. Now it's time for your gorgeous ass to return to the library so I have enough time and energy to get back here for this battle."

Mera pouted, the look only falling from her face when the lurch of our ship sent us all to the left. "Reece said we have to make land at the Guardians for more supplies," she said in a rush. "You told me you could portal from there as long as it's only you who returns. I can leave once I've gotten off this ship and had a proper look around."

Shadow's eyes narrowed until they were flaming slits. "I know what you're doing mate, and I promise you this is the last moon. Okay?"

Mera's smile was practically a beam as she shifted along the bench. "You're the best. I feel really good about all my new experiences. I think it's rounding me out as an eternal being."

I wasn't the only one hiding a smile; it had not escaped my notice that she hadn't agreed to Shadow's new terms. I'd already won the bet by default of Len losing—even if I wouldn't get the gems until after this battle because I didn't want to leave him short—but it was great to know that my guess had been accurate. I knew my best friend.

"Are you sure that Darin has allowed safe passage into the Guardian dynasty?" Len asked as he rolled a deep purple stone in this hand. The *enjette* gem was used for calming and strengthening a soul. I'd noticed him playing with that particular stone a lot lately, and it was clear we were all on edge.

It wasn't only the energy below us growing in strength, but also the unease in the Delfora too. I kept having the most vivid of dreams while meditating—dreams that tore me through a sea of bones and silver sand. The gods dragging me down so that my essence could rest with my sister's.

"Darin's last message assured me that we'll be welcome," Reece said shortly. "He advised us to replenish ourselves before we face Tsuma and the others. If there was another option, I'd take it, but this is our best chance."

"We should get some rest, then," Lucien said as he smoothly stood. "My plasma is almost out, so I'm hoping the Guardians have extra supplies. Otherwise I'll be heading back to the library with Shadow."

"Remind me again why we didn't just take a doorway in the

first place?" Alistair asked, voice raspy as he poured another cup of water over himself. "I think I missed the explanation in earlier conversations."

Reece leaned back in his chair, arms crossed over his broad chest as he said, "Only someone as powerful as Shadow could open an unapproved doorway this close to the Delfora, and he wouldn't have the strength to keep it open for all of us to cross. The same if I tried to transport all of us that far in my sands. This is the safest way to ensure we didn't use up all of our power getting there and have none for the battle."

Shadow nodded. "Yeah, it's going to be a struggle even for me. Luckily I only have to return with myself because the more I take, the harder it will be."

Mera's face fell. "Fuck, I've been a selfish bitch," she said in a rush, standing as fast as she could with her belly. "My need to stay with you outweighed the truths you've been telling me all along. We should go now, I won't have you weakened for this sort of battle."

Shadow reached out and took her hand, halting her. "Sunshine, I won't be further weakened by one more moon. We can stay for you to see the Guardians."

She examined his face closely, searching out the truth. "Please don't lie to me. I won't put any of you in danger."

Her mate stood as well, towering over all of us while still having to crouch to fit in the cabin. "There is no additional danger. You will see the Guardians and then go to the library." He took his eyes off her for a beat to look around. "And with that in mind, Mera needs to rest."

She didn't argue, clearly exhausted. This close to the end of her pregnancy, she'd been a trooper for staying this long. I was also fairly sure that while Mera thought she was convincing her mate to stay, he'd been secretly happy to keep an eye on her for as long as possible.

Unfortunately, it seemed that the Guardians would be her last stop, and I was going to miss my best friend. Worrying about her was second nature now, but in this situation, she would be safer away from this world. Even if we won this battle, there was a decent chance that some of us could be badly injured or killed in the Delfora, but that wasn't to be Mera's fate. The only event she had to worry about was the baby arriving while we were gone, and in that case, Gaster was powerful and well-versed in healing energy.

Mera and our baby would be okay, which allowed all of us to be clear-minded in this final mission.

When Shadow and Mera left, the others soon dispersed, everyone aware that Reece's sands controlled the ship when he didn't, so they were free to rest. As I moved to clean the table, Reece got there first, sweeping away the dishes with his sands.

"It wouldn't kill you to use your hands," I snarled, feeling extra tense for many reasons. "Sure, it's a few minutes longer, but we're in no rush this moon. Why waste your energy? Once it's gone, it's hard to reclaim."

Before I could say another word, his hands were around my waist as he hauled me back against his body. "What if I want to use those few minutes for something else," he murmured near my ear. "What if my energy is renewable, or at least refillable, and I would sacrifice it all to taste you."

And just like that, my mood dramatically improved.

My head dropped back, and I swallowed my moan as his lips grazed along my cheek.

"Can you be quiet, Angel?" he asked, and for once he didn't make that name sound like a disease on his tongue. "Can you swallow your screams and keep our secret?"

Our secret. I'd forgotten to tell him that Mera and Shadow knew, which really wasn't important when he turned me around, slipped the strap of my black tank to one side, and pressed his lips lower to caress my collarbone and the tops of my breasts.

"They have exceptional hearing and are only a few meters away," I murmured, my hands cupping the back of his head to keep him in place. His chuckle was low and delicious, and as he sucked on my nipple through the shirt, I had to squeeze my legs tightly together. Once again, too many days had passed since we'd had sex, and already the throbbing tension in my center was spiraling.

Reece stripped my shirt off in one smooth movement, leaving me naked from the waist up. "Fucking beautiful," I thought I heard him murmur.

Before I could take another breath, he lifted me to place me back on the newly cleared table, his hands grazing across my bare skin as his lips closed over my left nipple, working it into a hard and sensitive peak. At this point I was literally digging my fingers into the pamolsa material on either side of me to stop from crying out. I felt the wood crumble under my touch, but there was little else I could do. A few finger marks in the table wouldn't destroy its usefulness, and there was no way I could stay silent without that focus.

Reece's kisses grew hotter along my skin, his touch firm as his fingers followed the path, tracing every naked valley and peak, bringing my power to the surface in a way that, hopefully, wouldn't visibly light up this cabin. When his kisses reached my pants, they were stripped from me the same way my shirt had been, and since my feet were bare, there was nothing to stop him from having me naked in seconds.

As he leaned down, he pressed his lips to my lower stomach before his tongue scraped over the junction of my thighs. Just when I was about to say fuck it and scream in frustration, he reached the seam of my aching pussy, swiping at the moisture there. His groan was barely audible, and it seemed staying silent was going to be a challenge for both of us.

A challenge I would probably lose.

It had been too many days, and as we'd reach the Guardians at the next new-moon, this was our last chance to really take advantage of our situation.

On the eve of battle, you never let an opportunity slip you by.

Not when you knew it could be your last.

CHAPTER THIRTY-NINE

Reece's tongue was a talent that had no equal. Before my time with him, I'd have scoffed at the notion that someone's mouth could bring me to the brink of insanity within seconds, and yet here we were. As my breaths grew harsh and deep, I pressed my lips so tightly together that if I'd been more breakable, the skin would've shattered.

Not crying out grew more impossible as time went on, and all I could do was hold onto the table for dear fucking life and pray to the creation gods that it didn't crumble completely under the strain—especially as the ship started to lurch again and we had to fight not to get flung across the small room.

Reece's tongue picked up speed, flicking and sucking in a rhythm that had my ass lifting as I arched dramatically in time to the swelling of pleasure. Winding his hands under my thighs, he parted me wider so he could really slam his tongue into me, over and over, until audible whimpers spilled from between my pressed lips.

I was going to scream if he kept that up, and I didn't even care. He was eating me out on the dining table like I was the last damn meal he'd ever have. As one of his long fingers stroked my clit in time to his tongue, the swelling of pleasure grew too strong to contain, and as my body slammed back onto the table with the force of my orgasm, silent screams tore up my throat.

Reece didn't ease up, even as I jerked and tore off a small section of the pamolsa. By the time he was finished devouring every ounce of my pleasure, I was a limp rag on the table. I offered up no resistance as he reached out and lifted me, then I was flipped over so I faced away from him. He pulled my ass back toward his cock, and the heat of his body burned into my skin until I had to bite my lip again to stop from moaning.

I was positioned on the edge of the table, Reece's hands around my parted thighs as he slid in between them. The thick head of his cock found little resistance as he pushed it slowly inside; I was wet already, my muscles hugging his length as he continued to ease into me slowly, inch by damn inch, until he was fully seated.

I'd never had sex in this position before, but it was immediately obvious that I couldn't really move with Reece holding my thighs and controlling our pace. This didn't bother me as much as the fact that I couldn't see his face, but as he started to thrust, slowly at first and then faster, I stopped caring because I was once again holding on for the ride.

His cock slid deep, hitting spots that had to be illegal. Nerve endings fired, and I realized that this was what Mera always talked about with her G-spot. It was intense. My body attempted to arch and rock for relief, but Reece's firm grip on my thighs prevented me from moving too much.

His pace picked up, and I was choking on screams again, unable to let them free but needing to because I felt like I was going to explode. Like... literally explode.

How was I supposed to handle this pleasure? The surge of my power? Fire in my belly?

My toes curled as my fingers dug into a new part of the table, and I knew I was close. Again.

Fuck's sake, I really wasn't a warrior when it came to sex, with zero discipline in drawing out my orgasms. My vision went dark as the explosion I'd been anticipating slammed into me. Long mewling sounds escaped before I could stop them, and even though they'd been quiet, everyone on this ship had amazing hearing.

Luckily, I was past giving a fuck.

Reece lifted me higher, thrusting full lengths into me as I rode out the last of my orgasm, and I started to pray that this arrangement between us didn't end after the Delfora. There was no way I could give this up once we left the Desert Lands. Reece was the only male I'd been with, and it went against every instinct I possessed to even think of giving myself to another in the same way. Would I have to wait centuries again to be ready to move on? Could I ever move on?

Surely, since even in his anger he'd never been with another, he felt the same way too.

Before I could get lost in hazy worries, Reece slowed, his body rolling now rather than thrusting, giving me a moment to catch my breath. It felt so good... amazing... destructive... heart-breaking.

He groaned as he came, slow and deep thrusts sending literal tingles down my spine. He turned me then, our eyes meeting as he lifted me higher until my legs were wrapped around his waist. With his hands on my ass, he moved us to the wall.

The ship had been relatively stable during our first round of sex, but our luck ran out as a huge surge in the sand had us nearly keeling over. Reece stayed standing purely through his own strength and powers, and he didn't miss a beat, thrusting into me once more, his cock as hard as ever, despite his orgasm.

"No more heavy thoughts," he murmured near my ear, sensing the darkness hovering around me.

Before I could respond, his lips landed on mine, and I was groaning into his mouth, tasting his strength and power in that kiss. Our mouths never parted again, not in all the time he thrust in and out of me, until I lost all sense of time and space.

When I came again, eyes closed, Reece absorbed my cries with his mouth, his groans joining mine as he dragged out releases for us both. When I collapsed against him, he used his energy to clean us up before he carried me to the top deck where he'd been sleeping. Tonight, for maybe the first time since I'd arrived in this damn world with all its ghosts, I was going to truly rest and not be alone. I prayed this wasn't the last chance I had to experience the sort of peace I only felt around Reece.

No matter what else happened, this could not die in the Delfora.

Chapter Forty

I'd never stepped foot on the sands of the Guardians' territory. It was close to the Delfora and Rohami, so I'd sailed past it, but this was my first time entering their rich, midnight sands.

When our ship entered the docks, I was one of the first to rush down the plank and onto solid land. Time was running out, and the call of the sacred lands was growing harder to ignore. It thrummed inside my chest, competing with the bonds and power that filled my well. As I stepped closer to the village, where we would meet Darin and the others, a surge of energy almost slammed me to my knees. Reece caught me a moment before I would have hit the deck.

"I feel it too," he murmured, pulling me up. "But I'm used to the Delfora's call. You need to adjust your power."

It took only a few seconds for me to throw up some blocks to ensure I could handle the whirls of unease rocking the underbelly of the desert's power.

"It's not just the Delfora," Shadow said, pressing in behind us, Mera at his side. "That spell sent out by Tsuma is colliding with the impending power moon. The swelling of power is set on a path of destruction."

It would not stop until it destroyed the wards in the Delfora and gave its creator a pumped-up power to raise the gods. It all boiled down to one truth: We were running out of time.

"I'm going to talk with the sentinels," Reece said, quickly, his fingers grazing across my skin—deliberately, of course—as he released me. "They may know a more specific time of arrival for their princeps."

No one could have missed the intensity of his gaze as it held mine or the brush of his thumb across my cheek. But not one of them blinked an eye or showed any surprise. Probably thanks to the sex show we gave them all last night in the boat— no matter how quiet we'd attempted to be, their hearing was beyond exceptional.

That was how you knew you had amazing and loyal friends. They understood that Reece and I were too volatile for teasing, at this stage anyway, so they were following our lead. When we were ready to discuss the relationship, then they'd chime in.

Reece left, walking toward the black-and-bronze gates, which were made of sand and glass in a combination strong enough to withstand an attack. Beyond that was a city in the same dark tones of the land but without an ominous feel. Maybe it was the glow of power or the gently curving design of their homes, but the Guardians' land was quite homey.

As Reece pressed a hand to the huge double gates, they eased open, and four males stepped out, clad in black tunics. My focus didn't waver until it was clear that they were friendly, then I could turn back to the group. Just as I did, another surge of energy slammed into the land. This time I was blocking, so it only jolted me an inch, but Mera almost lost her balance completely. Shadow got her in time, of course, so she was just left a little shocked and breathless.

"I hope Darin is a Desertlandian of his word," she gasped, shaking her head. "You all need to refuel and get the hell to the Delfora before this world is rocked off its axis."

"It's time to leave, Sunshine," Shadow said, pulling her more firmly into his hold. "The dangers are growing too strong to ignore."

She opened her mouth, no doubt to argue, but this time I was backing the snarly beast. "He's right, Meers."

Her head jerked toward me, and despite being safely cradled in her mate's embrace, she looked devastated. "The dangers have increased since last moon, haven't they?"

I could only answer that honestly. "I feel it deep in my energy, and these warning shots are just the beginning."

"Why do you feel it in your energy?"" Mera asked as Len, Galleli, and Alistair pushed in closer to our circle. Lucien was on his way to join Reece at the gate. "I mean, more than the physical jolt of it, you're getting an actually connected beat between your energy and the Delfora... But you're not Desertlandian."

"I have a lot of history with this world," I reminded her. "The bones of my ancestors are buried here. My blood has spilled here. I bled my soul into these sands, and I think that maybe, through all of that, there's a connection between me and the Desert Lands that can never be broken..."

I trailed off at the heavy clomp of boots in the sands. Reece and Lucien were done with the sentinels. At first, I didn't think he'd heard the conversation, but then he said, "The reason Angel feels a connection is because we're bonded."

Everyone stilled at that rather casual statement, like he was discussing the damn weather and not an eternal bond. He continued, "When we were in our youth, I claimed her. We bonded our essence and energy, and with my close ties to the Delfora, there's no surprise that it would extend to my mate."

Did he just... *What in the actual demons of the deep?*

I opened my mouth, emotions spilling out of me so fast that I had no idea what I was going to say. "Matc?" was all that emerged.

Great, Melalekin. You're a fucking wordsmith.

Reece's smile was cocky. "You've known all along, Lale. We might have lost our way for a few centuries, but there was only one future for us."

When he was done, it seemed that I was the only one glued to the sands, basically speechless. The others let out a cheer as they rushed forward to hug us. It was clear that no one here was remotely surprised by what he'd said, but I felt like he'd just slammed me in the chest and knocked the air from me.

Reece was close, his big body wrapping around mine until our scents were so mingled I couldn't tell one from the other. And oddly... it calmed me. "Fight it all you want, Lale," he murmured. "We know the truth."

For a split second I turned to mush, my head so clouded that I'd all but forgotten I could kill in a second using four hundred different moves. Apparently, I'd sold my warrior soul for orgasms and some desert charm. I mean, incredible orgasms, but still...

Forcing my breaths to even out, I shook my head—Reece and I had too much history for this "mate" claim to just settle. We needed time and healing, and we couldn't get that until our mission here was complete. "Let's focus on what needs to be done now," I said, thankful to not sound breathless. "No point worrying about mates if we all die in the Delfora."

My nickname wasn't *Sunshine* for very good reason.

"What did the sentinels say?" I asked Reece directly. "Are our supplies ready; can we just leave?"

Reece's smirk faded into a dark scowl. "Darin is standing firm with his request that we wait for them so that we might approach this together. They've offered us rooms to rest and clean up, and they're preparing a banquet."

"We don't have time for this!" I snapped, agitated in a way I didn't want to examine.

The energy has not reached the Delfora, Galleli said, standing near the edge of the docks and swirling sands that formed the deeps. *Neither have Tsuma or her comrades. They will stay hidden until the last moment.* His wings extended as he looked out to the horizon. *We have time, and we should refuel. I sense this is a battle we're unprepared for, and if we lose, it will be over for the worlds.*

A slither of unease filtered through our group, grim faces replacing any that had been amused by Reece and me. We'd all learned to take his warnings seriously, and considering that, I could trust that we had enough time to refuel our energies before we found ourselves in a fight for the worlds. On the positive side, some of our team needed these few hours to restore their powerbase—like Reece, who had been controlling the ship and keeping us moving for moons; Lucien, who had run low on his plasma; Alistair, who needed to soak in a tub of liforina; and Shadow, who was about to make the difficult journey from this area to the library and back.

Mera must have had the same thought. "Take me now, Shadow," she said in a rush, twisting in his arms to face him. "Then you'll have time to replenish before walking into battle."

Wanting to ease her worry, because stress was not good for the baby, I quickly said, "We're strong together. No matter what happens, we won't leave anyone behind." Her teary eyes met mine as I continued. "This might be a difficult battle, but I believe there are no warriors stronger than the ones standing here. You hold the fort back home and hold onto that baby until we can return."

Her left hand fell from Shadows chest and pressed to her stomach as we both felt a stab of pain. I cursed that slip up; with children of power, there was no tempting fate. Mera recovered in a moment, but that flash of discomfort remained deep in her eyes. "I'll be fine," she said, waving off the concern that was no doubt written all over my face. Shadow's too, since he would have felt that stabbing sensation as well. "You all take care and make it through this because if any of you die, I will bring you back and kill you again for making me love you and then leaving me."

Silence, until a snort of laughter escaped Len, and somehow that broke the tension which had been holding us tight. The others moved forward and hugged Mera... after Shadow reluctantly allowed her to stand one foot from his body. If the men held on too long, he growled, and it was only Reece who risked his wrath by lifting her from the sands and twirling her around.

She laughed, and then coughed. "Enough! Enough. This baby does not like the spinning game."

Shadow, who was clearly on edge, rumbled louder than ever, his flames slapping out at the desert god, who only laughed and wiped them away like they were annoying flies and not lethal weapons.

"Take your mate home," Reece said. "We'll see you back here once you've secured the base and left Gaster, Inky, and Midnight in charge."

Shadow's fire calmed minutely, and at that, the pair clasped hands.

"Awww, Shadow and Shadow the Second." Mera sighed. "It's a true bromance."

Shadow's glare could have melted the damn ice lands. "I'm

going to enjoy removing that word from your vocabulary, mate," he rumbled.

She looked about as far from worried as a being could get. "Promises, promises."

Shadow stepped forward, clearly intending to scoop her up, but I hadn't had my chance at a goodbye yet, so I darted between them before he could. I wrapped my arms around her first, holding on as tightly as I could, breathing in the fiery scent that was all power and sass and Mera.

"I love you," she choked into my shoulder. "Like, forever best friends and sisters. Twin souls, remember. Do. Not. Die."

I laughed to cover up the depth of my worry that I would never see her again. "The Nexus would bring me back again."

She pulled away to glare at me. "We don't know for sure that would happen. Maybe next time your soul will be so tired that you'll choose rest. So, with that in mind, don't forget my previous warning. I need you to stay alive and keep the rest of my merry band of assholes alive too."

Before I could respond, she spun and leveled all of us with her Mera glare. "Work together. Use your brains. Don't under-estimate this enemy, and don't take stupid risks. You might be saving the worlds again, but if it looks like you can't win tomor-row, then get out of there. We can regroup and come back again, stronger than ever. But if you're all dead, there's no regrouping."

"We promise," Lucien said, flashing some fang as his need for plasma grew stronger. "Take care, *ma petite*."

Mera swallowed roughly, but for once didn't yell at him for his flirty ways. Instead, she appeared to be looking at all of us, memorizing our faces. I did the same to her, taking in the wild mass of red curls, her hair untamed for days, and the way she was dressed in a black shift dress and no shoes. She looked fierce and strong, ready to protect her family, and I sent out every prayer to every god—except the fucking ancients—that this was not our last moment together.

Shadow, done waiting, finally got his arms around her, scooping her up so she rested against his chest. Before any of us could say another word, he turned and walked back in the direction of the docks and the ship. The further he was from the black sands, the less energy it would require to open a doorway.

Just as his broad shoulders were about to disappear onto the ship, Mera poked her head around the side of his shoulder and yelled goodbye, her voice fading as they both disappeared from sight. Another jolt in my chest followed, filled with pain. Only this time, it was not baby-ready-to-enter-the-world pain. This was heart pain.

"We'll see her again," Len said, slinging his arm around my shoulders. "Don't let your focus be divided."

He was right, and with that in mind, I pulled myself together, falling into my normal prep-before-a-battle mindset. Just as I was about to shake off Len's hold because I needed to stand on my own, he was hit with a hard nudge from Reece.

"Too close, fae," he growled.

The pair exchanged a heated stare, but Len didn't push it. He wouldn't after the desert god's declaration that I was his mate. Staring between them, I briefly contemplated slamming their heads together, but instead leveled them with a withering glare and continued toward the front gates.

Reece was making some very public claims now, but there was no time to figure out why or what it meant. Anything that messed with my focus had to be pushed aside.

For now, my aim was to wash off the long journey on the ship, fuel up with the seeds we'd been saving, and prepare to fight for my life. All of our lives.

After all, I had a Mera-promise to keep.

CHAPTER FORTY-ONE

Guardians were well known for their stance on "silence is best." It was no surprise when they herded us without a word of conversation toward the rooms which had been set up for our brief stay. That didn't stop me from asking a few pressing questions. "How long have you been hit with these surges of power?" I asked a bald male in black robes.

"Disturbances for some time, but only minor," he said. "We feel the swell now as it approaches the Delfora. It has enough power to break the wards and securities."

"Have you seen any sign of Tsuma or others going to the Delfora?"

He shook his head, and that was apparently all the answer I would get, as he hurried away.

"There has to be other layers of security," Alistair said, voice raspy. His skin was drier than I'd ever seen as some of it flaked away into pale, blue-green sheets. "Beyond the valley of the dead."

Reece nodded. "There are, but with the power moon and this gathered energy from all the dynasties, they will be able to circumvent them. This power moon is so rare that if I hadn't heard about the last one from my parents, I would not have believed it possible."

That reminded me I still had to ask him if that moon was the reason for his existence. Another time, though.

"It will rise with the new-moon tomorrow?" Len asked. "That's the sixth day, right?"

"Not the new-moon," Reece said shortly. "If past stories are correct, it will take some time for the twin to form. My prediction is that between the mid- and half-moon there will be a fissure, and then power unseen for thousands of years will wash over our land."

Our timing would have to be so precise tomorrow. And we'd have one damn shot.

"It stands to reason that we can only defeat Tsuma once she gets to the Delfora," I stated, needing to run the facts through my mind. "She'll be hidden until that point. There's going to be a fine line between reaching the sacred lands and stopping their actions. What happens if we're too late and the gods rise?"

I knew the overall *the worlds will end* big picture, but this time, I wanted the smaller details.

Reece's expression turned darker. "If the rest of our information is correct, the gods themselves are the power that keeps Death from rising, so if the ancients find their way back to sentience, then there will be nothing to stop them from smashing through the final barrier."

"Why would they though?" Alistair asked, grabbing a small jug of water that had been set out and tipping it over his head. The relief that crossed his face only added to my secret stress over his health.

"Because Death is the ultimate vacuum of life essence," Reece said shortly, "and the gods will be able to use its energy to restore all of their power very quickly."

"We can't let them get that far," I bit out. "We must prevent Death from rising, whatever the cost."

Whatever the cost. Words that no ancient bandied about with ease, but we were in a critical situation. This was the precipice of an extinction level event, and we had to go all in. This was not the time for holding back.

"Angel is right," Reece said, backing me in a way I still wasn't used to. "But for now, let's enjoy the hospitality of the Guardians. We have made the decision to recharge and go in, all powers blazing, in the new-moon, so take advantage. Trust me when I say that you should utilize their bathing rooms."

Before anyone could comment on that, he wrapped his hand around my shoulders, drawing me into the hard muscles on his right side. "We'll meet back here soon for dinner."

Not one expression changed, our friends still following our cues in responding to this massive change in our relationship status. Reece and I ended up back in one of the farthest rooms, which was small, containing just a bed and what I hoped was an entrance into a bathing room. As soon as the heavy door closed behind us, Reece wasted no time tearing off my clothing —without actually destroying them this time. Useful, since I didn't really want to head into this battle naked.

Needing to feel and taste him, I did the same, pulling every item from his body until he was as naked as me. Desperation tinged our kisses as he walked us backward, the warm stone floor caressing my feet. I managed to open my eyes long enough to see that this bathing room was a rainfall design, with warm water already cascading from the ceiling to the floor, vanishing into the heated stones. It was obvious from the design that the liforina would cycle continuously, filtering through the stone and sands before returning to the ceiling above. I had no idea what particular magic they used for this, but I needed one in the meadows.

Reece swiped his tongue across my lips, and I lost all focus on the shower, especially as our kisses picked up speed and intensity again. Before I knew it, we were under the water, desert life soaking across our bodies, cleansing and healing us. Reece's low groan reminded me that he found pleasure in water as much as I did. It was an oddity for beings of his race to feel that way, same as mine, and yet here we were. Neither of us lived by the "rules," hence the reason we'd bonded our two races together so long ago.

Reece's hands traced over my sides, and I pressed mine to the words carved across his stomach. The ancient language had been lost, but he'd figured it out. "What does this mean?" I whispered, wondering if we had reached enough peace between us to share real truths.

His eyes held mine for so long that I was burning by the time he reached up and brushed his thumb over my lower lip, swiping at the water beading there. "I'll tell you if we survive," he murmured. "Call it incentive to make it through this battle."

Normally that shit would make me rage, but for some reason, I wanted this to look forward to. Thoughts of the future might be off my radar until I was sure there was one for all of us, but this little incentive... I could live with that. And until then, we had some existing in the moment to do.

Bending my legs, I launched myself at Reece, and he caught me with ease, hands sliding under my ass as my legs wrapped his waist. I was too far gone for foreplay, so I lifted my body and angled myself to slide right onto his hard length. His cock burned as the thick head pushed inside, stretching me to capacity, and I was starting to crave this hit of pleasure-pain. This stimulation of all my nerve endings.

My breath quickened as my body relaxed, growing wetter with each incremental slide deeper. Reece groaned as his patience snapped, and when he tightened his hold on my ass, he lifted me enough to slam the final inches of that impressive cock inside. I cried out, head falling back so that the waterfall droplets caressed my face.

"Sorry, Lale," he rumbled, "I can't be slow for you tonight."

I would have laughed, but there was no time before he was lifting me again, thrusting into me one more time. "Are you ever slow?" I choked out.

Reece's chuckle was throaty, followed by another groan as his pace picked up. We'd only just started and already the brutal thrusts were destroying me. I couldn't stop from crying out, craving every hard pound of our bodies. As I opened my eyes, teetering on the edge of an orgasm, it was to find Reece watching me, absorbing the signs of my pleasure. It was more of a turn-on than I'd ever imagined having his focus so completely on my being.

Just as my orgasm was about to explode, he slowed his pace. "Are you ready to push your boundaries," he murmured, mouth on mine in the same breath.

My mind immediately went to the ass play he was clearly a fan of, and at that very thought, my orgasm exploded, pleasure arching my spine as I cried out. When I finally returned to this plane of damn existence, it was to find Reece letting out amused, groaning laughs. "Guess I have my answer," he said with the most perfect fucking smile.

Slowly he lifted me off him until his length left my body completely. "What do you want, Lale?" he asked, his blue gaze filling my vision.

This time I didn't hesitate, need blasting through any nerves. Despite the orgasm I'd just had, I was so far from done. "Fuck me, Reece. Finish what you started in the grotto."

His eyes darkened. "Where do you want me to fuck you?"

This bastard loved this game. "In my pussy," I murmured, forcing away my smirk.

We both knew he was after another answer, but hey, two could play this game.

"I could fuck your pussy all day, Angel," he rasped, lips pressing against the side of my throat as he dragged his mouth across the surface, lapping up the water. "But is that all?"

A groan escaped me again. "No," I said before I could think it over. "I want more."

"More of what?" Another kiss, this time near the corner of my mouth, and my body jerked into him involuntarily, needing relief from the intense need inside. He was driving me insane. At one point I'd have waited to see who would break first, but now, I wasn't wasting one more second of our time together.

"Fuck me in the ass, Reece." I didn't whisper it, not remotely shamed by my wants. "But for the love of our creator, ease me into it." He wasn't small, and even though my body would heal whatever happened, I really wanted this to feel as good as it had in the grotto.

His chest rumbled, and I felt the surge of his energy. Before another word was spoken, he flipped me over, his sands drifting in to cradle me on all fours a few feet above the stones. Arching, I backed myself up and let out a breathy sigh when I made contact with his heat.

Reece wasted no time, the thick head of his cock pushing into my pussy, and while it felt fucking amazing, I was ready for this new experience. "Reece," I groaned. "Do you need an anatomy lesson?"

A heavy hand landed on my ass, the sound loud in this bathing room, and I let out a small whimper that was definitely not from pain. "Patience, Melalekin," he murmured. "You wanted me to ease you into it."

Dammit, I had asked for that. There were no more words from me since I was barely able to breathe and moan in time to his thrusts, turning me into a writhing mess. As I cried out, he used his finger to swipe through the liquid pooling between us, which he then slid to my ass, pushing that digit inside the tight muscles. For a few minutes he thrust into my ass and pussy at the same time, and I wondered if this was the actual event—in my thousands of years—that was going to take me out.

Death by double penetration. It was the way Mera wanted to go, and now I finally understood.

Stars spun before my eyes as my hands dug into the sands, desperate for something to hold onto. Just as I was about to explode again, Reece withdrew his fingers and cock from my body, and even as my vagina complained, the rest of me was about to shatter from the sensation of him finally focusing on my ass.

He entered me slowly, and I actually choked on my next breath. The muscles were tight, never having been stretched like this, and while it burned, a tingle of pleasure kept it from being too uncomfortable.

"Godsdamn, Lale," Reece groaned, sounding strained. "I never fucking imagined..."

Yeah, same. So much the same.

When it felt like he was maybe halfway inside me, he leaned over to press his lips to my spine while his hand snaked around and stroked my clit in time to his slow thrusts. The initial, mildly uncomfortable sensation faded as new swirls of pleasure started low in my gut, and already I could tell it was a deeper and more intense build up.

"Mine," Reece rumbled again, sounding much less like his normal self. The desert god had lost control, and I never thought I'd want to hear that one word from a male before. It was so possessive and domineering and claiming, and if Reece said it during normal conversation, I'd most likely stab him. But in this moment, another first for us both, it felt... right.

My essence had been reborn in the Nexus, but the dual

nature of my energy wasn't the part that defined me in this moment. Reece did, the god who was tearing down my walls and rebuilding me into a completely new being.

At this point, Reece's pace increased, and I wanted him as deep inside as he could go. There was no way I'd fit his full length, but my ass was handling this much better than I'd anticipated. Gold fucking star.

Still, it was lucky I healed quickly, otherwise I wouldn't be walking into battle tomorrow.

I'd be hobbling.

My breaths rushed out fast and shallow, leaving me gasping so hard I couldn't catch my breath. My legs started to tremble as the ball of energy in my center swelled... "I'm going to come," I said in a rush, right as my entire body caught fire, and I all but screamed Reece's name, arching and writhing against his hard length.

Reece let out a low rumble from behind me, and I swore I could hear the sands react to his pleasure, lifting to coat us as he thrust a few more times, the heat of his release burning with my own. My body was still jerking at the intensity, and I was thanking every damn being I knew that Reece had decided to push my boundaries.

Whether this lasted forever or ended the next moon, no part of me could regret this time with him.

CHAPTER FORTY-TWO

By the time we needed to leave to meet Darin and the others, I was beyond sated. I was also happy. At least for a moment, until reality called, forcing all of us back into warrior mode.

Standing in the bathing area, I was dressed in my magically cleaned clothing, along with the bronze armor and weapons I'd called from the ship. Reece watched as I braided my hair, adjusting it to fit around the longswords I had in a hilt down my spine.

This moon I'd decided to wear multiple weapons because one never knew what attack was waiting around the corner. This sword, along with my curved blades sheathed on either side of my body, gave me a sense of comfort.

"We need to leave now," he said softly, pushing up to stand, looking massive and powerful, dressed in his long sleeve black shirt, black cargo pants, and a few strategically placed armor plates. He didn't use any weapons, because his sands were always present to take that role. My energy could do the same, but for the most part, I was old-fashioned and preferred the clash of real steel.

"Let's do it," I murmured.

When we left the room, the others were waiting for us, each dressed in their own version of battle gear. Most of them wore black like Reece, except for Len, of course, who was flashing a lot of gem-dotted silver, visible whenever his coat parted.

A Guardian we hadn't met before led us from our area into the main streets and to a large domed building that, I would estimate, was about center of this particular village. The dark-moon outside hadn't shown us much, but once we were inside, more than a few desert lights highlighted a banquet table, dominating the center of the space.

Our guide indicated that we should move toward the table, which was low to the ground and surrounded by cushions. He left us as soon as we were seated—I ended up with Reece on one side and Lucien on the other. Len, Alistair, and Galleli sat across from us. Within a minute, a dozen or so Guardians hurried in, taking seats around us.

Darin was last, skin moon-kissed and much browner than the last time I'd seen him. "Welcome," he said, spreading his arms wide and flashing all of those perfect teeth. "Thank you for waiting for us. I've arranged energy foods to refresh everyone before we leave again in the new-moon." As he sat at the head of the table, conversation picked up between the other Guardians who'd been on their ship, while Darin continued to focus on us. "I even have some desert flower elixir, which has been brewing for many moons."

Reece's power spiked in our bond, and just as he opened his mouth to say *something not very nice*, I would wager, I reached out and grasped his hand under the table. His eyes clashed with mine, and I shot him a small smile. We didn't need to waste our energy battling Darin too.

With a long sigh, he turned back to the princeps. "Thank you. We appreciate the hospitality."

He almost sounded like he meant it this time.

"What's desert flower elixir?" Lucien asked, leaning forward to see Darin.

The princeps smiled. "It's brewed from a rare flower that only grows in two parts of our world."

"Let me guess," I said with a soft laugh, "one part is the land of the Guardians."

His smile grew broader. "Excellent guess. But yes, it grows here and the Delfora. It can boost energy threefold and give us all an edge before we head into battle tomorrow."

"It can also have the same effect as alcohol on humans," Reece warned. "Thankfully, the more negative influences will be out of our system by the new-moon, leaving only the extra energy. So, just beware for now."

Darin clapped him on the shoulder before quickly retrieving his hand at the look the desert god shot his way. "Reece is correct. If you sleep off the effects, it will definitely be worth it in the new-moon."

Reaching down, I ran my hand over my blades, calming at the touch of metal. The impending battle had us all on edge, but we shouldn't waste time when we could be discussing strategy. "We need to leave in the early hours of the new-moon," I said, "if we want to have a shot at reaching the Delfora at the same time or, hopefully, a little before Tsuma and the others."

"As long as we beat the power moon," Reece said, "they will have no advantage."

A moon we were only guessing about the time of arrival

There's only so much we can plan, Galleli said. Darin and others jumped, but they didn't say a word against his form of communication. *At this point, we've just got to do our best and let the sands fall where they are destined to lie.*

"Cryptic and somewhat terrifying, as per usual," Lucien said with a snort.

The food started to arrive then, and the conversations down the table switched to more lighthearted topics as everyone focused on refueling. All of us had been on rations by the end of our trip down the sand rivers, so this fresh array of energy-restoring foods was most welcome.

"We even had some high-quality plasma brought in for you," Darin said to Lucien. "It took a few days to trade for it, and it's not going to be as good as what you get on Valdor, but it should sustain you for this battle."

Lucien lifted the glass cup that had been placed before him a few minutes ago, and as he took a sip, his face relaxed. "This is perfect. Same as what we had on the ship."

Already his color was more golden, skin shining as his cells sucked in the freshly harvested energy he required to keep regenerating. Alistair was the same, seemingly flush in water here, his curls no longer dull and limp, skin without a single flake. Stopping might have cost us some time, but in the end, we were heading into this battle at our strongest.

An advantage I knew from experience could spell the difference between life and death.

Focusing on the fruits before me, I filled my plate to assuage the ache in my stomach that now required physical sustenance. We also cracked open the fae seeds Galleli had brought from the boat, sharing the contents with any who wanted to try them. I split the shell and lifted out a small, brown seed. Sniffing it, I found it had a slight chocolate scent. Mera had said that her favorite food originated from a tree, and it seemed that this seed was very similar.

Only this tree originated in Faerie and was almost as rare as the desert flower. The princeps had showed their support for our mission by including these nearly priceless seeds in our storage—as much as Darin did sharing the elixir with us. Everyone was putting in their all to win this war.

"Will the seeds and elixir have any odd effect together?" I asked as I swallowed the seed, which had almost no taste but did leave a burning path down my chest until it settled in my center. Tingles sparked under my skin, my blood soon buzzing as I was filled with a sense of power and freedom.

"Together they will heighten each other and inflate both negative and positive symptoms of the power boosts," Reece said, his lips twitching. "It could get wild around here tonight."

Already feeling that, I laughed louder than normal, happy to feel this buzz if it meant that tomorrow we'd be successful.

We had a true chance, and even if there were no guarantees in life, I was determined that this time, no bones would be left in these lands.

CHAPTER FORTY-THREE

Despite the underlying tension that continued to exist between Reece and Darin, the rest of the dinner went by with relative calm as we ate, drank, and focused on strategies for the new-moon. By the time we were full and ready for whatever tomorrow would bring, I marveled at the true calm I felt. It wasn't unusual; I'd often found a sense of peace when the battle was close and no more planning or training could take place. One way or another, this would all be over soon.

The elixir arrived just as everyone was done eating, small glasses filled with its milky substance. "Drink it slowly," Reece warned us as he lifted his. "It's been known to drop powerful beings on their asses." With a smirk, he threw it back in one gulp. Arrogant bastard.

I stared at the cloudy, pink liquid before lifting it to my nose to find it smelled like a more potent version of purple desert flowers, which were probably a hybrid version of this much rarer plant.

Breathing in deeply, I threw the liquid back in one shot and gasped at the duality of sweet-fire burning down my throat and into my center, joining the seed.

Reece let out a low laugh beside me. "You don't have to do the opposite of what I say to prove a point. I promise, nothing bad will happen if you just take my word for it."

I couldn't answer at first, too busy dealing with the heat expanding in my body, sapping my breath. Eventually all that energy settled, joining the well of power that I'd been holding from the Honor Meadows.

"You shot it in one go," I reminded him when I could talk again. "Not to mention I've never blindly taken another's orders. You know me better than that." I crossed my arms as my head spun. "Taking orders is not in my nature, just like having a true mate isn't in yours."

Well, shit. Seemed that the power items were already loosening my tongue. Reece looked amused as he leaned back on his cushion, arms braced to either side, making him look even larger. The only outward sign of the elixir affecting him was the slightest tinge of pink in his cheeks, which just made him more handsome. "Seems my little Lale has something to say to me." He laughed. "Never been a better time than right now, with your barriers down."

"Do *you* have something to say to me?" I shot back.

Yep, so while it was clear that these power items increased energy, they definitely did not help with snappy comebacks.

"More than I could convey in this short conversation," he said, sobering up. "But this is not the time or place. First we have to survive our battle."

I was on my feet in a flash, the burning inside assisting both speed and agility. "How can I even trust that as soon as we're done here you won't go back to the same old Reece? The one that ignored and hated me for goddamn centuries."

Fuck. My mouth was out of control, and even knowing I

was acting irrationally, I couldn't stop myself. I had to get out of here. Before he could respond, I spun and started toward the exit. Of course, in my quest to escape, I stupidly didn't take into account that all of the other idiots at the table had partaken of the seeds and elixir, and some had even less tolerance than me.

Len was lucky that I felt his energy right before he wrapped his arms around me and dragged me away from the exit. "I will stab you if you don't let me go," I snapped, reaching for my sword in its scabbard.

"Come on and dance with me," he said without a moment of worry that I was heavily armed and not in my right mind.

As he, once again, started to drag me toward an open space where a few Guardians were already dancing, my head felt even fuzzier. "Have you lost your damned mind?" I said loudly. "There's no freaking music."

Someone must've heard that observation because in my next breath, a low, steady drumbeat filled the air. Len and I were soon surrounded by laughing, joking, drunk-as-fuck Guardians. Even Galleli ended up swaying nearby with a very beautiful brunette Guardian. She was almost as tall as he was, with light brown skin and prominent golden eyes.

"Everyone here had better hope Galleli doesn't decide to talk, thanks to the elixir," I said in a jumble of words.

"Relax, Angel-faced sweetheart," Len crooned. "You're too tense, and it's best to release those worries the night before a battle."

His hold on my hand tightened as he pulled me closer and wrapped one arm around me. In the same instant, there was a deep, low rumble from behind us. Recognizing the sound, scent, and energy that accompanied that sound, I wasn't surprised to turn and find Reece standing there, his eyes filled with midnight.

Len, appearing unconcerned, didn't loosen his grip, and

Reece's next growl was even deeper... more animalistic. Judging by the look on his face, I wasn't even sure he could speak. Before I could make a move, Reece all but disappeared in a flurry of sand, and then both Len and the desert god were gone. No one else followed, letting those two work their shit out once and for all. Len was famous for stirring the pot with his broody friend, but there was only so far Reece could be pushed.

Deciding I was done with dancing and drama for the night, I was about to exit the tent once more, when a strong energy crashed against my shields. Shadow appeared in the doorway looking pissed and ready for a fight. Flames sprinkled his skin, and I knew him well enough to sense that after leaving his pregnant mate in another world and walking into what looked like a dance party, he was pissed that we weren't taking the dangers of tomorrow's battle seriously.

When Shadow was pissed, beings died.

Without Reece, there were few in here who would risk his wrath by getting any closer, so I took one for the team, half-stumbling my way to where he stood. "Shadow," I said with force, hoping to snap him out of his fury. "They're under the influence of the fae seeds and a desert elixir, which we all took in preparation for tomorrow's battle. These items will help boost our energies, but it has some short-term intoxicating effects."

He slowly lowered that gaze to meet my eyes, and I wasn't at all surprised to see flames burning in his red and gold depths.

"You should have some too," I said, not giving him a chance to argue. "Restore what was lost by taking Mera back so close to the Delfora."

In return I got a low rumble, eerily similar to Reece's. Shadow was a being of few words normally, and without his mate, he was walking death—very similar to the Death we were trying to stop from rising tomorrow, with just a touch more humanity.

"Come on," I said, jerking my head to indicate he should follow. "There's one waiting here for you."

Surprisingly, he followed me to the table and shrunk his height so he could sit on a cushion. I handed him a seed and a drink that hadn't been claimed, and he threw both back without question. Shadow had been around for a long time, and neither of these items would be a new experience for him. Even as they settled into his aura, there was barely a change in his energy levels.

"How is Mera," I asked both needing to know and needing the distraction. "Her energy feels steady, but there was a twinge of pain when she left."

Shadow turned and lifted another elixir, throwing it back just as quickly. "She's okay." His voice was a husky rasp, but speaking at all was a good sign that he'd dragged himself back from the beast. "The baby is close, but we have time. Sunshine is mostly annoyed that she's being excluded."

He fell silent after that, and I didn't speak either, content just to sit and allow the effects of the elixir to wear off before I did anything stupid under the influence. Like...

"Dance with me."

Darin stood before me looking kind of nervous as he held out a hand. Shadow let out a rumble at my side, and I had a sneaking suspicion that he was annoyed at this Desertlandian for stepping into what he considered his best friend's territory. I'd known these males for a very long time, and they were nothing if not predictable.

"She has a mate," he said, sounding somewhat casual, but I knew him better. "Move along."

Darin stepped back, as did every male when faced with the wrath of Shadow, but I gave him props for not turning tail and running. "Just a dance. I'll ensure it's in no way romantic," he spluttered out. "We're having fun before our battle, and Angel is an amazing dancer."

I really loved to dance. I'd missed it, and since Reece was off being a moron, why the hell shouldn't I have a fun dance? Darin knew the score now, so there was no issue. "Sure," I said, deep in the midst of making a bad decision. "Why the hell not. We should live while we have the chance."

Shadow dropped one of his oversized hands on my arm, and I immediately shook him off. "Don't overstep," I warned him in a hiss. "We do not want to go to war, Shadow."

His expression softened, and it was so unexpected that it halted me. "Mera loves you like a sister, which makes you my sister. I'm looking out for you. Don't wave a red flag in front of the bull; he will charge."

I read between the lines of everything he'd just said, but it was one damn dance. I wasn't planning on sleeping with Darin. And sure, a part of me deep down that wasn't under the influence of the elixir knew I was making a bad decision, but I just couldn't stop myself. Maybe I wanted to test Reece's claim on me, or maybe I really wanted to dance. Either way, I'd made my choice.

Darin tightened his grip and pulled me to my feet, leading me onto the dance floor. A faster beat started almost at the same time, and I recognized this number as one where everyone formed a large circle, moving around the room in a side-stepping and twirling pattern. For a nonromantic dance, Darin had chosen the perfect number.

"Let's do this," I said with a laugh, my legs thankfully stronger than my fuzzy brain as we got into position, facing each other but not touching. The intro began, and I threw myself into it, the steps coming back to me just as they had done with the dance in the Ostealon. Darin only had to touch me a few times, moving me around his body as we swirled and twirled. I couldn't even feel his hold through my armor, and I found that was how I preferred it. Despite my last stand of independence, Reece's hands were the only ones I wanted on my body.

As the beat picked up, I threw my head back, braid flying around. Laughter spilled from me; the elixir had me feeling completely out of control again. In a way, the buzz under my skin reminded me of the first time I'd used my wings alone, soaring across the lands. It'd been exhilarating. The only other event to ever come close to that feeling, was the moment I'd met Reece. He'd buzzed my energy too, and it seemed that he always would.

Unlike flying, I'd never gotten used to the affect he had on me.

And what the fuck was I doing dancing with another male?

Of all the stupid decisions I'd ever made, this one was on top.

Just as I tilted my head up to politely excuse myself, Darin swung me toward him, and I was baffled about this out-of-step move, until his lips crashed against mine. There was a split-second of shock before my fury broke through. With a growl, I slammed my hands into his chest, stepping to the side and hooking my foot around the back of his ankle to send him sprawling across the ground. "What in all the fucking sands do you think you're doin—" My shout was cut off as silence descended over the room, the music silencing midbeat.

I looked down at Darin to find him moving in slow motion, sand surrounding him as he attempted to break free. That was when I knew... *Reece had caught that kiss.*

I found him in a heartbeat as he stalked across the room, and even though I'd never admit it under torture, my heart raced at the power and fury spinning from him. I didn't fear for

my physical safety around this Desertlandian, but my heart...
that was another matter.

Reece's sands held everyone in the room, but as he got
closer, he released Darin. The princeps jumped to his feet, but
he had nothing that could stand against Reece's rage. It was
shaking the ground we stood on. No lie, it was an impressive
display, and I took a moment to internally fan my vagina
because she was far more excited by his strength than was
appropriate for the situation.

"Reece, I already dealt—"

He ignored my words, sand and male clashing into Darin,
who did his best to try and remain standing under the assault.
Tried and failed. The princeps ended up on his knees before
taking a massive blow to the chin that sent him sprawling across
the ground. The desert god didn't use his power at all, just
brute strength, as he seemed determined to destroy the other
Desertlandian with his bare hands.

When Darin was all but unconscious, I decided that
enough was enough. Jumping between them, I didn't pull my
weapons, but I did swing my leg out in a solid kick, smashing
Reece right in the side. He clearly hadn't expected me to fight
him, and I used that to my advantage, throwing myself forward
to wrap my body around his and flip him to the ground. From
this position I could hold him until he'd calmed enough that he
wouldn't murder Darin and take away our allies for the battle.
Which probably wouldn't be until the elixir and seed effects
wore off for him. Reece was always volatile, but this night he
was definitely worse.

He shifted to throw me over his shoulder and reverse our
positions, but even with his advantageous longer reach, I'd
already anticipated that move and got out of the way. We were
both on our feet in a heartbeat, and as my head spun, I cursed

the damn elixir. The elixir and Darin, who apparently was all about challenging mate-bonds.

"I had it under control," I said to Reece, even as guilt for even letting the dance happen hit me.

"You let him touch you," Reece rumbled, gaze hypnotic and filled with fire. "His hands... his lips should never be near you, Lale. For that, he will die."

"It was a dance," I shot back because I had nothing else. "We said a friends-only number. I have no idea why he got so carried away, but I'd already dealt with that."

Reece's eyes darkened, and it wasn't like when he was turned on. This was an out-of-control, everyone's-going-to-die sort of darkening. Here, in his domain, so close to the Delfora, Reece outpowered us all. A fact made obvious by the way everyone—even Shadow—remained trapped in his sands.

"Let them go," I murmured, leaning in so our faces were close. "I promise you that Darin will never come near me again. It was only supposed to be a dance, but clearly, he wanted to push his luck."

Sand sprung up around us, blocking everyone else from view, pushing in tight so we were trapped together.

Reece reached for me, gripping the back of my neck as he pulled me close, his mouth hovering over mine. "It can never happen," he snapped, fierce and furious. "I will destroy them all. I'm the only one to touch these lips." He kissed me hard, and unlike with Darin, my body responded immediately. Reece was my aphrodisiac. My Achilles heel.

As I sank against him, my hips flexed forward to meet his hard erection, arousal taking over. Reece didn't break the kiss, but I felt his sands remove my weapons and then my armor. Within minutes we were naked, and as Reece took us to the ground—me on top again—the wrestling was all about pleasure. I sank down onto his hard length, crying out as he pushed through my tight muscles without hesitation. I wasn't prepped, but neither of us gave a fuck. I cried out again as he thrust roughly, my body moving against each stroke. "Ride me, Lale," he commanded, the low, husky rumble sending a hot burst of heat through my pussy before it settled in my throbbing clit.

"You don't get to command me," I lied breathlessly, even as he was buried inside, claiming my body.

Reece's laughter was dark and raspy. "I called you mate, and while there's been no time to cement what that means, here are the basics." His scent and energy wrapped around me, holding me prisoner to his intense gaze as his voice lowered to a harsh whisper. "You are mine, Melalekin. For this day and all of our fucking days. Don't fight me on this, because I won't hesitate to wipe out Darin and any other who has ever touched you. I'm barely holding on."

I saw the truth in his face, and that was when I accepted that the reason I'd danced with Darin was not because I was living out my last drunken night before the battle. The truth was, I'd been too scared to fully accept his words... his claim on me. Scared that it was all talk and, eventually, he would leave me again, just as he had the last time.

"This is forever?" I whispered.

Reece reached up and cupped my cheek, holding onto my face like it was precious. "Until the sands fade."

My chest was so tight I couldn't breathe, but at that eternal statement, my soul settled. Whatever cracks had been in our bond cemented—a physical happening I could feel inside.

"We are mates," I whispered, and then I was moving again, unable to stop myself from sinking deep onto him and rising again.

"Mates, destined, everlasting," he replied, reaching up and brushing a thumb over my cheek, all the while meeting my movements with thrusts that were so strong I could barely stay seated.

We needed this moment. This claiming. I needed it like I needed my next breath, and considering Reece still held a room hostage in his sands, there was no time to waste.

Increasing my pace, I rolled my hips harder and faster, and as my clit brushed against his body, bursts of pleasure slammed into me over and over. Stars danced before my eyes, and I threw my head back, all but grinding against him. I cried out when the intensity sent me spiraling over the edge of reality, and this time, for once, Reece was close behind.

His hands tightened on my hips, holding me in place so his powerful body could drive into mine, faster than ever. His breathing was harsh as he rumbled my name, cock swelling within me as he came too, his movements slowing as we rode out the orgasm. Despite the energy from the elixir and fae seed, my system was so overwhelmed with not just the sex but also the cementing of a true bond that I found myself collapsing against his chest. Reece's arms wrapped around me, holding me, and I felt a slight desperation in that grip. A desperation I understood because now that I had him in the way I'd always dreamed of, I was greedy for more.

The fact that we couldn't stay like this forever was a real tragedy... The ones trapped in the sands would probably disagree.

"We need to move," I finally said. "They're not going to take lightly to you holding them with your power."

The next sound from his mouth was a grumbling complaint, but he did get us to our feet after my body reluctantly released his hard length. I stared down at his big warrior's body, crowned by an even bigger...

If there was ever an incentive to survive an upcoming battle —outside of saving the worlds, of course—it was the knowledge that pleasure beyond my wildest imagination was waiting for me.

With my... true mate. Fuck.

Before I could get lost in the overwhelming emotions attacking my system, Reece distracted me as his energy cleaned us and gathered our clothing. When we were both dressed again, I took a chance and stepped to his side, wrapping my arms around his neck so I could kiss him. I'd never had the confidence to initiate contact, because he'd always controlled our path. My screwup centuries ago had given him more power, and it hadn't been balanced.

But now... now we felt balanced. We'd both suffered and we'd both proven ourselves.

Our future was finally bright.

Outside of those fuckers trying to raise the gods.

"You didn't accept my claim when I first made it, did you?" Reece said, pulling away just far enough to see my face. "But you do now. What changed?"

Swallowing roughly, I slid a hand between us and pressed it to his chest. "I was so scared to lose you again," I admitted, "that subconsciously, part of me rejected the bond before it could reject me. I was the one holding us back, even when I thought it was you. Blaming you for playing it hot and cold, believing you still judged me for past hurts. It's clear to me now that all along, it was me."

Heavy emotion burned deep in his eyes, and it killed me as I pressed higher for another kiss. "I'm sorry, Reece," I whispered, "but just know... I'm all in now. Until the sands fade."

Fire burned between us, but there was no time for more sealing of this bond. We had to release the room and get back to business. The red cloud that had given us privacy dropped, sand scattering, and with it, the others were freed from their cages. Part of me felt guilty that we'd stopped for some sex while they were trapped, but it was a fairly small part that I could easily ignore.

We'd needed that bonding moment, and unfortunately, everyone else had to deal.

Glancing down, I noted that Darin was still out cold, sprawled on the ground. But his chest was moving, and I could feel the steady thrum of his energy. He was fine. As was everyone else in the tented room, even if more than a few glares headed our way. Despite this, no one actually approached us except for Shadow, who prowled across the room. I backed up to stand at Reece's side, prepared to do battle if needed. Shadow had already been on edge, and he never took well to being trapped in another's power.

I heard a chuckle from the desert god to my left, but I didn't look away as I lowered my arms so that my curved blades on my belt were in easy reach.

"Calm, my little warrior," Reece murmured, reaching out to take my hand.

Bond or not, I was going to punch him if he slowed me in this fight.

Reece, still holding me, faced his best friend. The pair were eye to eye, huge warriors filling the space with their energy and stupidly broad shoulders. Neither of them said a word, but if the stare-off was any indication, plenty was being said silently.

Finally, Shadow spoke out loud. "Are we okay now?" he asked.

I was surprised by that relatively unaggressive question before I remembered that Mera had softened this beast somewhat. If anyone understood the power of a true mate bond claiming, it was Shadow.

"We're fine," Reece replied, sounding just as calm. "Darin here," he shot a dark look at the figure, who'd just started to twitch his fingers, "overstepped with Lale, and since I claimed her centuries ago, he can count himself lucky that he's still alive."

A few of the Guardians heard this statement, and the glares they'd been sending Reece's way faded fast. Touching someone's claimed mate was forbidden, an act that generally resulted in death. No doubt everyone in this room was now counting themselves lucky they hadn't defended their princeps and suffered the same fate as he had.

At this point, Darin was awake, shaking his head as he pushed up to stand. He ran a hand over his face before focusing on Reece. The red marks on his cheeks were already healing, but it spoke of how hard he'd been struck that it was taking this long.

As he took a step forward, I was surprised to see him look contrite. "I have shamed you and my family," he said slowly. "Your friend told me Angel was claimed, but I thought it merely an attempt to get one over on me again. I soon figured out how wrong my intentions were when Angel sent me on my butt."

Reece barely glanced at the other male when he rumbled, "You're lucky I didn't tear you to pieces, but with the impending battle, you are needed. There's a chance for you to prove yourself, but this is your last warning. I will tolerate no more."

"Me either," I added drily, even though this was the sort of contest I had the wrong parts for.

Darin nodded as he spun and faced the room. "Everyone get some rest," he yelled. "We leave at first new light."

Without another word, he left the tent, all of his Guardians following.

Len, Lucien, Alistair, and Galleli drifted over to where we stood, none of them even bothering to mention what Reece had done. If these six friends had anything going for them, it was that they'd been through a lot and accepted each other's flaws without judgement.

It was a friendship everyone should envy.

A family they should crave to belong to.

It had taken me more years than I'd care to admit, but there was no point denying it any longer: I wanted Reece and every part of what that entailed.

The mate. The family.

Even the danger that all powerful beings attracted.

"We should also rest," Reece told his friends, and no one argued. As we made our way to the tents, I stayed close to my mate, settling in at his side, his arm around me. This desperate need to touch had been ramped up in the acceptance and repair of our bond, and I sure as hell wasn't about to complain. It felt as perfect as it always looked when Mera and Shadow were joined.

A feeling of warmth, safety, and... home.

When we reached our tents, everyone went to rest. My plan initially had been to head toward an energy pad, an ochre formation of Ostealon sands and pamolsa branches designed to allow a closer link to the power that lay below the sands. Before I could take two steps in that direction, though, Reece tightened his hold and all but lifted me across the main rooms and into the bedroom we'd used earlier.

He didn't say a word as he stripped me of my armor for the second time this dark-moon, and I didn't question or fight this new path. When we were both naked, he dragged me across the bed and wrapped his big body around me. The connection of our bond settled again, stronger, a tangible binding of our powers that veritably hummed between us in the quiet darkness.

His hand traced along my side, slowly sliding over the bare skin, and despite my body's reaction to that touch, it was also soothing. He loved me one more time that night, and afterward I found myself drifting off into a deep meditative state, all the while knowing that this was so much stronger than any energy pad.

A mate bond was the true definition of peace and healing.

Thank the Nexus I hadn't missed this moment, because the culmination of my dreams had finally come to pass. Now we just had to survive tomorrow.

CHAPTER FORTY-FOUR

As we boarded the ship the next day, the new-moon had just begun to spread across the sky, casting tendrils of red through the darkness. I palmed my blade for the tenth time, feeling somewhat reassured by the familiar weight of the weapon. At the docks beside us, Darin and his guardians were outfitted in full black armor, boots, and more than a few weapons of their own, including curved swords with thick blades.

Reece and the others were dressed more casually, their weapons contained to whatever power they possessed. Even with the Delfora's ability to influence and restrict their abilities, they would still be a force to be reckoned with. In the end, we were all that stood between the worlds and these ancient gods rising—us and whatever power we carried into the sacred lands, since nothing from the outside world could be pulled toward us once we'd entered those sands. We just had to hope we were enough.

As soon as Reece made his way to the higher deck, accompanied by Shadow, the engines started to hum below us. Lucien and Alistair released the power cords binding us to the docks, and then we were sent out into the surging swells of the sands.

"Hold on," Reece called, his voice almost lost in the raging winds as we moved out of the shallower Guardian stream. "The powers of the spell and the impending power moon are on us."

I fought my way across to the railing of the ship, contemplating releasing my wings for balance. I'd learned over the years how to use them as both weapons and extra limbs, but in this situation, the winds would probably catch onto their lengths. It wouldn't be worth the fight.

Our ship picked up speed as we left the docks and entered the deep sands; in the Desert Lands, this was the equivalent of being in the middle of the ocean. It was wild out here this moon, to the point that not another ship—outside of Darin's—or creature could be seen around us.

The fact that there was no sign of Tsuma didn't sit well with me. The hope that at some point we'd catch sight of what we were up against kept me focused on the scenery, even if there was nothing around except raging black and ochre sands.

Unease unexpectedly rocked through my chest... my bonds. It hadn't come from me, and a quick check of Mera told me it hadn't originated from her either. So that left...

My gaze shot up to the higher deck, and sure enough, when I probed our newly cemented bond, I found the unease was from Reece. The dark spike of restless power, as I pushed deeper into it, felt a lot like the Delfora. Reece's connection to this land was the reason we were here, and it was calling him into its depths.

As if he'd felt me poking around in his energy, Reece's gaze left the horizon and found mine. At first, he wore no expression, but then his face softened. I had to press my hand to my chest, feeling this newly reinforced connection as it burned between us.

This bond—even when I'd suppressed and all but forgotten about it—was the reason we'd both refused to take another lover or mate.

The reason we could never let go of our past, even when it felt as if anger and shame and accusations were all that remained between us.

The reason we were fighting for a brighter future, as cliché as that was.

A smile tilted up my lips, and it kept growing as my happiness filled every empty and broken crevice in my soul. Reece closed his eyes for a moment, breathing in the emotions I was spilling all over the place, and when I felt like literal light was about to burst from my skin, I released the power. Finally, I'd found the peace that I'd been looking for during my blessing in the Honor Meadows.

Turned out that, all along, my restlessness had nothing to do with the two sides of my reborn essence needing connectivity. It had been about Reece and our unfulfilled bond.

Feeling stronger, I looked down to see that my skin was glittering with golden energy, which usually only happened when I pumped myself up with layers of my land. This time, though, I was filled with a combination of Reece's power and my own. Together, we were the strength that Tsuma was going to regret going up against.

By the time we reached the middle of the deep between the Guardians and the Delfora, the ship was surging higher than ever. Behind and below us, a desert storm raged and built, set to destroy everything in its path. For now, though, it was helping to push us at a much faster pace, and hopefully, we'd have enough time to make it onto land before the full force hit.

Flexing my fingers on the railing, I fought to control my buzzing energy that came from a true mate bond, fae seed, and the elixir we'd consumed. By the time the power moon rose, I'd be fucking glowing like a gold statue.

When the Delfora came into view, Darin's ship had fallen back, but we'd all made great time. The new-moon was bright above us, its heat expanding my energy as well, but the power moon had not split the sky yet. It was building, just like the energy below us. I couldn't see the power at this point, but I felt the impending explosion.

As the ship surged higher than ever, I tightened my grip, riding out the swell as my gaze landed on the flat planes of this land. The very land where I'd lost my sister. This was the first time I'd been back here, and it hit me as hard as I'd expected. The memories... their insidious dark tendrils tried to wrap around me... to remind me how it felt to lie in those black sands and clutch her lifeless body. But for once, I was strong enough that they couldn't take hold.

The past had to stay there for this moon.

There was no way to bring my sister back to life, but I could prevent more death.

Focus was the key to prevent me from falling into the abyss of that pain. It was also the key to winning this battle.

"Have you been beyond this front flat section?" Len asked, standing only a few feet from me, but I barely heard his words.

"No," I shot back. "Beyond the planes is the valley of the dead. It's surrounded by canyons, so that valley is the only way to move further into the Delfora. But of course, the dead do not surrender their territory that easily."

Hence why Tsuma needed this spell and the power moon to blast past those "ghosts."

As far as I knew, no one had stepped into the valley and returned except Reece's parents, and even with an apparent power moon back then, he'd told me they made it no more than a few feet from the entrance.

"Literal dead, right?" Len said, raising his voice.

I nodded. "Yes, bones from the many who have fallen in the sacred-land-battles over the years. Even though the living never make it past the flats, the dead end up buried under the valley. Deep in the sands, fueling the Delfora's power." I paused. "This is where my sister rests."

The fae fell silent again, and even with bursts of my power fueling me, the impending battle pressed against my strength. I just needed this to be over, once and for all.

CHAPTER
FORTY-FIVE

When we finally reached the edge of the Delfora, there were two ships docked, engines running, still hot from their journey. We might not have seen Tsuma and the others in our crossing, but thankfully, it didn't appear that we were that far behind them.

Stepping down the ramp toward the black sands, it was near impossible for us to talk now over the roar of the world beneath us. As my boots hit the Delfora, I jumped a foot at the buzz of power racing like an electrical current below. Before anyone else had a chance to reach me, I was already running. The spell was about to explode, and if we didn't get to the valley of the dead, we would not reach it before being completely engulfed.

Fighting the spell would weaken us, giving Tsuma and the others the time they needed to use the power moon, which... I looked up quickly to see that a fissure was finally visible in the orb. This was it, the culmination as everything prepared to hit at once.

The others fell in behind me, powering across the black

sands. A glance back told me that Darin and the others, who had just docked, were only a few paces ahead of the surging energy. It was going to be touch and go for all of us, and with that in mind, I faced the valley and ran as fast as my power allowed.

The buzz and roar grew under our feet, black sands flying up and covering us as we closed in on the valley. The two compacted sand cliffs rose before us, and seeing our destination spurred me on faster. Just a few more miles and we'd be there.

Ahead, I finally saw Tsuma and the others, at least two dozen of them, also racing for the entrance. We all knew that if you weren't in that valley when the power storm hit and the moon split, you wouldn't be making it past the planes.

Risking another glance behind, I almost lost my balance and face-planted. The sands that we'd just crossed had lifted from the deeps and onto the Delfora, forming a massive sand wave. Darin and his Guardians were barely staying ahead of the raging storm cell, but they hadn't fallen yet.

"Move, Lale," Reece shouted, wrapping an arm around me as he went past, yanking me along the path. Shadow, on my other side, reached out and hauled me along, too, both holding me until my feet got back underneath me, moving without help.

We'd made it into the Delfora just in time; a sand wave of that size would have crushed us and our ships into dust. It could still crush us now if we didn't move our asses. Some of us might be able to put ourselves back together, but not in time to save the worlds.

"The power moon," Reece shouted again, and as my gaze lifted briefly, I caught the moment the red moon fissured down the center, splitting into two equally powerful orbs. Everything shuddered around us, and Tsuma, who'd been waiting centuries for this event, finally crossed into the valley ahead of us, disappearing from sight.

When we got within touching distance of the valley, the two massive cliffs blocked some of that intense energy from the moon. As we entered the valley, an icy shock of ancient power jabbed into mine. That touch was a warning, and normally if we'd ignored that warning, we'd be thrown back out into the Delfora. But on this particular moon, the other powers overwhelmed it and we made it through.

Shadow and the others fell back in the valley, more affected by its struggling wards. Reece didn't feel a thing, his connection to the Delfora giving both of us an advantage, and without waiting, we pushed forward, knowing Tsuma had to be stopped. The securities were already falling, and she had a head start. Time was running out.

The further we moved through this valley, the darker it grew above us until only slivers of red light illuminated in long arcs across our path. That didn't mean the power from those moons was any less, but it did block some of the impact.

At some point the roaring of the sands behind us eased, and Reece and I looked back to find that the wave had stopped surging forward, caught on the cliffs, unable to move into the valley at more than a trickle. Thankfully, all our allies, including Darin and the Guardians had made it through. And now we had a shot.

Unfurling my wings, I prepared to fly high and see where Tsuma and the others had ended up. Any information about what we were up against could help, and a bird's-eye view was an advantage. As I flapped hard, my feet left the sands, but I got no more than about five feet into the air when I hit a barrier.

The valley's securities were still strong enough to fight me from above, leaving only our narrow path to traverse. Frustrated, I landed and resumed my sprint, understanding that there was to be no shortcut here.

"We're not making any ground on her," I cursed as I tried to move faster, but I was already maxed out.

"She's pumped up on the spell's power," Reece bit out, not sounding remotely out of breath, despite our pace. "It's giving her unnatural abilities."

Explained why she'd been able to get here as quickly as we did and stay undetected along her journey. "That's okay, she won't get to use it for long," I said, palming my blades, ready for whatever we came up against.

The path started to curve, winding and growing narrower. At this point there was no option but to move single file, and I followed Reece, his broad shoulders almost scraping the sides at some sections. In the small glimpses I caught from around him, I was certain we were near the end of the valley.

"Something is in the sands ahead," Reece called back, and I ducked lower to see what he meant. It almost looked as if debris was littering the path...

It was only when the black sands crunched under my boot that I could see exactly what was rising from the sands: bones. The ones that should have been buried deep in this land, fueling its security and increasing the power that ran here.

"The ritual is underway," Reece sounded pissed, "and if we don't hurry, she'll succeed and the sands will wash us all away."

We were already moving at super speeds, but we found the strength to go faster, the crunching louder as more bones filled the path. It killed me to know that the dead were being ripped from their resting place and disrespected, especially when one was my sister, but there was nothing I could do to fix it right now. If we didn't move our asses, we would be joining them in their eternal rest, and that was unacceptable.

Reece rounded one final corner, and the path opened wide

for the first time in minutes, spanning out farther than it had at any other point. This was the last of the valley, the junction before the resting place of the gods. The source of the cold, biting energy.

This was our final chance to stop Tsuma before the ancients rose and destroyed us all.

CHAPTER FORTY-SIX

Being one of the first to ever see this section of the Delfora stirred the parts of me that loved history and books. My entire life, I'd always devoured information, embraced cultures, and studied battle. It would have been nice if instead of battle, I was here to examine the two ancient pillars filled with sprawling script, that framed the resting place of ancient gods. Maybe if we survived, I'd finally learn this world... this language. But until then, my focus had to be on those who'd let their craving for power destroy their common sense.

Tsuma and all the Desertlandians she'd recruited to her cause.

Their numbers scattered in our direction, more than I'd initially counted, leaving only Tsuma behind between the two twenty-foot pillars. We were close enough now that I saw the script across them was familiar but unreadable. The language of the gods and the rules that Reece had spoken of all those moons ago.

The same writing tattooed across Reece's stomach.

This was also where the spells to stop the gods from rising

were carved, and Tsuma was in the perfect position to break them all.

"All the dynasties," Reece cursed as we slowed, prepared to battle the Desertlandians who were racing toward us, determined to protect Tsuma.

"Traitors," Darin roared from nearby, having clearly noted the wash of tunics in all shades of the sand.

That was all the time we had for conversation because we were about to battle. I lifted my curved blades as my wings sprung free. I used their strength to give me more momentum. Even boxed in by the barrier above, I flew over the top of the first group to cut off the second lot, breaking their ranks. My aim was to get through this lot and to Tsuma before she could fuck the worlds.

The first Desertlandian I slashed my blades across was a pale skinned female from Shale, her brown tunic shimmering slightly in the low light. Forcing myself to ignore her youthful energy—she had no more than a few decades of life—I did not temper my attack. Slashing twice in quick succession, I was surprised when she dodged the blows and reached out to swipe her hand across my skin. A hand that was covered in a deep magenta, like it had been dipped in paint or... blood. Was this part of the ritual they were using to break the spell? What sort of weapon was it that they chose it over blades?

Needing to know what we were up against, I deliberately let her touch my skin the next time she tried, and the burn of a dark energy started deep under my muscle and connective tissue. A burn I'd felt before, even if it had never been administered this way.

She bore the power of blood-sacrifice energy, and risking a quick glance at Tsuma, I noted that she too wore hands of red, lifting them to place against the pillars. Searching further with the seconds I had, I saw what looked like a body lying in the sands before her, half-covered and unmoving. Shit, we were in trouble now.

The gathered dynasty power and the moons had gotten them here, but the final step was, as always, death. In all of its irony, death in the Delfora brought life.

My fury rose, and ignoring the burn under my skin, I swung my body to the side and released a curved blade with as much force and speed as I could. It never wavered, loyal and strong, bonded to me through many battles. The Shale female screamed as the curve sliced through her hands, both appendages hitting the sands to shrivel and burn.

"Remove their hands," I shouted to the others. "If they touch you, their magic will burn you from the inside out."

My energy still hadn't healed my burn, but I was strong enough to stop it from spreading and possibly destroying other parts of me. Some of my family weren't as powered up, and this sort of dark energy could kill them.

Especially Alistair, who was already struggling with the drier air.

There were too many combatants between us for me to check on him, so I had to hope he would be safe while I worked as fast as I could to take the others out.

I faced a male from Holinfra; the grey of his tunic was insipid in this lighting, perfectly matching his face. He snarled as he dove for me, hands out front since that was their weapon of choice this moon. Or should I say moons, since the power on their hands was probably thanks to the twins above.

Waiting until he almost collided with me, I dropped and slid under his grasp, popping up behind him. Another Holinfra waited there, so I was surrounded on both sides, but I wasn't worried. Kicking out at the one who had his back to me, I released my curved blades into their sheaths and whipped my sword from its scabbard. Its length gave me enough reach to stay away from their hands, and when I sliced through the second Holinfra's right wrist, he was backtracking to escape.

With a grin, I spun for momentum and released the sword in a straight line, sending it into the base of his throat, all but severing his head. Before his shout had even died off, the first Holinfra was back, and I used some of my energy to pin him to the ground while holding out a hand for my sword. It returned at my call, and I was in the perfect position to plunge the blade deep into the first Holinfra's chest.

These Desertlandian traitors were pumped up on power, fast and deadly, but they lacked fighting experience, which would be their downfall.

As I got back to my feet, prepared for the next wave, a ripple of heat and sand hit me, and I looked over to find Shadow and Reece tearing through the remaining traitors. They'd been somewhat handicapped until now, not able to use their full powers with all of us so close, but now they were determined to get to... My eyes tracked their path, right to Alistair.

Everything inside of me stilled, the world seeming to slow around the events that I could already see unfolding. Alistair had been my biggest worry since this entire mission started, and right now, he was fighting for his life. The Desertlandians had backed him against the side of the valley as he used blades of water to remove their hands. He was holding his own, but I could see what had his brothers in a panic.

His skin was near white and scaled.

He'd given everything he had and was weakening against enemies who were pumped up on sacrificial energy. It would only take one slipup.

Reece and Shadow felt the ticking tides of fate...

I was running and screaming, my blade cutting through any that stood in my way, but I would be too late. I'd had a sense of this from the first moment Alistair stepped onto the ship. I'd hoped against the inevitability of his passing, but as a Rohami ducked under his arm and slammed his hand against bare and flaking Karn skin, I knew that this was where Alistair's journey ended.

My sword released as fast as Shadow's flames and Reece's sands, but we were all too late. Racing toward him, sand flying around me, it was clear that our friend wasn't the only victim, with many of Darin's Guardians down too, but I couldn't focus on that. Not now.

Alistair fell to his knees, and as his eyes met Reece, who was almost at him, they were wide with this damn look of surprise. It was clear that he'd truly believed he had what it took to survive here.

He would have, too, if it weren't for their blood ritual drawing directly on the fire of this world.

Reece's energy blasted the Rohami against the cliff, crushing every bone in his body, but it was too late to save Alistair. When my mate dropped down to cradle his fallen brother, my chest heaved as I fought against the darkness pressing in around me. This death let the memories I'd been able to block earlier surge forward, overwhelming my system. It was Leka all over again, the death of someone I loved in the dark Delfora sands.

We'd failed in our mission. We'd failed Mera.

We'd failed Alistair.

Falling in beside Reece, I reached out and wrapped my hands around Alistair. Despite the prophetic way I'd felt on this journey, part of me was still praying that he was strong enough to fight the fire. Praying there was a chance to save him.

But it was not meant to be.

The moment the empty hollowness of his essence hit me, I let out a wailing battle cry, and I wasn't the only one. Shadow's beast form stood over me as he raged, sending flames out to wipe the world clean. I could only hope our other friends got out of the way because no one could survive that fire.

Lowering my head over Alistair's body, I manically whispered rapid prayers, desperate to send him into the afterlife blessed as the warrior he was. All the while, my heart cracked and bled, the past and present mingling so strongly that for moments all I could see was Leka. Her beautiful face. Her empty essence.

My power spilled from me, slamming into the land around us and mingling with that of the Delfora. As much as I knew I had to pull myself together and get to Tsuma, I couldn't reel it back in. I couldn't stem the tides any longer. My ability to compartmentalize and focus was shot to shit, and there was nothing to do except hold on for the ride and hope my mourning pain didn't destroy us all.

Reece and Shadow were the only ones who could get close to me as my power spanned out like a protective shield around us, but in the same breath, everything around us went silent—the sort of silence that spoke of danger approaching.

Except I knew we'd destroyed all of Tsuma's minions. Shadow's fire had taken care of any that had been missed in the battle.

Was this Tsuma finishing the ritual?

With a final whisper over Alistair, I managed to push to my feet, my limbs shaking as I felt for my weapons, unsurprised to find they'd returned to their sheaths and scabbard. At least one part of my life was going according to plan. One part out of hundreds.

In my grief, energy swirled within me, and I was ready to face the ancients. It wasn't over until I said it was, and right now, I was ready to fight.

"Lale," Reece whispered.

That one word drew all of my attention, and as my gaze snapped up, expecting to see Tsuma puffed up with power, I instead...

My next breath choked from me as I stared at the two ghosts standing in the path.

Floating above the very bones of the valley.

CHAPTER FORTY-SEVEN

I had no idea how I'd moved so fast. Even for me, it was a mere moment in time before I was halfway toward Tsuma, heading right for the two spectral figures. Reece was at my side, and even through the cacophony of pain and disbelief, there was a flicker of peace in knowing I wasn't facing this alone. Not anymore.

"Is it really them?" I asked, sobbing through each word.

He cleared his throat. "I don't know," he finally said. "But either way, there's still a moment to stop Tsuma, and we have to go through them to do it."

The ghosts were not just anyone, but Leka and Rhett. The translucent pair floated in the path, looking exactly as they had all those years ago, decked out in battle gear with smiles on their faces. Both had a love for life that apparently lasted through death and to the other side.

When I was a few feet away, I slowed my pace but didn't stop. We needed to know if they were a physical barrier or not. Leka winked as I passed right through her, and in another pop, she was now in front of me again. This time, she waved her hands on, but as she opened her mouth to say something, no sound emerged.

A barrier kept the living and the dead apart, and while I could see her, we could not talk. But I read lips well enough to understand what she was saying. *Run. Hurry.*

"They're not here to stop us," I said in a rush to Reece. "They're helping."

This gave me a final jolt of energy to cross the sand and smash into Tsuma, sending her flying into the pillar she stood before. In the same instant, Reece's sands formed glasslike weapons, slicing her hands clean off. He didn't stop there; his fury over Alistair and the overall betrayal driving him to punish her.

I was about to do the same, when a roar from behind us had me spinning to see that the giant wave of sand energy from earlier, which had been struggling to get through the valley, was now barreling rapidly toward us. I screamed at Shadow, who was already moving into action, sending up a flame-filled barrier that wrapped around the rest of our friends and Alistair's body.

He would protect them, which meant Reece and I were all that remained to stop the ancients from rising. Turning, I found him holding that disloyal bitch up with his sands, while she laughed manically. "Your parents would have been here if they were still alive," she taunted. "They craved power, same as the rest of us born too close to the Delfora. You are evidence of that."

"Reece," I yelled over the roar of the spell he hadn't seemed to notice in his rage. "How can we stop the sands?"

This finally got through to him, and he turned icy blue eyes my way before they looked along the valley. "The others?" he asked, his voice unnaturally deep.

"Shadow has them in a protective shield, but that can only

last so long," I shouted, the roar growing louder. The sands were at Shadow now, so we had only a few seconds until they engulfed us too.

I grabbed a fistful of Tsuma's tunic. "How do we stop this?" I yelled in her face. "All of your followers are dead, and you're about to join them. There's no one to control the gods now!"

Her face finally went blank. "There's no way to stop it," she whispered. "The ritual was complete when the blood of the sacrifice filled the final space." She looked toward the pillar, and I saw the deep burgundy dripping along the script I could not read, filling it all.

Before I could say another word, Leka and Rhett appeared before us, jumping and shouting, waving us past the pillars into the desert where the ancients rested. They were telling us what we already knew: Time was up, and our only option was to get out of this valley before the sands smashed into us.

Leaving Tsuma sprawled on the ground, we took off. Behind us, a clanking and shattering of bones echoed between the canyon walls, and the heat of this power's rage burned down my spine. This was the reason that Desertlandians were not welcome in this part of the Delfora. The powers here were strong and unpredictable, and when mixed with energies of all eight dynasties and a power moon? Well, the wall of destructive sand energy was the end result.

Tsuma should have known better; her greed for power might now destroy us all.

The two ancient pillars had stood as a barrier to the resting place of the gods for an eternity—since the ancient days—and as we tried to cross, I expected to be flung back. But in the last second, our ghosts wrapped around us, sending us into unchartered territory. The dead could cross where the living were not welcome.

The sands that had been right behind us hit the pillar

barriers and remained where they were, unable to cross after us. That didn't mean there was no power on this side, though. Tsuma had broken the spells holding the gods, and beneath our feet the ripples and bucking of the sands could already be felt. A particularly large jolt sent Reece and me up into the air, but my wings, still tucked in behind me from the fight, opened without thought and I caught us both. Not that Reece needed my help, but it was nice to save him for once.

When we were back on the land, standing under the bright light of a power moon, I knew that we were too late.

The ritual was complete, and the gods were about to rise.

I felt a hand on my shoulder, and knowing it couldn't be Reece from that angle, I spun to find Leka at my side, looking very un-spirit like. "You can touch me?" I burst out.

"You don't have much time," she said, and I had to reach out and hold onto her when my legs weakened at the sound of her musical voice. "You called us in your grief, and we knew we had to come to get you through the gateway, but the other realm is calling us back." Her golden eyes locked on mine. "The ancients awake."

My chest heaved as I clutched her; having her back for these few seconds meant more than I ever imagined. "How do we stop this from happening?" I managed to choke out.

"You have to put them to rest again," Rhett said from where he appeared beside Reece, looking like a slightly blonder and darker-skinned version of his brother.

Reece shook his head. "You did not die in these lands; your bones don't even rest here. How is this possible?"

Rhett shifted his gaze to stare right at Leka. "Where her soul goes, so goes mine. Our fates were always intertwined."

Even in this moment where everything had gone to shit and the worlds might possibly end, that was a ray of light to soothe away a small fraction of my pain. I hadn't known their bond was so strong... as strong as Reece's and mine.

My sister smiled at him; her face softer than it had ever been in this realm.

Before I could fall into my feelings over this, Leka returned her focus to me. Reaching up, she tucked a strand of my braid that had fallen free back behind my ear. "You can stop them, Mel. You're finally embracing all sides of yourself, including the side that was born to exist in the Desert Lands. Use it all now. Use your bond with Reece, and return the gods to their resting place."

She flickered, almost disappearing completely, and I tried desperately to hold onto her, needing one last touch before she was lost forever again. In my grief over Alistair, while in this land of power, I'd managed to call her soul. But she was not mine to keep.

"I love you, Leka," I whispered. "Until our souls meet again."

She hugged me hard, and for a second, we were twin souls again.

But then it was over.

By the time I opened my eyes, Leka and Rhett were gone. *Be happy.* I heard on the breezes before their energy returned to a realm I could not find. Not yet anyway. As I met Reece's gaze, a bittersweet emotion lingered between us. We were happy to know they'd found each other in the next life, but not having them here with us any longer was a wound that would never fully heal.

"At least I know now why Rhett was never the same after that battle," Reece said with a shake of his head.

"That battle felt like it took everything," I said swallowing roughly as I stepped to his side, "but it didn't take us. We're still standing here, centuries later, and we can finish this."

Reece, face set in the hard lines of his warrior expression, nodded. "Do you have any ideas?"

I took a second to look around, noting that the resting place of the ancients was a large, perfectly circular canyon, with cliffs curving overhead to define the shape. Behind us was the valley, its pillars the only part visible since the sands were smashed against the barrier, hiding everything else. In front of us was another set of pillars, which I could only imagine were guarding an even greater threat than the ancients beneath our feet.

"Whatever we do, we should do it fast," I finally said. "Because I have no idea how long Shadow can shield them from that deluge."

"They're still alive," Reece assured me, his hand against his chest. "I can feel their lifeforce, but time is running out."

It was, but for once, I wasn't facing this alone. "True mates," I reminded him. "We will face this together."

Always.

CHAPTER FORTY-EIGHT

Reece wrapped his arms around my waist and pulled me against his side. "You were always my greatest wish and my most destructive defeat," he murmured, pressing his lips to my cheek. His hand slid down to grip his shirt. "No matter what happens, I need you to know..." My eyes scanned down his torso to where he'd lifted the hem to reveal the words etched on his skin. "The day we fought, I got this inked on me. Our names are entwined with *until the sands fade* in ancient script."

Finally. Finally, I knew what he'd felt was so important that he'd permanently marked his skin. I was shattered by the realization that even when he'd hated me, he'd never let me go. "All this time?" I managed to say.

His scoff was low and broken. "Since the day you walked into my life. My anger was strong, but I never doubted our fate."

The beat of his energy matched the beat of mine, and as our lips met for what I really hoped wasn't the last time, I felt him inside my soul. We gave ourselves this moment, a mere second, before we pulled away knowing worlds were not going to save themselves.

Our addled "mate brains" had to be shelved for our warrior sides.

"How do we stop them from rising," I asked, once again cataloguing the sands around us. "What is beyond those other pillars?"

Reece turned toward the second set fifty yards from us. "I've never been this far, but I can only assume that beyond is more wards and the resting place of Death and all that comes with it."

As I'd expected. "How did they force the ancients to rest in the first place?"

Reece's answer was immediate. "I wasn't here, but the stories speak of a similar method to what Tsuma used to wake them. She was breaking the spells, while the original would have involved etching those ancient words into the stones. It takes sacrifice and power. A lot of power."

It made sense and explained why Tsuma had had to wait until the world was basically brimming with energy to break through those ancient spells. "We have a lot of power and a connection to this world," I reminded Reece. "More than anyone else. I think if we combine everything and bleed that essence onto another pillar, we might be able to stop them from fully regenerating."

Reece's red sands were suddenly visible and whipping around us. "There's a chance," he confirmed. "The ancients are still in the process of rising, and so there's a window of vulnerability."

A chance was better than nothing.

Reece, appearing to calculate it all, swirled his sands around for a moment, staring down into the Delfora. His gaze returned to the pillars at the valley junction, where black swirled maniacally, blocking our view of everything, including our friends somewhere beyond.

Trapped in the power.

"We need that energy," he murmured. "Of the dynasties."

Before I could ask for more details, he was running toward the pillars. I was only a few steps behind. When we reached it, he pressed his hands to the barrier but was blocked from moving past the sands. "Normally we'd be able to get through," he said distractedly, his gaze running up and down the pillars, "since this spell was designed to block in one direction. But there's too much power on the other side. I can't penetrate it, and it won't ease until the power moon above fades."

"But you need that sand for the pillar?" I confirmed.

He nodded. "I do, and I think there's a way to get it if I siphon it off in small increments."

"Hurry, then," I said quickly, feeling the continued destruction of wards below us, along with a sense that that the foundation of our worlds was shifting. My family line was an original power, all of us born to keep the balance. This was how I felt extinction level events, and I knew we were on the precipice of one now.

Reece's hands burned against the sand barrier and heat burst around us. Within a few moments, the sand turned to black glass, but he didn't stop there. Strain lined his face as he fought the barrier. I wanted to offer my support and energy, but unless he asked for it, I could not risk throwing him off task.

The heat grew as Reece removed his hand, and to my surprise, the glass followed, hot and pliable as he pulled it from the spelled sands. The rumble below us grew stronger, almost knocking me off my feet, but Reece didn't shift. He just continued to pull that sand through in slow, agonizing increments. "They're close," he huffed, "but so am I. Will you share your power with me?"

I nodded as I stumbled closer. "Yes, everything I have. This deep in the Delfora, I can't get more from the meadows, though."

Reece nodded, his focus still on the glass he was weaving into a pillar, building on what he'd taken from the barrier. "We'll just have to ensure it's enough."

I was willing to drain every part of myself to keep him and my friends alive.

"Get ready, Lale," he said, building faster until the pillar was almost as tall as he was. "I'm about to write the spell, and in doing so, we need to bleed power to secure the binding."

He closed his hand over the tip of the pillar, which was cylindrical and about ten inches in diameter now. Pressing firmer, his knuckles turned a few shades lighter than his skin as he closed his eyes and murmured spells in the ancient language. On the previously smooth piece, words and scripts began to appear, and with each new line, Reece looked more drained, especially when blood finally oozed from his palm, running fast along the pillar.

By now, the rumbling below us was near deafening, and over my shoulder the sands were falling away as the gods rose.

"Your turn, Lale," Reece shouted, bringing my gaze back to him as he ripped his hand free and a deep ochre blood sprayed us. I didn't hesitate, slamming my hand onto the same spot his had been, near the peak of the pillar. Spikes I hadn't noticed embedded into my skin, cutting through with ease, but the pain was easily ignored. The deep red of my blood, changed since my rebirth, spilled with my power. Both mingled with Reece's, intertwining like old friends. Like true mates.

"Don't give too much, Lale," he warned, hovering nearby. The vibration of the land caused him to stumble. I was fairly certain that was one of the only times he'd ever been thrown off balance in the sands.

"This is our chance," I reminded him though gritted teeth. "One shot. I will give it all and then some."

His chest was rumbling like the land itself, but he didn't argue, instead choosing to work with me by placing his hands on the glass just under mine, our essence and energy mingling and sealing this pillar's strength.

He started to read the words again, over and over, using the strength of both of us to ensure that we succeeded here. His low, deep voice gave me a moment of comfort, even as I weakened and slumped forward. I wanted to speak with him in this foreign, ancient tongue that seemed familiar but truly wasn't. I didn't know the language, so I couldn't do more than bleed power and life into the sands below and pray that we were giving enough.

Pray that the sands stopped shaking and parting.

It was our only hope.

CHAPTER FORTY-NINE

To my great relief, by the time I was slumped against the glass, feeling as drained as I ever had, the land was finally calming. And the buzz of power beneath us was definitely easing. Reece quieted, letting the ancient language ease from his lips as he took my weight, keeping me from collapsing onto the sand. The words etched into the glass were filled with our blood now, the sands below as well, and the pillar appeared to be stronger and more powerful than the originals.

"Did it work?" I rasped, barely conscious.

He tightened his hold on me, and I didn't like his hesitation when he said, "The sands are still falling."

I lifted my heavy head to see a huge chunk of sand disappear. "It didn't work," I sobbed.

We'd been so close. I'd felt it.

"We didn't give them the sacrifice," Reece bit out.

"Death is what holds them," I whispered, thinking of the bones that lay in the valley. We'd been fools to think we could circumvent that final part of their binding.

Through the gap in the sand, the gods rose until six of

them hovered across from us. Each was at least fifteen feet tall, and wearing ornately detailed robes in ivory and silver. There was no way to tell they'd been buried for centuries, with no dust or decay to be seen about their pristine outfits or long, flowing hair. Their skins were luminous in shades of brown and gold. Stunningly beautiful, each and every one, but also terrifying as they turned their completely white eyes in our direction. Silver lights reflected in their depths, and while it appeared as if they were blind, I knew they could see us.

"Do you know their names?" I whispered to Reece. "Maybe they have reason? If we appeal to them...?"

"Do not use their names, for they hold power," he murmured. "And there's no reasoning with them."

As he said that, he released me so he could sidle in front, drawing all their attention. He spoke in the ancient language, words I did not understand, and if we lived through this, he was teaching it to me. If there was one thing I hated, it was being disadvantaged by a lack of knowledge.

A goddess who stood in front of the others moved closer to Reece. Her hair was the color of snow, contrasting with her brown skin and perfectly pink lips. As she raised her hands and said something musical, I noticed a second set of arms and hands nestled below the main two she was using.

I had a vague idea that this was *Labinte,* the ancient goddess of plenty, who brought rain and crops and food. Along with destruction and devastation, depending on her mood. Whoever she was, when she locked eyes with Reece, I saw more than interest in her expression.

I saw desire.

These gods had been sleeping for a long time, and they had awoken with a craving for power. Among other things. When she spoke, I fought against the urge to cover my ears. The sound wasn't loud, but in my drained state, it pierced the center of my essence.

"She's thanking us for raising them," Reece said in a voice so low I could barely hear him. "She recognizes my energy holds tendrils of theirs and is offering me a chance to stand with them as they bring their power back to the worlds."

"Great," I muttered, pushing closer to his spine. Of course the stunning, scary, and power-hungry goddess would be interested in Reece.

All freaking females were. Still, I was his mate, and weakened or not, she'd have to pry him from my cold, dead hands. Her voice filled my head once more, and I caught the tic in Reece's jaw at whatever she was saying. "They don't have their full powers, yet," he said a little louder. "They need another influx of energy."

"And how do they plan on getting that energy?" I asked, sensing that the tic in his jaw was about to be explained.

"Our assumptions about what is buried beyond this circle are correct."

Great, fucking Death was next.

At that, two of the gods near the back—one with long black hair, four eyes, and no visible mouth and the other with shoulder-length ivory curls and an impressive set of magenta horns curving from her forehead—turned and started to walk toward those far-off pillars. It was their turn to bleed now, and when they did, the original vacuum would once again walk the worlds.

If the rumors were true, Death made Dannie look like a baby supervillain.

I was distracted as that white-haired goddess took another long-legged step forward, reaching for Reece with her first set of hands, her sharp tone turning more coaxing. While he had her distracted, I attempted to figure out my next course of action, already palming my blades. I had no idea if they would pierce a god's skin, but they were all I had at the moment.

What we really needed was a damn grotto.

Leaning forward, I wrapped my hand around Reece's biceps. "Are there silver sands here buried with the gods?"

Before he could answer, the goddess—who'd finally noticed me—struck out with her power, a lightning bolt slicing between us, and even at a relatively low strength, her shot was powerful enough to blow Reece and me apart. My wings caught me before I hit the sand, and I used them to pump myself up a few feet off the ground.

Searching for Reece in the same breath, I blinked at how damn close he was to the gods now. I'd been blasted away, but he was right in their clutches.

"Reece," I shouted, diving toward him, only to find myself slamming against a barrier of sand that had sprung up around me so fast I hadn't seen it coming. At first, I thought it was magic from the goddess of four arms, until I saw the red Rohami sands. Rohami sands that almost blocked me from view, except for a few gaps I could see through.

"Reece! I screamed again, slamming my hands against the side, cursing my current weakness. We'd given our all to stop them from rising, but we'd failed. And in doing so, I was more vulnerable than I'd ever been.

His eyes found mine, swirling pools of blue in this desert of black, and my hands stilled at the expression he wore: resignation and acceptance. Whatever he had planned, I wasn't going to like it, and I liked even less that he'd taken my choice away by locking me in this cage.

When he turned away from me to face the ancients again, my chest ached. My bond with him tangled inside as pain pulsed between us. Why the hell had he locked me over here in a cage of sand? Whatever his plan was, I could have helped.

Stronger together. I'd be stuck in this damn barrier until he lifted it or died—

The pain hit me so hard I almost fell to my knees. Reece pressed his hand to his chest, feeling my agony through our connection, but he didn't look my way. We both knew the plan now; Reece was giving it one last shot to return them into the sands.

A true sacrifice.

With his energy and connection to this land, he knew he was the only one who could do this. The only one strong enough. He was about to destroy himself... and me in the process.

If there was one thing I'd learned in the many years without my true mate, it was that there was no light in my life when he was gone. I wouldn't do it again. Just as Rhett had said about Leka, it was the same for me.

Where Reece went, I would follow.

CHAPTER FIFTY

The twin moons still burned brightly across the sky, and I prayed that their energy would be enough for me to regroup and fight my way out of here. My eyes never left Reece, who looked calm, showing no indication that he had set a suicide plan in motion to save the worlds.

Part of me wanted to rage at the unfairness of our path; it was too much to ask of us. We'd already spent centuries apart, and now, when we finally had a chance to live, it would be ripped from us one more time. But if we did this together...

Palming my blades, I sliced at the sand holding me, and while the energy-infused tip did part the barrier, it wasn't open long enough for me to slip through the shield. Reece didn't turn my way as I fought, but I knew he felt my fire and sorrow. All to no avail.

If only I could figure out a way to harness the power moon —an event that happened once in thousands of years. If I could tap into that power, we'd have a shot. Maybe we wouldn't even have to die, since the gods were still weak, and until Death rose, we had a chance.

I released my blades as an idea hit me. Maybe my way to

the moon's power was through my bond with the desert god. He could tap into parts of this land that I'd never be able to, even at full strength. Closing my eyes, I dropped to the ground and fisted my hands into the sand, drawing on the bond that was deep in my essence. Filtering through my normal strengths, I dug deeper to find the power of the Desert Lands, and it was there, strong and perfect. But no matter how many times I tried to grasp onto its core, the essence slipped through my hold.

My scream was near deafening as I released my frustration, my eyes still closed as I pushed deeper into my power well. Deeper than I'd ever gone before. This was the part of myself I'd cut off when Reece was no longer in my life. Where my pain lived. My shame. Every part of my soul hurt in there, and I was instantly reminded why ignoring this depth of myself was a favorite pastime. It was a cut that would never mend. A burn that seared deeper and deeper, even as I tried to exorcise the ruined flesh. In any other circumstances I'd give up the fight, too weak to crush the demons here, but this moon I would never stop.

I took the pain and used it to fuel my determination.

The sand heated under my hands, and at the same time, there was a flutter deep in my stomach. A foreign sort of flutter that caught all my attention. I choked out a cry at what I felt there. *Impossible.* I'd been searching for Reece's energy to use the sands, and I'd found it, only...

How in the damn worlds had this happened?

Before I could break down at the achingly tragic truth of my new existence, so perfect and so bittersweet, there was a roar from outside of my sand bubble, and I finally had to open my eyes. Pushing up against the sands to stand, I choked on my next breath to see the gods surrounding Reece. Despite their alien features, with too many or too few parts, it was still obvious that they were furious. Reece must have given up on his pretense of joining them, and as he stepped back, I was the only one to notice he was leading them to the blood-infused glass pillar he'd created.

Just as his back touched it, he lifted his hands into the air, and the land rumbled as he drew on its energy. Turning in my cage, I found another gap in his sand, and through it, I saw the pillars trembling as black sands smashed against them.

At least, I thought it was the sands, until bones burst into our clearing, the barrier no problem for them. The dead crossed where the living couldn't, and I knew every part of his plan now. Reece was using the bones, those powerful guards, and he was about to set them free on the ancient gods to give himself enough time for the sacrifice.

Ivory, gold, black and bronze bones from many races closed over the top of the ancients, and as Reece tilted his head back, he clapped his hands together. The shockwave knocked me a few steps away, and I scrambled back to the small gap in my sand in time to see every bone was now ash, showering down to cover the gods, who raged at this unexpected attack.

Reece turned, then, and met my gaze, and there was so much regret and pain and resignation in that one look that I lost conscious thought, screaming and smashing my arms against the sands, begging him not to do this. Not now. Not when we had so much to live for.

He just needed to give me time, a chance to save us all. I could do it, if he'd only wait—

His lips parted as he called my name, and then, with a final sigh of air, he threw himself up and onto the glass pillar. Time and space lost all meaning as my rage and agony took over, washing all other senses and emotions away. After some seconds, I noticed the ringing in my ears, and that was when I registered the screams. *My screams.*

Falling to my knees again, I could no longer hide from the

truth of what was happening. Reece had sacrificed himself to save the worlds, and all I could do was watch as his body slid down the glass, lifeforce slowly expelling from him. Normally, a pillar such as that would not kill a being of Reece's strength, but through our bond, I felt his solution to that problem.

Our eyes were locked together; he hadn't looked away from me as he died, and he was fucking killing me. As I pressed into the sand, I felt his power building. Building in the only way an eternal could destroy themselves: an explosion of his essence.

The gods started to howl then, but they were trapped in the bones, which had already started to pull them back into the sands where they would be held forevermore.

Reece's plan was working, which meant fuck all to me if I still lost him.

Forcing my frantic mind to calm, I stood and released my hair, needing the calming ritual of braiding before battle to get into a frame of mind that might include a solution before it was too late. As the long strands covered my shoulders, I reached up to braid it again, settling my brain into warrior mode. I was all that Reece had left in his corner, and I would not let him down again.

As I worked through the thick strands, I reached a small knot. Transcendents didn't get knots, a quirk of our magical energy, and yet here it was. Tugging at it, because I needed my braid done to focus completely, I tried to ignore the swells of Reece's power that told me he was almost gone.

The sharp pain against my scalp was brief, and as the hair finally released, a single speck of silver dust drifted in front of my eyes. It took me a fraction of a heartbeat to understand what I was seeing.

Silver sand.

Catching the fleck with one hand, my other hand dropped to my stomach as I put the pieces together. What I'd felt before was a miracle, and that explained this second miracle clutched against my palm. There was no time to truly marvel at this as Reece's energy swelled stronger, and I knew this was my last chance to stop him. I'd been given a gift, and I could not waste it.

Slamming the hand with my speck against the barrier, I gasped at the silvery shimmer that burst through the red sands, dissolving his barrier like it had never been there. My body moved on instinct, tearing toward its mate, our bond vibrating in my chest.

"Reece! Wait!" I cried, hoping he would give me the seconds I needed.

Just as I was within touching distance, red sands rose to cover his body, and as my fingertips scraped across his arm, the world went dark. In the darkness there was a second of still reflection, and then the explosion blew me across the clearing.

CHAPTER FIFTY-ONE

For many minutes the sands rose up and blocked all light, and even the two strong moons were unable to break through what felt like the land mourning Reece. When the dust settled, I found myself alone, the black sands smooth and calm with no sign of gods, bones, or... my mate. All that remained in this clearing, outside of my broken soul, was the glass pillar, which was now huge, as large as the two in the valley. It was also a shimmering red, a memorial to the Desertlandian god who'd sacrificed everything to save the worlds.

"Reece." My whisper was harsh as I dragged myself toward the pillar.

When I pressed my hand against the shiny surface, I felt his energy, and I crumbled forward and sobbed my guts out, all but vomiting the empty contents of my stomach. As I heaved and coughed, our bond twanged weakly in my chest, and I wondered why death had not severed our connection.

Would I keep that part of him? Or was it only because I carried another part of him at the moment? A part he would never know.

Tilting my head back, I let out a long, mournful cry, and with it, I sent my energy out to my world. It was a similar call to the one I'd made for Alistair, only this time, no ghosts joined my mourning as I lay in the sands, staring up into a world I wasn't sure I wanted to be in.

Above, the twin moons were wavering, their strong energy starting to fade. It was almost over now, the power moons, the gods... my mate. Needing something in my moment of grief, I drew on the power of the Honor Meadows, the layers my only hope of not fading under the sands with Reece. As much as I wanted to, I had to be strong for more than myself now.

Normally, this deep into the Delfora, there'd be no chance of ever touching another world, but in this circle of ancients, with Reece's essence coating everything and the final rays of the moons above, I could feel every layer. My family... my sister... my heritage.

The layers came to me, surrounding my body, and as I opened my eyes and sobbed into the heavens, a few grains of red sand landed on my cheek.

Reece's energy was still so strong... *He was still here.*

My mate was all but a god, with eternal energy, and while he'd sacrificed his vessel, his power remained in the valley. I sat up suddenly.

Vessels could be repaired, and if I got to his soul before he passed to the next realm...

If the Nexus had taught me anything, it's that rebirth is possible for all, if enough power was involved. At that thought, the two red moons moved together, narrowing my window of opportunity to attempt this crazy-ass plan. Without thought, I opened my well of power and sucked in every layer of the meadows. Thousands rushed into my center, until I was literally spilling energy all over the sand. Only this time, it wasn't just gold that sprinkled my skin, but also silver.

When my sister's layers moved into the collective, followed by my parents, I whispered goodbye, while thanking them for everything they'd done in my life. This was the last time I'd feel them, but I had to give it a shot. The ironic full circle of my last time in this land.

Reece would never face his battles alone, not while I had power to share.

By the time I was done, all that remained in the meadows was one final layer, my forest home, and it was only to ensure that I wasn't dragged into the afterlife by expelling all my power. My plan was a longshot, and it would fundamentally change every part of me. My recovery would take centuries, but if it saved Reece, it would all be worth it.

Under the waning energy of the merging moons, I sent the world-destroying level of power from my body in one bundle, forcing it to swirl into a giant sandstorm above my head. The fire of my Nexus side tried to leave as well, but I held it back. This moon I needed restoration, not destruction.

Closing my eyes, my hair whipping all over my face in the onslaught, I released my hold on the storm. It whirled from me in a rage, gathering up every last speck of red sand, Reece's essence, to bring my mate back to me. As the power detached, I fell to my knees, empty and cold, the warmth of my family no longer mine to hold. The storm was a physical entity, swirling, perfect, and deadly as the final bright bursts of moonlight washed over the clearing.

Weakened, I closed my eyes and prayed that this was enough to save him. I'd given everything I could, and if I'd had more, I'd have given that as well.

When I landed in the sands, everything felt heavy and empty, and the next time I closed my eyes, I couldn't force them open again. But I could have sworn, just as I succumbed to the weakness of my energy, a shadow stepped out of the swirling storm built of the meadows and the deserts. A ray of hope sparked in my chest.

Reece.

CHAPTER FIFTY-TWO

Reece

I'd lived my life following the ancient rules. Loyalty, strength, never betray the sands. I'd let those rules cloud my mind, and in my younger years, when Lale had broken my trust, I'd acted like a stupid fuck and lost the best part of my life.

For years I'd forced my feelings for her deep inside, unable to move past my anger, but also unable to let her go. But I had never forgotten her, and even when I didn't deserve her, I craved the bond. Lale was branded across my body... and in my damned soul.

Melalekin of the Honor Meadows was my destiny and always had been.

My sacrifice in the Delfora felt like the bare minimum she deserved from me, and no matter how long it took, my soul would find hers in the afterlife.

Like Rhett and Leka, where she went, I would always follow.

At the final explosion of my power, the world went briefly

dark, before I found myself standing in the power moons with Rhett. For a long beat, we stared silently out into the universe, as we'd done many times in our younger years. "You sacrificed much, Reece," he finally said, turning to me.

I nodded. "And I would again to keep her safe."

His hand clasped on my shoulder. "She feels the same way, and because of that, I think our time together will be short."

In that moment, I did not fully understand what he meant, and as he faded out into the moon's light, I expected to follow, only... I was stuck. Not just stuck, but the darkness was lifting until I could see the Delfora again, as clearly as if I stood a few steps above it. Not just the Delfora, but Lale.

She was on her knees, power spiraling from her, and I had spent enough time in her world to feel the essence of her family. "Until the sands fade, my brother," I heard Rhett call as he stepped back into the veil, but I had no time to respond as I was sucked into the storm of meadow power.

When the cells of my body reformed, infused with all the magic of the power moon and Lale, I truly understood the sacrifice she'd made for me. My strong, fierce, stunningly beautiful mate was one of a handful of beings in the world with access to enough power to restore a vessel and retrieve a soul before it entered the veil and was out of reach. Power that had been built from her family, which was all she had left of them.

She'd given it all to save me, and as I stepped free from the storm, feeling whole—if not stronger than ever—I saw her sprawled across the black sand. Fury and panic boiled within me, and as I raced toward her, I noted that the sand under my boots was turning to glass as heat poured off me faster than had ever happened before. Like Lale and Mera, I'd been reborn, and my essence felt more powerful... closer to the gods. Those insane fucks who'd almost cost me everything. Part of me really wanted to dig them up and tear their vessels into a billion pieces.

In fact, once I'd gotten to my mate and sorted out current world issues, I was going to figure out a way to remove the threat of the ancients permanently. A third pillar and the lack of another power moon for centuries meant we were most likely safe, but it wasn't worth the small chance that in the future, they would rise again.

When I reached Lale's side, I brushed my hands over her body, infusing my power into her. Through our bond I could feel that she was alive, but her energy felt cold. Empty. She had sacrificed so much for me, and while I didn't deserve it, I had lifetimes now to prove my worth to her.

"Love," I murmured, lifting her with ease and pulling her against me. Heat bloomed where we touched, twisting a fierce and protective need inside as a sense of *rightness* settled deep in my gut. This woman owned me, every fucking part of me, and I would destroy anything and anyone who ever got between us again.

She stirred as I carried her across the calm sands. No one would be able to tell that below this surface, there was a prison covered in bones, blood, and sacrifice. Too much sacrifice. Not only from Lale and me, but also... Alistair. My fury and pain spiked, heat seeping from me until the entire surface of the sand where I walked was glass.

As I crossed into the valley of the dead, there were no more sands or barriers, not for me. On the other side, it was empty, except for one giant blockade. Shadow stood unmoving, his face devoid of any expression, but I knew him well enough to feel the swell of fire within. I sensed that he'd parked himself there the moment the others were safe from the sands and hadn't moved since.

"You're alive," he said shortly, eyes full of flames even as the rest of him was a statue.

"Barely," I bit out. "Lale sacrificed all of her family power to save my ass, and right now I need to get her in a healing chamber."

What I actually needed was to get her into my grotto. Silver sands would return her natural strength, even if the rest was lost forever. "Where are the others?" I asked. "Where is Alistair?"

I hated the sliver of hope inside me. I knew he was gone, and yet... I couldn't quite let go.

Shadow's flames spanned down his cheeks and across his face. "The others returned him to Karn, to his waters and ancestors."

My own burning energy rose, sands melting into a puddle of glass and debris beneath my boots. "He will be honored," I managed to get out, wishing like fuck this wasn't necessary.

When would the sacrifices be enough?

Shadow dropped his head, and for the first time, my oldest friend looked weary. "As long as we get him back to the waters before his vessel disintegrates, he will find his honor in the afterlife."

It was a small comfort, one all warriors held onto. This life wasn't our only journey, and one day, all of our souls would meet again. "We will join them in the farewell," I told Shadow, "but first I need to restore my mate's energy."

He nodded, and Lale stirred in my arms, moaning gently. I sent more power into her through our bond, and almost instantly she calmed. "I will return to the library soon," I said quickly. "Mera's okay?"

Some of his fury eased, and I finally understood the calming effect of a true mate's presence. I also understood the raging fire if she was in danger. No one was safe around me if Lale wasn't safe.

"She's fine," he rumbled, "if a little anxious. Bring Angel back before my mate destroys me with her fury and tears."

Reaching out, I clapped my hand against his shoulder before once again wrapping it around the most precious being in my world. "Thanks for your help, brother."

Shadow let out a frustrated sigh. "I did nothing. Thank you for your sacrifice; I felt when your energy exploded. All of us fucking owe you."

I waved him off. "We've all paid our power to the worlds. This time it was my turn."

His heavy hand was the one to land on me now. "You saved my mate and unborn child. If I didn't already owe you a hundred times over, I would owe you everything now."

The moment between us was filled with a deeper under-standing of who we were now and how much had changed in our lives. "No owing," I reminded him. We'd all lost count of the number of times someone had saved the other. "I'm just thanking the fucking sands that I'm not burying the rest of my family this moon. It's bad enough we lost Alistair, but it could have been everyone."

"We will ensure that never happens again," Shadow said.

A look passed between us, and no words had to be spoken to tell me we were on the same page. One day, when we figured out a way, we would eliminate the threat of the gods once and for all. But not this moon.

Shadow followed me as I moved along the valley, picking up the pace until I was sprinting back to the flat planes. As we left, I felt the wards close in again, protecting us from the powers that wanted to destroy the worlds. Tsuma had wanted to raise the gods, and ironically, now her bones would be part of the very security system she'd tried to break.

When I reached the docks, it was to find Darin's ship still there, the princeps standing on board as if he'd been waiting for my return. "Is she okay?" he called down to me.

The fire of my power surged within me, but luckily for him, this day my arms were full and I had no time to beat this overstepping motherfucker to death. "She's fine. I take care of my mate."

He held both hands up, and I didn't bother to tone my energy down. I was without reason when it came to Lale, and any male that thought to go near her would learn how little tolerance I truly had. Darin was only alive because I'd needed him here in the Delfora.

His bravery this moon had saved him, but there were no more chances.

Ignoring everything else, I called my sands to surrounded Lale and me, hating how small she felt in my arms. For the first time in more years than I cared to remember, she was vulnerable, having sacrificed her massive powerbase. But it didn't matter, because she was strong in her own right, and I had more than enough power for us both.

My entire mission in life, from this point forward, was to protect and love my mate. Fuck, she would be so sick of me by the end she'd probably pull her blades on me. Honestly, I couldn't wait.

There was no hotter moment than when she kicked my ass.

Truth was, I could not live without this stubborn, frustrating, and beautiful female.

From this day forward, all threats against us would be eliminated without thought. The raging deserts had nothing on me and my need to protect her.

Until the sands faded.

CHAPTER FIFTY-THREE

Never in all my many years had I experienced the sort of emptiness that was sucking me into the darkness now. The loss of power was such a shock to my system it had shut itself down to protect us. Me and the miracle I carried. That flutter of foreign energy I'd felt inside when I was desperately searching for a way to save Reece was not actually foreign at all. It was a life we'd created in the silver sands, and it was only thanks to that power that I'd been able to save Reece.

Despite my fatigue, I knew my mate was with me, his hot sands and energy carrying us across the Desert Lands. As much as I wanted to open my eyes and see the sands below, there was no way I could until some of my base energy was restored.

Which happened the moment we stepped into the silver sands.

Reece had taken me to the grotto.

As water washed over my body, I let out a low moan, my senses bursting to life. Opening my eyes, I met a searing set of blue ones, those thick, heavy lashes framing hooded eyes. Eyes

I'd never thought I'd see in this realm again. "Mate," I whispered, choking up.

Reece always looked perfect, but there was a weariness around his eyes. "You scared the fuck out of me, Lale," he said, voice a harsh bark. "Don't ever sacrifice your power like that again."

I waited for him to finish berating me, a smile trying to force its way across my lips. Just hearing this stubborn asshole side of him again was the greatest gift. "I gave you everything," I told him. "And I would do it again in a heartbeat. The only reason I held back even the one layer was I needed to ensu—"

My word was cut off when his lips crashed onto mine. His taste, spice, and power filled my mouth, and I briefly forgot everything, including my name. When he pulled away, still cradling me in the water, both of us breathing heavy, he lifted me closer. "Just heal, Lale," he told me. "Let the grotto refill what you naturally hold, and we'll worry about the rest later."

"I have to tell you something," I said in a rush, before he distracted me with his damn sexiness again. "When I was searching through our bond, trying to use your power over the sands to save you, I felt a flutter of foreign energy deep in my power. Deeper than I'd ever gone before."

I had his full and silent attention now, even as he held me tight against his body.

"I got out of your barrier because a speck of silver sand fell from my hair."

His brow furrowed a beat as I paused to let that sink in. "You cannot take the sand with you," he said slowly.

I nodded. "And yet I did."

"Foreign energy inside?" he repeated, before understanding dawned in his expression; once again, that genius brain had put the pieces together in no time.

His hand trembled as he slid it down my body to press

against the armor over my stomach. "How can this be possible?" he murmured.

Bonded or not, we should never be able to have children together. Transcendents did not carry young with any outside of our light, but Reece and I were breaking all the rules now.

"It had to be the silver sands," I said, having had more time to think it over. "After our moon in the grotto, I left with a speck of sand and a miracle. The grotto allowed me to take sand because I carry a child of its essence. Our child."

Reece closed his eyes, heat under his hand seeping into me as he searched through our bond just as I had done back in the Delfora. The moment he felt the spark of life, it fluttered under his touch. "Fuck," he rasped, clearing his throat. "We had so much to lose. I almost missed this moment—and every fucking moment after."

His hands shook as he wrapped them around me, holding on desperately. "Fuck," he repeated, and it was unusual to see him in shock like this. Reece never let anything phase him, but this moon, he was unable to keep it together. The truth of what we'd almost lost was hitting him hard.

Been there, done that, had the mental triggers to show for it.

Reece's chest rumbled as his left hand traveled up into my loose hair, fingers tangling into the length as he pulled me into him for a kiss. As our lips met, a tinge of desperation burned between us. Both of us were struggling with the *almost* we'd just experienced. *Almost* dying. *Almost* losing our chance to be a family. *Almost* failing in our mission.

Needing to be closer, I slid across his lap, pressing into his body, wanting to feel every inch of him. Reece's hands and energy stripped my clothing away in seconds, the armor and weapons sailing across to the sand. Tearing at his shirt, I pressed my lips to his chest, which rumbled under my touch.

"Are you strong enough?" he rasped, holding onto my hair again, his tongue licking the water from my skin as well.

"More than strong enough," I moaned. My energy was well above the level needed to love my mate, and if anything was going to heal the empty parts of my soul, it was Reece.

Needing this more than my next breath, I groaned. "We have to hurry. I honestly don't think I can wait."

This spurred Reece on. As he lifted me higher, I managed to get rid of his pants and boots while running my hands along the length of his burning body. His cock was the hottest part of all, jerking in my hand when I wrapped my palm around his length. In this moment, we were need and want, moving without thought, the recent events pushing our instincts to base level.

Some might think it was uncaring to make love on the same moon others had lost their lives, especially Alistair, but the truth was, we took this opportunity because none of us were promised tomorrow. I'd watched Reece die in front of me, felt that cold emptiness of our bond dissolving. This moment here in the grotto was one I'd never expected to have, and I wouldn't waste a second.

As I lifted my body so I could slide down his hard length, I groaned when I ended up fully seated, the emptiness all but gone now. Reece had so much power, and with our bond and his cock filling me, there was no room to feel my losses. Rocking into him, the pleasure was instant, everything heightened by what we'd lived through. Reece soon took control, the slow movements picking up speed as he lifted me to strongly thrust into my aching pussy. He leaned down and wrapped his lips around my right nipple, sucking the erect tip into his mouth. I cried out, my hands closing around the back of his head, holding him in place, while also giving me leverage to stay seated.

He moved onto the left nipple, biting down, and my orgasm hit hard as my hips moved more erratically, riding out my release. Reece didn't stop there, turning me on his lap so that I was facing the opposite way. This angle allowed him to thrust more powerfully, and even as my head spun from the sensation, my second release was already building.

His fingers played with my clit in time to the thrusts, and as I cried out again, his hand slid back around my body to my ass, parting my cheeks so he could push against my entrance there.

"Are you ready for another first?" he murmured. "Another boundary I want to push with you?"

"Yes," I moaned without hesitation. There was very little in this world that Reece could do to me that I wouldn't enjoy.

His laugh was low and satisfied. "That's my warrior."

The heat of his power slid over my spine, and I arched, but his cock never left my pussy as I'd expected. Instead he continued to fuck me in slow, forceful thrusts, and... damn. Just when I was about to ask some questions, because hello... pushing boundaries, I saw his red sands mingling with the silver sands before me. The pair swirled and merged, accompanied by a blast of heat that melted them into a very smooth phallus-shaped object.

When it disappeared over my head, controlled by his energy, I had a very good idea what the plan was.

Fire burned through me as Reece's palm on my spine pushed me vertical. He still fucked me with those long, sure strokes, and as I cried out, face only inches from the water, the smooth head of his dildo pressed against my ass. As the tip entered me, a golden-red light illuminated the air, and I turned my head to see that Reece, filled with power, was looking much more godlike than he had before his rebirth.

"Wha—" I groaned, my words cut off as he pushed his new toy further into my ass, slow at first, even as the thrusts of his cock never eased. By the time the smooth piece was deep inside me, my body felt so full. Reece let out a low groan. "Fuck, Lale. I've never seen anything hotter than this moment, fucking your ass and pussy."

I cried out, screaming as my body tightened over both "cocks," sending me into an orgasm so intense I was fairly sure I was about to black out again. Reece's energy was the only thing that kept me from drowning in the waters, his strength holding me up as I rode out the longest release of my damn life. All too soon, Reece followed me over the edge, and I thanked every damn being that we were still alive to have this moment.

Alive and finally able to plan a future.

Together.

CHAPTER FIFTY-FOUR

By the time we'd been in the grotto long enough to recover my energy from the fight—and for Reece to give me a dozen or more orgasms—no part of my essence felt empty or alone. My family remained with me in my heart and memories—a truth I saw clearly now that I'd lost all the layers of my worlds.

I'd held onto those layers with a sort of desperation that shamed me. True power could never be taken away; the layers were a crutch I'd clung to for far too long.

"We need to return to the library," Reece murmured when we were dozing on the silver sands, warm and content. "But there's somewhere I want to take you first."

Lifting my right hand, I pressed it to my chest. "I can feel Mera in our bond," I said. "She's calm, if a little irritated. We have some time."

He was up in a flash, and before I knew it, we were out of the grotto. This time, silver sands remained on my body. "Your connection to our child and grotto grows stronger," Reece noted.

I rubbed a few grains between my fingers and smiled at the

silver power filling my well. "This is going to take some getting used to," I noted.

Reece wrapped his arms around me, red sands rising up to lift us from the ground. "We'll figure it out together," he told me, and for once, I let that push all other thoughts aside.

Together was exactly what we needed.

As his sands took us across the deserts, I figured out quickly where we were heading: Rohami.

"Why are we going home?" I asked, lifting my face to breathe in the familiar scent and energy of his land. Even if, technically, he was more closely connected to Delfora, Rohami was his blood.

His hold around me tightened, both of us sailing the breezes as one. "I want to renew our bond in the same spot where we originally committed to each other."

Our bond was already so strong, pulsing between us, but this gesture spoke of a true rebinding of what we'd neglected for years. "Some might think you're turning into a bit of a softy, desert god," I murmured, turning so I could wrap my arms around his neck.

He grumbled out a low laugh. "Some might be right."

Before I could join him in laughter, his mirth faded, to be replaced by a deeper emotion. "I prayed for this, you know?" His tone was serious. "Even when I knew you deserved more than me, I couldn't let you go. You have always been mine."

Exactly how I'd felt, even when I'd been so angry with him. "You hid it better than me," I said with a sad laugh.

Reece shook his head. "Love and hate are so close, and it was easy to pretend that the reason for my obsession with you, with your movements, with your life, was because I hated you. But I think we both know the real reason."

We were quite the pair, already bonded for an eternity... obsessed for an eternity.

And now we got to be happy for an eternity.

"Let's never compartmentalize our emotions again," I said as the stunning red sands passed below us. "We missed out on so much and could have died before we ever got to experience a true bond." I reached down and pressed my hand to my stomach to feel the flutter of life. Already our child was developing fast, and for that reason, I would keep all the silver sands I had on me, just in case we needed them in the future.

"No more talk of dying," Reece said, pulling me into him, his lips meeting mine.

By the time I came up for air, we were at his village, and as our sands lowered toward the entrance, I noticed a few changes in the years I'd avoided this place. Including some stock yards with hundreds of butle, brought in from the eastern planes. Those large, bull-like animals came in a range of red and black coats, and with their huge plates of horns on either side of their heads, were always impressive.

Reece brought us closer, and I peered over the side of his sands to see clearer. "New gates?" I asked. The red pillars appeared to be much larger than the old ones, crowning pieces to the red fences that encircled the entire village.

"Sandstorm tore through our old ones a couple hundred years ago," Reece said, zooming over the gates. He was the only one in this city with the permission to do so. "I was away from the Desert Lands at the time, but we got stronger pillars up."

His words reminded me that there was a stronger pillar in the Delfora too. So, hopefully, we'd never have to worry about the gods rising again.

The guards below saluted Reece, even though only our heads were visible, his sands keeping the rest of our naked forms hidden. "We've spent a lot of time naked in this world," I noted.

He laughed, shaking his head, and damn, if he didn't look

more relaxed than I'd ever seen. "If I had my way, Lale, you would never wear clothing."

I couldn't help but laugh too, euphoria bubbling in a way I hadn't felt since I was a youngling. "Kinda feel the same about you, but I also know we'd never get one thing done."

He didn't argue with me, because there was no lie in that statement.

We were now over the first circle of the seven that made up the structure of this village. Each of the first few were filled with stalls and shops and carts, the areas where goods were sold and exchanged and bartered. In some ways, this world was far more primitive than humanity's, who loved their technology, but Desertlandians were happy in their simpler lives. They never strove for more, content to exist in their bubbles of serenity. Everyone in this world had enough, with no homelessness or poverty, and maybe in the end, that was the sign of an evolved society.

Reece's family home was near the fifth circle, on the outer perimeter. "I always wondered if you would find your own space and leave your parents," I said as he landed, sands still swirling around us. They remained as we walked up the short path to the stately red front door, which had been hand carved with images of dunes and pamolsa and the Delfora. It was an impressive piece that his mother had commissioned, if I remembered correctly.

"I'm so rarely here," he shrugged, "and when I am, I'm alone. It just didn't seem worth creating my own place."

I grasped his hand. "No more loneliness for you."

He twisted his palm so our fingers could thread together. "For you either, mate. I know you must be worried about returning to the Honor Meadows now that your territory is so empty, but I promise, we will get through it together."

I was worried, but not to the level I'd have expected before this moon. "I know the loss will hit me hard once I'm there," I admitted, "but there's a new part of my family blooming now. Is it odd that I'm almost relieved?"

He lifted an eyebrow, expression encouraging me to talk the emotions out. "I'm free," I said simply. "No more power to protect. No more worry of letting my family down by misusing their gifts. I can move forward, and seeing my sister only cemented my belief that I'll find them again one day."

Reece nodded. "You will, but no time soon."

I smiled, needing some levity in this moment. "Definitely not soon."

We had too much to live for, and even though much of my eternal power was gone, now that I was bonded to Reece, I'd stay in this world as long as I wanted.

And with him, that was forever.

CHAPTER FIFTY-FIVE

Reece found us clothing first—basic shift shirts and light loose pants. Once we were dressed, I explored his home, which was exactly as I remembered it. Huge open windows to let in the moonlight and desert breezes, sparse furnishings and thick rugs on every floor giving the sense of being away from the sands, even if they were still filling all the corners.

After a time, he started to edge me toward his back garden, but on our way out we passed his wall of weapons and sacred pieces. I ground to a halt and stared at a very familiar set, displayed center stage.

"What in the worlds?" I gasped, stepping forward to brush my hand over my armor.

It dominated the wall, surrounded by a frame of red glass, which looked smooth and worn, as if it had been touched many times. Turning to see him, I pressed a hand to my chest, trying to get it together. "You had my armor?" I breathed. "You never told me."

His expression was soft and warm, but there was pain burning deep in his blue eyes. "When you died in the Shadow

Realm, I lost my mind." He let out a harsh breath. "I didn't allow anyone to touch your armor, and since I couldn't figure out how to return it to the Honor Meadows, I sent it here."

He brushed his hand over the smooth glass. "This was my comfort, and the moment I decided that I was done hiding in the past, I forced Mera to come to the Ostealon, knowing it would ensure you were also there. I never intended to let you leave."

I was gasping again, feeling like my eyes were so wide that my eyeballs could pop right the fuck out. "You... You did?"

Now he was laughing at me. "You never had a chance, mate. Even when you thought we had a 'hate-fucking' arrangement, I always knew it was the beginning of our love journey. Hate be damned."

I was so puffed up with emotions I wondered if maybe I was going to float away. Pushing myself as high as I could, I wrapped my arms around him, holding on tight and feeling every one of my blessings. Reece hugged me back with as much strength, and at this point I doubted we needed to cement this bond. We'd done that all on our own, but since we were here...

Outside in his yard, there were huge fences on all sides, giving a sense of privacy among the many pamolsa trees and desert flowers. This had always been a peaceful oasis, and not much had changed in the many years, outside of the trees along the back wall being about fifty feet taller.

In front of them was a small sand pond, the fast-moving energy there home to some *tretas* swimming about. These dark red, fish-lizard creatures were friendly, and when we walked by, a few jumped out of the sand by way of greeting.

Reece led me to a carved red bench in front of the largest pamolsa plant. As we sat, the memories hit me hard, and I remembered how young and full of hope we'd been that night we'd promised to bond our power for the rest of our days. "How do you know the language of the ancients?" I asked him. Even that day, his words had been spoken in their lilting tongue.

His gaze never left mine. "I was born knowing it, and while my parents warned me never to use it outside of the Delfora, that day I couldn't help myself."

"Like the words written across your skin?"

Those spectacular lashes briefly swept closed before our gazes met again. "Yes. It was a constant reminder that I'd lost you. I punished myself as hard as I punished you."

"Until the sands fade," I repeated. He'd etched that there with our names.

"There's more."

That got my full attention. "What else?"

His lips brushed across mine. "Love, Lale. It was always love."

Tears were not generally part of my disposition, and yet I felt them slide down my cheeks at the poignant confession. "I've loved you for almost my entire life," I said, my voice showing no signs of my overwhelmingly emotional state. "And now that our bond has been realized, I feel complete. Even without my family power, there's no weakness within me." My hand lifted his shirt so I could trace the words across his skin. "I want these words on me too."

Reece's eyes darkened. "I'll need Len's help, but I will make the marks. No one else touches your skin."

Possessive bastard. "Deal."

Okay, I kind of liked it.

We stood then, the bond humming powerfully between us, stoked brighter by the third member of our family that in some unknown amount of time would join our world—a blessing that *almost* made our centuries apart worth it.

"Your power feels stronger," I noted, tilting my head to

examine him closer. "It's beating within our bond like a power moon."

He didn't show surprise at my statement. "Between your power and the moons, I believe that I had been reformed stronger and closer to the Delfora. The gods will have more of a fight on their hands next time."

I waved him off, even as my chest tightened. "No *next time*, please."

His face hardened, and it could have been my imagination, but it felt like the world got darker too. "Their future is uncertain. I will not let them rise again."

"It would be more difficult, right?" I asked quickly. "The third pillar adds another layer of security, and there're no power moons for a long time."

He cupped my face, easing my worries with that one touch. "It will be harder, but nothing is impossible. I just have to figure out how to destroy them without bringing Death into our midst."

Examining his features, I knew that nothing I said would deter him, and if he made this a path in his life, I would stand by his side. From here on out, we were as one.

A twinge in my chest distracted me as I pressed a hand there, delving into the bond.

"Mera is in some discomfort," I said in a rush. "We should head back to the library."

He didn't argue, wrapping his sands around us again so we could head to an area for an easy doorway. "Is the baby coming now?" he asked as we lifted.

Probing the bond again, I shook my head. "Not yet, but it's close."

Which reminded me of our own child. "Any guesses on the gestation period of our Silver one?" There was no precedent for a Desertlandian god and transcendent hybrid. It could be weeks, months, or years, and in the end... it really didn't matter.

We were eternal, so this child was free to come when it was ready. But I'd be a liar if I didn't admit to a twinge of impatience over wanting to meet them.

"If the growing strength of their energy is any indication," Reece said with a soft smile, "it's not going to be too long. The library might have two children destroying it very soon."

My laughter was freer than it had been in centuries, just like my heart. "Even with all of us, we're going to be in over our heads."

Mera and Shadow's child would be powerful, born of two Nexus gods, and now Reece's and mine, conceived in the silver sands.

New powers coming into the world.

New futures for all of us.

CHAPTER FIFTY-SIX

We'd returned to find that Mera's discomfort was due to planning Alistair's farewell, a ceremony I was happy we hadn't missed, even if it hurt to finally grieve and let him go. Karn was a world I'd been to only a couple of times in my life, and now that we were here, floating above the vibrant green waters with the bright red sun high in the sky, sending down warmth and healing energy, I wished that I'd come more often. With Alistair.

He'd have tamed so many waters in this world, but now, I'd never know about them.

Mera, silently sobbing at my side, clutched onto Shadow, her stomach—larger than ever—out in front and covered by her stretchy blue dress. All of us were dressed in the greens and blues that Alistair loved so much.

We were silent while the sprites, wings fluttering around us, started to sing their songs of the dead, which, interestingly, were also their songs of life since they believed it was a never-ending circle. Alistair's vessel floated peacefully between the large gathering of Karns, which included more than the sprites. Some of his warrior race of brethren swam forward, adding their voices to the song, and when his youngest sibling rose up, I had to briefly close my eyes because he looked so much like our fallen friend.

Reece's face was hard, his hand gripping mine as the blue of his eyes swirled. Shadow was the same, the flames in his irises a consistent glow. Len and Lucien were off to the side where I couldn't see them, but I knew they would be mourning just the same. Galleli was above, where he felt most comfortable.

The sprites began to circle faster in the water forming a whirlpool. "This is the representation of their belief," I heard Shadow whisper to Mera. "There's no beginning or end of their life, but a circular path that will bring Alistair back into our lives again at some point."

Mera, with her views still strongly cemented in shifter and human beliefs, didn't appear to be bolstered by this notion. She was too deep in mourning, sensing that whether he returned to us or not, it wouldn't be the same Alistair we knew and loved.

The whirlpool grew in intensity as the sprites swirled, their translucent bodies and multiple limbs moving through the water with a grace that most beings would never have. The water was their world, and they were stunning in their beauty. Alistair's body began to swirl, then, too, caught in the current until he slipped below to join his warrior people.

His vessel would rest in the garden of their dead, and as he vanished from our view, Mera let out a loud sob. Turning, she buried her face in Shadow's side, and he held her as tight as he dared, keeping her together. Reece released my hand and wrapped an arm around me, and I was surprised by how much I needed that support. Both of us did.

As the last lilt of the Karn song faded, we all remained silently staring into the perfect sky above, our energies holding us above the water, even as our friend sank below. Eventually

Mera reminded us that we still had to have our own celebrations for Alistair's life. Shadow opened the doorway, and we stepped through silently.

A flutter in my tummy reminded me that I hadn't told them about our news yet because the time since we'd returned from the deserts had been about Alistair. He deserved our total focus, so I would keep it to myself a little longer.

When we returned to the library, there was already a gathering; Gaster had taken Mera very seriously when she'd asked if he could find all of those who'd been touched by Alistair's presence.

The room was filled with his friends, and unlike on Karn, this was a more lighthearted affair, all of us sharing a drink in his honor.

Shadow was the first to stand and speak. "Alistair has been my brother for more years than I care to remember," he rumbled, sadness pulling at his lips as Mera stared at him, tears streaming down her cheeks. "His bravery was renowned, but it was his lightheartedness, his humor, that pulled me back from the darkness many times."

There was a lot of truth in that, and as others stepped up to speak, we were regaled with tales of Alistair's youth and love of pranks. Eventually, his friends and acquaintances left the library until all that remained was our group and a few goblins cleaning up the mess. Shadow stepped in to assist them with his energy, and as the library obeyed his command, order was returned in no time.

This was always the point that the true loss kicked in. Once that farewell and the celebration of life were done, it was time to move on. Without them.

"You need to eat and rest," Reece said when he found me standing before some Karn shelves, looking at the many texts and tomes I'd read, wishing I'd done more to connect with Alistair.

"So many mysteries," I said, somewhat ignoring him. "I barely scratched the waters of Karn. Now that Alistair is gone, I feel that I should have cared more."

"Don't do that to yourself," Reece said, pulling me into his warmth. "It was my fault that you weren't part of our world for all of these years. I'm the one who needs to make amends, and when the time is right, I will show you the secrets of Karn that I learned from my brother. There's so much below the surface."

"We're both to blame," I reminded him. "And I would like that very much."

The others joined us then, and Mera looked completely wrecked, rubbing at her red and swollen eyes. The fact that she wasn't healing as quickly was an indicator that not only had she basically been continuously crying today, but also her baby was preparing to enter the world. This was always a draining time on an eternal's energy.

"How are you feeling?" I asked, stepping away from Reece so I could hug her. "Are the birth pains getting stronger?"

She nodded, clearing her throat. "Oh yeah. It's hectic, but I sense that our little one is not quite ready yet. They're building up for a dramatic grand entrance."

There were a few chuckles, and it was nice to feel some normalcy return. Even Mera brightened a touch as she mouthed, *Dramatic like their father.* Which Shadow caught, of course, then swept her up in his arms and dragged her off to the dining room as he demanded she eat.

The beast was obsessed with feeding his mate and keeping her healthy, just like Reece. Feeling somewhat drained from the grief of today, I didn't fight as he led me down the familiar hall and into my seat. Mera was, as always, on one side of me, but for once Reece took the other seat, and damn, if that didn't make my ancient heart skip a few damn beats.

"Who would have thought it," Mera said with a laugh. "Reece on our side of the table and not glaring us down with those baby blues and impossibly long lashes."

Reece leveled a glare at her for old time's sake before shaking his head and dropping an arm around my shoulders. "I was a fool, but thankfully, not so foolish that I haven't learned from my mistakes."

Mera's smile washed away more of her grief-stricken features. "You know what that means, don't you?"

Everyone was staring at her, and I couldn't wait to hear the next words out of her mouth. She was always so unpredictable. "Couple names," she cried, slapping her hands on the table, "and boy, do we have some doozies to choose from."

A snort of laughter escaped me, and I realized that I'd never feel empty with a family like mine. Reece, shooting me that sexy fucking smirk, winked, and *just stab me now, I had zero boundaries with this male.*

"Okay, so there're Reece and Angel combos," Mera started excitedly. "Rangel could work, but it's not very sexy. And I'm not too keen on Relalekin either because, come on."

"Rale?" Lucien suggested, looking amused as he toyed with some plasma that had been placed before him.

At that, Reece shook his head. "Fucking hell. You're all terrible at this."

Mera narrowed her eyes at him. "Look, it's not our fault your names are crap when put together. Maybe we should just call you Angel and the Asshole."

Laughter burst from me, but I stifled it when Reece caught my gaze, the blue in his eyes darkening. It was clear that while he could give zero shits about a couple name, he was truly happy we were together. Leaning over, I pressed my mouth to his, tasting all that power and sighing at how perfect he was. When I pulled away, I could tell he was ready to drag me out of here.

"DesertAngel is our couple name," he told the others, his focus never wavering from me. "The past and the future. You'll always be Lale to me, but you're also Angel."

"And you are the desert god," I said with a wink, heartbeat slamming in my chest.

Mera clapped her hands together. "Let's go with it. Shadowshine and DesertAngel. Fucking perfect." She looked around the table. "Who's next?"

Everyone laughed, Len waving his hands like he wanted nothing to do with this conversation. The others got to ordering food then, and as I leaned back into Reece, I figured that now was better than any time to give our news. We had a couple name, after all.

I cleared my throat. "Reece and I have an announcement."

Everyone fell silent, turning their attention to us, and I wondered how this news would be received.

"We're having a baby," Reece said before I could. "A powerful child that, outside of my Lale, is the greatest fucking gift I'll ever have."

Bastard stole my announcement, but since he was a pretty amazing mate, I'd probably forgive him. Mera squealed first, attempting to shift her stomach enough that she could hug me properly. "Oh, my freaking gods, our kids are going to be best friends like us, and this is the most amazing news we could get today. With so much loss, there's also life."

Shadow leaned around her to see Reece. "How is this possible?" he asked, finally slowing Mera's excitement. She was the only one not in shock, having no idea that this wasn't a normal possibility between two mates from our worlds.

"Reece found a grotto," I said simply. "The silver sands

within have magical properties that originated with the ancients. We didn't realize at the time, but... yeah, apparently, in these sands the normal rules do not apply."

That was all the explanation they needed, and cheers and congratulations rang out after that. We celebrated the new life even amid the grief of death. Warmth filled me from both Mera and Reece, the bonded ones in my soul, and I felt like every part of me was growing wings. Finally I was at peace with all sides of myself.

Reece lifted his hand and cupped my face, leaning in until his lips landing on mine. Heat sprang up between us, and I breathed in the desert scents, finally home.

THIS IS the end of Angel and Reece's story, but if you want to see more of this world, don't forget to check out Lucien and Simone's story in Compelled.

Pre-order here: Compelled

Turn over for a sneak peek...

Compelled

The incessant buzzing of my alarm grated against my sensitive hearing, and in my half-awake state, I almost tossed my phone out the window. One would think after twenty-five years of hating the screech of nails across a board, I wouldn't use it as an alarm. But alas, I was a fucking terrible morning person, and if not for the nails, I'd sleep half the day away.

Groaning, I dragged myself out of my crappy twin bed, trying not to think about the fact that, once again, I'd spent my Saturday night at home, alone, living my best damn life with popcorn and Teen Wolf. Yeah, it was a touch ridiculous that a shifter enjoyed watching shifter shows, especially when they got so many of the details wrong, but it was my secret indulgence.

Unlike dating, which was now a proven recipe for disaster.

I'd had exactly five dates in the past year, and each of them had bored me to the point that on my last date two weeks ago, I'd almost smashed my face into the main course when I fell asleep and my head slipped off my hand. In my defense, that Tucson pack shifter had droned on about horticulture for thirty-seven minutes.

Yeah, suffice it to say, there would be no second date.

Checking the time before I jumped into the shower, I noted that I had to be at the shop in twenty minutes, and since I now lived in my best friend Mera Callahan's crappy former apartment across Torma, I needed to haul ass.

It was my shop, and I took my role as a businesswoman seriously.

If it wasn't for all the morons in this town who thought literature was reading the back of a can of soda, I'd be rolling in green. Instead, I was barely making ends meet... which had absolutely nothing to do with the wicked collection of stories I kept in stock.

My aim this week was to get online and get my books into hands that would appreciate them. The longer I spent in Torma, the more I was convinced that I should have left years ago. Without Mera—and my parents—there was nothing here for me any longer.

The shop had been a great project and I still loved it, but I could open a business in any shifter pack. Maybe another one out there was my destiny, and if I did live for a few hundred more years, did I really want to waste them in this shithole? It was a circular argument I'd had many times. I'd lived my entire life in Torma, a shifter village in California, and for a long time we were the strongest pack in America. I'd been happy here with my Mera.

Of course, all of that had come to an end when she was rejected by the alpha, terrorized by this fucking pack, and then kidnapped by a scary-ass shifter god... who, luckily, turned out to be her true mate. My bestie-for-life was now living a best life that didn't include Teen Wolf, and I missed her more than I'd ever thought possible.

She'd cleaned up Torma before she left, but it didn't matter... I had nothing here without her. Hence my need to start a new adventure. Hell, maybe there was a growly, sexy, change-his-size shifter waiting out there for me too. Couldn't be worse than the horticulturist.

After ten minutes under the hottest stream I could get from this shitty shower, I finally felt somewhat awake, and throwing on underwear, black skinny jeans, a red flannel shirt with the sleeves rolled up, and a pair of black flats, I was ready to get to work. There was no need for makeup since I had no one to impress, and a quick brush was all it took to have my long, thick hair smooth and shiny—a gift of the Japanese heritage on my mom's side. My parents were no longer in Torma, having been exiled when Mera cleaned house, but we still stayed in touch with the occasional text and call.

As former enforcers for our crazy-ass alpha, they'd always been less than interested in me, so it was no huge loss that they were out of the pack. Still, it was one more thing that had tied me to Torma that was now gone.

The street was quiet at this time of day, but soon the pack school bell would chime, and with it, all the late students would rush across town. I'd be in my shop before that of course, and it was a blessing to no longer be part of school life.

My shop appeared on the horizon, nestled in the main street of businesses here in Torma. It had a stunning red brick front with a deep green awning. I'd picked that out as my first step in revamping the space, and I still loved the way the color contrasted to the brick.

After unlocking the door, I found the shop dark and cool inside, but as the spring days heated up, I'd have to get all the fans running to keep the small space from turning into a sauna.

Hitting the lights near the front, I took a second to appreciate each flickering beam highlighting a shelf below filled to the brim with all manner of stories.

Like Mera, I preferred my books heavy on romance and filled with angst and drama. In my store I included a few other genres in the hope that no matter who walked through that door, there would be something in here to tickle their fancy. I mean, who was I to tell someone when their taste in books sucked? *Cough*—biography—*cough cough*. If I wanted real life, I'd watch the damn news.

Books were my escape, one I hadn't truly understood until the last few years, but I was a full convert now. Some might call me obsessed.

Just as I was storing my keys and phone in the drawer, the door dinged, and I looked up to see my neighbor, Ethel. She was an ancient shifter who looked a million years old but was probably only a hundred and fifty. She ran the craft supply store two doors down. "Sim," she called, hobbling over, stretching out her back as she walked. "Slept funny again last night. Can you help an old wolf out?"

Anndddd there you have it, the full extent of my current social interactions. "Sure," I said with a sigh. "Happy to help."

We'd done this many times now, and as I twisted her arm to the side and pulled gently, I heard a few pops as everything went somewhat back into place. Ancient shifters stopped healing like the rest of us, but she still made it to work every single day. Lady had some strong vagina energy, which was much more impressive than big dick energy. Or so I'd heard.

Not a lot of dicks around, big or not, to test that theory.

Ethel left soon after, and it was just me, my store... and a new box of books, which were waiting to be sorted and priced. As I tore open the tape, no lie, I breathed in the scent of new books the same way others might breathe in food. This girl was straight up crack-addicted to this shit, and no matter where my path took me, I would never not have a bookstore now.

I lifted out the top paperback with a broad-shouldered and tattooed male on the cover, fire swirling around him as he raged, his back muscles tensed. When I placed it on the desk to grab the next, I felt a flicker of energy from within the same drawer I'd thrown my stuff. *Mera!* Ripping the drawer open, I shifted the top layer to find the paper I needed.

The parchment had an ancient feel to it, made from a material not found on Earth, and as more energy shot up from it, writing appeared in quick, jagged script.

Simone. Mera is in labor.

The moment I read that sentence, it disappeared, part of the safety in these hidden messages.

Another jolt of energy.

Inky on its way. Do not delay.

The parchment fell from my hands as I bounced on the spot, having had no idea that today would be the fucking day. The day that my best friend had her baby, and I got a little adventure out of this town. Grabbing up my phone, I shot a text to Sam, my friend in another shifter town, letting her know Mera was in labor and I'd be MIA for some time.

All I got in return was a smiling emoji and a thumbs up.

Like, fuck. Thumbs up should be banned as a response tool.

At least it seemed she was alive, even if she would only talk to me on the phone for five minutes a week. Clearly, she was in the middle of some shit over in her pack, and as much as I wanted to swoop in and save her ass, she was a grown woman who wanted to handle this on her own.

Lucky for her, Mera had been busy growing a baby and saving the worlds, otherwise she'd have been the one dragging

Sam out by her hair. Probably once this baby arrived, she'd still be the one doing that.

There was no one else to tell, so I just went around shutting off the lights again and making sure everything would be good for a few days without me. Nerves rolled in my stomach at the thought of being back in the Library of Knowledge. Back in the Solaris System gateways. Back near... him.

Funnily enough, my boring life hadn't always been this way, but in a concerted effort to keep the past in the past, I spent my time now dating horticulturists and not master vampires.

Safer for everyone.

Compelled

I nky showed up a few minutes after I'd shut everything down inside. This entity had scared the crap out of me the first time I'd seen it, being that it was a literal black cloud of power, originating in another world—the Shadow Realm—and was bonded to the Shadow Beast himself. I was used to it now, though.

Since most shifters were not cool with clouds of power, I ushered it inside, so it could open a doorway in privacy to send me into the magical library that connected worlds.

As we moved through the doorway, I sprinted along the hallway toward the library. Labor was not an act I was familiar with, but I had watched enough shows to know it was fast for some and slow for others. Mera never did shit half-assed, and I did not want to miss holding her hand when she birthed her child. Neither of us had ever thought we'd be moms, so it hadn't been a childhood dream for us, but now that it was happening, I couldn't imagine a different path for her.

"Will I make it in time?" I huffed to Inky as I ran along the hall.

It bobbed up and down, and I took that as encouragement.

My flats slapped against the ground as I ran. A more appropriate footwear would have been useful, but there was no time to change. Depending on how long I ended up staying this time, there were always spares in Mera's magical wardrobe, aka, the beast's way of dressing his mate in the sexy-ass outfits he liked to see her in.

Again, I would never be jealous of my best friend, but girl did get a mate, a library, and a fucking magical wardrobe. Least she could do was share some of her goodies.

Not the mate, he terrified me, but the clothing I'd take.

When we reached the swirling portal, I stepped right through into the Library of Knowledge, a hub that connected the worlds of the Solaris System and had books from all the different worlds lining the many shelves. The information here was priceless, and it always took my breath away and got my heart pounding when I entered its space.

Today, though, I had one focus.

Inky continued on, and I didn't bother to glance at the many beings here, each of them from one of the worlds, some very alien while others were more humanlike. We ended up at the farthest end, where Shadow's domain was. I'd never been into this space—the beast was very territorial with everyone except Mera—but when Inky zoomed through, I figured I'd follow.

There was no resistance, and when I ended up in the forbidden zone, I barely managed not to gasp at what lay beyond. "That bitch has two libraries?" I gasped. "We really need to talk about sharing."

Inky couldn't reply, but I liked to think that it agreed with me as it grew larger and started to spark. It was either that or he wanted me to hurry up, and with that in mind, I ignored the long expanse of heavy wooden shelves, gorgeous chandeliers, and the scent of books and followed the mist deep into the beast's lair.

We ended up at a bedroom, or, at least, I assumed it was because where else would Mera be having her child? The nondescript wooded door opened before I'd even reached it, and words spilled out.

The moment I heard, *"You fucking did this to me, you stupid, oversized beast,"* some of my panic faded.

That was Mera, my best friend for life, and she appeared to be doing just fine. I hadn't missed the birth yet... We were right in the cursing-your-mate-for-knocking-you-up stage. This was going to be fun.

As I was about to step through the door, I felt a strong wash of power. Ever since I'd gone to Valdor and... all the shit that'd happened there... my senses had been stronger. My shifter side might be weaker, but the rest of me was powered up like crazy. Hence how I knew Lucien, master fucking vampire and thorn in my damn side, was right behind me.

A huge part of me wanted to open the door and get inside before I had to see him, but another part was curious at how I'd feel after all this time. Would he still stir my body in a way I had no experience with and yet craved desperately? Would he send fire through my veins and anger into my heart? Would I hate him, while at the same time craving what could never be?

There was only one way to find out.

"B," he said softly. "I've been waiting for you to enter the lair, and I need to tell you something."

My throat hurt at the nickname, and not only because this pointy-fanged fucker liked to call me by my blood type—the cunt—but because I had missed hearing that smooth, sexy rasp of his voice.

Knowing it would hurt less if I just ripped the Band-Aid off, I turned and faced him. "Can I fucking help you, Lester?"

The master vampire was still the most beautiful man I'd ever seen. A huge, muscular body, blond hair, and piercing green eyes with this golden, sun-kissed skin that always looked like a fake tan advertisement, only there was nothing fake about this vamp. He was sex on legs, and seeing him again hit me harder than I'd expected.

His lips twitched, even if annoyance burned deep in his eyes. "Lester? I don't think so, sweetheart. You remember my name."

Faking boredom, I stared at my nails. "Sorry, Linc, but I'm super busy right now. My best friend is about to have a baby, and I kind of don't want to miss it. Was there something you needed to tell me?"

At this, Lucien sobered. Yeah, the bastard was right—I'd never forget his name.

"I've been waiting for you to return for the birth," he said. "I put this off as long as I could, but the masters have spoken. You have to return to Valdor."

My body went cold. I'd had to go to his vampiric world a year or so ago when the library had been compromised. The situation at the time had been life or death, and in that place I'd learned that I was nothing more than a walking blood bag for those fuckers. Shit had gone down and I'd broken a rule or two, but...

"I thought it was all sorted." Lucien had promised me.

"The masters just have some questions for you," he said softly. "Trust me, B. I will not let anything happen to you, but if you don't return, they will send others to bring you back."

A second power joined his, and a moment later Len, the fae, arrived. "You're here too?" I burst out.

He nodded. "Yes, we're all waiting for the child to be born, but once it's safe, we will accompany you and Lucien to Valdor. Vampire politics be damned, nothing will happen to Mera's best friend."

A scream echoed from the partially open door, and I was already inside the bedroom taking a step toward Mera, when Lucien's power wrapped around me, nearly rendering me motionless. I had to turn back and immediately got lost in the depthless green of his gaze. "You broke the rules, baby B," he said, reminding me of the worst day of my life, "and now you must answer to them."

As he walked away, the door closed between us, and my body burned even as my soul screamed.

Lucien was right. I did break the rules, but he'd tried to save me.

Looked like he was finally done.

Mera shouted again, swearing as she sobbed, and I pushed my worries away. Today I would be by my best friend's side as she brought a god-baby into the world, and tomorrow...

Tomorrow I would return to the land that had almost stolen everything from me.

Including my life.

STAY CONNECTED

The best way to stay up to date with the Shadow Beast Shifters world and all new releases, is to join my Facebook group here:

www.facebook.com/groups/jayminevenerdherd

We share lots of book releases, fun posts, sexy dudes, and generally it's a happy place to exist.

Next best place is www.facebook.com/JayminEve.Author

And my newsletter at www.jaymineve.com

xx

AFTERWORD

Well well well, what do we have here... no cliffhanger. Told you I could do it (teaser for the next book doesn't count).

Right?

LOL

In all honesty, I have absolutely loved being back in this world, and I'm beyond excited that there are two more spinoffs still to come. These stories are swirling around my head, and I'm hoping to get them out sooner rather than later.

Thank you all for the support you've shown toward this series and all the characters. I am so grateful that you took a chance on my books, and I hope you continue to enjoy the stories I still have to tell.

Thank you to Jane, my amazing PA, for all the teasers and support and friendship. You freaking rock.

Thank you to Tamara, cover extraordinaire. You take my vague instructions and turn them into masterpieces. You are invaluable to me.

Thank you to Jax for the edits. Your hard work and eye for details helped this story shine in its best light. You are amazing!

Thank you to my review team and the Nerd Herd for always giving support, feedback, and love. I wouldn't be here without you all, and for that, I'm feeling pretty damn blessed.

Hope to see you all again in Simone and Lucien's story!

Jaymin

Xxx

JAYMIN EVE

Demon Pack (PNR/Urban Fantasy 18+)

Book One: Demon Pack (Release Oct 2021)

Shadow Beast Shifters (PNR/Urban Fantasy 18+)

Book One: Rejected

Book Two: Reclaimed

Book Three: Reborn

Book Four: Deserted

Book Five: Compelled (Release 2022)

Book Six: Glamoured (Release 2022)

Supernatural Prison Trilogy (Complete UF series 17+)

Book One: Dragon Marked

Book Two: Dragon Mystics

Book Three: Dragon Mated

Book Four: Broken Compass

Book Five: Magical Compass

Book Six: Louis

Book Seven: Elemental Compass

Supernatural Academy (Complete Urban Fantasy/PNR 18+)

Year One

Year Two

Year Three

Royals of Arbon Academy (Dark, complete Contemporary Romance 18+)

Book One: Princess Ballot

Book Two: Playboy Princes

Book Three: Poison Throne

Titan's Saga (PNR/UF. Sexy and humorous 18+)

Book One: Releasing the Gods

Book Two: Wrath of the Gods

Book Three: Revenge of the Gods

Dark Legacy (Complete Dark Contemporary high school romance 18+)

Book One: Broken Wings

Book Two: Broken Trust

Book Three: Broken Legacy

Secret Keepers Series (Complete PNR/Urban Fantasy)

Book One: House of Darken

Book Two: House of Imperial

Book Three: House of Leights

Book Four: House of Royale

Storm Princess Saga (Complete High Fantasy)

Book One: The Princess Must Die

Book Two: The Princess Must Strike

Book Three: The Princess Must Reign

Curse of the Gods Series (Complete Reverse Harem Fantasy 18+)

Book One: Trickery

Book Two: Persuasion

Book Three: Seduction

Book Four: Strength

Novella: Neutral

Book Five: Pain

NYC Mecca Series (Complete - UF series)

Book One: Queen Heir

Book Two: Queen Alpha

Book Three: Queen Fae

Book Four: Queen Mecca

A Walker Saga (Complete - YA Fantasy)

Book One: First World

Book Two: Spurn

Book Three: Crais

Book Four: Regali

Book Five: Nephilius

Book Six: Dronish

Book Seven: Earth

Hive Trilogy (Complete UF/PNR series)

Book One: Ash

Book Two: Anarchy

Book Three: Annihilate

Sinclair Stories (Standalone Contemporary Romance)

Songbird